# Praise for *New York Times* bestselling author Diana Palmer

"Palmer proves that love and passion can be found even in the most dangerous situations."
—*Publishers Weekly* on *Untamed*

"You just can't do better than a Diana Palmer story to make your heart lighter and smile brighter."
—*Fresh Fiction* on *Wyoming Rugged*

"Diana Palmer is a mesmerizing storyteller who captures the essence of what a romance should be."
—*Affaire de Coeur*

"The popular Palmer has penned another winning novel, a perfect blend of romance and suspense."
—*Booklist* on *Lawman*

"Diana Palmer's characters leap off the page. She captures their emotions and scars beautifully and makes them come alive for readers."
—*RT Book Reviews* on *Lawless*

Dear Reader,

I can't believe that it has been thirty years since my first Long, Tall Texans book, *Calhoun*, debuted! The series was suggested by my former editor Tara Gavin, who asked if I might like to set stories in a fictional town of my own design. Would I! And the rest is history.

As the years went by, I found more and more sexy ranchers and cowboys to add to the collection. My readers (especially Amy!) found time to gift me with a notebook listing every single one of them, wives and kids and connections to other families in my own Texas town of Jacobsville. Eventually the town got a little too big for me, so I added another smaller town called Comanche Wells and began to fill it up, too.

You can't imagine how much pleasure this series has given me. I continue to add to the population of Jacobs County, Texas, and I have no plans to stop. Ever.

I hope all of you enjoy reading the Long, Tall Texans as much as I enjoy writing them. Thank you all for your kindness and loyalty and friendship. I am your biggest fan!

Love,

*Diana Palmer*

*NEW YORK TIMES* BESTSELLING AUTHOR

# DIANA PALMER

## LONG, TALL TEXANS:
### *Kingman*
### *Blake*

Previously published as
*The Princess Bride* and *Boss Man*

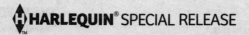

 **HARLEQUIN**® SPECIAL RELEASE

ISBN-13: 978-1-335-62186-3

Long, Tall Texans: Kingman/Blake

Copyright © 2019 by Harlequin Books S.A.

First published as The Princess Bride
by Harlequin Books in 1998 and
Boss Man by Harlequin Books in 2005.

The publisher acknowledges the copyright holder
of the individual works as follows:

The Princess Bride
Copyright © 1998 by Diana Palmer

Boss Man
Copyright © 2005 by Diana Palmer

PLEASE RECYCLE
THIS PRODUCT IS RECYCLABLE

Recycling programs
for this product may
not exist in your area.

**Printed in U.S.A.**

HARLEQUIN®
™ www.Harlequin.com

# CONTENTS

KINGMAN                                                    7

BLAKE                                                    171

A prolific author of more than one hundred books, **Diana Palmer** got her start as a newspaper reporter. A *New York Times* bestselling author and voted one of the top ten romance writers in America, she has a gift for telling the most sensual tales with charm and humor. Diana lives with her family in Cornelia, Georgia. Visit her website at dianapalmer.com.

## Books by Diana Palmer

### Long, Tall Texans

*Fearless*
*Heartless*
*Dangerous*
*Merciless*
*Courageous*
*Protector*
*Invincible*
*Untamed*
*Defender*
*Undaunted*

### The Wyoming Men

*Wyoming Tough*
*Wyoming Fierce*
*Wyoming Bold*
*Wyoming Strong*
*Wyoming Rugged*
*Wyoming Brave*

### Morcai Battalion

*The Morcai Battalion*
*The Morcai Battalion: The Recruit*
*The Morcai Battalion: Invictus*
*The Morcai Battalion: The Rescue*

Visit the Author Profile page
at Harlequin.com for more titles.

# KINGMAN

For Matt and Elisha

# CHAPTER ONE

TIFFANY SAW HIM in the distance, riding the big black stallion that had already killed one man. She hated the horse, even as she admitted silently how regal it looked with the tall, taciturn man on its back. A killer horse it might be, but it respected Kingman Marshall. Most people around Jacobsville, Texas, did. His family had lived on the Guadalupe River there since the Civil War, on a ranch called Lariat.

It was spring, and that meant roundup. It was nothing unusual to see the owner of Lariat in the saddle at dawn lending a hand to rope a stray calf or help work the branding. King kept fit with ranch work, and despite the fact that he shared an office and a business partnership with her father in land and cattle, his staff didn't see a lot of him.

This year, they were using helicopters to mass the far-flung cattle, and they had a corral set up on a wide flat stretch of land where they could dip the cattle, check them, cut out the calves for branding and separate them from their mothers. It was physically demanding work, and no job for a tenderfoot. King wouldn't let Tiffany near it, but it wasn't a front-row seat at the corral that she wanted. If she could just get his attention away from the milling cattle on the wide, rolling plain that led to the Guadalupe River, if he'd just look her way...

She stood up on a rickety lower rung of the gray wood fence, avoiding the sticky barbed wire, and waved her creamy Stetson at him. She was a picture of young elegance in her tan jodhpurs and sexy pink silk blouse and high black boots. She was a debutante. Her father, Harrison Blair, was King's business partner and friend, and if she chased King, her father encouraged her. It would be a marriage made in heaven. That is, if she could find some way to convince King of it. He was elusive and quite abrasively masculine. It might take more than a young lady of almost twenty-one with a sheltered, monied background to land him. But, then, Tiffany had confidence in herself; she was beautiful and intelligent.

Her long black hair hung to her waist in back, and she refused to have it cut. It suited her tall, slender figure and made an elegant frame for her soft oval face and wide green eyes and creamy complexion. She had a sunny smile, and it never faded. Tiffany was always full of fire, burning with a love of life that her father often said had been reflected in her long-dead mother.

"King!" she called, her voice clear, and it carried in the early-morning air.

He looked toward her. Even at the distance, she could see that cold expression in his pale blue eyes, on his lean, hard face with its finely chiseled features. He was a rich man. He worked hard, and he played hard. He had women, Tiffany knew he did, but he was nothing if not discreet. He was a man's man, and he lived like one. There was no playful boy in that tall, fit body. He'd grown up years ago, the boyishness burned out of him by a rich, alcoholic father who demanded blind obedience from the only child of his shallow, runaway wife.

She watched him ride toward her, easy elegance in the saddle. He reined in at the fence, smiling down at her with faint arrogance. He was powerfully built, with long legs and slim hips and broad shoulders. There wasn't an ounce of fat on him, and with his checked red shirt open at the throat, she got fascinating glimpses of bronzed muscle and thick black hair on the expanse of his sexy chest. Jeans emphasized the powerful muscles of his legs, and he had big, elegant hands that hers longed to feel in passion. Not that she was likely to. He treated her like a child most of the time, or at best, a minor irritation.

"You're out early, tidbit," he remarked in a deep, velvety voice with just a hint of Texas drawl. His eyes, under the shade of his wide-brimmed hat, were a pale, grayish blue and piercing as only blue eyes could be.

"I'm going to be twenty-one tomorrow," she said pertly. "I'm having a big bash to celebrate, and you have to come. Black tie, and don't you dare bring anyone. You're mine, for the whole evening. It's my birthday and on my birthday I want presents—and you're it. My big present."

His dark brows lifted with amused indulgence. "You might have told me sooner that I was going to be a birthday present," he said. "I have to be in Omaha early Saturday."

"You have your own plane," she reminded him. "You can fly."

"I have to sleep sometimes," he murmured.

"I wouldn't touch that line with a ten-foot pole," she drawled, peeking at him behind her long lashes. "Will you come? If you don't, I'll stuff a pillow up my dress and accuse you of being the culprit. And your reputation will be ruined, you'll be driven out of town on a rail, they'll tar and feather you…"

He chuckled softly at the vivid sparkle in her eyes, the radiant smile. "You witch," he accused. "They'd probably give me a medal for getting through your defenses."

She wondered how he knew that, and reasoned that her proud parent had probably told him all about her reputation for coolness with men.

He lit a cigarette, took a long draw from and blew it out with faint impatience. "Little girls and their little whims," he mused. "All right, I'll whirl you around the floor and toast your coming-of-age, but I won't stay. I can't spare the time."

"You'll work yourself to death," she complained, and she was solemn now. "You're only thirty-four and you look forty."

"Times are hard, honey," he mused, smiling at the intensity in that glowering young face. "We've had low prices and drought. It's all I can do to keep my financial head above water."

"You could take the occasional break," she advised. "And I don't mean a night on the town. You could get away from it all and just rest."

"They're full up at the Home," he murmured, grinning at her exasperated look. "Honey, I can't afford vacations, not with times so hard. What are you wearing for this coming-of-age party?" he asked to divert her.

"A dream of a dress. White silk, very low in front, with diamanté straps and a white gardenia in my hair." She laughed.

He pursed his lips. He might as well humor her. "That sounds dangerous," he said softly.

"It will be," she promised, teasing him with her eyes. "You might even notice that I've grown up."

He frowned a little. That flirting wasn't new, but it was disturbing lately. He found himself avoiding little Miss Blair, without really understanding why. His body stirred even as he looked at her, and he moved restlessly in the saddle. She was years too young for him, and a virgin to boot, according to her doting, sheltering father. All those years of obsessive parental protection had led to a very immature and unavailable girl. It wouldn't do to let her too close. Not that anyone ever got close to Kingman Marshall, not even his infrequent lovers. He had good reason to keep women at a distance. His upbringing had taught him too well that women were untrustworthy and treacherous.

"What time?" he asked on a resigned note.

"About seven?"

He paused thoughtfully for a minute. "Okay." He tilted his wide-brimmed hat over his eyes. "But only for an hour or so."

"Great!"

He didn't say goodbye. Of course, he never had. He wheeled the stallion and rode off, man and horse so damned arrogant that she felt like flinging something at his tall head. He was delicious, she thought, and her body felt hot all over just looking at him. On the ground he towered over her, lean and hard-muscled and sexy as all hell. She loved watching him.

With a long, unsteady sigh, she finally turned away and remounted her mare. She wondered sometimes why she bothered hero-worshiping such a man. One of these days he'd get married and she'd just die. God forbid that he'd marry anybody but her!

That was when the first shock of reality hit her squarely between the eyes. Why, she had to ask herself, would a man like that, a mature man with all the worldly advantages, want a young and inexperienced woman like her at his side? The question worried her so badly that she almost lost control of her mount. She'd never questioned her chances with King before. She'd never dared. The truth of her situation was unpalatable and a little frightening. She'd never even considered a life without him. What if she had to?

As she rode back toward her own house, on the property that joined King's massive holdings, she noticed the color of the grass. It was like barbed wire in places, very dry and scant. That boded ill for the cattle, and if rain didn't come soon, all that new grass was going to burn up under a hot Texas sun. She knew a lot about the cattle business. After all, her father had owned feedlots since her youth, and she was an only child who worked hard to share his interests. She knew that if there wasn't enough hay by the end of summer, King was going to have to import feed to get his cattle through the winter. The cost of that was prohibitive. It had something to do with black figures going red in the last column, and that could mean disaster for someone with a cow-calf operation the size of King's.

Ah, well, she mused, if King went bust, she supposed that she could get a job and support him. Just the thought of it doubled her over with silvery laughter. King's pride would never permit that sort of help.

Even the Guadalupe was down. She sat on a small rise in the trees, looking at its watery width. The river, like this part of Texas, had a lot of history in it. Archaeologists had found Indian camps on the Guadalupe that dated back seven thousand years, and because of that, part of it had been designated a National Historic Shrine.

In more recent history, freight handlers on their way to San Antonio had crossed the river in DeWitt County on a ferryboat. In Cuero, a nice drive from Lariat, was the beginning of the Chisolm Trail. In nearby Goliad County was the small town of Goliad, where Texas patriots were slaughtered by the Mexican army back in 1836, just days after the bloodbath at the Alamo. Looking at the landscape, it was easy to imagine the first Spanish settlers, the robed priests founding missions, the Mexican Army with proud, arrogant Santa Anna at its fore, the Texas patriots fighting to the last breath, the pioneers and the settlers, the Indians and the immigrants, the cowboys and cattle barons and desperadoes. Tiffany sighed, trying to imagine it all.

King, she thought, would have fitted in very well with the past. Except that he had a blasé attitude toward life and women, probably a result of having too much money and time on his hands. Despite his hard work at roundup, he spent a lot of time in his office, and on the phone, and also on the road. He was so geared to making money that he seemed to have forgotten how to enjoy it. She rode home slowly, a little depressed because she'd had to work so hard just to get King to agree to come to her party. And still haunting her was that unpleasant speculation about a future without King.

Her father was just on his way out the door when she walked up from the stables. The house was stucco, a big sprawling yellow ranch house. It had a small formal garden off the patio, a swimming pool behind, a garage where Tiffany's red Jaguar convertible and her father's gray Mercedes-Benz dwelled, and towering live oak and pecan trees all around. The Guadalupe River was close, but not too close, and Texas stretched like a yellow-green bolt of cloth in all directions to an open, spacious horizon.

"There you are," Harrison Blair muttered. He was tall and gray-headed and green-eyed. Very elegant, despite his slight paunch and his habit of stooping because of a bad back. "I'm late for a board meeting. The caterer called about your party…something about the cheese straws not doing."

"I'll give Lettie a ring. She'll do them for her if I ask her nicely," she promised, grinning as she thought of the elderly lady who was her godmother. "King's coming to my party. I ran him to ground at the river."

He looked over his glasses at her, his heavily lined face vaguely reminiscent of an anorexic bassett hound; not that she'd ever have said anything hurtful to her parent. She adored him. "You make him sound like a fox," he remarked. "Careful, girl, or you'll chase him into a hollow stump and lose him."

"Not me," she laughed, her whole face bright with young certainty. "You just wait. I'll be dangling a diamond one of these days. He can't resist me. He just doesn't know it yet."

He only shook his head. She was so young. She hadn't learned yet that life had a way of giving with one hand, only to take back with the other. Oh, well, she had plenty of years to learn those hard lessons. Let her enjoy it while she could. He knew that King would never settle for a child-woman like his beautiful daughter, but it was something she was going to have to accept one of these days.

"I hope to be back by four," he said, reaching down to peck her affectionately on one cheek. "Are we having champagne? If we are, I hope you told the caterer. I'm not breaking out my private stock until you get married."

"Yes, we are, and yes, I told them," she assured him. "After all, I don't become twenty-one every day."

He studied her with quiet pride. "You look like your mother," he said. "She'd be as proud of you as I am."

She smiled faintly. "Yes." Her mother had been dead a long time, but the memories were bittersweet. The late Mrs. Blair had been vivacious and sparkling, a sapphire in a diamond setting. Her father had never remarried, and seemed not to be inclined toward the company of other women. He'd told Tiffany once that true love was a pretty rare commodity. He and her mother had been so blessed. He was content enough with his memories.

"How many people are we expecting, by the way?" he asked as he put on his Stetson.

"About forty," she said. "Not an overwhelming number. Just some of my friends and some of King's." She grinned. "I'm making sure they're compatible before I railroad him to the altar."

He burst out laughing. She was incorrigible and definitely his child, with her keen business sense, he told himself.

"Do you reckon they'll have a lot in common?"

She pursed her pretty lips. "Money and cattle," she reminded him, "are always a good mix. Besides, King's friends are almost all politicians. They pride themselves on finding things in common with potential voters."

He winked. "Good thought."

She waved and went to call Lettie about doing the cheese straws and the caterers to finalize the arrangements. She was a good hostess, and she enjoyed parties. It was a challenge to find compatible people and put them together in a hospitable atmosphere. So far, she'd done well. Now it was time to show King how organized she was.

The flowers and the caterer had just arrived when she went down the long hall to her room to dress. She was nibbling at a chicken wing on the way up, hoping that she wouldn't starve. There was going to be an hors d'oeuvres table and a drinks bar, but no sit-down dinner. She'd decided that she'd rather dance than eat, and she'd hired a competent local band to play. They were in the ballroom now, tuning up, while Cass, the housekeeper, was watching some of the ranch's lean, faintly disgusted cowboys set up chairs and clear back the furniture. They hated being used as inside labor and their accusing glances let her know it. But she grinned and they melted. Most of them were older hands who'd been with her father since she was a little girl. Like her father, they'd spoiled her, too.

She darted up the staircase, wild with excitement about the evening ahead. King didn't come to the house often, only when her father wanted to talk business away from work, or occasionally for drinks with some of her father's acquaintances. To have him come to a party was new and stimulating. Especially if it ended the way she planned. She had her sights well and truly set on the big rancher. Now she had to take aim.

# CHAPTER TWO

TIFFANY'S EVENING GOWN was created by a San Antonio designer, who also happened to own a boutique in one of the larger malls there. Since Jacobsville was halfway between San Antonio and Victoria, it wasn't too long a drive. Tiffany had fallen in love with the gown at first sight. The fact that it had cost every penny of her allowance hadn't even slowed her down. It was simple, sophisticated, and just the thing to make King realize she was a woman. The low-cut bodice left the curve of her full breasts seductively bare and the diamanté straps were hardly any support at all. They looked as if they might give way any second, and that was the charm of the dress. Its silky white length fell softly to just the top of her oyster satin pumps with their rhinestone clips. She put her long hair in an elaborate hairdo, and pinned it with diamond hairpins. The small silk gardenia in a soft wave was a last-minute addition, and the effect was dynamite. She looked innocently seductive. Just right.

She was a little nervous as she made her way down the curve of the elegant, gray-carpeted staircase. Guests were already arriving, and most of these early ones were around King's age. They were successful businessmen, politicians mostly, with exquisitely dressed wives and girlfriends on their arms. For just an instant,

Tiffany felt young and uneasy. And then she pinned on her finishing-school smile and threw herself into the job of hostessing.

She pretended beautifully. No one knew that her slender legs were unsteady. In fact, a friend of one of the younger politicians, a bachelor clerk named Wyatt Corbin, took the smile for an invitation and stuck to her like glue. He was good-looking in a tall, gangly redheaded way, but he wasn't very sophisticated. Even if he had been, Tiffany had her heart set on King, and she darted from group to group, trying to shake her admirer.

Unfortunately he was stubborn. He led her onto the dance floor and into a gay waltz, just as King came into the room.

Tiffany felt like screaming. King looked incredibly handsome in his dark evening clothes. His tuxedo emphasized his dark good looks, and the white of his silk shirt brought out his dark eyes and hair. He spared Tiffany an amused glance and turned to meet the onslaught of two unattached, beautiful older women. His secretary, Carla Stark, hadn't been invited—Tiffany had been resolute about that. There was enough gossip about those two already, and Carla was unfair competition.

It was the unkindest cut of all, and thanks to this redheaded clown dancing with her, she'd lost her chance. She smiled sweetly at him and suddenly brought down her foot on his toe with perfect accuracy.

"Ouch!" he moaned, sucking in his breath.

"I'm so sorry, Wyatt," Tiffany murmured, batting her eyelashes at him. "Did I step on your poor foot?"

"My fault, I moved the wrong way," he drawled, forcing a smile. "You dance beautifully, Miss Blair."

What a charming liar, she thought. She glanced at King, but he wasn't even looking at her. He was talking and smiling at a devastating blonde, probably a politician's daughter, who looked as if she'd just discovered the best present of all under a Christmas tree. *No thanks to me*, Tiffany thought miserably.

Well, two could play at ignoring, she thought, and turned the full effect of her green eyes on Wyatt. Well, happy birthday to me, she thought silently, and asked him about his job. It was assistant city clerk or some such thing, and he held forth about his duties for the rest of the waltz, and the one that followed.

King had moved to the sofa with the vivacious little blonde, where he looked as if he might set up housekeeping. Tiffany wanted to throw back her head and scream with outrage. Whose party was this, anyway, and which politician was that little blonde with? She began scanning the room for unattached older men.

"I guess I ought to dance with Becky, at least once," Wyatt sighed after a minute. "She's my cousin. I didn't have anyone else to bring. Excuse me a second, will you?"

He left her and went straight toward the blonde who was dominating King. But if he expected the blonde to sacrifice that prize, he was sadly mistaken. They spoke in whispers, while King glanced past Wyatt at Tiffany with a mocking, worldly look. She turned her back and went to the punch bowl.

Wyatt was back in a minute. "She doesn't mind being deserted," he chuckled. "She's found a cattle baron to try her wiles on. That's Kingman Marshall over there, you know."

Tiffany looked at him blankly. "Oh, is it?" she asked innocently, and tried not to show how furious she really was. Between Wyatt and his cousin, they'd ruined her birthday party.

"I wonder why he's here?" he frowned.

She caught his hand. "Let's dance," she muttered, and dragged him back onto the dance floor.

For the rest of the evening, she monopolized Wyatt, ignoring King as pointedly as if she'd never seen him before and never cared to again. Let him flirt with other women at her party. Let him break her heart. He was never going to know it. She'd hold her chin up if it killed her. She smiled at Wyatt and flirted outrageously, the very life and soul of her party, right up to the minute when she cut the cake and asked Wyatt to help her serve it. King didn't seem to notice or care that she ignored him. But her father was puzzled, staring at her incomprehensibly.

"This party is so boring," Tiffany said an hour later, when she felt she couldn't take another single minute of the blonde clinging to King on the dance floor. "Let's go for a ride."

Wyatt looked uncomfortable. "Well… I came in a truck," he began.

"We'll take my Jag."

"You've got a Jaguar?"

She didn't need to say another word. Without even a glance in King's direction, she waved at her father and blew him a kiss, dragging Wyatt along behind her toward the front door. Not that he needed much coaxing.

He seemed overwhelmed when she tossed him the keys and climbed into the passenger seat of the sleek red car.

"You mean, I can drive this?" he burst out.

"Sure. Go ahead. It's insured. But I like to go fast, Wyatt," she said. And for tonight, that was true. She was sick of the party, sick of King, sick of her life. She hurt in ways she'd never realized she could. She only wanted to get away, to escape.

He started the car and stood down on the accelerator. Tiffany had her window down, letting the breeze whip through her hair. She deliberately pulled out the diamond hairpins and tucked them into her purse, letting her long, black hair free and fly on the wind. The champagne she'd had to drink was beginning to take effect and was making her feel very good indeed. The speed of the elegant little car added to her false euphoria. Why, she didn't care about King's indifference. She didn't care at all!

"What a car!" Wyatt breathed, wheeling it out onto the main road.

"Isn't it, though?" she laughed. She leaned back and closed her eyes. She wouldn't think about King. "Go faster, Wyatt, we're positively crawling! I love speed, don't you?"

Of course he did. And he didn't need a second prompting. He put the accelerator peddle to the floor, and twelve cylinders jumped into play as the elegant vehicle shot forward like its sleek and dangerous namesake.

She laughed, silvery bells in the darkness, enjoying the unbridled speed, the fury of motion. Yes, this would blow away all the cobwebs, all the hurt, this would…!

The sound of sirens behind them brought her to her senses. She glanced over the seat and saw blue bubbles spinning around, atop a police car.

"Oh, for heaven's sake, where did he come from!" she gasped. "I never saw the car. They must parachute down from treetops," she muttered, and then giggled at her own remark.

Wyatt slowed the car and pulled onto the shoulder, his face rapidly becoming the color of his hair. He glanced at Tiffany. "Gosh, I'm sorry. And on your birthday, too!"

"I don't care. I told you to do it," she reminded him.

A tall policeman came to the side of the car and watched Wyatt fumble to power the window down.

"Good God. *Wyatt?*" the officer gasped.

"That's right, Bill," Wyatt sighed, producing his driver's license. "Tiffany Blair, this is Bill Harris. He's one of our newest local policemen and a cousin of mine."

"Nice to meet you, Officer—although I wish it was under better circumstances," Tiffany said with a weak smile. "I should get the ticket, not Wyatt. It's my car, and I asked him to go faster."

"I clocked you at eighty-five, you know," he told Wyatt gently. "I sure do hate to do this, Wyatt. Mr. Clark is going to be pretty sore at you. He just had a mouthful to say about speeders."

"The mayor hates me anyway," Wyatt groaned.

"I won't tell him you got a ticket if you don't." Bill grinned.

"Want to bet he'll find out anyway? Just wait."

"It's all my fault," Tiffany muttered. "And it's my birthday…!"

A sleek, new black European sports car slid in behind the police car and came to a smooth, instant stop. A minute later, King got out and came along to join the small group.

"What's the trouble, Bill?" he asked the policeman.

"They were speeding, Mr. Marshall," the officer said. "I'll have to give him a ticket. He was mortally flying."

"I can guess why," King mused, staring past Wyatt at a pale Tiffany.

"Nobody held a gun on me," Wyatt said gently. "It's my own fault. I could have refused."

"The first lesson of responsibility," King agreed. "Learning to say no. Come on, Tiffany. You've caused enough trouble for one night. I'll drop you off on my way out."

"I won't go one step with you, King…!" she began furiously.

He went around to the passenger side of the Jag, opened the door, and tugged her out. His lean, steely fingers on her bare arm raised chills of excitement where they touched. "I don't have time to argue. You've managed to get Wyatt in enough trouble." He turned to Wyatt. "If you'll bring the Jag back, I think your cousin is ready to leave. Sorry to spoil your evening."

"It wasn't spoiled at all, Mr. Marshall," Wyatt said with a smile at Tiffany. "Except for the speeding ticket, I enjoyed every minute of it!"

"I did, too, Wyatt," Tiffany said. "I… King, will you stop dragging me?"

"No. Good night, Wyatt. Bill."

A chorus of good-nights broke the silence as King led an unwilling, sullen Tiffany back to his own leather-trimmed sports car. He helped her inside, got in under the wheel and started the powerful engine.

"I hate you, King," she ground out as he pulled onto the highway.

"Which is no reason at all for making a criminal of Wyatt."

She glared at him hotly through the darkness. "I did not make him a criminal! I only offered to let him drive the Jaguar."

"And told him how fast to go?"

"He wasn't complaining!"

He glanced sideways at her. Despite the rigid set of her body, and the temper on that lovely face, she excited him. One diamanté strap was halfway down a silky smooth arm, revealing more than a little of a tip-tilted breast. The silk fabric outlined every curve of her body, and he could smell the floral perfume that wafted around her like a seductive cloud. She put his teeth on edge, and it irritated him beyond all reason.

He lit a cigarette that he didn't even want, and abruptly put it out, remembering belatedly that he'd quit smoking just last week. And he was driving faster than he normally did. "I don't know why in hell you invited me over here," he said curtly, "if you planned to spend the whole evening with the damned city clerk."

"Assistant city clerk," she mumbled. She darted a glance at him and pressed a strand of long hair away from her mouth. He looked irritated. His face was harder than usual, and he was driving just as fast as Wyatt had been.

"Whatever the hell he is."

"I didn't realize you'd even noticed what I was doing, King," she replied sweetly, "what with Wyatt's pretty little cousin wrapped around you like a ribbon."

His eyebrows arched. "Wrapped around me?"

"Wasn't she?" she asked, averting her face. "Sorry. It seemed like it to me."

He pulled the car onto the side of the road and turned toward her, letting the engine idle. The hand holding the steering wheel clenched, but his dark eyes were steady on hers; she could see them in the light from the instrument panel.

"Were you jealous, honey?" he taunted, in a tone she'd never heard him use. It was deep and smooth and low-pitched. It made her young body tingle in the oddest way.

"I thought you were supposed to be my guest, that's all," she faltered.

"That's what I thought, too, until you started vamping Wyatt whats-his-name."

His finger toyed with the diamanté strap that had fallen onto her arm. She reached to tug it up, but his lean, hard fingers were suddenly there, preventing her.

Her eyes levered up to meet his quizzically, and in the silence of the car, she could hear her own heartbeat, like a faint drum.

The lean forefinger traced the strap from back to front, softly brushing skin that had never known a man's touch before. She stiffened a little, to feel it so lightly tracing the slope of her breast.

"They…they'll miss us," she said in a voice that sounded wildly high-pitched and frightened.

"Think so?"

He smiled slowly, because he was exciting her, and he liked it. He could see her breasts rising and falling with quick, jerky breaths. He could see her nipples peaking under that silky soft fabric. The pulse in her throat was quick, too, throbbing. She was coming-of-age tonight, in more ways than one.

He reached beside him and slowly, blatantly, turned off the engine before he turned back to Tiffany. There was a full moon, and the light of it and the subdued light of the instrument panel gave him all the illumination he needed.

"King," she whispered shakily.

"Don't panic," he said quietly. "It's going to be delicious."

She watched his hand move, as if she were paralyzed. It drew the strap even further off her arm, slowly, relentlessly, tugging until that side of her silky bodice fell to the hard tip of her nipple. And then he gave it a whisper of a push and it fell completely away, baring her pretty pink breast to eyes that had seen more than their share of women. But this was different. This was Tiffany, who was virginal and young and completely without experience.

That knowledge hardened his body. His lean fingers traced her collarbone, his eyes lifted to search her quiet, faintly shocked face. Her eyes were enormous. Probably this was all new to her, and perhaps a little frightening as well.

"You're of age, now. It has to happen with some-one," he said.

"Then… I want it to happen…with you," she whispered, her voice trembling, like her body.

His pulse jumped. His eyes darkened, glittered. "Do you? I wonder if you realize what you're getting into," he murmured. He bent toward her, noticing her sudden tension, her wide-eyed apprehension. He checked the slow movement, for an instant; long enough to whisper, "I won't hurt you."

She leaned back against the leather seat as he turned toward her, her body tautening, trembling a little. But it wasn't fear that motivated her. As she met his smoldering eyes, she slowly arched her back, to let the rest of the bodice fall, and saw the male desire in his dark eyes as they looked down at what the movement had uncovered.

"Your breasts are exquisite," he said absently, that tracing hand moving slowly, tenderly, down one tip-tilted slope, making her shudder. "Perfect."

"They ache," she whispered on a sob, her eyes half closed, in thrall to some physical paralysis that made her throb all over with exquisite sensations.

"I can do something about that," he mused with a brief smile.

His forefinger found the very tip of one small breast and traced around it gently, watching it go even harder, feeling it shudder with the tiny consummation. He heard the faint gasp break from her lips and looked up at her face, at her wide, misty eyes.

"Yes," he said, as if her expression told him everything. And it did. She wanted him. She'd let him do anything he wanted to do, and he felt hot all over.

She moved against the seat, her body in helpless control now, begging for something, for more than this. Her head went back, her full lips parting, hungry.

He slid his arm under her neck, bringing her body closer to his, his mouth poised just above hers. He watched her as his hand moved, and his lean fingers slowly closed over her breast, taking its soft weight and teasing the nipple with his thumb.

She cried softly at the unexpected pleasure, and bit her lower lip in helpless agony.

"Don't do that," he whispered, bending. "Let me…"

His hard lips touched hers, biting softly at them, tracing them warmly from one side to the other. His nose nuzzled against hers, relaxing her, gentling her, while his hand toyed softly with her breast. "Open your mouth, baby," he breathed as his head lowered again, and he met her open mouth with his.

She moaned harshly at the wild excitement he was arousing in her. She'd never dreamed that a kiss could be so intimate, so sweetly exciting. His tongue pushed past her startled lips, into the soft darkness of her mouth, teasing hers in a silence broken only by the sounds of breathing, and cloth against cloth.

"King," she breathed under his lips. Her hands bit into his hair, his nape, tugging. "Hard, King," she whispered shakily, "hard, hard…!"

He hadn't expected that flash of ardor. It caused him to be far rougher than he meant to. He crushed her mouth under his, the force of it bending her head back against his shoulder. His searching hand found first one breast, then the other, savoring the warm silk of their contours, the hard tips that told him how aroused she was.

He forgot her age and the time and the place, and suddenly jerked her across him, his hands easing her into the crook of his arm as he bent his head to her body.

"Sweet," he whispered harshly, opening his mouth on her breast. "God, you're sweet…!"

She cried out from the shock of pleasure his mouth gave her, a piercing little sound that excited him even more, and her body arched up toward him like a silky pink sacrifice. Her hands tangled in his thick black hair, holding him there, tears of mingled frustration and sweet anguish trailing down her hot cheeks as the newness of passion racked her.

"Don't…stop," she whimpered, her hands contracting at his nape, pulling him back to her. "Please!"

"I wonder if I could," he murmured with faint self-contempt as he gave in to the exquisite pleasure of tasting her soft skin. "You taste of gardenia petals, except right…here," he whispered as his lips suddenly tugged at a hard nipple, working down until he took her silky breast into his mouth in a warm, soft suction that made her moan endlessly.

His steely fingers bit into her side as he moved the dress further down and shifted her, letting his mouth press warmly against soft skin, tracing her stomach into the soft elastic of her briefs, tracing the briefs to her hips and waist and then back up to the trembling softness of her breasts.

She found the buttons of his jacket, his silk shirt, and fumbled at them, whimpering as she struggled to make them come apart. She wanted to touch him, experience him as he was experiencing her. Without a clue as to what he might want, she tugged at the edges until he moved her hand aside and moved the fabric away for her. She flattened her palm against thick hair and pure man, caressing him with aching pleasure.

"Here," he whispered roughly, moving her so that her soft breasts were crushed against the abrasive warmth of his chest.

He wrapped her up tight, then, moving her against his hair-roughened skin in a delirium of passion, savoring the feel of her breasts, the silkiness of her skin against him. His body was demanding satisfaction, now, hard with urgent need. His hand slid down her back to her spine and he turned her just a little so that he could press her soft hips into his, and let her know how desperately he wanted her.

She gasped as she felt him in passion, felt and understood the changed contours of his body. Her face buried itself in his hot throat and she trembled all over.

"Are you shocked, Tiffany?" he whispered at her ear, his voice a little rough as if he weren't quite in control. "Didn't you know that a man's body grows hard with desire?"

She shivered a little as he moved her blatantly against him, but it didn't shock her. It delighted her. "It's wicked, isn't it, to do this together?" she whispered shakily. Her eyes closed. "But no, I'm not shocked. I want you, too. I want...to be with you. I want to know how it feels to have you..."

He heard the words with mingled joy and shock. His whirling mind began to function again. *Want. Desire.*

*Sex.* His eyes flew open. She was only twenty-one, for God's sake! And a virgin. His business partner's daughter. What the hell was he doing?

He jerked away from her, his eyes going helplessly to her swollen, taut breasts before he managed to pull her arms from around his neck and push her back in her seat. He struggled to get out of the car, his own aching body fighting him as he tried to remove himself from unbearable temptation in time.

He stood by the front fender, his shirt open, his chest damp and throbbing, his body hurting. He bent over a little, letting the wind get to his hot skin. He must be out of his mind!

Tiffany, just coming to her own senses, watched him with eyes that didn't quite register what was going on. And then she knew. It had almost gone too far. He'd started to make love to her, and then he'd remembered who they were and he'd stopped. He must be hurting like the very devil.

She wanted to get out of the car and go to him, but that would probably make things even worse. She looked down and realized that she was nude to the hips. And he'd seen her like that, touched her...

She tugged her dress back up in a sudden flurry of embarrassment. It had seemed so natural at the time, but now it was shameful. She felt for the straps and pulled the bodice up, keeping her eyes away from her hard, swollen nipples. King had suckled them...

She shuddered with the memory, with new knowledge of him. He'd hate her now, she thought miserably. He'd hate her for letting him go so far, for teasing him. There were names for girls who did that. But she hadn't pulled away, or said no, she recalled. He'd been the one to call a halt, because she couldn't.

Her face went scarlet. She smoothed back her disheveled hair with hands that trembled. How could she face her guests now, like this? Everyone would know what had happened. And what if Wyatt should come along in the Jaguar…?

She looked behind them, but there was no car in sight. And then she realized that they were on King's property, not hers. Had he planned this?

After another minute, she saw him straighten and run a hand through his sweaty hair. He rebuttoned his shirt and tucked it back into his trousers. He did the same with his evening jacket and straightened his tie.

When he finally turned back to get into the car, he looked pale and unapproachable. Tiffany glanced at him as he climbed back in and closed the door, wondering what to say.

"I'll drive you home," he said tersely. "Fasten your seat belt," he added, because she didn't seem to have enough presence of mind to think of it herself.

He started the car without looking at her and turned it around. Minutes later, they were well on the way to her father's house.

It was ablaze with lights, although most of the cars had gone. She looked and saw the Jaguar sitting near the front door. So Wyatt was back. She didn't know what kind of car he was driving, so she couldn't tell if he'd gone or not. She hoped he had, and his cousin with him. She didn't want to see them again.

King pulled up at the front door and stopped, but he didn't cut the engine.

She reached for the door handle and then looked back at him, her face stiff and nervous.

"Are you angry?" she asked softly.

He stared straight ahead. "I don't know."

She nibbled her lower lip, and tasted him there. "I'm not sorry," she said doggedly, her face suddenly full of bravado.

He turned then, his eyes faintly amused. "No. I'm not sorry, either."

She managed a faint smile, despite her embarrassment. "You said it had to happen eventually."

"And you wanted it to happen with me. So you said."

"I meant it," she replied quietly. Her eyes searched his, but she didn't find any secrets there. "I'm not ashamed."

His dark eyes trailed down her body. "You're exquisite, little Tiffany," he said. "But years too young for an affair, and despite tonight's showing, I don't seduce virgins."

"Is an affair all you have to offer?" she asked with new maturity.

He pursed his lips, considering that. "Yes, I think it is. I'm thirty-four. I like my freedom. I don't want the commitment of a wife. Not yet, at least. And you're not old enough for that kind of responsibility. You need a few years to grow up."

She was grown up, but she wasn't going to argue the point with him. Her green eyes twinkled. "Not in bed, I don't."

He took a deep breath. "Tiffany, there's more to a relationship than sex. About which," he added shortly, "you know precious little."

"I can learn," she murmured.

"Damned fast, judging by tonight," he agreed with a wicked smile. "But physical pleasure gets old quickly."

"Between you and me?" she asked, her eyes adoring him. "I don't really think it ever would. I can imagine seducing you in all sorts of unlikely places."

His heart jumped. He shouldn't ask. He shouldn't… "Such as?" he asked in spite of himself.

"Sitting up," she breathed daringly. "In the front seat of a really elegant European sports car parked right in front of my house…"

His blood was beating in his temple. She made him go hot all over with those sultry eyes, that expression…

"You'd better go inside," he said tersely.

"Yes, I suppose I had," she murmured dryly. "It really wouldn't do, would it, what with the risk of someone coming along and seeing us."

It got worse by the second. He was beginning to hurt. "Tiffany…"

She opened the door and glanced back at his hard, set face. He was very dark, and she loved the way he looked in evening clothes. Although now, she'd remember him with his shirt undone and her hands against that sexy, muscular chest.

"Run while you can, cattle baron," she said softly. "I'll be two steps behind."

"I'm an old fox, honey," he returned. "And not easy game."

"We'll see about that," she said, smiling at him. "Good night, lover."

He caught his breath, watching her close the door and blow him a kiss. He had to get away, to think. The last thing he wanted was to find himself on the receiving end of a shotgun wedding. Tiffany was all too tempting, and the best way to handle this was to get away from her for a few weeks, until they both cooled off. A man had to keep a level head, in business and in personal relationships.

He put the car in gear and drove off. Yes, that was what he should do. He'd find himself a nice business trip. Tiffany would get over him. And he'd certainly get over her. He'd had women. He'd known this raging hunger before. But he couldn't satisfy it with a virgin.

He thought about her, the way she'd let him see her, and the aching started all over again. His face hardened as he stepped down on the accelerator. Maybe a long trip would erase that image. Something had to!

Tiffany went back into the house, breathless and worried that her new experiences would show. But they didn't seem to. Wyatt came and asked where she and King had been and she made some light, outrageous reply.

For the rest of the evening, she was the belle of her own ball. But deep inside she was worried about the future. King wasn't going to give in without a fight. She hoped she had what it took to land that big Texas fish. She wanted him more than anything in the whole world. And she wasn't a girl who was used to disappointments.

# CHAPTER THREE

"WELL, KING'S LEFT the country," Harrison Blair murmured dryly three days after Tiffany's party. "You don't seem a bit surprised."

"He's running scared," she said pertly, grinning up at her father from the neat crochet stitches she was using to make an afghan for her room. "I don't blame him. If I were a man being pursued by some persistent woman, I'm sure that I'd run, too."

He shook his head. "I'm afraid he isn't running from you," he mused. "He took his secretary with him."

Her heart jumped, but she didn't miss a stitch. "Did he? I hope Carla enjoys the trip. Where did they go?"

"To Nassau. King's talking beef exports with the minister of trade. But I'm sure Carla took a bathing suit along."

She put in three more stitches. Carla Stark was a redhead, very pretty and very eligible and certainly no virgin. She wanted to throw her head back and scream, but that would be juvenile. It was a temporary setback, that was all.

"Nothing to say?" her father asked.

She shrugged. "Nothing to say."

He hesitated. "I don't want to be cruel," he began. "I know you've set your heart on King. But he's thirty-four, sweetheart. You're a very young twenty-one. Maturity takes time. And I've been just a tad overprotective about you. Maybe I was wrong to be so strict about young men."

"It wouldn't really have mattered," she replied ruefully. "It was King from the time I was fourteen. I couldn't even get interested in boys my own age."

"I see."

She put the crochet hook through the ball of yarn and moved it, along with the partially finished afghan, to her work basket. She stood up, pausing long enough to kiss her father's tanned cheek. "Don't worry about me. You might not think so, but I'm tough."

"I don't want you to wear your heart out on King."

She smiled at him. "I won't!"

"Tiff, he's not a marrying man," he said flatly. "And modern attitudes or no, if he seduces you, he's history. He's not playing fast and loose with you."

"He already told me that himself," she assured him. "He doesn't have any illusions about me, and he said that he's not having an affair with me."

He was taken aback. "He did?"

She nodded. "Of course, he also said he didn't want a wife. But all relationships have these little minor setbacks. And no man really wants to get married, right?"

His face went dark. "Now listen here, you can't seduce him, either!"

"I can if I want to," she replied. "But I won't, so stop looking like a thundercloud. I want a home of my own and children, not a few months of happiness followed by a diamond bracelet and a bouquet of roses."

"Have I missed something here?"

"Lettie said that's how King kisses off his women," she explained. "With a diamond bracelet and a bouquet of roses. Not that any of them last longer than a couple of months," she added with a rueful smile. "Kind of them, isn't it, to let him practice on them until he's ready to marry me?"

His eyes bulged. "What ever happened to the double standard?"

"I told you, I don't want anybody else. I couldn't really expect him to live a life of total abstinence when he didn't know he was going to marry me one day. I mean, he was looking for the perfect woman all this time, and here I was right under his nose. Now that he's aware of me, I'm sure there won't be anybody else. Not even Carla."

Harrison cleared his throat. "Now, Tiffany…"

She grinned. "I hope you want lots of grandchildren. I think kids are just the greatest things in the world!"

"Tiffany…"

"I want a nice cup of tea. How about you?"

"Oolong?"

She grimaced. "Green. I ran out of oolong and forgot to ask Mary to put it on the grocery list this week."

"Green's fine, then, I guess."

"Better than coffee," she teased, and made a face. "I won't be a minute."

He watched her dart off to the kitchen, a pretty picture in jeans and a blue T-shirt, with her long hair in a neat ponytail. She didn't look old enough to date, much less marry.

She was starry-eyed, thinking of a home and children and hardly considering the reality of life with a

man like King. He wouldn't want children straight off
the bat, even if she thought she did. She was far too
young for instant responsibility. Besides that, King
wouldn't be happy with an impulsive child who wasn't
mature enough to handle business luncheons and the
loneliness of a home where King spent time only in-
frequently. Tiffany would expect constant love and attention, and King couldn't give her that. He sighed,
thinking that he was going to go gray-headed worrying
about his only child's upcoming broken heart. There
seemed no way to avoid it, no way at all.

TIFFANY WASN'T THINKING about business lunches or having King home only once in a blue moon. She was
weaving dreams of little boys and girls playing around
her skirts on summer days, and King holding hands
with her while they watched television at night. Over
and above that, she was plotting how to bring about his
downfall. First things first, she considered, and now
that she'd caught his eye, she had to keep it focused
on herself.

She phoned his office to find out when he was coming back, and wrangled the information that he had a
meeting with her father the following Monday just before lunch about a stock transfer.

She spent the weekend planning every move of her
campaign. She was going to land that sexy fighting
fish, one way or another.

SHE FOUND AN excuse to go into Jacobsville on Monday
morning, having spent her entire allowance on a new
sultry jade silk dress that clung to her slender curves

as if it were a second skin. Her hair was put up neatly in an intricate hairdo, with a jade clip holding a wave in place. With black high heels and a matching bag, she looked elegant and expensive and frankly seductive as she walked into her father's office just as he and King were coming out the door on their way to lunch.

"Tiffany," her father exclaimed, his eyes widening at the sight of her. He'd never seen her appear quite so poised and elegant.

King was doing his share of looking, as well. His dark eyebrows dove together over glittering pale eyes and his head moved just a fraction to the side as his gaze went over her like seeking hands.

"I don't have a penny left for lunch," she told her father on a pitiful breath. "I spent everything in my purse on this new dress. Do you like it?" She turned around, her body exquisitely posed for King's benefit. His jaw clenched and she had to repress a wicked smile.

"It's very nice, sweetheart," Harrison agreed. "But why can't you use your credit card for lunch?"

"Because I'm going to get some things for an impromptu picnic," she replied. Her eyes lowered demurely.

"You could come to lunch with us," Harrison began.

King looked hunted.

Tiffany saw his expression and smiled gently. "That's sweet of you, Dad, but I really haven't time. Actually, I'm meeting someone. I hope he likes the dress," she added, lowering her head demurely. She was lying her head off, but they didn't know it. "Can I have a ten-dollar bill, please?"

Harrison swept out his wallet. "Take two," he said,

handing them to her. He glared at her. "It isn't Wyatt, I hope," he muttered. "He's too easily led."

"No. It's not Wyatt. Thanks, Dad. See you, King."

"Who is it?"

King's deep, half-angry voice stopped her at the doorway. She turned, her eyebrows lifted as if he'd shocked her with the question. "Nobody you know," she said honestly. "I'll be in by bedtime, Dad."

"How can you go on a picnic in that dress?" King asked shortly.

She smoothed her hand down one shapely hip. "It's not *that* sort of picnic," she murmured demurely. "We're going to have it on the carpet in his living room. He has gas logs in his fireplace. It's going to be so romantic!"

"It's May," King ground out. "Too hot for fires in the fireplace."

"We won't sit too close to it," she said. "Ta, ta."

She went out the door and dived into the elevator, barely able to contain her glee. She'd shaken King. Let him stew over that lie for the rest of the day, she told herself, and maybe he'd feel as uncomfortable as she'd felt when he took his secretary to Nassau!

OF COURSE THERE was no picnic, because she wasn't meeting anyone. She stopped by a fish and chips place and got a small order and took it home with her. An hour later, she was sprawled in front of her own fireplace, unlit, with a trendy fashion magazine. Lying on her belly on the thick beige carpet, in tight-fitting designer jeans and a low-cut tank top, barefoot and with her long hair loose, she looked the picture of youth.

King's sudden appearance in the doorway shocked

her. She hadn't expected to be found out, certainly not so quickly.

"Where is he?" he asked, his hands in his slacks pocket. He glanced around the spacious room. "Hiding under the sofa? Behind a chair?"

She was frozen in position with a small piece of fish in her hand as she gaped at him.

"What a tangled web we weave," he mused.

"I wasn't deceiving you. Well, maybe a little," she acknowledged. Her eyes glared up at him. "You took Carla to Nassau, didn't you? I hope you had fun."

"Like hell you do."

He closed the door behind him abruptly and moved toward her, resplendent in a gray suit, his black hair catching the light from the ceiling and glowing with faint blue lights.

She rolled over and started to get up, but before she could move another inch, he straddled her prone figure and with a movement so smooth that it disconcerted her, he was suddenly full-length over her body on the carpet, balancing only on his forearms.

"I suppose you'll taste of fish," he muttered as he bent and his hard mouth fastened roughly on her lips.

She gasped. His hips shifted violently, his long legs insistent as they parted her thighs and moved quickly between them. His hands trapped her wrists, stilling her faint instinctive protest at the shocking intimacy of his position.

He lifted his mouth a breath away and looked straight into her eyes. One lean leg moved, just briefly, and he pushed forward against her, his body suddenly rigid. He let her feel him swell with desire, and something wickedly masculine flared in his pale, glittering eyes as new sensations registered on her flushed face.

"Now you know how it happens," he murmured, dropping his gaze to her soft, swollen mouth. "And how it feels when it happens. Draw your legs up a little. I want you to feel me completely against you there."

"King!"

He shifted insistently, making her obey him. She felt the intimacy of his hold and gasped, shivering a little at the power and strength of him against her so intimately.

"Pity, that you don't have anybody to compare me with," he mused deeply as his head bent. "But that might be a good thing. I wouldn't want to frighten you…"

His mouth twisted, parting her lips. It was so different from the night of her party. Then, she'd been the aggressor, teasing and tempting him. He was aroused and insistent and she felt young and uncertain, especially when he began to move in a very seductive way that made her whole body tingle and clench with sensual pleasure.

He heard the little gasp that escaped the lips under his hard mouth, and his head lifted.

He searched her eyes, reading very accurately her response to him. "Didn't you know that pleasure comes of such intimacy?" he whispered.

"Only from…books," she confessed breathlessly. She shivered as he moved again, just enough to make her totally aware of her body's feverish response to that intimate pressure.

"Isn't this more exciting than reading about it?" he

teased. His mouth nibbled at her lips. "Open them," he whispered. "Deep kisses are part of the process."

"King, I'm not…not…sure…"

"You're sure," he whispered into her mouth. "You're just apprehensive, and that's natural. They told you it was going to hurt, didn't they?"

She swallowed, aware of dizziness that seemed to possess her.

His teeth nibbled sensually at her lower lip. "I'll give you all the time you need, when it happens," he murmured lazily. "If I can arouse you enough, you won't mind if I hurt you a little. It might even intensify the pleasure."

"I don't understand."

His open mouth brushed over hers. "I know," he murmured. "That's what excites me so. Slide your hands up the back of my thighs and hold me against you."

"Wh…what?"

His mouth began to move between her lips. "You wore that dress to excite me. All right. I'm excited. Now satisfy me."

"I…but I…can't…" she gasped. "King!"

His hands were under her, intimate, touching her in shocking ways.

"Isn't this what you wanted? It's what you implied when you struck that seductive pose and invited me to ravish you right there on the floor of your father's office."

"I did not!"

His thumbs pressed against her in a viciously arousing way, so that when he pushed down with his hips, she lifted to meet them, groaning harshly at the shock of delight that was only the tip of some mysterious iceberg of ecstasy.

"Tell me that again," he challenged.

She couldn't. She was burning up, dying, in anguish. A stranger's hands fought her tank top and the tiny bra under it, pushing them out of the way only seconds before those same hands tugged at his shirt and managed to get under it, against warm muscle and hair.

While he kissed her, she writhed under him, shivering when she felt his skin against her own. Delirious with fevered need, she slid her hands down his flat belly and even as he dragged his mouth from hers to protest, they pressed, trembling, against the swollen length of him through the soft fabric.

He moaned something, shuddered. He rolled abruptly onto his side and drew her hand back to him, moving it softly on his body, teaching her the sensual rhythm he needed.

"Dear God," he whispered, kissing her hungrily. "No, baby, don't stop," he groaned when her movements slowed. "Touch me. Yes. Yes. Oh, God, yes!"

It was fascinating to see how he reacted to her. Encouraged, she moved closer and her mouth pressed softly, sensually, against the thick hair that covered his chest. He was shaking now. His body was strangely vulnerable, and the knowledge inhibited her.

He rolled onto his back, the very action betraying his need to feel her touch on him. He lay there, still shivering, his eyes closed, his body yielding to her soft, curious hands.

She laid her cheek against his hot skin, awash in new

sensations, touches that had been taboo all her life. She was learning his body as a lover would.

"Tell me what to do," she whispered as she drew her cheek against his breastbone. "I'll do anything for you. Anything!"

His hand held hers to him for one long, aching minute. Then he drew it up to his chest and held it there while he struggled to breathe.

Her breasts felt cool as they pressed nakedly into his rib cage where his shirt was pulled away. Her eyes closed and she lay there, close to him, closer to him than she'd ever been.

"Heavens, that was exciting," she choked. "I never dreamed I could touch you like that, and in broad daylight, too!"

That raw innocence caught him off guard. Laughter bubbled up into his chest, into his throat. He began to laugh softly.

"Do hush!" she chided. "What if Mary should hear you and walk in?"

He lifted himself on an elbow and looked down at her bare breasts. "She'd get an eyeful, wouldn't she?" He traced a taut nipple, arrogantly pleased that she didn't object at all.

"I'm small," she whispered.

He smiled. "No, you're not."

She looked down to where his fingers rested against her pale skin. "Your skin is so dark compared to mine..."

"Especially here, where you're so pale," he breathed. His lips bent to the soft skin he was touching, and he took her inside his mouth, gently suckling her.

She arched up, moaning harshly, her fists clenched beside her head as she tried to deal with the mounting delight of sensation.

He heard that harsh sound and reacted to it immediately. His mouth grew insistent, hot and hungry as it suckled hard at her breast. Her body clenched and suddenly went into a shocking spasm that she couldn't control at all. It never seemed to end, the hot, shameful pleasure he gave her with that intimate caress.

She clutched him, breathless, burying her hot face in his neck while she fought to still her shaking limbs, the faint little gasps that he must certainly be able to hear.

His mouth was tender now, calming rather than stirring. He pressed tender, brief kisses all over her skin, ending only reluctantly at her trembling lips.

Her shamed eyes lifted to his, full of tears that reflected her overwhelmed emotions.

He shook his head, dabbing at them with a handkerchief he drew from his slacks pocket. "Don't cry," he whispered gently. "Your breasts are very, very sensitive. I love the way you react to my mouth on them." He smiled. "It's nothing to worry about."

"It's…natural?" she asked.

His hand smoothed her dark hair. "For a few women, I suppose," he said. He searched her curious eyes. "I've never experienced it like this. I'm glad. There should be at least one or two firsts for me, as well as for you."

"I wish I knew more," she said worriedly.

"You'll learn." His fingers traced her nose, her softly swollen lips. "I missed you."

Her heart felt as if it could fly. She smiled. "Did you, really?"

He nodded. "Not that I wanted to," he added with such disgust that she giggled.

He propped himself on an elbow and stared down at her for a long time, his brows drawn together in deep thought.

She could feel the indecision in him, along with a tension that was new to her. Her soft eyes swept over his dark, lean face and back up to meet his curious gaze.

"You're binding me with velvet ropes," he murmured quietly. "I've never felt like this. I don't know how to handle it."

"Neither do I," she said honestly. She drew a slow breath, aware suddenly of her shameless nudity and the coolness of the air on her skin.

He saw that discomfort and deftly helped her back into her clothes with an economy of movement that was somehow disturbing.

"You make me feel painfully young," she confessed.

"You are," he said without hesitation. His pale eyes narrowed. "This is getting dangerous. I can't keep my hands off you lately. And the last thing on earth I'll ever do is seduce my business partner's only daughter."

"I know that, King," she said with an odd sort of dignity. He got to his feet and she laid down again, watching him rearrange his own shirt and vest and jacket and tie. It was strangely intimate.

He knew that. His eyes smiled, even if his lips didn't.

"What are we going to do?" she added.

He stared down at her with an unnerving intensity. "I wish to God I knew."

He pulled her up beside him. His big hands rested

warmly on her shoulders. "Wouldn't you like to go to Europe?" he asked.

Her eyebrows lifted. "What for?"

"You could go to college. Or have a holiday. Lettie could go with you," he suggested, naming her godmother. "She'd spoil you rotten and you'd come back with a hefty knowledge of history."

"I don't want to go to Europe, and I'm not all that enthralled with history."

He sighed. "Tiffany, I'm not going to sleep with you."

Her full, swollen lips pouted up at him. "I haven't asked you to." She lowered her eyes. "But I'm not going to sleep with anyone else. I haven't even thought about anyone else since I was fourteen."

He felt his mind whirling at the confession. He scowled deeply. He was getting in over his head and he didn't know how to stop. She was too young; years too young. She didn't have the maturity, the poise, the sophistication to survive in his world. He could have told her that, but she wouldn't have listened. She was living in dreams. He couldn't afford to.

He didn't answer her. His hands were deep in his pockets and he was watching her worriedly, amazed at his own headlong fall into ruin. No woman in his experience had ever wound him up to such a fever pitch of desire by just parading around in a silk dress. He'd accused her of tempting him, but it wasn't the whole truth. Ever since the night of her birthday party, he hadn't been able to get her soft body out of his mind. He wanted her. He just didn't know what to do about it. Marriage was out of the question, even more so was an affair. Whatever else she was, she was still his business partner's daughter.

"You're brooding," she murmured.

He shrugged. "I can't think of anything better to do," he said honestly. "I'm going away for a while," he added abruptly. "Perhaps this will pass if we ignore it."

So he was still going to fight. She hadn't expected anything else, but she was vaguely disappointed, just the same.

"I can learn," she said.

His eyebrow went up.

"I know how to be a hostess," she continued, as if he'd challenged her. "I already know most of the people in your circle, and in Dad's. I'm not fifteen."

His eyes narrowed. "Tiffany, you may know how to be a hostess, but you haven't any idea in hell how to be a wife," he said bluntly.

Her heart jumped wildly in her chest. "I could learn how to be one."

His face hardened. "Not with me. I don't want to get married. And before you say it," he added, holding up a hand, "yes, I want you. But desire isn't enough. It isn't even a beginning. I may be the first man you've ever wanted, Tiffany, but you aren't the first woman I've wanted."

# CHAPTER FOUR

THE MOCKING SMILE on his face made Tiffany livid with jealous rage. She scrambled to her feet, her face red and taut.

"That wasn't necessary!" she flung at him.

"Yes, it was," he replied calmly. "You want to play house. I don't."

Totally at a loss, she knotted her hands at her sides and just stared at him. This sort of thing was totally out of her experience. Her body was all that interested him, and it wasn't enough. She had nothing else to bargain with. She'd lost.

It was a new feeling. She'd always had everything she wanted. Her father had spoiled her rotten. King had been another impossible item on her list of luxuries, but he was telling her that she couldn't have him. Her father couldn't buy him for her. And she couldn't flirt and tease and get him for herself. Defeat was strangely cold. It sat in the pit of her stomach like a black emptiness. She didn't know how to handle it.

And he knew. It was in his pale, glittering eyes, in that faint, arrogant smile on his hard mouth.

She wanted to rant and rave, but it wasn't the sort of behavior that would save the day. She relaxed her hands, and her body, and simply looked at him, full of inadequacies and insecurities that she'd never felt before.

"Perhaps when I'm Carla's age, I'll try again," she said with torn pride and the vestiges of a smile.

He nodded with admiration. "That's the spirit," he said gently.

She didn't want gentleness, or pity. She stuck her hands into her jeans pockets. "You don't have to leave town to avoid me," she said. "Lettie's taking me to New York next week," she lied, having arranged the trip mentally in the past few minutes. Lettie would do anything her godchild asked, and she had the means to travel wherever she liked. Besides, she loved New York.

King's eyes narrowed suspiciously. "Does Lettie know she's going traveling?"

"Of course," she said, playing her part to the hilt.

"Of course." He drew in a heavy breath and slowly let it out. His body was still giving him hell, but he wasn't going to let her know it. Ultimately she was better off out of his life.

"See you," she said lightly.

He nodded. "See you."

And he left.

LATE THAT AUTUMN, Tiffany was walking down a runway in New York wearing the latest creation of one David Marron, a young designer whose Spanish-inspired fashions were a sensation among buyers. The two had met through a mutual friend of Lettie's and David had seen incredible possibilities in Tiffany's long black hair and elegance. He dressed her in a gown that was reminiscent of lacy Spanish noblewomen of days long past, and she brought the house down at his first showing of his new spring line. She made the cover of a major fashion magazine and jumped from an unknown to a familiar face in less than six months.

Lettie, with her delicately tinted red hair and twinkling brown eyes, was elated at her accomplishment. It had hurt her deeply to see Tiffany in such an agony of pain when she'd approached her godmother and all but begged to be taken out of Texas. Lettie doted on the younger woman and whisked her away with a minimum of fuss.

They shared a luxurious Park Avenue apartment and were seen in all the most fashionable places. In those few months, Tiffany had grown more sophisticated, more mature—and incredibly more withdrawn. She was ice-cold with men, despite the enhancement of her beauty and her elegant figure. Learning to forget King was a full-time job. She was still working on it.

Just when she was aching to go home to her father where her chances of seeing King every week were excellent, a lingerie company offered her a lucrative contract and a two-week holiday filming commercials in Jamaica.

"I couldn't turn it down," she told Lettie with a groan. "What's Dad going to say? I was going to help him with his Christmas party. I won't get home until Christmas Eve. After we get back from Jamaica, I have to do a photo layout for a magazine ad campaign due to hit the stands next spring."

"You did the right thing," Lettie assured her. "My dear, at your age, you should be having fun, meeting people, learning to stand alone." She sighed gently.

"Marriage and children are for later, when you're established in a career."

Tiffany turned and stared at the older woman. "You never married."

Lettie smiled sadly. "No. I lost my fiancé in Vietnam. I wasn't able to want anyone else in that way."

"Lettie, that's so sad!"

"One learns to live with the unbearable, eventually. I had my charities to keep me busy. And, of course, I had you," she added, giving her goddaughter a quick hug. "I haven't had a bad life."

"Someday you have to tell me about him."

"Someday, I will. But for now, you go ahead to Jamaica and have a wonderful time filming your commercial."

"You'll come with me?" she asked quickly, faintly worried at the thought of being so far away without any familiar faces.

Lettie patted her hand. "Of course I will. I love Jamaica!"

"I have to call Dad and tell him."

"That might be a good idea. He was complaining earlier in the week that your letters were very far apart."

"I'll do it right now."

She picked up the receiver and dialed her father's office number, twisting the cord nervously while she waited to be put through.

"Hi, Dad!" she said.

"Don't tell me," he muttered. "You've met some dethroned prince and you're getting married in the morning."

She chuckled. "No. I've just signed a contract to do

lingerie commercials and we're flying to Jamaica to start shooting."

There was a strange hesitation. "When?"

"Tomorrow morning."

"Well, when will you be back?" he asked.

"In two weeks. But I've got modeling assignments in New York until Christmas Eve," she said in a subdued tone.

"What about my Christmas party?" He sounded resigned and depressed. "I was counting on you to arrange it for me."

"You can have a New Year's Eve party for your clients," she improvised with laughter in her voice. "I'll have plenty of time to put that together before I have to start my next assignment. In fact," she added, "I'm not sure when it will be. The lingerie contract was only for the spring line. They're doing different models for different seasons. I was spring."

"I can see why," he murmured dryly. "My daughter, the model." He sighed again. "I should never have let you get on the plane with Lettie. It's her fault. I know she's at the back of it."

"Now, Dad…"

"I'm having her stuffed and hung on my wall when she comes back. You tell her that!"

"You know you're fond of Lettie," she chided, with a wink at her blatantly eavesdropping godmother.

"I'll have her shot!"

She grimaced and Lettie, reading her expression, chuckled, unabashed by Harrison Blair's fury.

"She's laughing," she told him.

"Tell her to laugh while she can." He hesitated and

spoke to someone nearby. "King said to tell you he misses you."

Her heart jumped, but she wasn't leaving herself open to any further humiliation at his hands. "Tell him to pull the other one," she chuckled. "Listen, Dad, I have to go. I'll phone you when we're back from Jamaica."

"Wait a minute. Where in Jamaica, and is Lettie going along?"

"Of course she is! We'll have a ball. Take care, Dad. Bye!"

He was still trying to find out where she was going when she hung up on him. He glanced at King with a grimace.

The younger man had an odd expression on his face. It was one Harrison couldn't remember ever seeing there before.

"She's signed a contract," Harrison said, shoving his hands into his pockets as he glared at the telephone, as if the whole thing had been its fault.

"For what?" King asked.

"Lingerie commercials," his partner said heavily. "Just think, my sheltered daughter will be parading around in sheer nighties for the whole damned world to see!"

"Like hell she will. Where is she?" King demanded.

"On her way to Jamaica first thing in the morning. King," he added when the other man started to leave. "She's of age," he said gently. "She's a woman. I don't have the right to tell her how to live her own life. And neither do you."

"I don't want other men ogling her!"

Harrison just nodded. "I know. I don't, either. But it's her decision."

"I won't let her do it," King said doggedly.

"How do you propose to stop her? You can't do it legally. I don't think you can do it any other way, either."

"Did you tell her what I said?"

Harrison nodded again. "She said to pull the other one."

Pale blue eyes widened with sheer shock. It had never occured to him that he could lose Tiffany, that she wouldn't always be in Harrison's house waiting for him to be ready to settle down. Now she'd flown the coop and the shoe was on the other foot. She'd discovered the pleasure of personal freedom and she didn't want to settle down.

He glanced at Harrison. "Is she serious about this job? Or is it just another ploy to get my attention?"

The other man chuckled. "I have no idea. But you have to admit, she's a pretty thing. It isn't surprising that she's attracted a modeling agency."

King stared out the window with narrowed, thoughtful eyes. "Then she's thinking about making a career of it."

Harrison didn't tell him that her modeling contract might not last very long. He averted his eyes. "She might as well have a career. If nothing else, it will help her mature."

The other man didn't look at him. "She hasn't grown up yet."

"I know that. It isn't her fault. I've sheltered her from life—perhaps too much. But now she wants to try her wings. This is the best time, before she has a reason to fold them away. She's young and she thinks she has the world at her feet. Let her enjoy it while she can."

King stared down at the carpet. "I suppose that's the wise choice."

"It's the only choice," came the reply. "She'll come home when she's ready."

King didn't say another word about it. He changed the subject to business and pursued it solemnly.

MEANWHILE, TIFFANY WENT to Jamaica and had a grand time. Modeling, she discovered, was hard work. It wasn't just a matter of standing in front of a camera and smiling. It involved wardrobe changes, pauses for the proper lighting and equipment setup, minor irritations like an unexpected burst of wind and artistic temperament on the part of the cameraman.

Lettie watched from a distance, enjoying Tiffany's enthusiasm for the shoot. The two weeks passed all too quickly, with very little time for sightseeing.

"Just my luck," Tiffany groaned when they were back in New York, "I saw the beach and the hotel and the airport. I didn't realize that every free minute was going to be spent working or resting up for the next day's shoot!"

"Welcome to the world of modeling." Lettie chuckled. "Here, darling, have another celery stick."

Tiffany grimaced, but she ate the veggie platter she was offered without protest.

At night, she lay awake and thought about King. She hadn't believed his teasing assertion that he'd missed her. King didn't miss people. He was entirely self-sufficient. But how wonderful if it had been true.

That daydream only lasted until she saw a tabloid at the drugstore where she was buying hair-care products. There was a glorious color photo of King and Carla right on the front page of one, with the legend, "Do wedding bells figure in future for tycoon and secretary?"

She didn't even pick it up, to her credit. She passed over it as if she hadn't seen it. But she went to bed that evening, she cried all night, almost ruining her face for the next day's modeling session.

UNREQUITED LOVE TOOK its toll on her in the weeks that followed. The one good thing about misery was that it attracted other miserable people. She annexed one Mark Allenby, a male model who'd just broken up with his long-time girlfriend and wanted a shoulder to cry on. He was incredibly handsome and sensitive, and just what Tiffany needed for her shattered ego.

The fact that he was a wild man was certainly a bonus.

He was the sort of person who'd phone her on the spur of the moment and suggest an evening at a retro beatnik coffeehouse where the patrons read bad poetry. He loved practical jokes, like putting whoopee cushions under a couple posing for a romantic ad.

"I can see why you're single," Tiffany suggested breathlessly when she'd helped him outrun the furious photographer. "And I'll bet you never get to work for *him* again." She indicated the heavyset madman chasing them.

"Yes, I will." He chuckled. "When you make it to my income bracket, you don't have to call photographers to get work. They call you." Mark turned and blew the man a kiss, grabbed Tiffany's hand, and pulled her along to the subway entrance nearby.

"YOU NEED A MAKEOVER," he remarked on their way back to her apartment.

She stopped and looked up at him. "Why?"

"You look too girlish," he said simply, and smiled. "You need a more haute couture image if you want to grow into modeling."

She grimaced. "I'm not sure I really do, though. I like it all right. But I don't need the money."

"Darling, of course you need the money!"

"Not really. Money isn't worth much when you can't buy what you want with it," she said pointedly.

He pushed back his curly black hair and gave her his famous inscrutable he-man stare. "What do you want that you can't buy?"

"King."

"Of which country?"

She grinned. "Not royalty. That's his name. King-man. Kingman Marshall."

"The tycoon of the tabloids?" he asked, pursing his chiseled lips. "Well, well, you do aim high, don't you? Mr. Marshall has all the women he wants, thank you. And if you have anything more serious in mind, forget it. His father taught him that marriage is only for fools. Rumor has it that his mother took his old man for every cent he had when she divorced him, and that it drove his father to suicide."

"Yes, I know," she said dully.

"Not that Marshall didn't get even. You probably heard about that, too."

"Often," she replied. "He actually took his mother to court and charged her with culpability in his father's suicide in a civil case. He won." She shivered, remembering how King had looked after the verdict—and, more importantly, how his mother had looked. She lost two-thirds of her assets and the handsome gigolo that she'd been living with. It was no wonder that King had such a low opinion of marriage, and women.

"Whatever became of the ex-Mrs. Marshall?" he asked aloud.

"She overdosed on drugs and died four years ago," she said.

"A sad end."

"Indeed it was."

"You can't blame Marshall for treating women like individually wrapped candies," he expounded. "I don't imagine he trusts anything in skirts."

"You were talking about a makeover?" she interrupted, anxious to get him off the subject of King before she started screaming.

"I was. I'll take you to my hairdresser. He'll make a new woman of you. Then we'll go shopping for a proper wardrobe."

Her pale eyes glittered with excitement. "This sounds like fun."

"Believe me, it will be," he said with a wicked grin. "Come along, darling."

They spent the rest of the day remaking Tiffany. When he took her out that night to one of the more fashionable nightspots, one of the models she'd worked with didn't even recognize her. It was a compliment of the highest order.

Lettie was stunned speechless.

"It's me," Tiffany murmured impishly, whirling in her black cocktail dress with diamond earrings dripping from her lobes. Her hair was cut very short and feathered toward her gamine face. She had just a hint of makeup, just enough to enhance her high cheekbones and perfect bone structure. She looked expensive, elegant, and six years older than she was.

"I'm absolutely shocked," Lettie said after a minute. "My dear, you are the image of your mother."

Tiffany's face softened. "Am I, really?"

Lettie nodded. "She was so beautiful. I always envied her."

"I wish I'd known her," she replied. "All I have are photographs and vague memories of her singing to me at night."

"You were very young when she died. Harrison never stopped mourning her." Her eyes were sad. "I don't think he ever will."

"You never know about Dad," Tiffany remarked, because she knew how Lettie felt about Harrison. Not that she was gauche enough to mention it. "Why don't you go out with us tonight?"

"Three's a crowd, dear. Mark will want you to himself."

"It isn't like that at all," Tiffany said gently. "He's mourning his girlfriend and I'm mourning King. We have broken hearts and our work in common, but not much else. He's a friend—and I mean that quite sincerely."

Lettie smiled. "I'm rather glad. He's very nice. But he'll end up in Europe one day in a villa, and that wouldn't suit you at all."

"Are you sure?"

Lettie nodded. "And so are you, in your heart."

Tiffany glanced at herself in the mirror with a quiet sigh. "Fine feathers make fine birds, but King isn't the sort to be impressed by sophistication or beauty. Besides, the tabloids are already predicting that he's going to marry Carla."

"I noticed. Surely you don't believe it?"

"I don't believe he'll ever marry anyone unless he's trapped into it," Tiffany said honestly, and her eyes were suddenly very old. "He's seen nothing of marriage but the worst side."

"It's a pity about that. It's warped his outlook."

"Nothing will ever change it." She smiled at Lettie. "Sure you won't come with us? You won't be a crowd."

"I won't come tonight. But ask me again."

"You can count on it."

MARK WAS BROODY as he picked at his mint ice cream.

"You're worried," Tiffany murmured.

He glanced at her wryly. "No. I'm distraught. My girl is being seen around town with a minor movie star. She seems smitten."

"She may be doing the same thing you're doing," she chided. "Seeing someone just to numb the ache."

He chuckled. "Is that what I'm doing?"

"It's what we're both doing."

He reached his hand across the table and held hers. "I'm sorry we didn't meet three years ago, while I was still heart-whole. You're unique. I enjoy having you around."

"Same here. But friendship is all it can ever be."

"Believe it or not, I know that." He put down his spoon. "What are you doing for Christmas?"

"I'll be trying to get back from a location shoot and praying that none of the airline pilots go on strike," she murmured facetiously.

"New Year's?"

"I have to go home and arrange a business party for my father." She glanced at him and her eyes began to sparkle. "I've had an idea. How would you like to visit Texas?"

His eyebrows arched. "Do I have to ride a horse?"

"Not everyone in Texas rides. We live in Jacobsville. It's not too far from San Antonio. Dad's in business there."

"Jacobsville." He fingered his wineglass with elegant dark fingers that looked very sexy in the ads he modeled for. "Why not? It's a long way from Manhattan."

"Yes, it is, and I can't bear to go home alone."

"May I ask why?"

"Of course. My own heartbreaker lives there. I told you about him. I ran away from home so that I could stop eating my heart out over him. But memories and heartache seem to be portable," she added heavily.

"I could attest to that myself." He looked up at her with wickedly twinkling black eyes. "And what am I going to be? The competition?"

"Would you mind?" she asked. "I'll gladly do the same for you anytime you like. I need your moral support."

He paused thoughtfully and then he smiled. "You know, this might be the perfect answer to both our headaches. All right. I'll do it." He finished his wine.

"I've been asked to fill a lot of roles. That's a new one." He lifted his glass and took a sip. "What the hell. I'll tangle with Kingman Marshall. I don't want to live forever. I'm yours, darling. At least, for the duration of the party," he added with a grin.

She lifted her own glass. "Here's to pride."

He answered the toast. As she drank it, she wondered how she was going to bear seeing King with Carla. At least she'd have company and camouflage. King would never know that her heart was breaking.

## CHAPTER FIVE

TIFFANY AND MARK boarded the plane with Lettie the day before New Year's Eve. Tiffany looked sleek and expensive in a black figure-hugging suit with silver accessories and a black-and-white-striped scarf draped over one shoulder. Mark, in a dark suit, was the picture of male elegance. Women literally sighed when he walked past. It was odd to see a man that handsome in person, and Tiffany enjoyed watching people react to him.

Lettie sat behind them and read magazines while Mark and Tiffany discussed their respective assignments and where they might go next.

It wasn't as long a flight as she'd expected it to be. They walked onto the concourse at the San Antonio airport just in time for lunch.

Tiffany had expected her father to meet them, and sure enough, he was waiting near the gate. Tiffany ran to him to be hugged and kissed warmly before she introduced Mark.

Harrison scowled as he shook hands with the young man, but he gathered his composure quickly and the worried look vanished from his features. He greeted Lettie warmly, too, and led the three of them to the limousine near the front entrance.

"Mark's staying with us, Dad," Tiffany said. "We're both working for the same agency in Manhattan and our holidays coincided."

"We'll be glad to have you, Mark," Harrison said with a forced warmth that only Tiffany seemed to notice.

"How is King?" Lettie asked.

Harrison hesitated with a lightning glance at Tiffany. "He's fine. Shall we go?"

Tiffany wondered why her father was acting so peculiarly, but she pretended not to be interested in King or his feelings. Only with Mark.

"Did you manage to get the arrangements finalized?" Harrison asked his daughter.

She grinned. "Of course. Long distance isn't so long anymore, and it wasn't that hard. I've dealt with the same people for years arranging these 'dos' for you. The caterer, the flowers, the band, even the invitations are all set."

"You're sure?" Harrison murmured.

She nodded. "I'm sure."

"You didn't forget to send an invitation to King and Carla?" her father added.

"Of course not! Theirs were the first to go out," she said with magnificent carelessness. "I wouldn't forget your business partner."

Harrison seemed to relax just a little.

"What's wrong?" she asked, sensing some problem.

"He's out of town," he said reluctantly. "Rather, they're out of town, and not expected back until sometime next week. Or so King's office manager said. I hadn't heard from him, and I wondered why he was willing to forgo the party. He never misses the holiday bash. Or, at least, he never has before."

Tiffany didn't betray her feelings by so much as the batting of an eyelash how much that statement hurt. She only smiled. "I suppose he had other plans and wasn't willing to change them."

"Perhaps so," he said, but he didn't look convinced.

Mark reached beside him and caught Tiffany's hand in his, pressing it reassuringly. He seemed to sense, as her father did, how miserable she felt at King's defection. But Mark asked Harrison a question about a landmark he noticed as they drove down the long highway that would carry them to Jacobsville, and got him off on a subject dear to his heart. By the time they reached the towering brick family home less than an hour later, Mark knew more about the siege at the Alamo than he'd ever gleaned from books.

Tiffany was too busy with her arrangements to keep Mark company that day or the next, so he borrowed a sedan from the garage and set about learning the area. He came back full of tidbits about the history of the countryside, which he seemed to actually find fascinating.

He watched Tiffany directing the traffic of imported people helping with the party with amused indulgence.

"You're actually pretty good at this," he murmured. "Where did you learn how to do it?"

She looked surprised. "I didn't. It just seemed to come naturally. I love parties."

"I don't," he mused. "I usually become a decoration."

She knew what he meant. She learned quickly that very few of the parties models attended were anything but an opportunity for designers to show off their fashions in a relaxed setting. The more wealthy clients who were present, the better the opportunity to sell clothes. But some of the clients found the models more interesting than their regalia. Tiffany had gravitated toward Mark for mutual protection at first. Afterward, they'd become fast friends.

"You won't be a decoration here," she promised him with a smile. "What do you think?"

She swept her hand toward the ballroom, which was polished and packed with flowers and long tables with embroidered linen tablecloths, crystal and china and candelabras. Buffets would be set up there for snacks, because it wasn't a sit-down dinner. There would be dancing on the highly polished floor to music provided by a live band, and mixed drinks would be served at the bar.

"It's all very elegant," Mark pronounced.

She nodded absently, remembering other parties when she'd danced and danced, when King had been close at hand to smile at her and take her out onto the dance floor. She hadn't danced with him often, but each time was indelibly imprinted in her mind. She could close her eyes and see him, touch him. She sighed miserably. Well, she might as well stop looking back. She had to go on, and King wanted no part of her. His absence from this most special of all parties said so.

"I think it'll do," she replied after a minute. She gave him a warm smile. "Come on and I'll show you the way I've decorated the rest of the house."

TIFFANY WORE A long silver-sequined dress for the party, with a diamond clip in her short hair. She'd learned how to walk, how to move, how to pose, and even people who'd known her for years were taken aback at her new image.

Mark, at her side, resplendent in dark evening dress, drew feminine eyes with equal magnetism. His Italian ancestry was very evident in his liquid black eyes and olive complexion and black, black hair. One of Tiffany's acquaintances, a pretty little redhead named Lisa, seemed to be totally captivated by Mark. She stood in a corner by herself, just staring at him.

"Should I take pity on her and introduce you?" she asked Mark in a teasing whisper.

He glanced toward the girl, barely out of her teens, and she blushed as red as her hair. Seconds later, she rushed back toward her parents. He chuckled softly.

"She's very young," he mused. "A friend?"

She shook her head. "Her parents are friends of my father's. Lisa is a loner. As a rule, she doesn't care as much for dating as she does for horses. Her family has stables and they breed racehorses."

"Well, well. All that, and no beaux?"

"She's shy with men."

His eyebrows arched. He looked at the young woman a second time, and his eyes narrowed as they caught her vivid blue ones and held them relentlessly. Lisa spilled her drink and blushed again, while her mother fussed at the skirt of her dress with a handkerchief.

"How wicked," Tiffany chided to Mark.

"Eyes like hers should be illegal," he murmured, but he was still staring at Lisa just the same. He took Tiffany's arm and urged her toward the group. "Introduce me."

"Don't..." she began.

"I'm not that much a rake." He calmed her. "She intrigues me. I won't take advantage. I promise." He smiled, although his eyes were solemn.

"All right, then." She stopped at Mrs. McKinley's side. "Will it stain?" she asked gently.

"Oh, I don't think so," the older woman said with a smile. "It was mostly ice. Lisa, you remember our Tiffany, don't you?" she added.

Lisa looked up, very flustered as her eyes darted nervously from Mark's to Tiffany. "H...hi, Tiffany. Nice to see you."

"Nice to see you, Lisa," Tiffany replied with a genuine smile. "I'm sorry about your dress. Have you met Mark Allenby? He works with me. We're both represented by the same modeling agency in New York. You might have seen him in the snack food commercials with the puppet...?"

"G...good Lord, was that you?" Lisa choked. "I thought he...you...looked familiar, Mr. Allenby!"

He smiled lazily. "Nice of you to remember it, Miss McKinley. Do you dance?"

She looked as if she might faint. "Well, yes..."

He held out a hand. "You'll excuse me?" he said to Tiffany and Lisa's parents.

Lisa put her hand into his and let him lead her onto the dance floor. Her eyes were so full of dreams and delight that Mark couldn't seem to stop looking down at her.

"He dances beautifully," Mrs. McKinley said.

"Not bad," her gruff husband agreed. "Is he gay?"

"Mark?" Tiffany chuckled. "No. Very straight. And

quite a success story, in fact. His parents are Italian. He came to this country as a baby and his father held down two jobs while his mother worked as a waitress in a cafeteria. He makes enough to support both of them now, and his three young sisters. He's very responsible, loyal, and not a seducer of innocents, just in case you wondered."

Mrs. McKinley colored. "I'm sorry, but he was an unknown quantity, and it's very easy to see the effect he has on Lisa."

"I wouldn't worry," she said gently. "He's just broken up with his long-time girlfriend and his heart hurts. He's not in the market for an affair, anyway."

"That's a relief," the older woman said with a smile. "She's so unworldly."

Because she'd been as sheltered as Tiffany herself had. There were great disadvantages to that overprotection in today's world, Tiffany thought miserably. She stared into her champagne and wondered why King had declined the invitation to the party. Perhaps he was making the point that he could do nicely without Tiffany. If so, he'd succeeded beyond his wildest dreams.

She got through the long evening on champagne and sheer willpower. Mark seemed to be enjoying himself immensely. He hardly left Lisa all evening, and when she and her parents got ready to leave, he held on to her hand as if he couldn't bear to let it go.

They spoke in terse, quiet tones and as she left, her blue eyes brightened considerably, although Mrs. McKinley looked worried.

"I'm going over there tomorrow to see their horses.

You don't mind?" he asked Tiffany as the other guests were preparing to leave.

She stared up at him curiously. "She's very young."

"And innocent," he added, his hands deep in his pockets. "You don't need to tell me that. I haven't ever known anyone like her. She's the sort of girl I might have met back home, if my parents hadn't immigrated to America."

She was startled. "I thought you were grinding your teeth over your girlfriend?"

He smiled vaguely. "So did I." His head turned toward the front door. "She's breakable," he said softly. "Vulnerable and sweet and shy." His broad shoulders rose and fell. "Strange. I never liked redheads before."

Tiffany bit her lower lip. She didn't know how to put into words what she was feeling. Lisa was the sort of girl who'd never get over having her hopes raised and then dashed. Did he know that?

"She dances like a fairy," he murmured, turning away, his dark eyes introspective and oblivious to the people milling around him.

Harrison joined his daughter at the door as the last guests departed.

"Your friend seems distracted," he murmured, his eyes on Mark, who was staring out a darkened window.

"Lisa affected him."

"I noticed. So did everybody else. He's a rake."

She shook her head. "He's a hardworking man with deep family ties and an overworked sense of responsibility. He's no rake."

"I thought you said he had a girlfriend."

"She dumped him for somebody richer," she said

simply. "His pride was shattered. That's why he's here with me. He couldn't bear seeing her around town in all the nightspots with her new lover."

Harrison's attitude changed. "Poor guy."

"He won't hurt Lisa," she assured him, mentally crossing her fingers. She saw trouble ahead, but she didn't know quite how to ward it off.

He studied her face. "You're much more mature. I wouldn't have recognized you." He averted his eyes. "Pity King didn't get back in time for the party."

She froze over. "I didn't expect him, so it's no great loss."

He started to speak, and suddenly closed his mouth. He smiled at her. "Let's have a nightcap. Your friend can come along."

She took his arm with a grin. "That sounds more like you!"

THE NEXT DAY, Mark borrowed Harrison's sedan again and made a beeline for the McKinley place outside town. He was wearing slacks and a turtle-neck white sweater and he looked both elegant and expensive.

As Tiffany stood on the porch waving him off, a car came purring up the driveway. It was a black Lincoln. She fought down the urge to run. She didn't have to back away from King anymore. She was out of his reach. She folded her arms over the red silk blouse she was wearing with elegant black slacks and leaned against a post in a distinctive pose to wait for him. It surprised her just a little that he didn't have Carla with him.

King took the steps two at a time. He was wearing

dark evening clothes, as if he'd just come from a party. She imagined he was still wearing the clothes he'd had on the night before. Probably he didn't keep anything to change into at Carla's place, she thought venomously, certain that it explained his state of dress.

"Well, well, what brings you here?" she drawled, without any particular shyness.

King paused at the last step, scowling as he got a good look at her. The change was phenomenal. She wasn't the young girl he'd left behind months before. She was poised, elegant, somehow cynical. Her eyes were older and there was no welcome or hero-worship in them now. Her smile, if anything, was mocking.

"I came to see Harrison," he said curtly.

She waved a hand toward the front door. "Help yourself. I was just seeing Mark off."

He seemed suddenly very still. "Mark?"

"Mark Allenby. We work together. He came home with me for our holidays." She gave him a cool glance. "You've probably seen him in commercials. He's incredibly handsome."

He didn't say another word. He walked past her without speaking and went right into the house.

Tiffany followed a few minutes later, and found him with her father in the study.

Harrison glanced out the door as she passed it on her way to the staircase. "Tiffany! Come in here a minute, would you, sweetheart?"

He never called her pet names unless he wanted something. She wandered into the room as if King's presence made no difference at all to her. "What do you want, Dad?" she asked with a smile.

"King needs some papers from the safe at my office, and I promised I'd drive Lettie down to Floresville to visit her sister. Would you...?"

She knew the combination by heart, something her father had entrusted her with only two years before. But she sensed a plot here and she hesitated. King noticed, and his face froze over.

"You don't have anything pressing, do you?" Harrison persisted. "Not with Mark away?"

"I suppose not." She gave in. "I'll just get my jacket."

"Thanks, sweetheart!"

She only shrugged. She didn't even glance at King.

It WAS A short drive to the downtown office her father shared with King. It seemed a little strange to her that King didn't have the combination to Harrison's safe, since they were partners. She'd never really wondered why until now.

"Doesn't he trust you?" she chided as they went into the dark office together.

"As much as he trusts anyone," he replied. "But in case you wondered, he doesn't have the combination to my safe, either. Our respective lawyers have both. It's a safeguard, of a sort."

He turned on the lights and closed the door. The sprawling offices were vacant on this holiday and she was more aware than ever of being totally alone with him. It shouldn't have bothered her, knowing what she did about his relationship with Carla, but it did. It hadn't been long enough for her to forget the pleasure of his kisses, being in his arms.

She ignored her tingling nerves and went straight

to the concealed safe, opening it deftly. "What do you want out of here?" she asked.

"A brown envelope marked *Internet Proposals.*"

She searched through the documents and found what he wanted. She closed the safe, replaced the painting that covered it, and handed the envelope to King.

"Is that all you needed me for?" she asked, turning toward the door.

"Not quite."

She hesitated a few feet away from him. Her eyes asked the question for her.

He wasn't smiling. The friendly man of years past was missing. His eyes were wary and piercing. He didn't move at all. He just stared at her until she felt her heartbeat accelerate.

She lifted her chin. "Well?"

"Was it deliberate?"

She blinked. "Was what deliberate?"

"Leaving us off the guest list for the New Year's Eve party."

She felt an uncomfortable tension in the air. She frowned. "You and Carla were invited," she said. "I faxed the list of invitations straight to the printers. The two of you were the first two names on the list. In fact, they went straight to my father's secretary from the printer's, to be mailed. Carla knows Rita, Dad's secretary. I'm sure she knew that you were on the list."

His eyes narrowed. "She said that she checked the list. Our names weren't there."

"Someone's lying," Tiffany said quietly.

He made a sound deep in his throat. "I don't need two guesses for a name."

"You think I did it. Why?"

He shrugged. "Spite?" he asked with a mocking smile. "After all, I sent you packing, didn't I?"

Months of conditioning kept her face from giving away any of her inner feelings. She pushed a hand into her jacket pocket and lifted an eyebrow. "You did me a favor, as it happens," she said. "You needn't worry, I'm no longer a threat to you. Mark and I are quite an item about town these days. We both work for the same agency. We see a lot of each other. And not only on the job."

His narrow gaze went over her, looking for differences. "You've changed."

Her shoulders rose and fell. "I've only grown up." Her smile never reached her eyes. "I have a bright future, they tell me. It seems that my body is photogenic."

Something flashed in his eyes and he turned away before she could see it. "I thought you were going on a holiday, not to find a job."

"I didn't have much choice," she said, turning back to the door. "There was nothing for me here."

His fist clenched at his side. He turned, about to speak, but she'd already opened the door and gone out into the hall.

He followed her, surprised to find her headed not for the exit, but for Rita's computer. She sat down behind the desk that her father's secretary used, turned on the computer, fed in a program, and searched the files for the invitation list. She found it and pulled it up on the screen. Sure enough, King's name wasn't on it. Neither was Carla's. But one of the agency models was a computer whiz and she'd been tutoring Tiffany on the side.

"I told you our names weren't there," he said gruffly from behind her.

"Oh, don't give up yet. Wait just a sec…" She put up another program, one designed to retrieve lost files, and set it searching. A minute later, she pulled up the deleted file and threw it up on the screen. There, at the top of the list, were King's and Carla's names.

King scowled. "How did you do that? I didn't see your hands typing on the keyboard."

"They didn't. This file was deliberately erased and replaced. I'm sure if I look for the fax, I'll discover that it's been redone as well." She saved the file, cut off the computer, and got to her feet. She met his eyes coldly. "Tell Carla nice try. But next time, she'd better practice a little more on her technique."

She retrieved her purse and went out the door, leaving King to follow, deep in thought.

"Why do you think Carla tampered with the list?" he asked on the way home.

"She's a girl with aspirations. Not that I'm any threat to them," she added firmly. "I have a life in New York that I'm learning to love, and a man to shower affection on. You might tell her that, before she dreams up any new ideas to put me in a bad light."

He didn't answer her. But his hands tightened on the steering wheel.

SHE WAS OUT of the car before he could unfasten his seat belt.

The house was empty, she knew, because Harrison was supposed to be out, and she was certain that Mark was still at Lisa's house. She didn't want King inside.

She paused on the lowest step. "I'll tell Dad you got the information you needed," she said firmly.

His narrow eyes went from her to the front of the house. "Is he in there waiting for you?" he asked coldly.

"If he is, it's nothing to do with you," she said solemnly. "As you said on that most memorable occasion, I wanted to play house and you didn't. For the record," she added with cold eyes, "I no longer want to play with you, in any manner whatsoever. Goodbye."

She went to the door, unlocked it, let herself in, and threw the bolt home after her. If he heard it, so much the better. She didn't want him within three feet of her, ever again!

# CHAPTER SIX

TIFFANY WENT UPSTAIRS, almost shaking with fury at Carla's treacherous action, because certainly no one else could be blamed for the omission of those names on the guest list. Carla was playing to win and thought Tiffany was competition. It was funny, in a way, because King wanted no part of her. Why didn't Carla know that?

She went into her room and opened her closet. It was New Year's Day, and tomorrow she and Mark would have to fly back to New York and get ready to begin work again. It was going to be a hectic few weeks, with the spring showings in the near future, and Tiffany was almost certain that she'd be able to land a new contract. She was young and photogenic and her agent said that she had great potential. It wasn't as heady a prospect as a life with King, but it would have to suffice. Loneliness was something she was just going to have to get used to, so she...

"Packing already?"

The drawled question surprised her into gasping. She whirled, a hand at her throat, to find King lounging in the doorway.

"How did you get in?" she demanded.

"Kitty let me in the back door. She's cleaning the kitchen." He closed the door firmly behind him and started toward Tiffany with a strange glitter in his pale blue eyes. "It isn't like you to run from a fight. You never used to."

"Maybe I'm tired of fighting," she said through a tight throat.

"Maybe I am, too," he replied curtly.

He backed her against the bed and suddenly gave her a gentle push. She went down onto the mattress and his lean, hard body followed her. He braced himself on his forearms beside her head and stared into her eyes at a breathless proximity.

"I'm expecting Mark…" She choked.

"Really? Kitty says he's at Lisa McKinley's house, and very smitten, too, from the look of them at the party last night." His hand smoothed away the lapels of her jacket. His big hand skimmed softly over her breast and his thumb lingered there long enough to make the tip go hard. He smiled when he felt it. "Some things, at least, never change."

"I don't know what you…oh!"

She arched completely off the bed when his mouth suddenly covered her breast. Even through two layers of cloth, it made her shiver with pleasure. Her hands clenched at her ears and her eyes closed as she gave in without even a struggle.

His hands slid under her clothing to the two fastenings at her back. He loosened them and his hands found the softness of her breasts. "Good God, it's like running my hands over silk," he whispered as his head lifted. "You feel like sweet heaven."

As he spoke, his hands moved. He watched her pupils dilate, her lips part on whispery little sighs that grew sharp when his thumbs brushed her hard nipples.

"The hell with it," he murmured roughly. He sat up, drawing her with him, and proceeded to undress her.

"King…you can't…!"

"I want to suckle you," he said quietly, staring into her shocked eyes as he freed her body from the clothes.

The words fanned the flames that were already devouring her. She didn't speak again. She sat breathing like a track runner while he tossed her jacket and blouse and bra off the bed. Then his hands at her rib cage arched her delicately toward him. He bent and his mouth slowly fastened on her breast.

There was no past, no present. There was only the glory of King's hard mouth on her body. She sobbed breathlessly as the pleasure grew to unbelievable heights.

He had her across his knees, her head falling naturally into the crook of his arm, while he fed on her breasts. The nuzzling, suckling pressure was the sweetest sensation she'd ever known. It had been so long since he'd held her like this. She was alive again, breathing again.

"Easy, darling," he whispered when she began to sob aloud. "Easy, now."

"King…!" Her voice broke. She sounded as frantic as she felt, her heartbeat smothering her, the pressure of his hands all of heaven as he held her to his chest.

"Baby…" He eased her onto the bed and slid alongside her, his face solemn, his eyes dark with feeling. His mouth found hers, held it gently under his while his hands searched out the places where she ached and began to soothe them…only the soothing made the tension worse.

She moaned, tears of frustration stinging her eyes as his caresses only made the hunger more unbearable.

"All right," he whispered, easing down against her. "It's too soon, Tiffany, but I'm going to give you what you want."

He shifted her and his hand moved slowly against her body. She stiffened, but he didn't stop. He kissed her shocked eyelids closed and then smothered the words of protest she tried to voice.

She had no control over her body, none at all. It insisted, it demanded, it was wanton as it sought fulfillment. Her eyes remained tightly closed while she arched and arched, pleading, whispering to him, pride shorn from her in the grip of a madness like none she'd ever experienced.

She opened her eyes all at once and went rigid as a flash of pleasure like hot lightning shot through her flesh. She looked at him in shock and awe and suddenly she was flying among the stars, falling, soaring, in a shuddering ecstasy that none of her reading had ever prepared her for.

Afterward, of course, she wept. She was embarrassed and shocked by this newest lesson in passion and its fulfillment. She hid her face against him, still shivering gently in the aftermath.

"I told you it was too soon," he whispered quietly. He held her close, his face nuzzling her throat. "I took it too far. I only meant to kiss you." His arms tightened. "Don't cry. There's no reason to be upset."

"Nobody…*ever*…" She choked.

His thumb pressed against her swollen lips. "I know." His mouth moved onto her wet eyelids and kissed the tears away slowly. "And that was only the beginning," he whispered. "You can't imagine how it really feels."

He carried her hand to his body and shivered as he moved it delicately against him. "I want you."

She pressed her lips to his throat. "I know. I want you, too."

His teeth nipped her earlobe gently and his breath caught. "Tiffany, your father is my business partner. There's no way we can sleep together without having him find out. It would devastate him. He doesn't really belong to this century."

"I know." She grimaced slightly. "Neither do I, I suppose."

He lifted his head and looked down at her soft hand resting so nervously against his body. He smiled gently even through the pleasure of her touch. His hand pressed hers closer as he looked into her eyes hungrily. "I'm starving," he whispered.

She swallowed, gathering her nerve. "I could...?"

He sighed. "No. You couldn't." He took her hand away and held it tightly in his. "In my way, I'm pretty old-fashioned, too." He grimaced. "I suppose you'd better come into town with me tomorrow and pick out a ring."

Her eyelids fluttered. "A what?"

"An engagement ring and a wedding band," he continued.

"You don't want to marry. You said so."

He looked down at himself ruefully and then back at her flushed face. "It's been several months," he said pointedly. "I'm not a man to whom abstinence comes naturally, to put it modestly. I need a woman."

"I thought you were having Carla," she accused.

He sighed heavily. "Well, that's one of the little problems I've been dealing with since you left. She can't seem to arouse my…interest."

Her eyes widened. This was news. "I understood that any woman can arouse a man."

"Reading fiction again, are we?" he murmured dryly. "Well, books and instruction manuals notwithstanding, my body doesn't seem to be able to read. It only wants you. And it wants you violently."

She was still tingling from her own pleasure. She grimaced.

"What?" he asked.

"I feel guilty. This was all just for me," she faltered, still a little embarrassed.

"I'll run around the house three times and have a cold shower," he murmured dryly. "No need to fret."

She laid back on the bed, watching him sketch her nudity with quick, possessive eyes. "You can, if you want to," she whispered with a wicked smile, never so sure of him as she was at the moment. "I'll let you."

His high cheekbones actually flushed. "With Kitty in the kitchen and aware that I'm up here?" He smiled mockingly and glanced at his watch. "I'd say we have about two minutes to go."

"Until what?"

"Until you have a phone call, or I have a phone call," he remarked. "Which will have strangely been disconnected the minute we pick up the receiver."

She giggled. "You're kidding."

"I'm not." He got up and rearranged his tie, staring down at her with pure anguish. "I want to bury myself in you!" he growled softly.

She flushed. "King!"

It didn't help that her eyes went immediately to that part of him that would perform such a task and she went even redder. She threw herself off the bed and began to fumble to put her clothing back on.

He chuckled. "All that magnificent bravado, gone without a whimper. What a surprise you've got in store on our wedding night," he murmured.

She finished buttoning her blouse and gave him a wry look. "You really are a rake."

"And you'll be glad about that, too," he added with a knowing look. "I promise you will."

She moved close to him, her eyes wide and eloquent. "It won't hurt after what we've done, will it?"

He hesitated. "I don't know," he said finally. "I'll be as careful and gentle as I can."

"I know that." She searched his eyes with a deep sadness that she couldn't seem to shake. "It's only because you want me that we're getting married, isn't it?"

He scowled. "Don't knock it. Sex is the foundation of any good marriage. You and I are highly compatible in that respect."

She wanted to pursue the conversation, but there was a sudden knock at the door.

"Yes, what is it, Kitty?" Tiffany called, distracted.

"Uh, there's a phone call for Mr. Marshall, Miss Tiffany," she called nervously.

"I'll take it downstairs, Kitty. Thanks!" he added with a roguish look in Tiffany's direction.

"You're welcome!" Kitty called brightly, and her footsteps died away.

"Your father puts her up to that," he mused.

"He's sheltered me."

"I know."

She pursed her lips and eyed him mischievously. "I've been saved up for you."

"I'll be worth the effort," he promised, a dark, confident gleam in his eyes.

"Oh, I know that." She went to open the door, pushing back her disheveled hair. "Are you coming to dinner tonight?"

"Is your male fashion plate going to be here?"

"I'm not sure. Lisa was very taken with him, and vice versa."

He smiled. "I started up here bristling with jealousy. I could have danced a jig when Kitty stopped me to tell me about your houseguest and Lisa."

"You were jealous?" she asked.

He lifted an eyebrow and his eyes slid over her like hands. "We both know that you've belonged to me since you've had breasts," he said blatantly. "I kept my distance, almost for too long. But I came to my senses in time."

"I hope you won't regret it."

"So do I," he said without thinking, and he looked disturbed.

"I'll try to make you glad," she whispered in what she hoped was a coquettish tone.

He grinned. "See that you do."

She opened the door and he followed her out into the hall.

MARK WAS MORE amused than anything when he discovered that his gal pal was engaged to her dream man. He and Lisa had found many things in common and a romance was blooming there, so he had only good wishes for Tiffany and her King. But there was something in the way King looked that made him uneasy. That man didn't have happily ever after in mind, and he wasn't passionately in love with Tiffany—and it showed. He wanted her; that was obvious to a blind man. But it seemed less than honest for a man to marry a woman only because of desire. Perhaps her father was the fly in the ointment. He couldn't see the dignified Mr. Blair allowing his only daughter to become the mistress of his business partner.

Of course! That had to be the reason for the sudden marriage plans. King had manipulated Tiffany so that she was done out of a fairy tale wedding, so that she was settling for a small, intimate ceremony instead. It was unkind and Mark wished he could help, but it seemed the only thing he could do for his friend was wish her the best and step aside. King didn't seem like a man who'd want a male friend in his virgin bride's life....

LIFE CHANGED FOR Tiffany overnight. She went to one of the biggest jewelers in San Antonio with King, where they looked at rings for half an hour before she chose a wide antique gold wedding band in yellow and white gold, with engraved roses.

King hesitated. "Don't you want a diamond?" he asked.

"No." She wasn't sure why, but she didn't. She let

the salesman try the ring on her finger. It was a perfect fit and she was enchanted with it.

King held her hand in his and looked down at it. The sentiment of the old-fashioned design made him strangely uneasy. It looked like an heirloom, something a wife would want to pass down to a child. His eyes met hers and he couldn't hide his misgivings. He'd more or less been forced into proposing by the situation, but he hadn't thought past the honeymoon. Here was proof that Tiffany had years, not months, of marriage in mind, while he only wanted to satisfy a raging hunger.

"Don't you like it?" she asked worriedly.

"It's exquisite," he replied with a determined smile. "Yes, I like it."

She sighed, relieved. "Don't you want to choose one?" she asked when he waved the salesman away.

"No," he said at once. He glanced down at her. "I'm not much on rings. I'm allergic to gold," he added untruthfully, thinking fast.

"Oh. Oh, I see." She brightened a little. It had hurt to think he didn't want to wear a visible symbol of his married status.

In no time at all, they were caught up in wedding arrangements. King didn't want a big society wedding, and neither did Tiffany. They settled for a small, intimate service in the local Presbyterian church with friends and family. A minister was engaged, and although traditionally the groom was to provide the flowers, Tiffany made the arrangements for them to be delivered.

Her one regret was not being able to have the elegant

wedding gown she'd always imagined that she'd have. Such a dress seemed somehow out of place at a small service. She chose to wear a modern designer suit in white, instead, with an elegant little hat and veil.

She wished that her long-time best friend hadn't married a military man and moved to Germany with him. She had no one to be maid or matron of honor. There again, in a small service it wouldn't be noticeable.

King became irritable and withdrawn as the wedding date approached. He was forever away on business or working late at the office, and Tiffany hoped this wasn't going to become a pattern for their married life. She was realistic enough to understand that his job was important to him, but she wanted a big part in his life. She hoped she was going to have one.

The night before the wedding, King had supper with Tiffany and her father. He was so remote even Harrison noticed.

"Not getting cold feet, are you?" Harrison teased, and tensed at the look that raced across the younger man's face before he could conceal it.

"Of course not," King said curtly. "I've had a lot on my mind lately, that's all."

Tiffany paused with her glass in midair to glance at King. She hadn't really noticed how taut his face was, how uneasy he seemed. He'd never spoken of marriage in anyone's memory. In fact, he'd been quite honest about his mistrust of it. He'd had girlfriends for as long as Tiffany could remember, but there had never been a reason to be jealous of any of them. King never let himself become serious over a woman.

"Don't drop that," King murmured, nodding toward the loose grip she had on the glass.

She put it down deliberately. "King, you do want to marry me, don't you?" she asked abruptly.

His eyes met hers across the table. There was no trace of expression in them. "I wouldn't have asked you if I hadn't meant to go through with it," he replied.

The phrasing was odd. She hesitated for a few seconds, tracing patterns on her glass. "I could work for a while longer," she suggested, "and we could put off the ceremony."

"We're getting married Saturday," he reminded her. "I already have tickets for a resort on Jamaica for our honeymoon. We're scheduled on a nonstop flight Saturday afternoon to Montego Bay."

"Plans can be changed," she replied.

He laughed humorlessly. "Now who's got cold feet?" he challenged.

"Not me," she lied. She smiled and drained her glass. But inside, butterflies were rioting in her stomach. She'd never been more unsure of her own hopes and dreams. She wanted King, and he wanted her. But his was a physical need. Had she pushed him into this marriage after all, and now he was going to make the most of it? What if he tired of her before the honeymoon was even over?

She stopped this train of thought. It was absurd to have so little faith in her own abilities. She'd vamped him at her twenty-first birthday party, to such effect that he'd come home from his business trip out of his mind over her. If she could make him crazy once, she could do it twice. She could make him happy. She could fit in his world. It was, after all, hers, too. As for Carla, and the complications she might provoke, she could worry about that later. If she could keep King happy at home, Carla wouldn't have a prayer of splitting them up.

Her covetous eyes went over him as if they were curious hands, searching out his chiseled mouth, his straight nose, the shape of his head, the darkness of his hair, the deep-set eyes that could sparkle or stun. He was elegant, devastating to look at, a physical presence wherever he went. He had power and wealth and the arrogance that went with them. But was he capable of love, with the sort of loveless background he'd had? Could he learn it?

As she studied him, his head turned and he studied her, his eyes admiring her beauty, her grace. Something altered in the eyes that swept over her and his eyes narrowed.

"Am I slurping my soup?" she asked with an impish grin.

Caught off guard, he chuckled. "No. I was thinking what a beauty you are," he said honestly. "You won't change much in twenty years. You may get a gray hair or two, but you'll still be a miracle."

"What a nice thing to say," she murmured, putting down her soup spoon. "You remember that, in about six years' time. I'll remind you, in case you forget."

"I won't forget," he mused.

Harrison let out a faint sigh of relief. Surely it was only prenuptial nerves eating at King. The man had known Tiffany for years, after all, there wouldn't be many surprises for them. They had things in common and they liked each other. Even if love was missing at first, he knew it would come. It would have to. Nothing short of it would hold a man like King.

Tiffany glanced at her father's somber expression and lifted an eyebrow. "It's a wedding, not a wake," she chided.

He jerked and then laughed. "Sorry, darling, I was miles away."

"Thinking about Lettie?" she teased.

He glared at her. "I was not," he snapped back. "If they ever barbecue her, I'll bring the sauce."

"You know you like her. You're just too stubborn to admit it."

"She's a constant irritation, like a mole at the belt line."

Tiffany's eyes widened. "What a comparison!"

"I've got a better one," he said darkly.

"Don't say it!"

"Spoilsport," he muttered, attacking his slice of apple pie as if it were armed.

King was listening to the byplay, not with any real interest. He was deeply thoughtful and unusually quiet. He glanced at Tiffany occasionally, but now his expression was one of vague concern and worry. Was he keeping something from her? Perhaps something was going on in his life that she didn't know about. If she could get him alone later, perhaps he'd tell her what it was.

But after they finished eating, King glanced quickly at his watch and said that he had to get back to the office to finish up some paperwork.

Tiffany got up from the table and followed him into the hallway. "I thought we might have a minute to talk," she said worriedly. "We're getting married tomorrow."

"Which is why I have to work late tonight," he replied tersely. "It's been a very long time since I've given myself a week off. Ask your father."

"I don't have to. I know how hard you work." She looked up at him with real concern. "There's still time to back out, if you want to."

His eyebrows shot up. "Do you want to?"

She gnawed the inside of her lip, wondering if that was what he wanted her to admit. It was so difficult trying to read his thoughts. She couldn't begin to.

"No," she said honestly. "I don't want to. But if you do…"

"We'll go through with it," he said. "After all, we've got plenty in common. And it will keep the business in the family."

"Yes, it will go to our children…" she began.

"Good God," he laughed without mirth, "don't start talking about a family! That's years away, for us." He scowled suddenly and stared at her. "You haven't seen a doctor, have you?"

"For the blood test," she reminded him, diverted.

"For birth control," he stated flatly, watching her cheeks color. "I'll take care of it for now. But when we get back from our honeymoon, you make an appointment. I don't care what you choose, but I want you protected."

She felt as if he'd knocked her down and jumped on her feetfirst. "You know a lot about birth control for a bachelor," she faltered.

"That's why I'm still a bachelor," he replied coldly. He searched her eyes. "Children will be a mutual decision, not yours alone. I hope we've clarified that."

"You certainly have," she said.

"I'll see you at the church tomorrow." His eyes went over her quickly. "Try to get a good night's sleep. We've got a long day and a long trip ahead of us."

"Yes, I will."

He touched her hair, but he didn't kiss her. He laughed again, as if at some cold personal joke. He left her in the hallway without a backward glance. It was a foreboding sort of farewell for a couple on the eve of their wedding, and because of it, Tiffany didn't sleep at all.

# CHAPTER SEVEN

THE NEXT DAY dawned with pouring rain. It was a gloomy morning that made Tiffany even more depressed than she had been to start with. She stared at her reflection in the mirror and hardly recognized herself. She didn't feel like the old devil-may-care Tiffany who would dare anything to get what she wanted from life. And she remembered with chilling precision the words of an old saying: *be careful what you wish for; you might get it.*

She made up her face carefully, camouflaging her paleness and the shadows under her eyes. She dressed in her neat white suit and remembered belatedly that she hadn't thought to get a bouquet for the occasion. It was too late now. She put on her hat and pulled the thin veil over her eyes, picked up her purse, and went out to join her father in the downstairs hall. The house seemed empty and unnaturally quiet, and she wondered what her late mother would have thought of this wedding.

Harrison, in an expensive dark suit with a white rose in his lapel, turned and smiled at his daughter as she came down the staircase.

"You look lovely," he said. "Your mother would have been proud."

"I hope so."

He came closer, frowning as he took her hands and found them ice-cold. "Darling, are you sure this is what you want?" he asked solemnly. "It's not too late to call it off, you know, even now."

For one mad instant, she thought about it. Panic had set in firmly. But she'd gone too far.

"It will work out," she said doggedly, and smiled at her father. "Don't worry."

He sighed impotently and shrugged. "I can't help it. Neither of you looked much like a happy couple over dinner last night. You seemed more like people who'd just won a chance on the guillotine."

"Oh, Dad," she moaned, and then burst out laughing. "Trust you to come up with something outrageous!"

He smiled, too. "That's better. You had a ghostly pallor when you came down the stairs. We wouldn't want people to mistake this ceremony for a wake."

"God forbid!" She took his arm. "Well," she said, taking a steadying breath, "let's get it over with."

"Comments like that are so reassuring," he muttered to himself as he escorted her out the door and into the white limousine that was to take them to the small church.

Surprisingly, the parking lot was full of cars when they pulled up at the curb.

"I don't remember inviting anyone," she ventured.

"King probably felt obliged to invite his company people," he reminded her. "Especially his executive staff."

"Well, yes, I suppose so." She waited for the chauffeur to open the door, and she got out gingerly, keenly aware that she didn't have a bouquet. She left her purse in the limo, in which she and King would be leaving for the airport immediately after the service. A reception hadn't been possible in the time allocated. King would probably have arranged some sort of refreshments for his office staff, of course, perhaps at a local restaurant.

Tiffany entered the church on her father's arm, and they paused to greet two of King's vice presidents, whom they knew quite well.

King was standing at the altar with the minister. The decorations were unsettling. Instead of the bower of roses she'd hoped for, she found two small and rather scruffy-looking flower arrangements gracing both sides of the altar. Carelessly tied white ribbons festooned the front pews. Family would have been sitting there, if she and King had any close relatives. Neither did, although Tiffany claimed Lettie as family, and sure enough, there she sat, in a suit, and especially a hat, that would have made fashion headlines. Tiffany smiled involuntarily at the picture her fashionable godmother made. Good thing the newspapers weren't represented, she thought, or Lettie would have overshadowed the bride and groom for splendor in that exquisite silk dress. And, of course, the hat.

The minister spotted Tiffany in the back of the church with her father and nodded to the organist who'd been hired to provide music. The familiar strains of the "Wedding March" filled the small church.

Tiffany's knees shook as she and her father made their way down the aisle. She wondered how many couples had walked this aisle, in love and with hope and joy? God knew, she was scared to death of what lay ahead.

And just when she thought she couldn't feel any worse, she spotted Carla in the front pew on King's side of the church. With disbelief, she registered that the woman was wearing a white lacy dress with a white veiled hat! As if she, not Tiffany, were the bride!

She felt her father tense as his own gaze followed hers, but neither of them were unconventional enough to make any public scene. It was unbelievable that King would invite his paramour here, to his wedding. But, then, perhaps he was making a statement. Tiffany would be his wife, but he was making no concessions in his personal life. When confronted by the pitiful floral accessories, and her lack of a bouquet, she wasn't particularly surprised that he'd invited Carla. She and her dress were the final indignity of the day.

King glanced sideways as she joined him, her father relinquishing her and going quickly to his own seat. King's eyes narrowed on her trim suit and the absence of a bouquet. He scowled.

She didn't react. She simply looked at the minister and gave him all her attention as he began the ceremony.

There was a flutter when, near the end of the service, he called for King to put the ring on Tiffany's finger. King searched his pockets, scowling fiercely, until he found it loose in his slacks' pocket, where he'd placed it earlier. He slid it onto Tiffany's finger, his face hardening when he registered how cold her hand was.

The minister finished his service, asked if the couple had any special thing they'd like to say as part of the ceremony. When they looked uneasy, he quickly pronounced them man and wife and smiled as he invited King to kiss the bride.

King turned to his new wife and stared at her with narrowed eyes for a long moment before he pulled up the thin veil and bent to kiss her carelessly with cold, firm lips.

People from the front pews surged forward to offer congratulations. Lettie was first. She hugged Tiffany warmly, acting like a mother hen. Tiffany had to fight tears, because her new status would take her away from the only surrogate mother she'd ever known. But she forced a watery smile and started to turn to her father when she saw a laughing Carla lift her arms around King's neck and kiss him passionately, full on the mouth.

The minister looked as surprised as Tiffany and her father did. Harrison actually started forward, when Lettie took his arm.

"Walk me to my car, Harrison," Lettie directed.

Seconds later, King extricated himself and shook hands with several of his executives. Tiffany gave Carla a look that could have fried an egg and deliberately took her father's free arm.

"Shall we go?" she said to her two elderly companions.

"Really, dear, this is most…unconventional," Lettie faltered as Tiffany marched them out of the church.

"Not half as unconventional as forgetting which woman you married," she said loudly enough for King, and the rest of the onlookers, to hear her.

She didn't look at him, although she could feel furious eyes stabbing her in the back.

She didn't care. He and his lover had humiliated her beyond bearing, and on her wedding day. She was tempted to go home with her father and get an annulment on the spot.

As she stood near the limousine with Harrison and Lettie, debating her next move, King caught her arm and parceled her unceremoniously into the limousine. She barely had time to wave as the driver took off.

"That was a faux pas of the highest order," he snapped at her.

"Try saying that with less lipstick on your mouth, darling," she drawled with pure poison.

He dug for a handkerchief and wiped his mouth, coming away with the vivid orange shade that Carla had been wearing.

"My own wedding," she said in a choked tone, her hands mangling her small purse, "and you and that… creature…make a spectacle of the whole thing!"

"You didn't help," he told her hotly, "showing up in a suit, without even a bouquet."

"The bouquet should have come from you," she said with shredded pride. "I wasn't going to beg for one. Judging by those flower arrangements you provided, if you'd ordered a bouquet for me, it would have come with dandelions and stinging nettle! As for the suit, you didn't want a big wedding, and a fancy gown would have been highly inappropriate for such a small ceremony."

He laughed coldly, glaring at her. "You didn't say you wanted a bouquet."

"You can give Carla one later and save her the trouble of having to catch mine."

He cursed roundly.

"Go ahead," she invited. "Ruin the rest of the day."

"This whole damned thing was your idea," he snapped at her, tugging roughly at his constricting tie. "Marriage was never in my mind, until you started throwing yourself at me! God knew, an affair was never an option."

She searched his averted profile sadly. As she'd feared, this had been, in many ways, a shotgun wedding. She mourned for the old days, when they were friends and enjoyed each other's company. Those days were gone forever.

"Yes. I know," she said heavily. She leaned back against the seat and felt as if she'd been dragged behind the car. She'd lost her temper, but it wasn't really his fault. He was as much a victim as she was, at the moment. "I don't know why I should have expected you to jump with joy," she said when she'd calmed a little. "You're right. I did force you into a marriage you didn't want. You have every right to be furious." She turned to him with dead eyes in a face like rice paper. "There's no need to go on with this farce. We can get an annulment, right now. If you'll just have the driver take me home, I'll start it right away."

He stared at her as if he feared for her sanity. "Are you out of your mind?" he asked shortly. "We've just been married. What the hell do you think it will say to my executives and my stockholders if I annul my marriage an hour after the ceremony?"

"No one has to know when it's done," she said reasonably. "You can fly to Jamaica and I'll go back to New York with Lettie until this all blows over."

"Back to modeling, I suppose?" he asked curtly.

She shrugged. "It's something to do," she said.

"You have something to do," he returned angrily. "You're my wife."

"Am I?" she asked. "Not one person in that church would have thought so, after you kissed Carla. In fact, I must say, her dress was much more appropriate than mine for the occasion, right down to the veil."

He averted his eyes, almost as if he were embarrassed. She leaned back again and closed her own eyes, to shut him out.

"I don't care," she said wearily. "Decide what you want, and I'll do it. Anything at all, except," she added, turning her head to stare at him with cold eyes, "sleep with you. That I will not do. Not now."

His eyebrows arched. "What the hell do you mean?"

"Exactly what I just said," she replied firmly. "You can get…that…from Carla, with my blessings." She almost bit through her lip telling the flat lie. Pride was very expensive. She closed her eyes again, to hide the fear that he might take her up on it. "I've been living in a fool's paradise, looking for happily ever after, dreaming of satin and lace and delicious nights and babies. And all I've got to show for it is a secondhand lust without even the gloss of friendship behind it and an absolute edict that I'm never to think of having a child."

He sat back in his own seat and stared straight ahead. Yes, he'd said that. He'd been emphatic, in fact, about not having children right away. He'd withdrawn from her in the past two weeks, so deliberately that he'd given the impression of a man being forced to do something he abhorred. He'd arranged a quick ceremony, but he hadn't let his secretary—Carla—arrange the flowers. He'd left that duty to another subordinate. He wondered what the hell had gone wrong. Only two sparse and not-very-attractive flower arrangements had graced the church and Tiffany had been denied a bouquet. He knew that it was deliberate, that Carla was somehow involved, but there was no way to undo the damage. By the time he saw the flowers it was far too late to do anything. Carla's dress and the kiss had been as much a surprise to him as it had to Tiffany. She wouldn't believe it, though. She was thinking of the things he'd denied her.

She'd been denied more than just flowers, at that. She hadn't had a photographer, a ring bearer, flower girls and attendants, a reception—she'd lacked all those as well. And to top it all off, it looked as if he'd wanted to kiss his secretary instead of his new bride, in front of the whole assembly.

His eyes sought her averted face again, with bitter regret. He'd fought marrying her from the start, hating his weakness for her, punishing her for it. This had been a travesty of a wedding, all around. She was bitter and wounded, and it was his fault. He studied her drawn countenance with haunted eyes. He remembered Tiffany all aglitter with happiness and the sheer joy of living, teasing him, laughing with him, tempting him, loving him. He could have had all that, just for himself. But he'd let his fears and misgivings cloud the occasion, and Tiffany had suffered for them.

He drew in a long breath and turned his eyes back to the window. This, he thought wearily, was going to be some honeymoon.

IN FACT, IT was some honeymoon, but not at all the sort Tiffany had once dreamed about having. Montego Bay was full of life, a colorful and fascinating place with a long history and the friendliest, most welcoming people Tiffany could ever remember in her life.

They had a suite at an expensive resort on the beach, and fortunately it contained two rooms. She didn't ask King what he thought of her decision to sleep in the smaller of the two rooms; she simply moved in. She paid him the same attention she'd have paid a female roommate, and she didn't care what he thought about that, either. It was her honeymoon. She'd had no real wedding, but she was going to have a honeymoon, even if she had to spend it alone.

King had brought along his laptop with its built-in fax-modem, and he spent the evening working at the small desk near the window.

Tiffany put on a neat beige trouser suit and fixed her hair in a soft bun atop her head. She didn't even worry with makeup.

"I'm going to the restaurant to have supper," she announced.

He looked up from his monitor, with quiet, strangely subdued eyes. "Do you want company?"

"Not particularly, thanks." She went out the door while he was getting used to being an unwelcome tourist.

She sat alone at a table and ate a seafood salad. She had a piña colada with her meal, and the amount of rum it contained sent her head spinning.

She was very happy, all of a sudden, and when a steel

band began to play to the audience, she joined in the fun, clapping and laughing with the crowd.

It wasn't until a tall, swarthy man tried to pick her up that she realized how her behavior might be misinterpreted. She held up her left hand and gave the man a smile that held just the right portions of gratitude and regret. He bowed, nonplussed, and she got up to pay her bill.

King was out on the patio when she returned, but he looked at her curiously when she stumbled just inside the closed door and giggled.

"What the hell have you been doing?" he asked.

"Getting soused, apparently," she said with a vacant smile. "Do you have any idea how much rum they put in those drinks?"

"You never did have a head for hard liquor," he remarked with a faint smile.

"A man tried to pick me up."

The smile turned into a cold scowl. He came back into the room slowly. He'd changed into white slacks and a patterned silk shirt, which was hanging open over his dark-haired chest. He looked rakish with his hair on his forehead and his eyes glittering at her.

"I showed him my wedding ring," she said to placate him. "And I didn't kiss him. It is, after all, my wedding day."

"A hell of a wedding day," he replied honestly.

"If I hadn't gone all mushy, we'd still be friends," she said with a sad little sigh as the liquor made her honest. "I wish we were."

He moved a little closer and his chest rose and fell

roughly. "So do I," he admitted tersely. He searched her sad eyes. "Tiffany, I…didn't want to be married."

"I know. It's all right," she said consolingly. "You don't have to be. When we get back, I'll go and see an attorney."

He didn't relax. His eyes were steady and curious, searching over her slender body, seeking out all the soft curves and lines of her. "You shouldn't have grown up."

"I didn't have much choice." She smothered a yawn and turned away. "Good night, King."

He watched her go with an ache in his belly that wouldn't quit. He wanted her, desperately. But an annulment would be impossible if he followed her into her room. And she'd already said that she didn't want him. He turned back to the cool breeze on the patio and walked outside, letting the wind cool his hot skin. He'd never felt so restless, or so cold inside.

TIFFANY AWOKE WITH a blinding headache and nausea thick in her throat. She managed to sit up on the side of the bed in her simple white cotton gown. It covered every inch of her, and she was glad now that she'd decided not to pack anything suggestive or glamorous. She looked very young in the gown and without her makeup, with her dark hair in a tangle around her pale face.

King knocked at the door and then walked in, hesitating in the doorway with an expression of faint surprise when he saw the way she looked. His brows drew together emphatically.

"Are you all right?" he asked curtly.

"I have a hangover," she replied without looking at him. "I want to die."

He breathed roughly. "Next time, leave the rum to the experts and have a soft drink. I've got some tablets in my case that will help. I'll bring you a couple. Want some coffee?"

"Black, please," she said. She didn't move. Her head was splitting.

When he came back, she still hadn't stirred. He shook two tablets into her hand and gave her a glass of water to swallow them with. She thanked him and gave back the glass.

"I'll bring the coffee in as soon as room service gets here," he said. "I don't suppose you want breakfast, but it would help not to have an empty stomach."

"I can't eat anything." She eased back down on the bed, curled up like a child with her eyes closed and a pillow shoved over her aching head.

He left her against his better judgment. A caring husband would have stayed with her, held her hand, offered sympathy. He'd fouled up so much for her in the past few weeks that he didn't think any overtures from him would be welcomed. She didn't even have to tell him why she'd had so much to drink the night before. He already knew.

Minutes later, he entered the room with the coffee and found Tiffany on the floor, gasping for breath. She couldn't seem to breathe. Her face was swollen. Red-rimmed eyes looked up at him with genuine panic.

"Good God." He went to the phone by her bed and called for a doctor, in tones that made threats if one wasn't forthcoming. Then he sat on the floor beside her, his expression one of subdued horror, trying to reassure her without a single idea what to do. She looked as if she might suffocate to death any minute.

The quick arrival of the doctor relieved his worry, but not for long.

Without even looking at King, the doctor jerked up the telephone and called for an ambulance.

"What did she eat?" the doctor shot at him as he filled a syringe from a small vial.

"Nothing this morning. She had a hangover. I gave her a couple of aspirins a few minutes ago..."

"Is she allergic to aspirin?" he asked curtly.

"I...don't know."

The doctor gave him a look that contained equal parts of contempt and anger. "You are her husband?" he asked with veiled sarcasm, then turned back to put the needle directly into the vein at her elbow.

"What are you giving her?" King asked curtly.

"Something to counteract an allergic reaction. You'd better go out and direct the ambulance men in here. Tell them not to lag behind."

King didn't argue, for once. He did exactly as he was told, cold all over as he took one last, fearful glance at Tiffany's poor swollen face. Her eyes were closed and she was still gasping audibly.

"Will she die?" King choked.

The doctor was counting her pulse. "Not if I can help it," he said tersely. "Hurry, man!"

King went out to the balcony and watched. He heard the ambulance arrive an eternity of seconds later. Almost at once ambulance attendants came into view. He motioned them up the stairs and into Tiffany's bedroom.

They loaded her onto a gurney and carried her out. Her color was a little better and she was breathing much more easily, but she was apparently unconscious.

"You can ride in the ambulance with her, if you like," the doctor invited.

King hesitated, not because he didn't want to go with her, but because he'd never been in such a position before and he was stunned.

"Follow in a cab, then," the other man rapped. "I'll ride with her."

He muttered under his breath, grabbed his wallet and key, locked the door, and went down to catch a cab at the front of the hotel. It was a simple exercise, there was always a cab waiting and a doorman to summon it.

MINUTES LATER, HE was pacing outside the emergency room waiting for the doctor to come out. Strange how quickly his priorities had changed and rearranged in the past few minutes. All it had taken was seeing Tiffany like that. He knew that as long as he lived, the sight of her on the floor would come back to haunt him. It had been so unnecessary. He'd never bothered to ask if she was allergic to anything. He hadn't wanted to know her in any intimate or personal way.

Now he realized that he knew nothing at all, and that his ignorance had almost cost her her life this morning. Nothing was as important now as seeing that she had the best care, that she got better, that she never had to suffer again because of a lack of interest or caring on his part. He might not have wanted this marriage, but divorce was not feasible. He had to make the best of it. And he would.

## CHAPTER EIGHT

BUT THE THING that hadn't occurred to him was that Tiffany might not care one way or the other for his concern. When she was released from the hospital later that day, with a warning not to ever touch aspirin again in any form, her whole attitude toward her husband had changed. Every ounce of spirit seemed to have been drained out of her.

She was quiet, unusually withdrawn on the way back to the hotel in the taxi. Her paleness hadn't abated, despite her treatment. The swelling had gone, but she was weak. He had to help her from the taxi and into the hotel.

"I never asked if you had allergies," King said as he supported her into the elevator. He pushed the button for their floor. "I'm sorry this happened."

"The whole thing was my fault," she said wearily. "My head hurt so bad that it never occurred to me to question what you were giving me. I haven't had an aspirin since I was thirteen."

He studied her as she leaned back against the wall of the elevator, looking as if she might collapse any minute. "One way or another, you've had a hell of a wedding."

She laughed mirthlessly. "Yes, I have."

The elevator jerked to a stop and the doors opened. King abruptly swung her up into his arms and carried her to their room, putting her down only long enough to produce the key and open the door.

She let her head rest on his broad shoulder and closed her eyes, pretending that he loved her, pretending that he wanted her. She'd lived on dreams of him most of her life, but reality had been a staggering blow to her pride and her heart. They were married, and yet not married.

He carried her into the sitting room and deposited her gently on the sofa. "Are you hungry?" he asked. "Do you think you could eat something?"

"A cold salad, perhaps," she murmured. "With thousand island dressing, and a glass of milk."

He phoned room service, ordering that for her and a steak and salad and a beer for himself.

"I didn't know you ever drank beer," she mused when he hung up.

He glanced at her curiously. "We've lived in each other's pockets for as long as I can remember," he said. "Amazing, isn't it, how little we actually know about each other."

She pushed back her disheveled hair with a sigh and closed her eyes. "I don't think there's a drop of anything left in my poor stomach. I couldn't eat last night. I didn't even have breakfast this morning."

"And you don't need to lose weight," he stated solemnly. He scowled as he searched over her body. "Tiffany, you've dropped a few pounds lately."

"I haven't had much appetite for several months," she said honestly. "It wasn't encouraged when I was modeling. After I came home, and we…decided to get married, I was too busy to eat a lot. It's been a hectic few weeks."

He hadn't missed the hesitation when she spoke of their decision to marry. He hated the way she looked. The change in her was so dramatic that anyone who'd known her even a year before wouldn't recognize her.

His heavy sigh caught her attention.

"Do you want to go home?" she asked.

The sadness in her eyes hurt him. "Only if you do," he said. "There are plenty of things to see around here. We could go up and walk around Rose Hall, for example," he added, mentioning a well-known historical spot.

But she shook her head. "I don't feel like sightseeing, King," she told him honestly. "Couldn't we go home?"

He hesitated. She was worn-out from the rushed wedding, the trip over here, her experience with the allergic reaction. He wanted to tell her that a night's sleep might make all the difference, but the sight of her face was enough to convince him that she'd do better in her own environment.

"All right," he said gently. "If that's what you want. We'll leave at the end of the week. I'll try to get tickets first thing in the morning."

She nodded. "Thank you."

Room service came with their orders and they ate in a strained silence. Tiffany finished her salad and coffee and then, pleading tiredness, got up to go to bed.

She started for her own room.

"Tiffany."

His deep voice stopped her at the doorway. She turned. "Yes?"

"Sleep with me."

Her heart jerked in her chest. Her eyes widened.

"No," he said, shaking his head as he got to his feet. "I don't want you that way yet, honey," he said softly, to lessen the blow of the statement. "You don't need to be alone tonight. It's a king-size bed, and you won't need to worry that I'll take advantage."

It was very tempting. He'd hardly touched her in almost a month. And although he didn't know it, any fear of having him take advantage of the situation was nonexistent. She sometimes felt that she'd have given six months of her life to have him throw her down onto the nearest available surface and ravish her to the point of exhaustion. She wondered what he'd say if she admitted that. Probably it would be just one more complication he didn't want. And there was still Carla, waiting back home.

"All right," she said after a minute. "If you don't mind…"

"Mind!" He bit off the word and turned away before she could see his strained face. "No," he said finally. "I don't…mind."

He was behaving very oddly, she mused as she showered and then put on another of her white embroidered gowns. The garment was very concealing and virginal, and there was a cotton robe that matched it, with colorful pastel embroidery on the collar and the hem, and even on the belt that secured it around her trim waist.

When she walked into the other room and approached King's, through the slightly open door she heard him talking on the telephone.

"…be home tomorrow," he was saying. "I'll want

everything ready when I get to the office. Yes, we'll talk about that," he added in a cold, biting tone. "No, I wouldn't make any bets on it. You do that. And don't foul things up this time or it will be the last mistake you make on my payroll. Is that clear?"

He put down the receiver with an angry breath and ran a hand through his own damp hair. He was wearing an incredibly sexy black velour robe with silver trim. When he turned, Tiffany's knees went weak at the wide swath of hair-roughened chest it bared to her hungry eyes.

He was looking at her, too. The gown and robe should have been dampening to any man's ardor, because she looked as virginal as he knew she was. But it inflamed him. With her face soft in the lamplight, her eyes downcast, she made him ache.

"Which side of the bed do you want?" he asked curtly.

"I like the left, but it doesn't matter."

He waved her toward it. Trying not to notice that he was watching her obsessively, she drew off the robe and spread it across the back of a nearby chair before she turned down the covers and, tossing off her slippers, climbed under the sheet.

He looked at her with darkening, narrowed eyes. She could see his heartbeat, it was so heavy. While she watched, his hand went to the loop that secured the belt of his robe and loosened it, catching the robe over one arm to toss it aside. He stood there, completely nude, completely aroused, and let her look.

Her lips parted. It was a blatant, arrogant action. She didn't know what to do or say. She couldn't manage words. He was…exquisite. He had a body that would have made the most jaded woman swoon with pleasure. And, remembering the heated mastery of his lovemaking, her body throbbed all over. It was in her eyes, her flushed face, her shaking heartbeat.

"Take it off," he said in a husky soft tone. "I want to look at you."

She wasn't able to think anymore. She clammered out from under the sheet and onto her knees, struggling to throw off the yards of concealing cotton. At last, she tugged it over her head and threw it onto the floor. Her body was as aroused as his. He knew the signs.

He moved around the bed. As he came closer, he caught the rose scent of her. Forgotten was the rocky start to their honeymoon, the accusations, the sudden illness. He approached her like a predator.

She made a helpless little sound and abruptly reached beside her to sweep both pillows off the bed and onto the floor as she surged backward, flat on the sheet, her legs parted, her arms beside her head. She trembled there, waiting, a little afraid of the overwhelming masculinity of him, but hungry and welcoming despite it.

He came onto the bed, slowly, stealthily, as if he still expected her to bolt. One lean, powerful leg inserted itself between both of hers, his chest hovered above hers, his arms slid beside her, his fingers interlaced with her own and pinned them beside her ears.

"It's…pagan." She choked.

He understood. He nodded slowly, and still his eyes held hers, unblinking, as his leg moved against the inside of hers in a sinuous, sensual touch that echoed the predatory approach of his mouth to her parted lips.

It was like fencing, she thought half-dazed. His body teased her, his mouth teased her, every part of him was an instrument of seduction. It was nothing like their earlier lovemaking, when he'd kissed her, touched her, even pleasured her. This was the real thing, a prowling, tenderly violent stalking of the female by the male, a controlled savagery of pleasure that enticed but never satisfied, that aroused and denied all at the same time.

Her body shook as if with a fever and she arched, pleaded, pulled, twisted, trying to make him end it. The tension was at a level far beyond any that he'd ever subjected her to.

He touched her very briefly and then, finally— finally!—moved down into the intimacy that she'd begged for. But even as it came, it frightened her. She stiffened, her nails digging into his muscular arms, her teeth biting at her lower lip.

He stilled. His heart was beating furiously, but his eyes, despite their fierce need, were tender.

"First times are always difficult," he whispered. He held her eyes as he moved again, very gently. "Can you feel me, there?" he murmured wickedly, bending to brush his smiling lips against hers. They rested there as he moved again. "Talk to me."

*"Talk?"* She gasped as she felt him invading her. "Good… Lord…!"

"Talk to me," he chided, laughing as she clutched him. "This isn't a ritual of silence. We're learning each other in the most intimate way there is. It shouldn't be an ordeal. Look down my body while I'm taking you. See how it looks when we fit together like puzzle pieces."

"I couldn't!" she gasped.

"Why?" He stilled and deliberately lifted himself for a few seconds. "Look, Tiffany," he coaxed. "It isn't frightening, or sordid, or ugly. We're becoming lovers. It's the most beautiful thing a man and woman can share, especially when it's as emotional as it is physical. Look at us."

It was a powerful enticement, and it worked. But her shocked eyes didn't linger. They went quickly back to his, as if to seek comfort and reassurance.

"You're my wife," he whispered softly. He caught his breath as his next movement took him completely to the heart of her, and his eyes closed and he shivered.

Seeing him vulnerable like that seemed to rob her of fear and the slight discomfort of their intimate position. One of her hands freed itself and moved hesitantly to touch his drawn face, to sift through his thick, cool black hair. His eyes opened, as if the caress startled him.

It was incredible, to look at him and talk to him with the lights on while they fused in the most shocking way. But he didn't seem at all shocked. In fact, he watched her the whole time. When his hips began to move lazily against hers and the shock of pleasure lifted her tight against him, and she gasped, he actually laughed.

"For...shame!" She choked, shivering with each movement as unexpected pleasure rippled through her.

"Why?" he taunted.

"You laughed!"

"You delight me," he whispered, bending to nibble her lips as his movements lengthened and deepened. "I've never enjoyed it like this."

Which was an uncomfortable reminder that he was no novice. She started to speak, but as if he sensed what she was going to say, he suddenly shifted and she was overwhelmed by the most staggering pleasure she'd ever felt.

It possessed her. She couldn't even breathe. She arched up, helpless, her mouth open, her eyes dazed, gasping with each deliberate movement of his body. She was trying to grasp something elusive and explosive, reaching toward it with every thread of her being. It was just out of her reach, almost, almost, tantalizingly close…

"Oh…please!" she managed to say in a shuddering little cry.

He looked somber, almost violent in that instant. He said something, but she didn't hear him. Just as the tension abruptly snapped and she heard her own voice sobbing in unbearable pleasure, his face buried itself in her soft throat and his own body shuddered with the same sweet anguish.

For a long time afterward, his breathing was audible, raspy and unsteady at her ear. She gasped for air, but she was still clinging to him, as if she could retain just a fragment of that extraordinary wave of pleasure that had drowned her for endless seconds.

"It doesn't last," she whispered shakenly.

"It couldn't," he replied heavily. "The human body can only bear so much of it without dying."

Her hands spread on his damp shoulders with a sort of wonder at the feel of him so deep in her body. She moved her hips and felt the pleasure ripple through her unexpectedly.

She laughed at her discovery.

He lifted his dark head and his eyes, sated now, searched hers. "Experimenting?"

She nodded, and moved gently again, gasping as she found what she was searching for. But along with it came a new and unfamiliar stinging sensation and she stilled.

He brushed back her damp hair gently. "Your body has to get used to this," he murmured. "Right now, you need rest more than you need me." He moved very slowly and balanced himself on his hands. "Try to relax," he whispered. "This may be uncomfortable."

Which was an understatement. She closed her eyes and ground her teeth together as he lifted away from her.

He eased over onto his back with a heavy breath and turned his head toward her. "And now you know a few things that you didn't, before," he mused, watching her expressions. "Want a bath or just a wet cloth?"

The matter-of-fact question shouldn't have shocked her, but it did. Her nudity shocked her, too, and so did his. Without the anesthetic of passion, sex was very embarrassing. She got to her feet and gathered up her gown, holding it over her front.

"I... I think I'd like a shower," she stammered.

He got out of bed, completely uninhibited, and took the gown from her fingers, tossing it onto the bed. "None of that," he taunted softly. "We're an old married couple now. That means we can bathe together."

Her expression was complicated. "We can?"

"We can."

He led her into the bathroom, turned on the shower jets, and plopped her in before him.

It was an adventure to bathe with someone. She was alternately embarrassed, intrigued, amused, and scandalized by it. But she laughed with pure delight at this unexpected facet of married life. It had never occurred to her that she might take a shower with King, even in her most erotic dreams.

Afterward, they dried each other and he carried her back to bed, placing her neatly under the covers, nude, before he joined her and turned off the lights.

He caught her wandering hand and drew it to his hairy chest with a chuckle.

"Stop that," he murmured. "You're used up. No more for you tonight, or probably tomorrow, either."

She knew he was right, but she was still bristling with curiosity and the newness of intimacy.

His hand smoothed her soft hair. "We have years of this ahead of us," he reminded her quietly. "You don't have to rush in as if tonight was the last night we'd ever have together."

She lay against him without speaking. That was how it had felt, though. There was a sort of desperation in it, a furious seeking and holding. She didn't understand her own fears, except that she was fatally uncertain of Kingman Marshall's staying power. Carla still loomed in the background, and even if he'd found Tiffany enjoyable in bed, he was still getting used to a married status that he'd never wanted. She didn't kid herself that it was smooth sailing from now on. In fact, the intimacy they'd just shared might prove to be more of a detriment than an advantage in the cold light of day.

The worry slowly drifted away, though, as she lay in her husband's warm arms and inhaled the expensive scent of his cologne. Tomorrow would come, but for tonight, she could pretend that she was a much-loved wife with a long happy marriage ahead of her. King must know that she hadn't had time to see a doctor about any sort of birth control. But he apparently hadn't taken care of it as he'd said he would. He'd been too hungry for her to take time to manage it himself.

She thought of a child and her whole body warmed and flushed. He didn't want children, but she did, desperately. If he did leave her for Carla, she'd have a small part of him that the other woman could never take from her.

FROM PIPE DREAMS to reality was a hard fall. But she woke alone the next day, with her gown tossed haphazardly on the bed with her. King was nowhere in sight, and it was one o'clock in the afternoon!

She put on the gown and her slippers and robe and padded slowly out into the sitting room of the suite. It was empty, too. Perturbed, she went across into her own room and found some white jeans and a red-and-blue-and-white jersey to slip into. She tied her hair back in a red ribbon, slipped on her sneakers, and started to go out and look for King when she saw the envelope on the dresser.

Her name was on the front in a familiar bold black slash. She picked up the envelope and held it, savoring for a moment the night before, because she knew inside herself that whatever was in that envelope was going to upset her.

She drew out a piece of hotel stationery and unfolded it.

*Tiffany,*
*I've left your passport, and money for a return*
*ticket and anything else you need in your purse.*
*I've paid the hotel bill. An emergency came up*
*back home. I meant to tell you last night that I had*
*to leave first thing this morning, but it slipped my*
*mind. I managed to get the last seat on a plane to*
*San Antonio. We'll talk later.*
*King.*

She read it twice more, folded it, and put it into the envelope. What sort of emergency was so pressing that a man had to leave his honeymoon to take care of it?

That was when something niggled at the back of her mind, and she remembered the snatch of conversation she'd overheard before they'd gone to bed. King had said that he'd be home tomorrow—today. She drew in a harsh breath. *Carla.* Carla had phoned him and he'd left his wife to rush home. She'd have bet her last dollar that there was no emergency at all, unless it was that he was missing his old lover. Apparently, she thought with despair, even the heated exchange of the night before hadn't been enough for him. And why should it? She was a novice, only a new experience for him. Carla was probably as expert as he was.

With wounded pride stiffening her backbone, she picked up the telephone and dialed the international code and her father's private office number.

"Hello?" he answered after a minute.

The sound of his voice was so dear and comforting that she hesitated a few seconds to choke back hurt tears. "Hi, Dad," she said.

"What the hell's going on?" he demanded. "King phoned me from the airport and said he was on his way into the city to sort out some union dispute at one of the branch offices. Since when do we have a union dispute?" he asked irritably.

"I don't know any more than you do," she said. "He left me a note."

He sighed angrily. "I could have dealt with a dispute, if there had been one. I've been doing it longer than he has, and I'm the senior partner."

He didn't have to say that. She already knew it. "I'm coming home tomorrow," she told him. "I, uh, sort of had a bout with some aspirin and I'm feeling bad. I was ready to leave, but there was only one seat available on the morning flight. We agreed that I'd follow tomorrow," she lied glibly.

It sounded fishy to Harrison, but he didn't say a word about it. "You're allergic to aspirin," he said pointedly.

"I know, but King didn't. I had a splitting headache and he gave me some. He had to take me to the hospital, but I'm fine now, and he knows not to give me aspirin again."

"Damnation!" her father growled. "Doesn't he know anything about you?"

"Oh, he's learning all the time," she assured him. "I'll talk to you tomorrow, Dad. Can you have the car meet me at the airport? I'm not sure if King will remember me, if he's involved in meetings." *Or with Carla*, she thought. King hadn't said anything about her coming home at all in his terse little note. She was going to be a surprise.

There was an ominous pause. "I'll remember you. Phone me when you get in. Take care, darling."

"You, too, Dad. See you."

He put down the receiver, got out of his chair, and made the door in two strides. He went past his secretary and down the hall to King's office, pushed open the door on a startled Carla, and slammed it back.

She actually gasped. "Mr....Mr. Blair, can I do something for you?"

"You can stop trying to sabotage my daughter's marriage, you black-eyed little pit viper," he said with furious eyes. "First you fouled up the flowers, then you wore a dress to the ceremony that even to the most unprejudiced person in the world looked like a wedding gown. You kissed the groom as if you were the bride, and now you've managed to get King back here on some tom fool excuse, leaving his bride behind in Jamaica!"

Carla's eyes almost popped. "Mr. Blair, honestly, I never meant..."

"You're fired," he said furiously.

She managed to get to her feet and her cheeks flamed. "Mr. Blair, I'm King's secretary," she said through her teeth. "You can't fire me!"

"I own fifty-one percent of the stock," he told her with pure contempt. "That means I can fire whom I damned well please. I said, you're fired, and that means you're fired."

She drew an indignant breath. "I'll file a complaint," she snapped back.

"Go right ahead," he invited. "I'll call the tabloids

and give them a story that you'll have years to live down, after they do a little checking into your background."

It was only a shot in the dark, but she didn't know that. Her face went paper white. She actually shivered.

"Your severance pay will be waiting for you on the way out," he said shortly.

He went out the office door, almost colliding with King.

"I've just fired your damned secretary!" Harrison told King with uncharacteristic contempt. "And if you want a divorce from my daughter so you can go chasing after your sweet little paramour, here, I'll foot the bill! The two of you deserve each other!"

He shouldered past King and stormed away down the hall, back into his own office. The walls actually shook under the force with which he slammed the door.

King gave Carla a penetrating look. He walked into the office, and closed the door. Harrison had beaten him to the punch. He was going to fire Carla, but first he wanted some answers.

"All right," he said. "Let's have it."

"Have what?" she faltered. She moved close to him, using every wile she had for all she was worth. "You aren't going to let him fire me, are you?" she teased, moving her hips gently against his body. "Not after all we've been to one another?"

He stiffened, but not with desire, and stepped back. "What we had was over long before I married Tiffany."

"It never had to be," she cooed. "She's a child, a little princess. What can she be to a man like you? Nothing more than a new experience."

"You phoned and said there was a labor dispute," he reminded her. "I can't find a trace of it."

She shrugged. "Tom said there were rumors of a strike and that I'd better let you know. Ask him, if you don't believe me." She struck a seductive pose. "Are you going to let him fire me?" she asked again.

He let out a harsh breath. Harrison was breathing fire. Apparently he'd got the wrong end of the stick and Carla had done nothing to change his mind.

"You've made an enemy of him," King told her. "A bad one. Your behavior at the wedding is something he won't forget."

"You will," she said confidently. "You didn't want to marry her. You didn't even check about the flowers or a silly bouquet, because you didn't care, and she embarrassed you by wearing a suit to get married in." She made a moue of distaste. "It was a farce."

"Yes, thanks to you." He stuck his hands into his pockets and glowered at her. He wondered how far out of his mind he'd been to get involved with this smiling boa constrictor. She'd been exciting and challenging, but now she was a nuisance. "I'll see what I can do about getting you another job. But not here," he added quietly. "I'm not going against Harrison."

"Is that why you married her?" she asked. "So that you could be sure of inheriting the whole company when he dies?"

"Don't be absurd."

She shrugged. "Maybe it's why she married you, too," she said, planting a seed of doubt. "She'll have security now, even if you divorce her, won't she?"

Divorce. Harrison had said something about a divorce. "I have to talk to Harrison," he said shortly. "You'll work your two weeks' notice, despite what he said, and I'll see what's going at another office."

"Thank you, sweet," she murmured. She moved close and reached up to kiss him. "You're a prince!"

He went out the door with a handkerchief to his mouth, wiping off the taste of her on his way to his partner's office.

# CHAPTER NINE

HARRISON JUST GLARED at King when he went into the office and closed the door behind him.

"I don't care what you say, she's history," Harrison told the younger man. "She's meddled in my daughter's affairs for the last time!"

King scowled. He didn't like the look of his partner. "I haven't said a word," he said softly. "Calm down. If you want her to go, she goes. But let her work out her notice."

Harrison relaxed a little. His eyes were still flashing. He looked deathly pale and his breathing was unusually strained. He loosened his tie. "All right. But that's all. That silly woman," he said in a raspy voice. "She's caused... Tiffany...no end of heartache already, and now I've got...to cause her...more..." He paused with a hand to his throat and laughed in surprise. "That's funny. My throat hurts, right up to my jaw. I can't..." He grimaced and suddenly slumped to the floor. He looked gray and sweat covered his face.

King buzzed Harrison's secretary, told her to phone the emergency services number immediately and get some help into Harrison's office.

It was terribly apparent that Harrison was having a heart attack. His skin was cold and clammy and his lips were turning blue. King began CPR at once, and in no time, he had two other executives of the company standing by to relieve him, because he had no idea how long he'd have to keep it up before the ambulance came.

As it happened, less than five minutes elapsed between the call and the advent of two EMTs with a gurney. They got Harrison's heartbeat stabilized, hooked him up to oxygen and rushed him down to the ambulance with King right beside them.

"Any history of heart trouble in him or his family?" the EMT asked abruptly as he called the medical facility for orders.

"I don't know," King said irritably. For the second time in less than a week, he couldn't answer a simple question about the medical backgrounds of the two people he cared for most in the world. He felt impotent. "How's he doing?" he asked.

"He's stabilized, but these things are tricky," the EMT said. "Who's his personal physician?"

Finally, a question he could answer. He gave the information, which was passed on to the doctor answering the call at the medical center.

"Any family to notify?" the man relayed.

"I'm his son-in-law," King said grimly. "My wife is in Jamaica. I'll have to get her back here." He dreaded that. He'd have to tell her on the phone, and it was going to devastate her. But they couldn't afford the loss of time for him to fly down there after her. Harrison might not live that long.

The ambulance pulled up at the hospital, and Harrison, still unconscious, was taken inside to the emergency room. King went with him, pausing just long enough to speak with the physician before he found a pay phone and called the hotel in Jamaica. But more complications lay in store. Mrs. Marshall, he was told, had checked out that very morning. No, he didn't know where she'd gone, he was sorry.

King hung up, running an angry hand through his hair. Playing a grim hunch, he telephoned Harrison's house instead of his own. A maid answered the call.

"This is Kingman Marshall. Is my wife there?" he asked.

"Why, yes, sir. She got in about two hours ago. Shall I get her for you?"

He hesitated. "No. Thank you."

This was one thing he couldn't do on the phone. He told the doctor where he was going, hailed a taxi and had it drive him to Harrison's home.


TIFFANY WAS UPSTAIRS, UNPACKING. She paled when she saw King come in the door. She hadn't expected her father to be at home, since it was a working day. She hadn't expected to see King, either.

"Looking for me?" she asked coolly. "I've decided that I'm going to live here until the divorce."

Divorce! Everything he was going to say went right out of his mind. He'd left her after the most exquisite loving of his life. Hadn't he explained the emergency that had taken him from her side? It wasn't as if he hadn't planned to fly right back. He'd had no idea at all that Carla had manufactured the emergency.

"Tiffany," he began, "I flew back because there was an emergency…"

"Yes, and I know what it was," she replied, having

phoned the office just a while ago. "My father fired your secretary, and you had to rush back to save her job. I've just heard all about it from the receptionist, thanks."

"The receptionist?"

"I wanted to know if you were in. She talked to someone and said I should call back, you were in the middle of some sort of argument with my father…"

He let out a short breath. "We'll talk about that later. There's no time. Your father's had a heart attack. He's in the emergency room at city general. Get your purse and let's go."

She grasped her bedpost. "Is he alive? Will he be all right?"

"He was seeing the doctor when I left to fetch you," he replied. "Come on."

She went out with him, numb and shocked and frightened to death. Her life was falling apart. How would she go on if she lost her father? He was the only human being on earth who loved her, who needed her, who cared about her.

Through waves of fear and apprehension, she sat motionless as he drove her Jaguar to the hospital. When he pulled up at the emergency entrance and stopped, she leapt out and ran for the doors, not even pausing to wait for him.

She went straight to the clerk, rudely pushing in front of the person sitting there.

"Please." She choked, "My father, Harrison Blair, they just brought him in with a heart attack…?"

The clerk looked very worried. "You need to speak with the doctor, Miss Blair. Just one minute…"

King joined her in time to hear the clerk use her maiden name. Under different circumstances, he'd have been furious about that. But this wasn't the time.

The clerk motioned Tiffany toward another door. King took her arm firmly and went with her, sensing calamity.

A white-coated young doctor gestured to them, but he didn't take them into the cubicle where King had left her father. Instead, he motioned them farther down the hall to a small cluster of unoccupied seats.

"I'm sorry. I haven't done much of this yet, and I'm going to be clumsy about it," the young man said solemnly. "I'm afraid we lost him. I'm very sorry. It was a massive heart attack. We did everything we possibly could. It wasn't enough."

He patted her awkwardly on the upper arm, his face contorted with compassion.

"Thank you," King said quietly, and shook his hand. "I'm sure it's hard for you to lose a patient."

The doctor looked surprised, but he recovered quickly. "We'll beat these things one day," he said gently. "It's just that we don't have the technology yet. The worst thing is that his family physician told us he had no history of heart problems." He shook his head. "This was unexpected, I'm sure. But it was quick, and painless, if that's any comfort." He looked at Tiffany's stiff, shocked face and then back at King. "Bring her along with you, please. I'll give you something for her. She's going to need it. Any allergies to medicines?" he asked at once.

"Aspirin," King said. He glanced down at Tiffany, subduing his own sorrow at Harrison's loss. "Are you allergic to anything else, sweetheart?" he added tenderly.

She shook her head. She didn't see, didn't hear, didn't think. Her father was dead. King had argued with him over Carla. Her father was dead because of King.

She pushed his hand away. Her eyes, filled with hatred, seared into his mind as she looked up at him. "This is your fault." She choked. "My father is dead! Was keeping Carla worth his life?"

He sucked in a sharp breath. "Tiffany, that wasn't what happened…"

She moved away from him, toward the cubicle where the doctor was waiting. She was certain that she never wanted to speak to her husband again for as long as she lived.

THE NEXT FEW days were a total black void. There were the arrangements to be made, a service to arrange, minor details that somehow fell into place with King's help. The Blair home became like a great empty tomb. Lettie came to stay, of course, and King did, too, in spite of her protests. He slept in a bedroom down the hall from Tiffany's, watching her go through life in a trance while he dealt with friends and lawyers and the funeral home. She spoke to him only when it became necessary. He couldn't really blame her for the way she felt. She was too upset to reason. There would be plenty of time to explain things to her when she'd had time to recover. Meanwhile, Carla was on her way out of the office despite her plea to work out her notice. On that one point, King had been firm. She had her severance pay and a terse letter of recommendation. If only he could have foreseen, years ago, the trouble it was going to cause him when he put her out of his life, all this anguish with Tiffany might have been avoided. But at that time, Carla had been an exciting companion and he'd never considered marrying anyone. Now he was paying the price for his arrogance.

UNDAUNTED BY HER FIRING, Carla showed up at the funeral home, only to be escorted right back out again by King. She made some veiled threat about going to the tabloids with her story, and he invited her to do her worst. She was out of his life. Nothing she did would ever matter to him again, and he said so. She left, but with a dangerous glint in her cold eyes.

She didn't come to the funeral service, Tiffany noted, or to the graveside service. Apparently she'd been told that it wasn't appropriate. Some people, Lettie had said huffily, had no breeding and no sensitivity. She said it deliberately, and within King's hearing. He didn't react at all. Whatever he felt, he was keeping it to himself.

The only chip in his stony front came the night of the funeral, when he sat in Harrison's study with only a lamp burning and downed a third of a bottle of Harrison's fine Scotch whiskey.

Lettie intruded long enough to ask if he wanted anything else from the kitchen before the housekeeper closed it up.

He lifted the glass toward her. "I'm drinking my supper, thanks," he drawled.

Lettie closed the door behind her and paused in front

of the big antique oak desk, where his booted feet were propped on its aged, pitted surface.

"What are you going to do about the house?" she asked abruptly. Her eyes were red. She'd cried for Harrison almost as much as Tiffany had. Now her only concern was the girl's future.

"What do you mean, what am I going to do?" he asked. "It belongs to Tiffany."

"No, it doesn't," Lettie said worriedly. "Harrison was certain right up until the wedding ceremony that you weren't going to go through with the marriage. He wanted Tiffany provided for if something happened to him, and he didn't want her to have to be dependent on you. So he went to see his personal accountant about having everything he owned put in trust for her, including the house and his half of the business." She folded her hands at her waist, frowning worriedly. "But the accountant couldn't be located. Then Harrison found out that the man had been steadily embezzling from him for the past three years." She lifted her hands and spread them. "Just this week, he learned that a new mortgage had been taken out on the house and grounds and the money transferred to an account in a Bahamian bank." She grimaced as King lowered his feet to the floor and sat up. "He'd hired a private detective and was to see his attorney this afternoon after filing a lawsuit against the man before he skips the country with what's left of Harrison's fortune. If you can't stop him, Tiffany will be bankrupt."

"Good God!" King got to his feet, weaving a little. "No wonder he was so upset! Lettie, why the hell didn't you say something before this?"

"Because I wasn't sure that I had the right to involve you, except where the business is concerned," she said flatly. "You must know that Tiffany doesn't want to continue your marriage."

His face was drawn taut like a rope. "I know it."

She shrugged. "But there's no one else who can deal with this. I certainly can't. I can't even balance my checkbook. I wouldn't know how to proceed against the man."

King leaned forward with his head in his hands. "Get me a pot of strong coffee," he said through heavy breaths. "Then I want every scrap of information you have on the man and what Harrison planned."

Lettie brightened just a little. "We'll all miss him," she said gently as she turned toward the door. "But Tiffany most of all. He was both parents to her, for most of her life." She hesitated. "She needs you."

He didn't reply. She didn't seem to expect him to. She went out and closed the door behind her.

Tiffany was sitting on the bottom step of the staircase, looking pale and worn. Her eyes were red and she had a crumpled handkerchief in her hand. The long white gown and robe she was wearing seemed to emphasize her thinness.

"Child, you should be in bed," Lettie chided softly.

"I can't sleep." She stared at the study door. "Is he in there?"

Lettie nodded.

"What's he doing?"

"Getting drunk."

That was vaguely surprising. "Oh."

"I want to know why my father had a heart attack,"

she said grimly. "The receptionist wouldn't let me speak with King the day Daddy died because he and my father were arguing. Then at the funeral, one of his coworkers said it was a pity about the blow-up, because it was only seconds later when he collapsed. I know he fired Carla. Was that why King argued with him?"

"I don't know. Tiffany," she said, approaching the girl, "this is a vulnerable time for all of us. Don't say anything, do anything, that you'll have cause to regret later. King's hurt, too. He respected Harrison. Even if they did argue, they were friends as well as business partners for a long time."

"They were friends until I married King." Tiffany corrected her. "My father thought it was a mistake. He was right."

"Was he? It's early days yet, and some marriages can have a rocky beginning. It's no easy thing to make a life with another person. Fairy tales notwithstanding, even the most loving couples have to adjust to a shared coexistence."

"It helps if both partners work at it," Tiffany said.

"I agree. Get in there and do your part," her godmother prodded, jerking her red head toward the closed study door. "If you want answers, he's the only person who's got them."

Tiffany stared at the carpet for a minute and then got slowly to her feet.

"That's the idea," Lettie said. "I'm going to make him a pot of coffee. We have a few complications. Get him to tell you about them. Shared problems are another part of building a marriage."

Tiffany laughed, but without mirth. She went to the door after Lettie vanished down the hall and opened it.

King glanced at her from behind the desk as she came into the room. "I didn't plan to strand you in Montego Bay," he said pointedly. "I would have been on my way back that night."

"Would you?" She went to the chair in front of the desk, a comfortable burgundy leather armchair that she'd occupied so many times when she and her father had talked. She sighed. "The whole world has changed since then."

"Yes. I know."

She leaned back, sliding her hands over the cold leather arms, over the brass studs that secured it to the frame. "Tell me how he died, King."

He hesitated, but only for a second. His chiseled mouth tugged into a mocking smile. "So they couldn't wait to tell you, hmm? I'm not surprised. Gossip loves a willing ear."

"Nobody told me anything. It was inferred."

"Same difference." He spread his hands on the desk and stood up. "Okay, honey, you want the truth, here it is. He fired Carla and they had a royal row over it. I walked in and he started on me. I followed him to his office and got there just in time to watch him collapse."

She let out the breath she'd been holding. Her nails bit into the leather arms of the chair. "Why did you follow him? Were you going to talk him out of it?"

"No. But there's more to this than an argument over Carla," he added, searching for the right way to explain to her the tangled and devastating fact of her father's loss of wealth.

"Yes, there is. We've already agreed that I maneuvered you into a marriage you didn't want," she said curtly. "We can agree that what happened in Montego Bay was a form of exorcism for both of us and let it go at that," she added when he started to speak. "Charge me with desertion, mental cruelty, anything you like. Let me know when the papers are ready and I'll sign them."

His eyes flashed like black fires. "There won't be a divorce," he said shortly.

She was surprised by the vehemence in his tone, until she remembered belatedly just what her status was. As her father's heir, by a quirk of fate she was now his business partner. He couldn't afford to divorce her. What an irony.

She cocked her head and looked at him with cold curiosity. "Oh, yes, I forgot, didn't I? We're business partners now. How nice to have it all in the family. You won't even have to buy me out. What's mine is yours."

The look on his face was a revelation. Amazing how he could pretend that the thought had never occurred to him.

"That's a nice touch, that look of surprise," she said admirably. "I expect you practiced in front of a mirror."

"Why are you downstairs at this hour of the night?" he asked.

"I couldn't sleep," she replied, and was suddenly vulnerable. She hated having it show. "My father was buried today," she drawled, "in case you forgot."

"We can do without the sarcasm," he said. "Wait a minute." He reached into her father's top desk drawer and extracted a bottle. "Come here."

She stopped with the width of the desk between them

and held her hand out. He shook two capsules into her hand and recapped the bottle.

"Don't trust me with the whole bottle?" she taunted.

That was exactly how he felt, although he wasn't going to admit it. She'd had one too many upsets in the past few weeks. Normally as sound as a rock, even Tiffany could be pushed over the edge by grief and worry. He couldn't add the fear of bankruptcy to her store of problems. That one he could spare her. Let her think him a philanderer, if it helped. When she was strong enough, he'd tell her the truth.

"Take those and try to sleep," he said. "Things will look brighter in the morning."

She stared at the capsules with wounded wet eyes. "He was my rudder," she said in a husky whisper. "No matter how bad things got, he was always here to run to."

His face hardened. Once, he'd been there to run to, before they married and became enemies. "You'll never know how sorry I am," he said tightly. "If you believe nothing else, believe that I didn't cause him to have that heart attack. I didn't argue with him over Carla."

She glanced at him and saw the pain in his eyes for the first time. It took most of the fight out of her. She seemed to slump. "I know you cared about my father, King," she said heavily.

"And in case you're wondering," he added with a mocking smile, "she's gone. She has her severance pay and some sort of reference. You won't see her again."

She studied him silently. "Why?"

"Why, what?"

"Why did my father fire her?"

It was like walking on eggshells, but he had to tell her the truth. "Because she dragged me home from Jamaica with a nonexistent emergency, just to interfere with our honeymoon, and he knew it. He said he'd had enough of her meddling."

"So had I," she returned.

"Not half as much as I had," he said curtly. "Harrison beat me to the punch by five minutes."

"He did?"

"Come here."

He looked faintly violent, and he'd been drinking. She hesitated.

He got up and came around the desk, watching her back away. "Oh, hell, no, you don't," he said in a voice like silk. His arms slid under her and he lifted her clear of the floor. "I've listened to you until I'm deaf. Now you can listen to me."

He went back to his chair and sat down with Tiffany cradled stiffly in his arms.

"No need to do your imitation of a plank," he chided, making himself comfortable. "Drunk men make bad lovers. I'm not in the mood, anyway. Now, you listen!"

She squirmed, but he held her still.

"Carla wasn't supposed to have anything to do with the flowers for our wedding," he said shortly. "I gave that task to Edna, who heads the personnel department, because she grew up in a florist's shop. But I was out of the office and Carla went to her with a forged letter that said I wanted Carla to do it instead."

Tiffany actually gasped.

He nodded curtly. "And she didn't get those arrangements from a florist, she did them herself with wilted flowers that she either got from a florist, or from a florist's trash can! She never had any intention of bringing you a bouquet, either. The whole thing was deliberate."

"How did you find out?"

"I went to see Edna when I flew back from Jamaica and found there was no emergency. I gave her hell about the flowers," he said. "She gave it back, with interest. Then she told me what had really happened. I was livid. I'd gone straight to my office to have it out with Carla when I found your father there."

"Oh."

He searched her stunned eyes. "You don't think much of me, do you?" he asked quietly. "Regardless of how I felt about the wedding, I wouldn't have deliberately hurt you like that."

She grimaced. "I should have known."

"You wore a suit to be married in," he added. "That was a blow to my pride. I thought you were telling me in a nonverbal way that you were just going through the motions."

"And I thought that you wouldn't mind what I wore, because you didn't want to marry me in the first place."

The arm behind her shoulders contracted, and the big, warm hand at the end of it smoothed over her upper arm in an absent, comforting motion. "I drew away from you at a time when we should have been talking about our insecurities," he said after a minute. "We had too many secrets. In fact, we still have them." He took a quick breath. "Tiffany, your father's personal accountant just did a flit with the majority of your inheritance. I'll bet that's what really set your father off, not Carla, although she helped. He was upset because he knew he'd have to tell you what had happened when you came home."

Tiffany's eyes widened. "You mean, Daddy was robbed?"

"In a nutshell," he agreed. He smiled faintly. "So, along with all your other woes, my wife, you may have bankruptcy looming unless I can find that accountant and prosecute him."

"I'm broke?" she said.

He nodded.

She sighed. "There goes my yacht."

"What do you want with one of those?"

She kept her eyes lowered demurely. Her heart was racing, because they were talking as they'd never talked before. "I thought I'd dangle it on the waterfront for bait and see if I could catch a nice man to marry."

That sounded like the girl he used to know. His eyes began to twinkle just faintly and he smiled. "What are you going to do with the husband you've already got?"

She studied his lean face with pursed lips. "I thought you were going to divorce me."

One eyebrow levered up. His eyes dropped to her slender body and traced it with arrogant possession. "Think again."

## CHAPTER TEN

THE LOOK IN his eyes was electric and Tiffany watched him watching her for long, exquisite seconds before his head began to bend.

She lay in his arms, waiting, barely breathing as he drew her closer. It seemed like forever since he'd kissed her, and she wanted him. She reached up, barely breathing, waiting...

The sudden intrusion of Lettie with a tray of coffee and cookies was as explosive as a bomb going off. They both jerked.

She hesitated just inside the door and stared at them. "Shall I go away?" she asked, chuckling.

King recovered with apparent ease. "Not if those are lemon cookies," he said.

Tiffany gasped, but he got up and helped her to her feet with a rakish grin. "Sorry, honey, but lemon cookies are my greatest weakness."

"Do tell," she murmured with her hands on her hips.

He gave her a thorough going-over with acquisitive eyes. "My *second* greatest weakness," he said, correcting her.

"Too late now," she told him and moved a little self-consciously toward Lettie as King swept forward and took the heavy tray from her.

He put it on the coffee table and they gathered around it while Lettie poured coffee into thin china cups and distributed saucers and cookies.

"I'm going to be poor, Lettie," Tiffany told Lettie.

"Not yet, you're not," King murmured as he savored a cookie. "I'll get in touch with the private detective your father hired to trail your elusive accountant, not to mention Interpol. He'll be caught."

"Poor Daddy," Tiffany sighed, tearing a little as she thought of her loss. "He must have only found out."

"About two days before the heart attack, I think," Lettie said heavily. She leaned over to pick up her coffee. "I tried to get him to see a doctor even then. His color wasn't good. That was unusual, too, because Harrison was always so robust—" She broke off, fighting tears.

Tiffany put an arm around her. "There, there," she said softly. "He wouldn't want us to carry on like this."

"No, he wouldn't," King added. "But we'll all grieve, just the same. He was a good man."

Tiffany struggled to get in a deep breath. She bit halfheartedly into a cookie and smiled. "These are good."

"There's a bakery downtown, where they make them fresh every day," Lettie confided.

"I know where it is," King mused. "I stop by there some afternoons to buy a couple to go with my coffee."

Tiffany glanced at him a little shyly and smiled. "I didn't know you liked cookies."

He looked back at her, but he didn't smile. "I didn't know you were allergic to aspirin."

He sounded as if not knowing that fact about her really bothered him, too.

"It's the only thing," she replied. She searched his drawn features. "King, you couldn't have known about Daddy's heart. I didn't even know. You heard what the doctor said. There was no history of heart trouble, either."

He stared at his half-eaten cookie. "It didn't help to have him upset…"

She touched his hand. "It would have happened anyway," she said, and she was sure of it now. "You can only control so much in life. There are always going to be things that you can't change."

He wouldn't meet her eyes. His jaw was drawn tight.

"Yes, I know, you don't like being out of control, in any way," she said gently, surprising him. "But neither of us could have prevented what happened. I remember reading about a politician who had a heart attack right in his doctor's office, and nobody could save him. Do you see what I mean?"

He reached out his free hand and linked it with hers. "I suppose so."

Lettie sipped coffee, lost in her own thoughts. She missed Harrison, too. The house was empty without him. She looked up suddenly. "Good Lord, you only had a one-day honeymoon," she exclaimed.

"It was a good day," King murmured.

"Yes, it was," Tiffany said huskily, and his fingers contracted around hers.

"We'll finish it when we solve our problems here," King replied. "We have all the time in the world."

Tiffany nodded.

"It will be a shame if you can't catch that crook," Lettie said, looking around her at the beauty of the study. "This house is the beginning of a legacy. Harrison had hoped to leave it to his grandchildren."

Tiffany felt King stiffen beside her. Slowly, she unlinked her hand with his and put both hands around her coffee cup.

"We have years to talk about children," she told Lettie deliberately. "Some couples don't ever have them."

"Oh, but you will, dear," Lettie murmured dreamily. "I remember how we used to go shopping, and the nursery department was always the first place you'd stop. You'd touch little gowns and booties and smile and talk about babies…"

Tiffany got to her feet, hoping her sudden paleness wouldn't upset Lettie. She had no way of knowing that King didn't want a child.

"I'm so tired, Lettie," she said, and looked it. She smiled apologetically. "I'd like to try to go back to sleep, if you don't mind."

"Of course not, dear. Can you sleep now, do you think?"

Tiffany reached into the pocket of her robe and produced the two capsules King had given her. She picked up her half-full cup of coffee and swallowed them. "I will now," she said as she replaced the cup in the saucer. "Thank you, King," she added without looking directly at him.

"Will you be all right?" he asked.

She felt that he was trying to make her look at him. She couldn't bear to, not yet. She was thinking about the long, lonely years ahead with no babies. She didn't dare hope that their only night together would produce fruit. That one lapse wasn't enough to build a dream on. Nobody got pregnant the first time. Well, some people did, but she didn't have that sort of luck. She wondered if King remembered how careless he'd been.

"I hope you both sleep well," she said as she went from the room.

"You, too, dear," Lettie called after her. She finished her coffee. "I'll take the tray back to the kitchen."

"I'll do it," King murmured. He got up and picked it up, less rocky on his feet now that he'd filled himself full of caffeine.

"Are you going to try to sleep?"

He shook his head. "I've got too much work to do. It may be the middle of the night here, but I can still do business with half the world. I have to wrap up some loose ends. Tomorrow, I'm going to have my hands full tracing that accountant."

Lettie went with him to the kitchen and sorted out the things that needed washing.

King paused at the door, his face solemn and thoughtful. "Stay close to Tiffany tomorrow, will you?" he asked. "I don't want her alone."

"Of course, I will." She glanced at him. "Are you worried about Carla?"

He nodded. "She's always been high-strung, but just lately she seems off balance to me. I don't think she'd try to do anything to Tiffany. But there's no harm in taking precautions."

"I wish…" she began and stopped.

"Yes. I wish I'd never gotten involved with her, either," he replied, finishing the thought for her. "Hindsight is a grand thing."

"Indeed it is." She searched his bloodshot eyes. "You aren't sorry you married Tiffany?"

"I'm sorry I waited so long," he countered.

"But there are still problems?" she probed gently.

He drew in a long breath. "She wants babies and I don't."

"Oh, King!"

He winced. "I've been a bachelor all my life," he said shortly. "Marriage was hard enough. I haven't started adjusting to it yet. Fatherhood…" His broad shoulders rose and fell jerkily. "I can't cope with that. Not for a long time, if ever. It's something Tiffany will have to learn to live with."

Lettie bit down on harsh words. She sighed worriedly. "Tiffany's still very young, of course," she said pointedly.

"Young and full of dreams," King agreed. He stared at the sink. "Impossible dreams."

Outside the door, the object of their conversation turned and made her way slowly back upstairs, no longer thirsty for the glass of milk she'd come to take to bed with her. So there it was. King would never want a child. If she wanted him, it seemed that she'd have to give up any hopes of becoming a mother. Some women didn't want children. It was a pity that Tiffany did.

SHE DIDN'T HAVE to avoid King in the days that followed. He simply wasn't home. Business had become overwhelming in the wake of Harrison Blair's death. There were all sorts of legalities to deal with, and King had a new secretary who had to learn her job the hard way. He was very seldom home, and when he was, he seemed to stay on the telephone.

Lettie was still in residence, because Tiffany had begged her to stay. The house was big and empty without Harrison, but Lettie made it bearable. And on the rare occasions when King was home, their meals weren't silent ones. Lettie carried on conversations with herself if no one else participated, which amused Tiffany no end.

She hadn't paid much attention to the date. She'd grieved for two long weeks, crying every time she saw familiar things of her father's, adjusting to life without him. But just as she was getting used to the lonely house, another unexpected complication presented itself.

Tiffany suddenly started losing her breakfast. She'd never had any such problems before, and even if it was too soon for tests, deep inside she knew that she was pregnant. She went from boundless joy to stifling fear in a matter of seconds as she realized how this news was going to affect her husband. Her hands went protectively to her flat stomach and she groaned out loud.

She couldn't tell him. He wouldn't want the baby, and he might even suggest…alternatives. There wasn't an option she was willing to discuss. She was going to have her baby, even if she had to leave him and hide it away. That meant that she had to keep her condition secret.

At first it was easy. He was never home. But as the demands of business slowed a couple of weeks later, he began to come home earlier. And he was attentive, gentle with Tiffany, as if he were trying to undo their rocky beginning and start over.

It wounded her to the quick to have to withdraw from those sweet overtures, because she needed him now more than at any time in their shared past. But it was too great a risk to let him come close. Her body was changing. He wasn't stupid. If he saw her unclothed, there were little signs that even a bachelor might notice.

Her behavior surprised him, though, because they'd become much closer after Harrison's death. He'd had business demands that had kept him away from home, and he'd deliberately made very few demands on Tiffany just after her father's death, to give her time to adjust. But now, suddenly, she was talking about going back to modeling in New York, with Lettie to keep her company.

King worried about her attitude. He'd been kept busy with the transfer of authority and stocks and the implementation of Harrison's will, not to mention tracking down the elusive accountant. Perhaps she'd thought he wasn't interested in her feelings. That wasn't true. But when he tried to talk to her, she found dozens of excuses to get out of his vicinity.

Even Lettie was puzzled and remarked about Tiffany's coldness to the man, when he'd done so much for them. But Tiffany only smiled and ignored every word she said. Even from Lettie, the bouts of nausea were carefully concealed. No one was going to threaten her baby, Tiffany told herself. Not even Lettie, who might unwittingly let the cat out of the bag.

She talked about going to New York, but all the while, she was checking into possible escape routes.

She could fly anywhere in the world that she wanted to go. Even without her father's fortune, she had a legacy from her mother, which guaranteed her a tidy fixed sum every month paid into her personal checking account. She could live quite well and take care of her child. All she needed was a place to go.

King found her one afternoon poring over travel brochures, which she gathered with untidy haste and stuffed back into a folder as if she'd been caught stealing.

"Planning a trip?" he asked, scowling as he stood over her.

She sat forward on the sofa. "Who, me? No!" She cleared her throat. "Well, not immediately, at least. I thought…" She hesitated while she tried to formulate an answer that would throw him off the track.

"Heard from your friend Mark?" he asked abruptly.

"Mark?" She'd all but forgotten her modeling friend, although she saw Lisa occasionally, and Lisa certainly heard from him. They were becoming an item. "I believe he's in Greece," she added. "Doing a commercial for some swimwear company."

"Yes, he is," King replied thoughtfully. "I saw Lisa's father at a civic-club meeting this week. He said that the two of them are quite serious."

"I'm glad," Tiffany said. "Mark's had a hard life. So has Lisa, in some ways. She's always had money, but her father is a very domineering sort. I hope he isn't planning to throw a stick into their spokes."

"Apparently Lisa's threatened to run away if he does," he mused, and smiled. "Love does make a woman brave, I suppose."

She could have made a nasty remark about Carla, but she let it go and made some careless remark.

"Don't you eat breakfast anymore?" he asked abruptly.

She jumped. "I… Well, no, I don't, really," she stammered. "I've gotten into bad habits since Daddy died," she added with a nervous laugh. "Breakfast reminds me too much of him."

"Which is still no reason to starve yourself, is it?"

She shifted, tracing a flower in the pattern on her skirt. "I'm not starving myself. I just don't like eating breakfast at the table. I have it in my room."

He stood there without speaking, frowning, jingling the loose change in his pocket.

She glanced at the clock and then at him. "Aren't you home early?" she asked.

"Yes." He moved to the armchair beside the sofa and dropped into it. "I thought you might like to know that we've found the runaway accountant."

"Have you really!"

He chuckled at her radiance. "Vengeful girl. Yes, he thought he'd gotten clean away. He was passing the time in luxurious splendor on a private island in the Bahamas when some rogue popped a bag over his head, trussed him up like a duck, and carted him off to a sailboat. He was hauled onto the beach in Miami and summarily arrested."

"Do we know rogues who would do such a thing?" she asked.

He chuckled. "Of course we do!"

"Does he still have any money?"

"All but a few thousand," he replied. "He confessed

wholeheartedly when faced with a long prison term for his pains. He offered to give the money back without any prompting. To do him credit, he was sorry about Harrison."

"My father might still be here, if it hadn't been for that skunk. I won't shed any tears for him," she muttered. "I hope he isn't going to get off with a slap on the wrist."

"Not a chance," he replied. "He'll serve time. And he'll never get another job of trust."

"I suppose that's something. But it won't bring Daddy back."

"Nothing will do that."

She crossed her legs and glanced at King. He was restless and irritable. "What's wrong?" she asked.

"I wish I didn't have to tell you."

She sat up, bracing herself for anything. After what she'd just come through, she felt that she could take it on the chin, though, whatever it was. She was stronger than she'd ever been.

"Go ahead," she said. "Whatever it is, I can take it."

He looked at her, saw the new lines in her face, the new maturity. "How you've changed, Tiffany," he murmured absently.

"Stop stalling," she said.

He let out a hollow laugh. "Am I? Perhaps so." He leaned forward, resting his forearms across his knees. "I want you to see a doctor."

Her eyebrows arched. "Me? What for?"

"Because we're married," he replied evenly. "And I've gone without you for as long as I can. That being the case, you have to make some sort of preparation about birth control. We can't have any more lapses."

Steady, girl, she told herself. You can't give the show away now. She swallowed. "You said that you'd take care of it," she hedged.

"Yes, I did, didn't I?" he reflected with a laugh. "And you remember how efficiently I did it, don't you?" he asked pointedly.

She flushed. "It was…unexpected."

"And exquisite," he said quietly. "I dream about how it was. I've tried to wait, to give you time to get over the trauma of losing Harrison. But, to put it bluntly, I'm hurting. I want you."

She felt her cheeks go hot. She still wasn't sophisticated enough for this sort of blunt discussion. "All right," she said. "I'll see the doctor."

"Good girl." He got up and moved toward the sofa, reaching down to pull her up into his arms with a long sigh. "I miss you in my bed, Tiffany," he murmured as he bent to her mouth. "I want you so badly…!"

His mouth opened on hers and she moaned harshly at the pleasure of his embrace. She reached up and held him around the neck, pressing her body to his, moving provocatively, involuntarily.

He groaned harshly and his hands went to her waist to pull her closer. Then, suddenly, he stilled. Holding her rigidly, he lifted his head. His breath seemed to catch in his throat. His eyes looked straight into hers. And while she was trying to decide what had made him stop, his hands smoothed with deliberation over her thick waist and, slowly, down over the faint swell of her stomach.

His face changed. She knew the instant he began to suspect. It was all there, the tautness, the shock, the horror.

She jerked away from him, her face stiff with pain. The breath she drew was painful.

He let his arms fall to his sides. The look he sent to her belly would have won a photo contest.

"No, I won't." She choked out the words before he could speak. She backed toward the door. "I won't do anything about it, I don't care what you say, what you do! It's mine, and I'm going to have it! Do you hear me, I'm going to have it!"

She whirled and ran toward the staircase, desperate to reach the sanctuary of her room. She could lock the door and he couldn't get in, she could outrun him! But out of the corner of her eye, she saw him racing toward her. She'd never make the staircase, not at the speed he was running.

She turned at the last second and went toward the front door, panic in her movements, nausea in her throat. She jerked open the front door and forgot the rain that had made the brick porch as slick as glass. Her feet went out from under her and she fell with a horrible, sickening thud, right on her back.

"Tiffany!"

King's exclamation barely registered. She knew every bone in her body was broken. She couldn't even breathe, much less talk. She had the breath knocked completely out of her. She stared at his white face and didn't really see it at all.

"My...baby," she moaned with the only bit of breath she could muster.

King knelt beside her, his hands running over her gently, feeling for breaks while he strangled on every breath he took. There was a faint tremor in his long fingers.

"Don't try to move," he said uneasily. "Dear God…!" He got up and went back to the doorway. "Lettie! Lettie, get an ambulance, she's fallen!"

"Is she all right?" Lettie's wail came out the door.

"I don't know. Call an ambulance!"

"Yes, dear, right now…!"

King knelt beside Tiffany and took her cold, nerveless hand in his. The rain was coming down steadily beyond the porch, like a curtain between the two of them and the world.

Tiffany sucked in shallow breaths. Tears ran down her cheek. One hand lifted to her stomach. She began to sob. "My baby," she wept. "My baby!"

"Oh, God, don't!" he groaned. He touched her wet cheeks with the backs of his fingers, trying to dry the tears. "You're all right, sweetheart, you're going to be fine. You're going to be fine… Lettie! For God's sake!"

Lettie came at a run, pausing at the slick porch. "I've phoned, and they're on the way right now." She moved onto the wet surface and looked down at Tiffany. "Oh, my dear," she groaned, "I'm so sorry!"

Tiffany was beyond words. She couldn't seem to stop crying. The tears upset King more than she'd ever seen anything upset him. He found his handkerchief and dried her wet eyes, murmuring to her, trying to comfort her.

She closed her eyes. She hurt all over, and she'd probably lost the baby. She'd never get another one.

He'd make sure that she took precautions from now on, she'd grow old without the comfort of a child, without the joy of holding her baby in her arms…

The sobs shook her.

King eased down beside her, regardless of the wet floor, and his big hand flattened gently over her flat stomach, pressing tenderly.

"Try not to worry," he whispered at her lips. He kissed her softly, and his hand moved protectively. "The baby's all right. I know he is."

## CHAPTER ELEVEN

Tiffany couldn't believe what she'd just heard. Her eyes opened and looked straight into his.

"You don't want it," she whispered.

He drew in a rough breath and his hand spread even more. "Yes, I do," he said quietly. "I want both of you."

She could barely get enough breath to speak, and before she could find the words, the ambulance drowned out even her thoughts as it roared up at the front steps and two EMTs disembarked.

She was examined and then put into the ambulance. King went with her, promising Lettie that he'd phone the minute he knew anything.

Tiffany felt him grasp her hand as the ambulance started up again. "You're forever taking me away in ambulances," she whispered breathlessly.

He brought her hand to his mouth and kissed the palm hungrily. "Wherever you go, I go, Tiffany," he said. But his eyes were saying other things, impossible things. They took the rest of her breath away.

She was taken to the local emergency room and checked thoroughly, by the family physician who was doing rounds.

Dr. Briggs chuckled at her when he'd finished his tests and had the results, over an hour later. "I heard about your wild ride in Montego Bay. Now, here you are in a fall. Maybe marriage doesn't agree with you," he teased, having known her from childhood.

"It agrees with her," King murmured contentedly, watching her with open fascination. "So will having a baby to nurse." He glanced at Briggs. "Is she?"

He nodded, smiling complacently at Tiffany's gasp and radiant smile. "I don't imagine we'll have much trouble computing a delivery date," he added wickedly.

Tiffany flushed and King chuckled.

"One time," he murmured dryly. "And look what you did," he accused.

"What I did!" she exclaimed.

"I only plant. I don't cultivate."

She burst out laughing. She couldn't believe what she was hearing. All that talk about not wanting babies, and here he sat grinning like a Cheshire cat.

"He'll strut for a while," the doctor told her. "Then he'll start worrying, and he won't do any more strutting until after the delivery. You'll have to reassure him at frequent intervals. Expectant fathers," he said on a sigh, "are very fragile people."

"She'll have to have an obstetrician," King was murmuring aloud. He glanced at Briggs. "No offense."

"None taken," the doctor mused.

"A good obstetrician."

"I don't refer pregnant women to any other kind," he was assured.

"We'll need to find a good college, too—"

Tiffany started to protest, but King was at the window, talking to himself and Dr. Briggs held up a hand.

"Don't interrupt him," he told Tiffany. "He's considering all the other appropriate families in town who have baby daughters. He'll have to have the right wife—"

"It could be a girl," she interjected.

"Heresy!" the doctor said in mock alarm.

"Shouldn't we point that out?" she continued, glancing at King.

Dr. Briggs shook his head. "A man has to have dynastic dreams from time to time." He smiled. "You're fine, Tiffany. A few bruises, but nothing broken and that baby is firmly implanted. Just don't overdo during the first trimester. Call me Monday and I'll refer you to an obstetrician. I do not," he added, "deliver babies. I like sleeping at night."

"Are babies born at night?"

"From what I hear, almost all of them," he said with a chuckle.

King took her home, still reeling with his discoveries. He carried her inside, cradling her like a treasure.

Lettie met them at the door, wringing her hands. "You didn't phone," she said accusingly.

"He was too busy arranging the wedding," Tiffany replied.

Lettie looked blank. "Wedding?"

"Our son's."

"Son." Lettie still looked blank. Then her face flushed with glorious surprise. "You're pregnant!"

"Yes," she said.

Lettie gnawed her lip and shot a worried glance at King.

"I know," he said wearily. "I'll have to eat boiled crow for the next month, and I deserve to." He shrugged, holding Tiffany closer. "I didn't know how it was going to feel," he said in his own defense, and he smiled with such tenderness that electricity seemed to run through her relaxed body. "What an incredible sensation."

Tiffany smiled and laid her cheek against his shoulder. "I'm sleepy," she said, yawning.

King glanced at Lettie. "I'm going to put her to bed."

"That's the best place for her," Lettie said with a warm smile. "Let me know if you need anything, dear," she told Tiffany, and bent to kiss the flushed cheek.

"I'll be fine. Thank you, Lettie."

King was grinning from ear to ear all the way up the staircase, and he never seemed to feel her weight at all, because he wasn't even breathing hard by the time they reached the top.

"You don't want children," she murmured drowsily. "You said so."

"We're all entitled to one stupid mistake." He carried her to his room, not hers, and laid her gently on the coverlet. His eyes were solemn as he looked down at her. "For what it's worth, I do want this child. I want it very much. Almost as much as I want you."

She flushed. "King, Dr. Briggs said—" she began cautiously.

He put a finger over her lips. "He said that the first trimester is tricky," he replied. He nodded. "We won't make love again until the baby is at home." He bent and kissed her with aching tenderness. "But we'll sleep in each other's arms, as we should have been doing from the first night, when you were a virgin bride—my beautiful princess bride. If you're cold, I'll warm you. If you're afraid, I'll cuddle you." He pushed back her soft hair. His eyes looked deeply, hungrily into hers.

"And if you want to be loved, I'll love you. Like this."
His lips drew softly against her mouth, cherishing, tasting. His cheek rested on hers and he sighed. "I'll love
you with all my heart," he whispered a little roughly.
"For all my life."

Her caught breath was audible. "You love me?"

"As much as you love me," he agreed. He lifted his
head and searched her eyes. "Didn't you think I knew?"

She sighed. "No. Not really."

"That's the only thing I was ever sure of, with you.
And sometimes, I wondered why you loved me. I've
been a lot of trouble. Still want to keep me, in spite of
everything?"

She smiled slowly. "More than ever. Somebody has
to teach the baby how to take over corporations when
he or she is old enough."

He chuckled. "Well, you're stuck with me, whether
you want me or not." He touched her cheek and looked
at her with pale eyes that mirrored his awe and delight.
"I never dreamed that it would feel like this to belong
to someone, to have someone who belonged to me." He
sighed. "I didn't think I could."

"I know why," she replied, tracing his mouth with
her fingertip. "But we're not like your parents, King.
We won't have their problems. We'll have each other
and our child."

He began to smile. "So we will."

She drew him down to her lips and kissed him with
pure possession. "Now, try to get away," she challenged
under her breath.

He chuckled as he met her lips with his. "That works
both ways."

She thought what a wonderful godmother Lettie would be to the new arrival, and how proud her father would have been. It made her a little sad to think of him.

But then her husband's warm, strong arms tightened gently around her and reminded her that in life, for each pain, there is a pleasure. She closed her eyes and her thoughts turned to lullabies as the rain beat softly on the roof.

* * * * *

BLAKE

## CHAPTER ONE

VIOLET HARDY SAT at her desk and wondered why she'd ever taken this secretarial job in the first place. Her boss, Jacobs-ville, Texas, attorney Blake Kemp, didn't appreciate her at all. She'd only been trying to keep him from dying of a premature heart attack by changing his regular coffee to decaf. For her pains, she'd been on the receiving end of the worst insult she could ever imagine, and from the one man in the world she loved above all others. She knew her co-workers were as upset as she was. They'd been kindness itself. But nothing made up for the fact that Blake Kemp thought Violet was fat.

She looked down at her voluptuous body in a purple dress with a high neckline, frilly bodice and straight skirt, vaguely aware that the style did nothing for her. She would be wearing it today, of all days, when Kemp gave her that disapproving scrutiny. Her mother had tried to tell her, gently, that frills and big bosoms didn't match. Worse, a tight-fitting skirt only emphasized those wide hips.

She'd been trying so hard to lose weight. She'd given up sweets, joined a gym, and worked hard at cooking regular and weight-conscious meals for herself and her elderly mother, who had a heart condition. Her father had died the year before of an apparent heart attack.

But just lately there were rumors that her co-worker Libby Collins's stepmother might be responsible for Mr. Hardy's sudden death. Janet Collins had been suspected of poisoning an elderly man in a nursing home, and she'd taken Mr. Hardy for quite a sum of money before he died unexpectedly, just after being seen with her in a motel room. It had been too late for Mrs. Hardy to stop payment on the check, because she didn't realize the money was missing until well after the funeral.

Violet and her mother had been devastated, not only by his loss, but by the disastrous financial condition he'd left behind. They'd lost their nest egg, their home, their car, everything. The woman who'd convinced Mr. Hardy to give her a quarter of a million dollars couldn't be positively identified. And she'd run up accounts in department stores and even jewelry stores for which Mr. Hardy's estate was suddenly responsible. Her mother had had the first stroke just after the funeral. Violet's small, separate inheritance had been just enough to support them for a few months. But after it ran out, Violet had been forced to support them both. There had been a vacancy at Kemp's office, working with Libby Collins and Mabel Henry. Fortunately, Violet had taken a business course in spite of her father's disapproval. She'd never have to get a job, he'd said confidently.

It was nice working in Kemp's office and she was a good secretary. But her boss didn't appreciate her. Less today than ever before. She raged for five minutes, while her helpless co-workers listened and sympathized. She poured out her heart, including her feelings for her taciturn boss.

"Don't take it so much to heart, dear," Mabel said

finally, sympathizing with her despair. "We all have bad days."

"He thinks I'm fat," Violet said miserably.

"He didn't say anything."

"Well, you know how he looked at me and what he insinuated," Violet muttered, glaring down the hall.

Mabel grimaced. "He's had a bad day."

"So have I," Violet said flatly.

Libby Collins patted her on the shoulder. "Buck up, Violet," she said gently. "Just give it a couple of days and he'll apologize. I'm sure he will."

Violet wasn't sure. In fact, she'd have bet money that an apology was the last thing on her boss's mind.

"We'll see," she replied as she went back to her desk. But she didn't believe it.

She pushed back her long dark hair and her blue eyes were tearful, although she was careful to conceal her hurt feelings. It was far worse than just his insinuation that she was overweight. She'd overheard Mabel and Libby whispering that the intercom had been on when Violet had poured out her heart to her co-workers after Kemp's blistering attack over the decaffeinated coffee he'd been given. She was crazy about him. He'd heard that. How was she ever going to be able to face him again?

It was as bad as she feared. All day, he walked out to the front to meet clients, talk about appointments and get coffee. Every single time he walked in, he glared at Violet as if she were responsible for the seven deadly sins. She began to cringe when she heard his footsteps coming down the hall.

By the end of the day, Tuesday, she knew she

couldn't stay with him anymore. It was too humiliating all the way around. She was going to have to leave.

Libby and Mabel noticed her unusual solemnity. It got worse when she pulled a typed sheet from her printer, got up, took a deep breath, and walked down the hall to Kemp's office.

Seconds later, they heard him. "What the hell…?"

Violet came stalking back down the hall, red-faced and unnerved, with an enraged Kemp, minus his glasses, two steps behind, waving the sheet of paper at her back.

"You can't give me one day's notice!" he raged. "I have cases pending. You're responsible for sorting them out and notifying the petitioners…!"

She whirled, eyes flashing. "All that information is in the computer, along with the phone numbers! Libby knows what to do. She's had to help me keep track of your cases when I had to be home with Mother during her last stroke! Please don't pretend it matters who's doing the typing or making the phone calls, because I know it doesn't matter to you! I'm going to work for Duke Wright!"

He was seething, but he went suddenly quiet. "Going over to the enemy, then, Miss Hardy?"

"Mr. Wright is less excitable than you are, sir, and he won't rage about coffee. In fact," she said audaciously, "he makes his own!"

He looked for a retort, couldn't think up one, mashed his sensuous lips together, let out a word under his breath that could have had him up for charges of harassment, and stomped back down the hall still clutching the single sheet of paper. As an afterthought, he slammed his door.

Libby and Mabel tried not to laugh. Mr. Kemp had thrown two people out of the office onto the sidewalk in less than a month. His temper had gone from bad to worse, and poor Violet had caught the worst of it. Now she was leaving and it would be lonely without her. Sadly, Libby thought, her own workload had just doubled.

VIOLET APOLOGIZED TO her co-workers, but insisted that she couldn't take the working situation anymore. At the end of the day, she closed down her computer, noting that Mabel and Libby were both out the door before she could get her things together. Libby had already agreed to come back as soon as she had a bite to eat and finish up two cases that Kemp was presenting the next day. Violet would have offered to do it; poor Libby had problems of her own with her horrible stepmother trying to sell the Collins house out from under Libby and her brother, Curt. But Libby insisted she didn't mind.

Violet shouldered into her long sweater-jacket just as Kemp came stalking down the hall, still in a temper, his pale blue eyes flashing behind his glasses, his lean face taut with anger, his dark wavy hair slightly mussed in back from his restless fingers.

He stopped and glared at her. "I hope I've made my point about the coffee," he said bluntly. "Have you reconsidered your impulsive resignation, by the way?"

She swallowed. He'd made his point about a lot of things. She drew herself up to her full height and faced him bravely. "I have not. I'll be leaving as soon as you can get a replacement, Mr. Kemp."

His eyebrows arched. "Running away, Miss Hardy?" he asked sarcastically.

"You can call it that if you like," she replied.

His eyes glittered, angered all out of proportion by the reply. "In that case, you can consider this your last day and forget the measly notice. I'll get Libby to finish your work and I'll mail your two weeks' pay to you. If that's satisfactory."

Her face felt tight and uncomfortable at the taunting question, but she stood her ground. "That will be fine, Mr. Kemp. Thank you."

He glared at her. He was furious that he couldn't get a rise out of her. "Very well. Your office key, please."

She fumbled it off her key chain and handed it to him, careful not to let her fingers touch his. Her heart was going to break in two when the shock wore off. But she was too proud to let him see how devastated she was.

He stared down at her dark head of hair as she placed the key in his fingers. He felt an unfamiliar, uncomfortable surge of loss. He couldn't understand why. He had little to do with women these days, although he was only thirty-six. He'd lost the woman he loved years ago and had never had any inclination to risk his heart again.

Violet, however, threatened his freedom. She had a sort of empathy with people that was disturbing. She was easily hurt. He could see that this was killing her, being tipped out of his office, out of his life. But he had to let her go. She'd already gotten too close. He never wanted to feel again the pain of having his heart ripped out with the loss of a woman. His fiancée had died. He was through with love. So Violet had to go.

It was for the best, he told himself firmly. She was only infatuated with him. She'd get over it. He thought of how much she'd lost in the past year: her father, her home, her whole way of life. Now she had her invalid mother to care for, a burden she shouldered without a word of complaint. Now she had no job. He winced as he sensed the pain she must be feeling.

"It's for the best," he muttered uncomfortably.

She looked up at him, her blue eyes tragic in her rounded face. "It is?"

His jaw tautened. "You're confused about your feelings. You're only infatuated, Violet," he said as kindly as he could, watching her face flush violently. "It isn't love eternal, and there are eligible men elsewhere. You'll get over it."

Her lips actually trembled as she tried to find a comeback to that devastating revelation. She'd been afraid he'd overheard her confession of love, now she knew he had. His words made her feel like sinking into the floor. It was the worst humiliation she could ever remember feeling in her life. He couldn't possibly have made his own feelings any clearer.

"Yes, sir," she bit off, turning away. "I'll get over it."

She picked up her bits and pieces and moved toward the door. Predictably, he went to open it for her, a gentleman to the bitter end.

"Thank you," she choked, her eyes averted.

"Are you certain that Duke Wright will hire you?" he asked abruptly.

She didn't even look at him. "What do you care, Mr. Kemp?" she asked in a dull, miserable tone. "I'm out of your hair."

She walked toward her car with her heart around her ankles. Behind her, a tall man stood watching, brooding, as she walked out of his life.

SHE'D FORGOTTEN THE CAKE. She'd promised to drop it by the Hart ranch for Tess, but it was still sitting in Kemp's office. She no longer had a key, and she'd rather have died than phoned him to let her in to get the cake. He'd think it was a ruse, so that she could see him again.

She stopped by the bakery instead and got another cake. Luckily for her, Tess didn't want a message on it, just the cake. She stopped by the Hart ranch property at Tess and Cag's enormous house and handed it off to their housekeeper, with a beaming smile that never reached her eyes. Then she went home.

HER MOTHER WAS lying on the sofa, watching the last of her soap operas. "Hello, sweetheart," she said, smiling. "Did you have a nice day?"

"Very nice," Violet lied, smiling back. "How about you?"

"I've done very well. I made supper!"

"Mama, you aren't supposed to exert yourself," Violet protested, gritting her teeth.

"Cooking isn't exertion. I do love it so," the older woman replied, her blue eyes that were so like Violet's sparkling with pleasure. Her hair was silver now, short and wavy. She lay on the sofa in an old gown and housecoat, her feet in socks. Nights were still chilly, even though it was April.

"Want to eat in here on trays?" Violet offered.

"That would be lovely. We can watch the news."

Violet grimaced. "Not the news," she groaned. "Something pleasant!"

"Then what would you like to watch? We've got lots of DVDs," her mother added.

Violet named a comedy about a crocodile who ate people living around a lake.

Her mother gave her an odd look. "My, my. Usually when you want to watch that one, you've had an argument with Mr. Kemp." She was fishing.

Violet cleared her throat. "We did have a little tiff," she confessed, not daring to tell her mother that the family breadwinner was temporarily out of work.

"It will all blow over," Mrs. Hardy promised. "He's a difficult man, I imagine, but he's been very kind to us. Why, when I had to go to the hospital last time, he drove you there and even sat with you until they got me over the crisis."

"Yes, I know," Violet replied, without adding that Mr. Kemp would do that for anybody. It didn't mean anything, except that he had a kind heart.

"And then there was that huge basket of fruit he sent us at Christmas." The older woman was still talking.

Violet was on her way to her bedroom to change into jeans and a sweatshirt. She wondered how she was going to get another job without naming Mr. Kemp as a reference. He might give her one. She just hated having to ask him to. She'd told her co-workers, and Kemp, that she was going to work for Duke Wright, but it had been a lie to save face.

"Going to the gym tonight?" her mother asked when she reappeared and rifled through the DVD stack for the movie she wanted.

"Not tonight," Violet replied with a smile. Maybe never again, she was thinking. What use was it to revamp herself when she'd never see Mr. Kemp again, anyway?

Later, she cried herself to sleep, hating her own show of weakness. Fortunately, nobody else would see it. By dawn, she was up and dressed, her makeup on, her resolve firm. She was going to get a new job. She had skills. She was a hard worker. She would be an asset to any prospective employer. She told herself these things firmly, because her ego was badly hurt. She'd show Mr. Kemp. She could get a job anywhere!

ACTUALLY, THAT WASN'T quite the case. Jacobsville was a small town. There weren't that many office jobs available, because most people lucky enough to get them worked in the same place until they retired.

There was one hope. Duke Wright, a local rancher who had a real verbal war going with Mr. Kemp, couldn't keep a secretary. He was hard, cold, and demanding. At least one secretary had left his employment in tears. His wife had left him, along with their young son, and filed for divorce. He consistently refused to sign the final papers, which had led to a furious confrontation between himself and Blake Kemp. The fistfight escalated until Chief of Police Cash Grier had to step in and break it up. Duke threw a punch at Cash, missed the chief and landed in jail. There was certainly no love lost between Duke Wright and Blake Kemp.

With that idea in mind, and gathering up her courage, she phoned him from home the next morning while her mother was still asleep.

His deep voice was easily recognizable the instant he spoke.

"Mr....Mr. Wright? It's Violet Hardy," she stammered.

There was a surprised pause. "Yes, Miss Hardy?" he replied.

"I was wondering if you needed any secretarial help right now," she blurted out, embarrassed almost to tears just to ask the question.

There was another pause and then a chuckle. "Have you and Kemp parted ways?" he asked at once.

She felt her cheeks redden. "In fact, yes, we have," she said flatly. "I quit."

"Great!"

"Ex-excuse me?" she stammered, surprised.

"I can't get a secretary who doesn't see me as a matrimonial prospect," he told her.

"I certainly won't," she replied without thinking. "Uh, sorry!"

"Don't apologize. How soon can you get out here?"

"Fifteen minutes," she said brightly.

"You're hired. Come in right away. Be sure and tell Kemp who you're working for, will you?" he added. "It would make my day!"

She laughed. "Yes, sir. And thank you very much! I'll work hard, I'll do overtime, anything you want! Well, within reason."

"No need to worry, I'm off women for life," he said in a rough tone. "See you soon, Violet."

He hung up before she could reply. She had a job! She didn't have to tell her mother she was out of work and they wouldn't be able to afford rent payments and her car payment and food. It was such a relief that she sat staring at the phone blankly until she remembered that she had to go to work.

"I'll be home just after five, Mama," she told her mother gently, bending to kiss her forehead. It felt clammy. She frowned, standing erect. "Are you okay?"

Her mother opened pale blue eyes and managed a smile. "Just a little headache, darling, certainly nothing to worry about. I'd tell you. Honest."

Violet relaxed, but only a little. She loved her mother. Mrs. Hardy was the only person in the whole world who loved her. She had frequent unspoken terrors about losing her. It was scary.

"I'm okay!" her mother emphasized.

"You stay in bed today and don't get up and start trying to do cordon bleu in the kitchen. Okay?"

Mrs. Hardy reached out and caught Violet's hand. "I don't want to be a burden on you, darling," she said softly. "That was never what I intended."

"You can't help having a bad heart," she insisted.

"I wish I could. Your father might still be alive, if he hadn't been forced to…to go to another woman…for—" She broke off, tears brightening her eyes.

"Mama, you can't blame yourself for something you couldn't help," Violet told her, privately thinking that if she'd been married to the same man for twenty-five years and he had a stroke, she certainly wouldn't be running around on him while he was fighting just to stay alive. Her father hadn't really loved her mother, and it showed to everybody except Mrs. Hardy. The older woman was forever doing things to help other people. Until her illness, she'd always been active in the community, baking for fund-raising sales, working in her church group, taking food to bereaved families—anything she could do. Her father, a very successful Certified Public Accountant, went to work and came home and watched television. He had no sense of compassion. In fact, his mind was forever on himself, and what he needed. He and Violet had never been close, although he hadn't been a bad father, in his way.

But she couldn't say all that to her mother. Instead she bent and kissed her mother's temple again. "I love you. It's no burden to take care of you. And I mean that," she added, smiling.

"You tell that Mr. Kemp that I'm very proud he gave you the job. I don't know what we'd have done…"

Violet sat down beside her mother. "Listen, I have to tell you something."

"You're getting married?" the older woman asked hopefully, with bright eyes and a smile. "He's finally realized you're in love with him?!"

"He's realized it," Violet said, tight-lipped. "And he said I'd get over it quicker if I was working for somebody else."

Her mother's jaw fell. "And he seemed like such a nice man!" she exclaimed.

She held the other woman's hand hard. "I've got a new job," she said at once, before her mother could start worrying. "I'm going to start this morning." She smiled. "It's going to be great!"

"Start where? Working for whom?"

"Duke Wright."

Her mother's thin eyebrows arched and a twinkle came into her eyes. "He doesn't like Mr. Kemp."

"And vice versa," Violet stated firmly. "It will pay just as well as Mr. Kemp did," she added, mentally crossing her fingers, "and he won't complain about how I make coffee."

"Excuse me?" Mrs. Hardy asked.

Violet cleared her throat. "Never mind, Mama. It's going to be fine. I like Mr. Wright."

Mrs. Hardy pressed her hand again. "If you say so. I'm sorry, darling. I know how you feel about Mr. Kemp."

"Since he doesn't feel the same way, it's for the best if I don't go on working there and eating my heart out over him," Violet said realistically. "I daresay I'll find other company, someone who doesn't think I'm too fat…" She stopped at once and flushed.

Her mother looked furious. "You are not fat! I can't believe Mr. Kemp had the audacity to say something like that to you!"

"He didn't," Violet replied at once. "He just…insinuated it." She sighed. "He's right. I am fat. But I'm trying so hard to lose weight!"

Her mother held her hand tighter. "Listen to me, darling," she said softly. "A man who really cares about you isn't going to dwell on what he considers faults. Your father used that same argument to me," she added unexpectedly. "He actually said that he went to that other woman because she was slender and well-groomed."

"He…did?"

She grimaced. "I should have told you. Your father never loved me, Violet. He was in love with my best friend and she married somebody else. He married me to get even with her. He wanted a divorce two months later, but I was pregnant with you, and in those days, people really gossiped about men who walked out on a pregnant wife. So we stayed together and tried to make a home for you. Looking back," she said wearily, lying back down on her pillows, "perhaps I made a mistake. You don't know what a good marriage is, do you? Your father and I hardly ever did anything together, even when you were little."

Violet pushed back her mother's disheveled hair. "I love you very much," she told her parent. "I think you're wonderful. So do a lot of other people. It was my father's loss if he couldn't see how special you were."

"At least I have you" came the soft reply, with a smile. "I love you, too, darling."

Violet fought tears. "Now I really have to go," she said. "I can't afford to lose my new job before I start it!"

Her mother laughed. "You be careful!"

"I'll drive under the speed limit," she promised.

"Mr. Wright isn't married now, is he?" Mrs. Hardy wondered.

"Yes, he is. He refused to sign the final divorce papers." She laughed. "That's why he had the fight with Mr. Kemp."

"Is it spite, do you think, or does he still love her?"

"Everybody thinks he still loves her, but she's mak-

ing a fortune working as a lawyer in New York City
and she doesn't want to come back here."

"They have a little boy. Doesn't she think his father
has any right to see the child?"

"They're still arguing about custody."

"What a pity."

"People should think hard about having children,"
Violet said with conviction, "and they shouldn't ever
be accidents."

"That's just what I've always said," Mrs. Hardy replied. "Have a good day, darling."

"You, too. The phone's right here and I'm going to
write down Mr. Wright's number in case you need me."
She penciled it on the pad next to the phone, smiled,
and went to get her purse.

DUKE WRIGHT LIVED in a huge white Victorian house.
Local gossip said that his wife had wanted it since she
was a child, living in a poor section of Jacobsville.
She'd married Duke right out of high school and started
to college after the honeymoon was over. College had
opened a new world to her eyes. She'd decided to study
law, and Duke stood by and let her have her way, sure
that she'd never want to leave Jacobsville. But she got a
taste of city life when she went on to law school in San
Antonio, and she decided to work in a law firm there.

Nobody understood exactly why they decided to
have a child in her first year as a practicing estate lawyer. She didn't seem happy about it, although she had
the child. But a live-in nurse had to be employed because Mrs. Wright spent more and more time at the
office. Then, two years ago, she'd been offered a posi-

tion in a well-known law firm in New York City and she'd jumped at the chance. Duke had argued, cajoled, threatened, to try to get her to turn it down. Nothing worked. In a fit of rage, she moved out, with their son, and filed for divorce. Duke had fought it tooth and nail. Just this month, she'd presented him with divorce papers, demanding his signature, which also required him to remit full custody of his five-year-old son to her. He'd gone wild.

To look at him, though, Violet thought, he seemed very self-possessed and confident. He was tall and bronzed with a strong face, square chin, deep-set dark eyes and blondish-brown hair which he wore conventionally cut. He had the physique of a rodeo star, which he'd been before his father's untimely death and his switch from cowboy to cattle baron. He ran purebred red angus cattle, well-known in cattle circles for their pedigree. He had all the scientific equipment necessary for a prosperous operation, including high-tech methods of genetic breeding, artificial insemination, embryo transplantation, cross-breeding for leanness, low birth weight and daily weight gain ratio, as well as expert feed formulation. He had the most modern sort of operation, right down to lagoon management and forage improvement. He had the most modern computers money could buy, and customized software to keep up with his cattle. But his newest operation was organic ham and bacon that he raised on his ranch and marketed over the Internet.

Violet was staggered at the high-tech equipment in the office he maintained on his sprawling ranch outside town.

"Intimidated?" he drawled, smiling. "Don't worry. It's easier to use than it looks."

"Can you operate it all?" she asked, surprised.

He shrugged. "With the average duration of secretarial assistance around here, I have to be able to do things myself," he said heavily. He gave her a long look and stuck his lean hands in the pockets of his jeans. "Violet, I'm not an easy boss," he confessed. "I have moods and rages, and sometimes I blow up when things upset me. You'll need nerves of steel to last long here. So I won't blame you if you have reservations."

Her eyebrows arched. "I worked for Blake Kemp for over a year."

He chuckled, understanding her very well. "They say he's worse than me," he agreed. "Okay. If you're game, we'll give it two weeks. After that, you can decide if it's worth the money. That's another thing," he added, smiling. "I pay better than Kemp." He named a figure that made Violet look shocked. He nodded. "That's to make it worth the aggravation. Come on, and I'll show you around the equipment."

It WAS FASCINATING. She'd never seen anything like the tangle of spreadsheets and software that ran his empire. Even the feed was mixed by computer.

"Not that you'll have to concern yourself with the organic pork operation," he added quickly. "I have three employees who do nothing except that. But these figures—" he indicated the spreadsheet "—are urgent. They have to be maintained on a daily basis."

"All of them?" she exclaimed, seeing hours and hours of overtime in statistics before her.

"Not by hand," he replied. "All the cowboys are computer literate, even the old-timers. They feed the information into handheld computers and send it to the mainframe by internal modem, right from the pastures," he told her.

She just shook her head. "It's incredible," she replied. "I hope I'm smart enough to learn all this, Mr. Wright."

He smiled approvingly. "There's nothing I appreciate more than modesty, Miss Hardy," he replied. "You'll do fine. Ready to get started?"

"Yes, sir!" she replied.

It was a short day, mainly because she was so busy trying to learn the basics of Duke Wright's agricultural programs. She liked him. He might have a bad reputation, and she knew he could be hard to get along with, but he had saving graces.

She managed not to think about Mr. Kemp all afternoon, until she got home.

Her mother smiled at her from the sofa, where she was watching her daily soap operas. "Well, how did it go?" she asked.

"I like it!" Violet told her with a big smile. "I really do. I think I'm going to work out just fine. And, besides that, I'm going to be making a lot more money. Mama, we might even be able to afford a dishwasher!"

Mrs. Hardy sighed. "That would be lovely, wouldn't it?"

Violet kicked off her shoes and sat down in the recliner next to the sofa. "I'm so tired! I'm just going to rest for a minute and then I'll see about supper."

"We could have chili and hot dogs."

Violet chuckled. "We could have a nice salad and bread sticks," she said, thinking of the calories.

"Whatever you like, dear. Oh, by the way, Mr. Kemp came by a few minutes ago."

Violet's world came crashing down around her ears. She'd hoped to not even hear his name, at least for another few days.

"What did he want?" she asked her mother.

The older woman picked up a white envelope. "To give you this." She handed it to Violet, who sat staring at it.

"Well," she murmured. "I guess it's my final pay."

Mrs. Hardy muted the television set. "Why not open it and see?"

Violet didn't want to, but her mother looked expectant. She tore open the envelope and extracted a check and a letter. With her breath in her throat, she slowly unfolded it.

"What does it say?" her mother prompted.

Violet just stared at it, unbelieving.

"Violet, what is it?"

Violet drew in a breath. "It's a letter of recommendation," she said huskily.

## CHAPTER TWO

"I CAN'T BELIEVE he actually gave me one," Violet said huskily, her heart racing from just the thought that he'd backed down that far. "I didn't ask for it."

"He told me that," her mother replied. "He said that he felt really bad about the way you left, Violet, and that he hoped you'd be happy in your new job."

Violet looked up at her parent, hating herself for being so happy with these crumbs of Kemp's regard. "He did?" She caught herself. "Did you tell him where I was working?"

Mrs. Hardy shifted on the sofa. "Well, dear, he looked so pleasant and we had such a nice conversation. I thought, why upset the man?"

Violet laughed helplessly. "What did you tell him, Mother?" she asked gently.

"I said you were working in a local office for a very nice man, doing statistics," she said with a chuckle. "He didn't actually ask where. He started to, and I changed the subject. He said Libby and Mabel were splitting your work for the time being. He's going to advertise for a new secretary," she added.

Violet sighed. "I hope he's happy with whichever poor soul gets the job," she said.

"No, you don't. I know you hated to leave. But, dear,

if he doesn't feel the same way, it's a blessing in the
long run," her mother said wisely. "No sense eating
your heart out."

"That's what I thought when I quit," Violet admitted.
She got to her feet, putting the letter and check back in
the envelope. "I'll go fix something to eat."

"You could make a pot of coffee," her mother suggested.

Violet gave her a glare. "You don't need to be drinking caffeine."

"Don't we have any decaf?"

It reminded Violet too much of her ex-boss, and she
wasn't enthusiastic. But her mother loved coffee, and
missed being able to drink it. She didn't know about
the coffee wars in Kemp's office, either. Violet forced
a smile. "I'll see," she said, and left her mother to the
soap opera.

THE FIRST FEW days out of Kemp's office were the hard-
est. She couldn't forget how she'd looked forward to
every new day, to each morning's first glimpse of her
handsome boss. Her heart had jumped at the sound of
his voice. She tingled all over when, rarely, he smiled
at her when she finished a difficult task for him. Even
the scent of a certain masculine cologne could trigger
memories, because he always smelled of it. She felt de-
prived because her life would no longer contain even a
casual glimpse of him. She was working for his worst
enemy. Not much likelihood that Kemp would turn up
on Duke Wright's ranch in the near or distant future.

But as time passed, Violet slowly fell into a routine
at Duke's ranch. The spreadsheet programs were easy

to use once she learned what the various terms meant, like weight gain ratio and birth weight. She learned that Duke used artificial insemination to improve the genetics of his cattle, selecting for low birth weight, good weight gain ratios for offspring and lean cuts of meat in the beef cattle offspring that would eventually be generated by his purebred herd sires and dams.

She was fascinated to find that science was used to predict leanness and tenderness of beef cuts, that genetics could manipulate those factors to produce a more marketable product for consumers.

She was fascinated by the various pedigrees and the amount of history contained in his breeding programs. It was like an organic history of Texas just to look back over the first herds that had contributed to Duke's formidable beef concern. He kept photographic records as well as statistical ones, and she found the early beef sires short, stocky and woolly compared to modern ones. It graphically showed the progression of genetic breeding.

Her duties were routine and hardly exciting, but she made good wages and she liked the people she worked with. Duke had full-time and part-time cowboys, as well as a veterinary student who worked one semester and went to school one semester. He had three people who did nothing but work with his Internet Web site that sold his premium organic ham and bacon products.

But Violet's job was separate from that of the other workers. There was a new storefront that Duke had just opened in Jacobsville to market his organic pork. There was also a modern office complex adjacent to the enormous barn, where the production and lab staff were located. The barn, in addition to containing the pride of his purebred cattle herd, his expensive seed bulls, there was also a climate controlled room where the frozen sperm and embryos were kept for artificial insemination. The procedure itself was conducted in the barn. Purebred embryos from superior herd sires, as well as straws of semen from champion bulls who were now long dead, were kept in vats of liquid nitrogen. These were placed in surrogate mothers who might be Holsteins or even mixed breed cattle rather than the purebred heifers he also sold along with each new crop of yearling bulls from purebred sires.

Violet had a passing acquaintance with the employees who ran the lab, one of whom was a graduate biologist named Delene Crane, a young woman with a quirky sense of humor. They were nodding acquaintances, because she didn't have much free time to socialize. None of the staff did, for that matter. Routine at the ranch was chaotic because spring was the busiest time for everyone, with calves being born and recorded and branding in full swing.

She knew that Duke used not only hot branding, but also had computer chips on plastic tags that dangled from the ears of his cattle. These chips contained the complete history of each cow or bull. The information was scanned into a handheld computer and sent by modem to Violet's computer to be compiled into the spreadsheet program.

"It's just fascinating," Violet told Duke as she watched the information updating itself on her computer screen from minute to minute.

He smiled wearily. He was dusty. His chaps and boots were dirty and blood-stained because he'd been helping with calving all day. His red shirt was wet all over. His hair, under his wide-brimmed Stetson, was dripping sweat. His leather gloves, tight-fitting and suede-colored, were dangling from the wide belt buckle at his lean waist over his jeans.

"It's taken a lot of work to get this operation so far," he confessed, his eyes on the screen as he spoke, his voice deep and pleasant in the quiet office. "And a lot of cash. I've been in the hole for the past year. But I'm just beginning to show a profit. I think the pork operation may be what finally gets me in the black."

"Where are the pigs kept?" she wondered aloud, because she'd only seen cattle and horses so far. In addition to the cattle herd, Duke maintained a small herd of purebred Appaloosa horses.

"Far enough away that they aren't easy to smell," he replied with a grin. "They have their own complex about a mile down the road. It's remarkably clean, and purely organic. They have pastures to roam and a stream that runs through it all the year, and they're fed a carefully formulated organic diet. No pesticides, no hormones, no antibiotics unless they're absolutely necessary."

"You sound like the Harts and the Tremaynes and…" she began.

"…and Cy Parks and J. D. Langley," he finished for her, chuckling. "They did give me the idea. It's catching on. Christabel and Judd Dunn jumped on the wagon last year."

"It's been very profitable for them, I hear," Violet replied. "Mr. Kemp handles all the paperwork for the Harts and Cy Parks…" She bit her tongue as his face hardened and the smile faded. "Sorry, boss," she said at once.

He moved jerkily. "No harm done."

But she knew how he felt about Kemp. She opened a second window on the computer screen and diverted him with a question about another procedure.

He explained the process to her and smiled. "You're a diplomat, Violet. I'm glad you needed a job."

"Me, too, Mr. Wright," she replied, smiling.

He pulled his hat down over his eyes. "Well, I've played hooky as long as I can," he said with a grimace. "I'll get back to work before Lance comes in here and lassos me and drags me back out to the pasture. You go home at five regardless of the phone, okay?" he added. "I know you worry about your mother. You don't need to do overtime."

"Thanks," she said, and meant it. "It's hard for her to be alone in the evening. She gets scared."

"I don't doubt it. Oh, if you get a minute," he added from the door, "call Calhoun Ballenger and tell him I'm sending him a donation for his campaign."

She grinned. "I'll be happy to do that! I'm voting for him, too."

"Good for you." He closed the door carefully behind him.

Violet made the call, finished up her work, and left on time. She had to run by the post office on the way home to put Duke's correspondence into the mail.

As LUCK WOULD have it, Kemp was in the lobby when she walked in the door, having just put a last-minute letter into the outgoing post.

He stopped short when he saw her, his pale blue eyes narrow and accusing. She was keenly aware that her lipstick was long gone, that her hair was sticking out in comic angles from her once-neat braid, that one leg of her panty hose was laddered. She couldn't run into him when she looked neat and pretty, she thought miserably. To top it all off, she was wearing white jeans that were too tight and a red overblouse with ruffles that made her look vaguely clownish. She ground her teeth as she glared back at him.

"Mr. Kemp," she said politely, and started to go around him.

He stepped right into her path. "What's Wright been doing to you?" he asked. "You look worn to the bone."

Her thin eyebrows arched as she registered genuine concern in that narrow gaze. She cleared her throat. "It's roundup," she replied.

He nodded understanding. "The Harts are breaking out in hives already," he mused, and almost smiled. "They've had some problems with their exports to Japan as well. I suppose the cattle business is wearing on the nerves."

She smiled shyly. "Everybody's rushing to record all the pertinent information for every new calf, and there are a lot of them."

"He's opened a meat shop here in town," he remarked. "It sells organic hams and sausage and bacon."

"Yes. His employees run a Web site, too, so that he can sell his pork on the Internet." She hesitated. Her heart was racing like mad and she felt her knees weakening just from the long, shared looks. She missed him so much. "How...how are Libby and Mabel?"

"Missing you." He made it sound as if she'd left him in a bind.

She shifted to the other foot. If they'd been alone, she'd have had more to say about the accusing look he was giving her. But people were coming and going all around them. "Thank you. For the recommendation, I mean."

He shrugged. "I didn't think Wright would take you on," he said honestly. "It's no secret that he hates having women around the ranch since the divorce."

"Delene Crane works with him," she replied, curious. "She's a woman."

"He's known Delene since they were in college together," he told her. "He doesn't think of her as a woman."

Interesting, she mused, because Delene wasn't a bad-looking woman. She had red hair and green eyes and a milky complexion with a few freckles. She froze out the cowboys who gave her flirting glances, though. She was also strictly business with Duke, so maybe it was true that he didn't think of her as a romantic prospect. She wondered why Delene didn't feel comfortable around men...

"How's your mother?" Kemp asked abruptly.

She grimaced. "She does things they told her not to do," she lamented. "Especially lifting heavy stuff. The doctors said that she still has a tendency toward clots, despite the blood thinners they give her. They didn't say, but I know that once a person has one or two strokes, they're almost predisposed to have more."

He nodded slowly. "But there are drugs to treat that, now. I'm sure your doctor is taking good care of her."

"He is," she had to agree.

"Your mother is special."

She smiled. "Yes. I think so, too."

He looked past her. "It's clouding up. You'd better get your letters mailed, so you don't get soaked when you leave."

"Yes." She looked at him with pain in her eyes. She loved him. It was so much worse that he knew, and pitied her for it. She glanced away, coloring faintly. "Yes, I'd better...go."

Unexpectedly, he reached out and pushed back a long strand of black hair that had escaped her braid. He tugged it behind her ear, his gaze intent and solemn as he watched her heartbeat race at her bodice. He heard her breath catch at the faint contact. He felt guilty. He could have been kinder to Violet. She had enough on her plate just with her mother to care for. She cared about him. She'd shown it, in so many ways, when she worked with him. He hadn't wanted to encourage her, or give her false hope. But she looked so miserable.

"Take care of yourself," he said quietly.

She swallowed, hard. "Yes, sir. You, too."

He moved aside to let her pass. As she went by, a faint scent of roses drifted up into his nostrils. Amazing how much he missed that scent around his office. Violet had become almost like a stick of furniture in the past year, she was so familiar. But at the same time, he was aware of an odd, tender nurturing of himself that he'd never had in his adult life. Violet made him think of open fireplaces in winter, of warm lamplight in the darkness. Her absence had only served to make him realize how alone he was.

She walked on to the mail slots, unaware of his long, aching stare at her back. By the time she finished her chore, he was already out the door and climbing into his Mercedes.

Violet watched him drive away before she opened the door of the post office and went outside. It was starting to rain. She'd get wet, but she didn't care. The odd, tender encounter made her head spin with pleasure. It would be a kind thought to brighten her lonely life.

THERE WAS A lot of talk around town about Janet Collins. She'd gone missing and Libby and Curt were the subject of a lot of gossip. Jordan Powell had been seen with Libby, but nobody took that seriously. He was also seen with old Senator Merrill's daughter, Julie, doing the social rounds. Violet wondered if Libby felt the rejection as much as Violet felt it over Kemp. Her coworker had a flaming crush on Jordan in recent weeks, but it seemed the feeling wasn't reciprocated.

Violet's mother seemed to be weakening as the days passed. It was hard for Violet to work and not worry about her. She'd started going back to the gym on her way home from work three days a week, but it was only for a half hour at a time. She'd splurged on a cell phone and she kept it with her all the time now, just in case there was ever an emergency when she wasn't home. Her mother had a hot button on the new phone at home, too, so that she could push it and speed-dial Violet.

She had her long hair trimmed and frosted, and she actually asked a local boutique owner for tips on how to make the most of her full figure. She learned that lower cut blouses helped to diminish a full bosom. She also learned that a longer jacket flattered wide hips, and that straight lines made her look taller. She experimented with hairstyles until she found one that flattered her full face, and with makeup until she learned how to use it so that it looked natural. She was changing, growing, maturing, slimming. But all of it was a means to an end, as much as she hated to admit it. She wanted Blake Kemp to miss her, want her, ache for her when he looked at her. It was a hopeless dream, but she couldn't let go of it.

Kemp, meanwhile, spent far too much time at his home thinking about ways and means to get Violet to come back.

He stretched out on his burgundy leather couch to watch the weather channel with his two female Siamese cats, Mee and Yow, curled against his chest. Mee, a big seal-point, rarely cuddled with him. Yow, a blue-point, was in his lap the minute he sat down. He felt a kinship with the cats, who had become his family. They sat with him while he watched television at night. They curled up on the big oak desk when he worked there at his computer. Late at night, they climbed under the covers on either side of him and purred him to sleep.

The Harts thought his cat mania was a little overdone. But, then, they weren't really cat people, except for Cag and Tess. Their cats were mostly strays. Mee and Yow, on the other hand, were purebred. Blake had brought both of them home with him together from a pet store, where they'd been in cages behind glass for weeks, the last products of a cattery that had gone bank-rupt. He'd felt sorry for them. More than likely, he told himself, they'd set him up. Cats were masters of the subtle suggestion. It was amazing how a fat, healthy cat could present itself as an emaciated, starving orphan. They were still playing mind tricks on him after four years of co-existence. It still worked, too.

He thought about Violet and her mother, and remem-bered that the elderly Mrs. Hardy was allergic to fur. Violet loved animals. She kept little figurines of cats on her desk. He'd never asked her to his home, but he was certain that she'd love his cats. He imagined she'd have Duke Wright bringing calves right up to the porch for her to pet.

His eyes flashed at the thought of Violet getting involved with the other man. Wright was bitter over the divorce and the custody suit his wife had brought against him. He blamed Kemp for it, but Kemp was only doing what any other attorney would have done in his place. If the soon-to-be ex-Mrs. Wright was as happy as she seemed in that high-powered property law job she held in New York City, she wasn't likely to ever come home. She loved the little boy as much as Duke did, and she felt it was better not to have him dangling between two parents. Kemp didn't agree. A child had two parents. It would only lead to grief to deny access to either of them.

He shook his head. What a pity that people had chil-dren before they thought about the consequences. They never improved a bad marriage. Kemp's clientele shot that truth home every time he handled a divorce case. The children were always the ones who suffered most.

Beka Wright had never admitted it, and Kemp never pried, but local gossip had it that Duke had deliberately hidden her birth control pills at a critical time, hoping that a baby would cure her of ambition. It hadn't. He was an overbearing sort of man, who expected a woman to do exactly what he told her to do. His father had been the same, a domineering autocrat whose poor wife had walked in a cold rain with pneumonia while he was out of town one January weekend in a last, fatal attempt to escape him. Death had spared her further abuse. Duke had grown up with that same autocratic attitude and assumed that it was the way a normal man dealt with his wife. He was learning to his cost that marriage meant compromise.

Blake looked around at his house with its Western motifs, burgundy leather mingling with dark oak and cherry wood furniture. The carpet and the curtains were earth tones. He enjoyed a quiet atmosphere after the turmoil of his working life. But he wondered what a woman would do with the décor.

Mee curled her claws into his arm. He winced, and moved them. She was sound asleep, but when she felt his hand on her, she snuggled closer and started purring.

He laughed softly. No, he wasn't the marrying sort. He was a gourmet cook. He did his own laundry and housework. He could sew on a button or make a bed. Like most other ex-special forces officers, he was independent and self-sufficient. A veteran of the first war with Iraq, he mustered out with the rank of captain. He'd been in the Army reserves after he graduated from law school and started practicing in Jacobsville, and his unit had been called up. He and Cag Hart had served in the same mechanized division. Few people knew that, because he and Cag didn't talk much about the missions they'd shared. It forged bonds that noncombatants could not understand.

He reached for the remote control and changed the channel. He paused on the weather channel to see when the rain was going to stop, and then went on to the History channel, where he spent most of his free time in the evenings. He often thought that if he ever came across a woman who enjoyed military history, he might be coaxed into rejoining the social scene.

But then he remembered the woman he'd lost, and the ache started all over again. He turned up the volume and leaned back, his mind shifting to the recounting of Alexander the Great's final successful campaign against the Persian king Darius in 331 B.C. at Gaugemela.

VIOLET WAS LATE getting home the following Friday. She'd stopped by the gym and then remembered that there was no milk in the house. She'd gone by the grocery store as well. When she pulled up into the driveway of the small, rickety rental house, she found her mother sitting on the ground beside the small flower garden at the porch steps. Mrs. Hardy wasn't moving.

Panicking, Violet jumped out of her car without bothering to close the door, and ran toward her parent.

"Mama!" she screamed.

Her mother jerked, just faintly. Her blue eyes were startled as she turned her head and looked at her daughter. She was breathing heavily. But she laughed. "Darling, it's all right!" she said at once. "I just got winded, that's all! I'm all right!"

Violet knelt beside her. Tears were rolling down her cheeks. Her face was white. She was shaking.

"Oh, baby." Mrs. Hardy winced as she reached out and cuddled Violet close, whispering soft endearments. "I'm sorry. I'm so sorry. I wanted to weed my flower bed and put out those little seedlings I'd grown in the kitchen window. I just worked a little too hard, that's all. See? I'm fine."

Violet pulled back, terrified. Her mother was all she had in the world. She loved her so much. How would she go on living if she lost her mother? That fear was written all over her.

Mrs. Hardy winced when she saw it. She hugged Violet close. "Violet," she said sadly, "one day you'll have to let me go. You know that."

"I'm not ready yet," Violet sobbed.

Mrs. Hardy sighed. She kissed Violet's dark hair. "I know," she murmured, her eyes faraway as they looked toward the horizon. "Neither am I."

LATER, AS THEY sat over bowls of hot soup and fresh corn bread, Mrs. Hardy studied her daughter with concern.

"Violet, are you sure you're happy working at Duke Wright's place?" she asked.

"Of course I am," Violet said stolidly.

"I think Mr. Kemp would like it if you went back to work with him."

Violet stared at her with her spoonful of soup in mid-air. "Why would you say that, Mama?"

"Mabel, who works at your office, stopped by to see me at lunch. She says Mr. Kemp is so moody they can hardly work with him anymore. She said she thinks he misses you."

Violet's heart jumped. "That wasn't how he sounded when I ran into him in the post office the other day," she said. "But he was acting...oddly."

The older woman smiled over her soup spoon. "Often men don't know what they want until they lose it."

"Bring on the day." Violet laughed softly.

"So, dear, back to my first question. Do you like your new job?"

She nodded. "It's challenging. I don't have to deal with sad, angry, miserable people whose lives are in pieces. You know, I didn't realize until I changed jobs how depressing it is to work in a law office. You see such tragedies."

"I suppose cattle are a lot different."

"There's just so much to learn," Violet agreed. "It's so complex. There are so many factors that produce good beef. I thought it was only a matter of putting bulls and heifers in the same pasture and letting nature do its work."

"It isn't?" her mother asked, curious.

Violet grinned. "Want to know how it works?"

"Yes, indeed."

So Violet spent the next half hour walking her mother, hypothetically speaking, through the steps involved in creating designer beef.

"Well!" the elderly woman exclaimed. "It isn't simple at all."

"No, it isn't. The records are so complicated..."

The sudden ringing of the telephone interrupted Violet. She frowned. "It's probably another telemarketer," she muttered. "I wish we could afford one of those new answering machines and caller ID."

"One day a millionaire will walk in the front door carrying a glass slipper and an engagement ring," Mrs. Hardy ventured with a mischievous glance.

Violet laughed as she got up and went to answer the phone. "Hardy residence," she said in her light, friendly tone.

"Violet?"

It was Kemp! She had to catch her breath before she could even answer him. "Yes, sir?" she stammered.

He hesitated. "I have to talk to you and your mother. It's important. May I come over?"

Violet's mind raced. The house was a mess. She was a mess. She was wearing jeans and a shirt that didn't fit. Her hair needed washing. The living room needed vacuuming…!

"Who is it, dear?" Mrs. Hardy called.

"It's Mr. Kemp, Mama. He says he needs to speak to us."

"Isn't it nice that we have some of that pound cake left?" Mrs. Hardy wondered aloud. "Tell him to come right on, dear."

Violet ground her teeth together. "It's all right," she told Kemp.

"Fine. I'll be there in fifteen minutes." He hung up before Violet could ask him what he wanted.

She turned worriedly to her mother. "Do you think it might be something about me coming back to work for him?"

"Who can say? You should wash your hair, dear. You'll have just enough time."

"Not to do that and vacuum and pick up around the living room," she wailed.

"Violet, the chores can wait," her mother replied amusedly. "You can't. Go, girl!"

Violet turned like a zombie and went right to the bathroom to wash her hair. By the time she heard Kemp pulling up in the driveway, she had on a nice low-cut short-sleeved blue sweater and clean white jeans. Her hair was clean and she left it down, because she didn't have time to braid it. She was wearing bedroom shoes, but that wasn't going to matter, she decided.

She opened the door.

Kemp gave her a quiet going-over with his pale blue eyes. But he didn't remark about her appearance. He was scowling. "I have something to say that your mother needs to hear, but I don't want to upset her."

There went her dreams of being rehired. "What is it about?" she asked.

He drew in a sharp breath. "Violet, I want to have your father exhumed. I think Janet Collins killed him."

# CHAPTER THREE

VIOLET WASN'T SURE she was hearing right. She knew there was something going on with Janet Collins. Curt had come by her office when he carried a note to Duke from Jordan Powell, his boss. He'd told her that he and Libby were going to have to have their father exhumed because there were suspicions that Janet, their stepmother, might have killed him. She was suspected of killing at least one other elderly man by poison. Violet and her mother knew about the waitress Mr. Hardy had had his fling with. But they'd never questioned the cause of death. And they'd never found out who the waitress was. Now, a lot of questions she hadn't wanted even to ask were suddenly being answered.

Her lips parted on a husky sigh. "Oh, dear."

Kemp closed the door behind him and tilted Violet's chin up to his eyes. "I don't want to do this," he said softly. "But there's a very good chance that your father was murdered, Violet. You don't want Janet Collins to get away with it, if she's guilty. Neither do I."

"You're right," she agreed. "But what about Mama?"

He drew in a long breath. "I have to have her signature. I can't do it on yours alone."

They exchanged worried looks.

His eyes suddenly narrowed on her oval face in its

frame of dark hair. Her skin was clean and bright. She wasn't wearing makeup, except a touch of pink lipstick. And that sweater… His eyes slid down to her breasts with quiet sensuality. They narrowed, as he appreciated how deliciously full-breasted she was. She had a small waist, too. The jeans emphasized the nicely rounded contours of her hips.

"I've lost weight!" she blurted out.

"Don't lose any more," he murmured absently. "You're perfect."

Her eyebrows arched. "Sir?" she stammered.

"If I weren't a confirmed bachelor, you'd make my mouth water," he replied quietly, and the eyes that met hers were steady, intent.

Her heart began racing. Her knees were weak. He wasn't blind. Any minute, he was going to notice her helpless, headlong reaction.

"But I am a confirmed bachelor," he added firmly, as much for his own benefit as for hers. "And this isn't the time, anyway. May I come in?"

"Of course." She closed the door behind him, unsettled by what he'd said.

"I planned to come by your office and tell you," he said, his voice low, "but I got caught at the last minute and by the time I finished with an upset client, you'd already left Wright's place. I'd hoped to have a little time to prepare you for what we have to do." He glanced toward the living room door. "How is she?" he asked.

She bit her lower lip. "She's had a slight spell this week," she told him worriedly. "She thinks she's stronger than she really is. Losing Daddy and finding out about his affair ruined her life."

He bit back a harsh reply. "Should we have the doctor here while I tell her?"

She sighed wearily. "I don't think it will matter." She looked up at him. "She has to know. I don't want Janet Collins to get away with murder. Neither will she. We both loved Daddy, in our way."

"All right then." He nodded for her to go ahead of him and he followed her into the room.

Her mother looked up and smiled. "Mr. Kemp! How nice to see you again!"

He smiled, pausing in front of her to shake her hand gently. "It's good to see you, too, Mrs. Hardy. But I'm afraid I may have some upsetting news."

She put down her knitting and sat up straight. "My daughter thinks I'm a marshmallow," she said with an impish look at Violet. "But I'm tougher than I look, despite my rickety blood vessels." She set her lips firmly. "You just tell me what I need to know, and I'll do what I have to."

His blue eyes twinkled. "You are a tough nut, aren't you?" he teased.

She grinned at him, looking far younger than she was. "You bet. Go on. Spill it."

His smile faded. Violet sat on the arm of her mother's chair.

"It must be bad, if you're both expecting me to keel over," she said. "It's something about Janet Collins, isn't it?"

Violet gasped. Kemp's eyebrows arched over the frames of his glasses.

"I'm not a petunia. I don't just hang on the porch all the time," Mrs. Hardy informed them. "I get my hair done, I go to the doctor's office, I see a lot of people. I know that Libby and Curt Collins are up to their ears in trouble about their stepmother, and there's a lot of talk that she's been linked to the death of an old man in a nursing home. They said she took every penny he had. And then she went on to cheat Arthur and me out of our savings, a quarter of a million dollars. It wasn't ever proven that it was her."

"I've found an eyewitness who thinks she can place Janet Collins at the motel with Arthur the last day of his life," Kemp told her, "just before the ambulance came to take him to the hospital. She ran out the door and was seen. At the hospital the doctor, not aware of any foul play, diagnosed a heart attack from the symptoms. There was no autopsy."

"That's right," Mrs. Hardy said. She gave her audience a knowing look. "And you think she killed him, don't you?" she asked Kemp.

He was impressed. "Yes, I do," he told her honestly.

"I didn't want to think about that, but I've had my doubts," she said. "He never had heart trouble. There had been some mixup at a clinic in San Antonio and he ended up getting a heart catherization that he didn't really need. What it showed was that his heart and arteries were in fine shape, no blockages at all. So it came as something of a surprise when he died only a month later of a supposed heart attack. But I was far too upset at his affair and his sudden death to think clearly."

"If it's any consolation, Janet Collins had a way with men," Kemp replied. "She was known for playing up to older men, and she isn't a bad-looking woman. Most men react predictably to a head-on assault."

Violet was wondering irrelevantly if it would work with Kemp, but she pushed that thought to the back of her mind.

"Arthur had strayed before," Mrs. Hardy said surprisingly, and with an apologetic glance at Violet. "He was a handsome, vital man, and I was always quiet and shy and rather ordinary."

"You weren't ordinary," Violet protested.

"My people were very wealthy, dear," she told her daughter sadly. "And Arthur was ambitious. He wanted his own accounting firm, and I helped him get it. Not that he didn't work hard, but he'd never have made it without my backing. I think that hurt his pride. Maybe his...affairs...were a way of proving to himself that he could still appeal to beautiful women even as he got older. I'm sorry, Violet," she added, patting her daughter's thigh. "But parents are human, too. Arthur did love you, and he tried to be a good father, even if he wasn't a good husband."

Violet clenched her teeth. She could only imagine how it would have felt to her, if she'd been married and her husband thought nothing of having affairs with other women.

"By the time Arthur started straying," Mrs. Hardy continued, "I was too fragile to leave him and strike out on my own. There was Violet, who needed both her parents and a stable environment. And I could no longer take care of myself. Arthur paid a price to stay with me, under the circumstances. I don't really blame him for what he did."

She did, though, and it showed. Violet hugged her close. "I blame him," she murmured.

"So do I," Kemp said, surprisingly firm. "Any honorable man would have asked for a divorce before getting involved with another woman."

"Why, you Puritan," Mrs. Hardy accused with a smile.

"I've got company," he jerked his thumb at Violet.

Mrs. Hardy laughed. She folded her hands in her lap. "Okay, so we've settled that Arthur probably had an affair with Janet Collins and she may have been responsible for his death. But unless he's exhumed, and an autopsy done, we can't prove it. That's why you're here, isn't it, Mr. Kemp?"

"You're amazing, Mrs. Hardy," Kemp replied with admiration in his pale blue eyes.

"I'm perceptive. Ask Violet." The smile faded. "When do you want to do it?"

"As soon as possible. I'll make the arrangements, if you're willing. There will be papers to sign. It may make news as well."

"I can manage. So can Violet," Mrs. Hardy assured him, smiling up at her daughter.

"I can," Violet assured him. "We'll both do whatever's necessary. Whatever Daddy did, she had no right to kill him."

"Very well." Kemp got up from the sofa and shook hands with Mrs. Hardy one last time. "I'll be in touch as soon as I've got things underway. You're taking this very well."

"Surprised you, did I?" The elderly woman chuckled.

He nodded. "Pleasantly, at that," he said, adding a smile. "I'll see you." He glanced at Violet. "Walk me to the door."

She got up and followed him out into the hall, her eyes wide and curious on his face.

He paused with his hand on the doorknob and looked down at her for a long moment with narrow, intent eyes.

"I'll let you know the details as soon as I work them out with the proper authorities," he told her. "You think she'll handle it all right?" he added, alluding to her mother.

"She will," Violet replied with certainty. She looked up at him with soft, hungry eyes. "How is everything at work?"

He grimaced. "I have to make the coffee myself," he muttered. "Mabel and Libby don't make it strong enough. And Mabel is ready to tear her hair out over the extra work. So I guess we'll be advertising for a new secretary."

Violet didn't notice that he had a hopeful, anticipatory look on his face, because her eyes were downcast. She thought he was criticizing her for leaving him in the lurch, and after he'd all but forced her out of his office.

She squared her shoulders. "I'm sure you'll find someone to suit you, Mr. Kemp," she said in a subdued tone.

The formality and her lack of interest irritated him. He opened the door with a jerk. "I'll be in touch," he said, and left without even looking back.

Violet closed the door behind him, forcing herself not to look hungrily at his departing back as he left. She'd hoped just for a few seconds that he might be offering her back her old job. That was obviously not the case.

KEMP CLIMBED INTO his car, irritable and unsettled by
Violet's lack of response when he'd practically laid her
old job at her feet. Duke Wright wasn't bad-looking, and
he had an eye for a pretty woman. He was all but divorced now, too. Violet was attractive. He hoped Wright
wasn't trying to turn her head. He was going to check
into that. For Violet's own good, of course. He wasn't
interested in her himself.

Involuntarily, his mind went back eight years, to
the only woman he'd really ever loved. Shannon Culbertson had been eighteen the year they started dating. It had been love at first sight for both of them.
Kemp, who was already a junior partner in a local law
firm, having graduated from college late at the age of
twenty-eight, was in practice with Shannon's uncle.
They met at the office and started dating. Within a
month, they knew they were going to be married one
day. Shannon had gone to a party with a girlfriend, at
Julie Merrill's house. Nobody understood why Julie
wanted her worst enemy at the bash, least of all Shannon—but she thought maybe Julie was willing to bury
the hatchet over the rivalry of the two girls for senior
president. Someone, probably Julie herself, had put a
forerunner of the date rape drug into Shannon's soft
drink. She had an undiagnosed heart condition, and
the drug had killed her.

It still hurt Kemp to remember the aftermath. He'd
mourned her for months, blamed Julie, tried to have
her arrested for the crime. But her father was a state
senator and wealthy. The case never got to trial, despite
Kemp's best efforts.

He still resented the Merrills. He missed Shannon.

But since Violet had come to work for him, he'd thought less and less about his old love. In the mornings, he'd looked forward to Violet's smiling, happy face in his office. He was afraid of the feeling he got when she nurtured him. He didn't ever want to risk loving someone again. Tragedy had hallmarked his life. He'd had a sister, Dolores, who'd died in a swimming accident his senior year of high school. His mother had died of cancer soon afterward. There had only been the two of them, because his father had gone overseas to work for an oil company in the Middle East when he was only a child, fallen in love with a French woman, and divorced his mother. He had no contact with his father. He had no interest in him.

The experiences of his life had taught him that love was dangerous, and so was getting too used to people. Violet was still infatuated with him, but she'd get over it, he told himself firmly. Better to let her go. She was young and impressionable. She'd find someone else. Perhaps Duke Wright…

His teeth clenched hard on the thought. It was strangely uncomfortable to think of Violet in some other man's arms. Very uncomfortable.

VIOLET LOOKED UP from her typing one morning at the sound of approaching voices, and was surprised to find Curt Collins, Libby Collins's brother, standing at her desk.

"Curt's just joined the operation, Violet," Duke Wright told her with a grin. "We've stolen him from Jordan Powell."

"It wasn't much of a steal," Curt drawled with a grim smile. "I quit my job. Jordan's changed lately."

"Curt's going to help with the cattle operation," Duke told Violet. "If he needs any information, you can give it directly to him without having to ask me first," he added with a smile.

"Okay," she agreed.

"Come on, Curt, I'll show you around the rest of the operation," the older cattleman beckoned.

"See you later, Violet," Curt murmured.

She nodded, smiling. She watched them leave, frowning. Libby was crazy about Jordan Powell, and Curt had worked for him for years. What in the world was going on?

CURT CAME BY just as she was getting her things together. "I suppose you're wondering how I landed here," he said.

She nodded. "It's a bit of a surprise," she replied.

"Have you talked to Kemp lately?"

Her heart jumped just at the sound of his name, but she recovered quickly. "No. I haven't spoken to him for a week or two, I guess."

"There's been some unpleasantness, shall we say, between Libby and Julie Merrill."

Violet looked blank. "I wasn't aware that they even knew each other," she replied.

"They're not even acquaintances," Curt agreed. "But Julie wants Jordan, and Libby was getting in the way."

"I see."

"Anyway, Julie attacked Libby and Jordan didn't stand up for her. Jordan made some nasty remarks to

Libby." He shrugged. "I'm not working for any man who bad-mouths my sister."

"I don't blame you one bit. Poor Libby!"

"She can take care of herself on good days," he said. "But Julie has some unsavory friends. Sadly for her, she walked into Kemp's office while Libby was there."

"Excuse me?"

He smiled. "You don't know, do you? There's bad blood between Kemp and Julie. She had a party at her house eight years ago and invited Shannon Culbertson, who was all but engaged to Kemp at the time. There was a rivalry between Shannon and Julie for a class office at school. Somebody put something in Shannon's drink. She died. Julie got the office."

"She was poisoned?" Violet exclaimed, fascinated by this private look at her taciturn boss's life. So he had a woman in his past after all. Was that why he didn't have much to do with women now? It made her sad to think there was another woman in his life, even a ghost. How could a living woman compete with a perfect memory?

"She wasn't poisoned. She had a hidden heart condition," he corrected. "Anyway, she died. Kemp never got over it. He did his best to have Julie tried for it, but her father had plenty of money and plenty of influence. It was listed as a tragic accident with no explanation, and the case was closed. Kemp would hang Julie if he could ever find an excuse to get her in court." He leaned forward. "Just between you and me, that might happen. Senator Merrill got busted for drunk driving. Now he and his nephew the mayor are trying to get the arresting officers fired—and Chief Cash Grier, too."

Violet's mind had to jump-shift back to the subject

at hand. She was still taking in Kemp's secret past, one that she hadn't even expected. "That'll be the day, when Chief Grier will let his officers go down the drain without a fight."

"Exactly what most of us think," Curt said. "Grier is hell on drug traffickers. Which brings to mind one other rumor that's going around—that Julie has her finger in a nasty white powder distribution network."

Violet whistled. "Some news!"

"Keep it to yourself, too," he admonished. "But the point of the thing is, I was without a job and Duke said I could work for him."

"Welcome aboard, as one refugee to another."

"That's right, you and Kemp had a mixer, too, didn't you?" He smiled wryly. "Libby told me," he added when she looked surprised. "But I heard it from three other people as well. You don't keep secrets in a town like Jacobsville. We're all one big family. We know all about each other."

She smiled. "I suppose we do."

"How's your mother taking the exhumation?"

The smile faded. "She says it's not bothering her, but I know it is. She's very old-fashioned about things like that."

He looked angry. "We feel the same way. But we had to let them exhume Dad, too. Nobody wants Janet to walk away from another murder."

"That's how Mama and I feel," Violet agreed. "But it really is hard. Have you heard anything yet?"

He shook his head. "They say the results will take time. The state crime lab is backed up, so it won't be a quick process. That will make it worse, I guess."

She nodded. "But we'll get through it, won't we?" she added.

He smiled at her determination. "You bet we will."

BLAKE KEMP WAS FUMING. He'd been so busy with work that he'd forgotten the exhumations until Libby had actually asked him about them. He'd promised her that he'd get right on it. But the disturbing news had nothing to do with possible murders. It had to do with the fact that Curt Collins, Libby's brother, was taking Violet to Calhoun Ballenger's volunteer staff meeting at his ranch on the following Saturday.

He'd been worried about Violet letting Duke Wright turn her head, and here she was going on a date with a very eligible, upstanding member of a founding family of Jacobs-ville, Texas. Even Kemp couldn't claim descent from old John Jacobs himself. Duke might have a lot of warts, but Curt was a fine young man with a promising future. And Violet was going to date him.

He didn't understand his own violent opposition to that pairing. Violet was nothing to him, after all. She was just his ex-secretary. He had no right to care if she had a private life.

But he did care. The thought of her with Curt made him uneasy. He knew Calhoun Ballenger from years past. He frequently handled cases for him. He admired and respected the local feedlot owner. There was no reason he couldn't get himself invited to that meeting. He just wanted to make sure Violet didn't do something stupid, like falling into Curt's arms at the first opportunity. It was his duty to protect her. Sort of. He picked up the phone and dialed Calhoun's number, refusing to consider his motives in any personal way.

THE MEETING WAS RIOTOUS. There were people gathered around the big recreation room that Kemp hadn't seen face-to-face in years. Some were frankly a surprise, because at least two of the county's biggest Republican contributors were in the front row.

"Interesting, isn't it?" Police Chief Cash Grier asked him with a grin, noting the direction Kemp was staring. "Ballenger's crossing party lines all over the place. He's well-known in cattlemen's circles, and locally he's the original hometown boy who came out of poverty to become a millionaire. He did it without any under-the-table dealings as well, I hear."

"That's right," Kemp told him. "Calhoun and his brother, Justin, were the poorest kids around. They made their fortunes honestly. They both married well, too."

"Calhoun's wife was his ward, they say," Grier mused.

"Yes, and Justin married a direct descendant of Big John Jacobs, the founder of Jacobsville. Between them, they've got six boys. Not a girl in either family."

At the mention of children, Grier became quiet. He and his houseguest, Tippy Moore, a rising movie star, had lost their baby just before Tippy's little brother was kidnapped and held for ransom. Tippy had traded herself for him, an act of courage that still made Grier proud. Their relationship was rocky even now, and Tippy was a potential victim of one of the kidnappers who'd eluded police in Manhattan.

Kemp glanced at him, aware of the older man's discomfort. "Sorry," he murmured. He knew about the baby because the story, a false and very unflattering one, had played out in the tabloids when Tippy had miscarried.

Grier let out a long breath. "I never knew I wanted kids," he said quietly, not meeting Kemp's gaze. "Hell of a way to find out I did."

"Life evens out," Kemp said philosophically. "You have bad days, then you have good ones to make up for them."

Grier's dark eyes twinkled. "I'm due about two years of good days."

Kemp laughed without humor. "Aren't we all?"

Grier's attention was captured by someone behind Kemp. He pursed his lips. "Your ex-secretary sure has changed."

Kemp was aware of his heart jumping at the statement. He turned his head and there was Violet. But she looked very different. She was wearing a neat little black skirt with a dropped-waist blue top that was cut modestly low in front. Her hair was around her shoulders, but it had frosted tips. She looked ten pounds lighter, and very pretty.

She noticed Kemp and her heart raced. Beside her Curt was watching the byplay with amusement, because Kemp couldn't seem to help staring any more than Violet could.

"I need to talk to someone," he told Violet. "Can you manage without me for a few minutes?"

"Yes!" She curbed her enthusiasm. "I mean, yes, that would be all right, Curt. Thanks."

He chuckled, winked at her, and strolled off.

Kemp walked up to her. He was dressed in an open-necked shirt with a sports coat and navy slacks. He looked expensive, sophisticated, and good enough to eat. Violet could hardly keep her eyes off him.

He was having a similar problem. It was odd how much Violet had been on his mind lately. He saw her in the office even when she wasn't there. He'd been uneasy since he'd seen her at her mother's house, and they'd parted on a harsh note.

"Still like working for Duke?" he queried stiffly.

She shrugged. "It's a job."

His eyebrow jerked. "Your hair looks nice," he murmured, reaching out to take a strand of it in his strong fingers. "I don't like frosting as a rule, but it suits you. You've lost more weight, too, haven't you?"

"It may look like it, but I haven't really," she replied, lost in a haze because of contact with him. "I've just been learning how to dress to make the most of what I have."

His eyes slid up to meet hers. "That's what life is all about, Violet," he said gently. "Learning how to make do with what we're given. You don't need to lose any more weight. You look great."

She flushed and smiled radiantly. "Do you…really think so?"

He moved a step closer, aware of pleasure centers opening all over his mind as he looked down at her. "Do you like trout?"

It was an odd question. She blinked. "Trout? Well, yes."

"Why don't you come over for lunch tomorrow? I'll

fry trout and make a pasta salad to go with them. You can take some home to your mother."

Violet's jaw dropped. She stood gaping at him while she tried to decide, quickly, if she'd lost her mind and was having hallucinations.

## CHAPTER FOUR

HER LACK OF response made Kemp uneasy and provoked a sarcastic response. He'd thought she'd jump at the chance. "What's the matter?" Kemp taunted. "Afraid to be alone with me outside the office?"

Violet gaped at him. "I am not…no… I don't think… I didn't say…" She cleared her throat. "I love trout. So does Mama."

His eyes twinkled. So he hadn't been wrong. She did still care about him. "So do I," he replied. "I pan-fry it in butter and spices. I have my own herb garden, even in the winter."

"It sounds delicious," she said breathlessly.

He still had the strand of her hair in his fingers. They became caressing, and his deep voice dropped even lower. "Do you like cats?"

She nodded.

"You may have a little trouble with Mee and Yow at first, but they'll get used to you."

Violet felt as if she'd stepped off a precipice and solved the mystery of free flight. She was ecstatic. "I think cats are beautiful."

"Mine are Siamese. They're unique."

She smiled slowly. "I'll enjoy meeting them."

He let go of her hair and touched her soft cheek

with his fingertips. They seemed to tingle at the contact. "About one in the afternoon tomorrow suit you?"

She nodded, speechless.

"Know how to get to my house?"

"Oh, yes," she said, and could have bitten her tongue for sounding so enthusiastic.

Kemp was eating it up. He knew it was a bad idea, encouraging her. At some point he was going to have to back away from her. He didn't want commitment. Not yet. But Violet was soft to the touch and lovely to look at. He'd been without a woman in his life for a long time. He was lonely. Surely it wouldn't hurt to have the occasional meal with her. Of course it wouldn't. He was enjoying her rapt expression. She made him feel as if he could conquer the world. For once in his life he was going to jump in with both feet without counting the cost.

"Then I'll expect you," he added.

She smiled up at him, her blue eyes wide and soft and hungry. "I'll look forward to it," she said huskily.

"So will I," he replied, and the smile faded for an instant as he searched her eyes for so long that she flushed and her breath rustled wildly in her throat.

"Kemp! Glad you could make it!" Tall, handsome Calhoun Ballenger moved forward to shake Kemp's hand and greet Violet. "Kemp, there's someone I'd like to introduce you to. Violet, you don't mind?"

"No, not at all," she lied.

"Tomorrow, at one," Kemp added before he walked away with Calhoun.

"Tomorrow," she replied.

CURT HAD TO ask her twice if she was ready to leave. She hadn't had the opportunity to talk to Kemp any further, and he'd been called away suddenly to meet with a man who'd just been arrested. Before he left, he'd looked back at Violet with pale blue eyes that absolutely smoldered. She was still tingling an hour after he'd gone.

"What?" she asked abruptly, facing Curt. She flushed when he grinned. "Sorry," she began.

"Oh, I'm not upset," he replied, chuckling. "I'm glad to see that your ex-boss finally realized what he was missing."

She flushed even more. "It's not like that."

"I'm a man, Violet," he reminded her as they walked out to his car after making their goodbyes to their host. "I know a smitten man when I see one. Kemp's got it bad."

"Do you really think so?" she asked hopefully.

"I think so. Just go slowly," he advised. "He's pretty much a loner and he doesn't play around."

"I knew that already."

He turned toward her, serious for once. "What I meant," he said softly, "is that he's more vulnerable than a man who plays the field. And everybody knows he's not a marrying man, at least not visibly. You just step carefully, okay?"

"I will. Thanks for the advice, Curt."

He shrugged. "Story of my life. I'm always someone's big brother."

She grinned. "One day some lucky girl will carry you off," she promised.

He smiled back. "I hope it's a few years coming. I'm

no more ready to settle down than your friend Kemp is. At least he's got a profession. I'm still drifting."

"Libby said you wanted to open a feed store."

He nodded. "It's the dream of my life."

"I hope you get to do it, Curt. I mean that."

He opened the door for her. "So do I. You're a nice girl, Violet."

"You're a nice man."

He chuckled. "Well, I'm accommodating, at least. Calhoun had quite a crowd today," he added when he'd climbed in under the wheel of his and Libby's old pickup truck.

"A big one. And some big money, too. I think he just may beat Senator Merrill for the Democratic nomination."

"I wouldn't be a bit surprised myself."

Violet told her mother about Kemp's invitation, and Mrs. Hardy grinned from ear to ear. "And how long have I been telling you that Mr. Kemp had more interest in you than a boss in his secretary?" she asked.

"It's only to eat a trout," Violet replied.

"He can eat trout by himself," her mother said sagely. "It's also interesting that Mr. Kemp, who never advertises his political affiliations, suddenly turned up at a campaign meeting."

"He likes Mr. Ballenger."

Mrs. Hardy pursed her lips. "I think somebody told him you were going to the meeting with Curt Collins."

She gasped. "Really?"

"Sometimes a man doesn't appreciate what he's got until some other man wants it. Or he thinks another man wants it." Mrs. Hardy's eyes twinkled. "We'll see, won't we, dear?"

Violet colored prettily and suggested a television program.

SHE DIDN'T SLEEP. All night long, she saw Blake Kemp's eyes drilling into her own, she heard his voice, felt the touch of his fingers on her face. She tried on everything in her closet the next morning before she finally decided on a nice ankle-length sky-blue knit jumper with a white blouse under it and her embroidered denim jacket over it. She left her hair long.

"You look fine," Mrs. Hardy said from her bed when Violet went in to say goodbye.

"Are you sure you feel all right?" Violet worried.

"I'm just going to have a lazy Sunday," the older woman replied, smiling. "I wouldn't lie to you."

"All right. But if you need me…"

"The phone's right here, darling." Mrs. Hardy indicated it on the bedside table. "Now go and have a good time. I won't expect my trout anytime soon, by the way, and I've already had my breakfast."

"I'll bring you back something nice," Violet promised.

"Drive carefully."

Violet kissed her. "Always!"

She stopped on the front porch and looked down at her black loafers, worn with knee-high hose. She grimaced, because one of them was scuffed. But, she reasoned, Kemp was going to be more interested in the rest of her than in her shoes. She straightened her purse's shoulder strap over her shoulder and walked resolutely to her old but reliable car.

KEMP WAS ON the front porch of his house when she drove up. It was a Victorian, with gingerbread patterned woodwork and a real turret room. The whole thing was painted white, brilliant and new-looking, and there was a porch swing and rocking chairs on the long, wide front porch. There were bird feeders everywhere. In the flower gardens flanking the porch, seeds were sprouting and rosebushes were putting out buds.

Violet took her purse and locked the car involuntarily before she pocketed her car key and walked up the steps.

"You like birds!" she exclaimed.

He laughed. He was dressed casually, as she was, in khaki slacks and a blue knit designer shirt darker than the shade of his eyes behind the metal rims of his glasses.

"Yes, I like birds. But so do Mee and Yow, so I have to make sure they're both inside before I fill the feeders," he said on a chuckle.

"I have bird feeders at our place, too," Violet replied shyly. "I especially like the little birds, like the wrens and titmice."

"I prefer cardinals and blue jays."

"They're still birds," Violet said on a laugh.

He felt as if his feet were off the floor as he looked at her. Smiles transformed her oval face, made it bright and radiant—almost beautiful.

"Do you hire a gardener, or do you work in the yard

yourself?" she asked, enthusiastic about the mass of flowering shrubs around the front yard.

"I do it," he replied. "I need to unwind from time to time."

"Yes, gardening is good for stress," she admitted. "I go through a lot of it myself. But I plant vegetables in our little garden, and I can or freeze them for the winter." She stopped suddenly, embarrassed, because the garden was a necessity for Violet and her mother, who had to budget furiously just to make ends meet. She doubted seriously if Kemp had ever budgeted in his life.

"I don't grow vegetables," he confessed. "Unless you count catnip, for the cats, and some herbs. I enjoy cooking."

"Me, too," she said. "Mama can do it, but I don't like to let her. She favors cast iron cookware, and it's heavy."

"She shouldn't be lifting it," he agreed. "I hope you're hungry."

She smiled. "I didn't even eat breakfast."

He smiled back. "Come in, then. It's all ready."

He opened the front door and let her walk in. There was a long hall with an elephant umbrella stand and a coatrack, with rooms opening off it on either side.

"Down the hall, to the left," he directed as he closed the front door.

The hall was painted a pale blue, with a chair rail in a darker shade, and wallpaper up to the crown. There was a pale blue carpet as well.

"You're probably thinking that it's hard to keep clean," Kemp remarked as he followed behind her. "And you're right. I have a cleaning crew come in to steam it frequently."

"I love the color," she remarked. "It reminds me of the ocean."

He laughed out loud. "It's the color of Yow's eyes," he added. "And she knows it. She loves to sprawl on the carpet. Mee prefers the couch or my bed."

Violet caught her breath as she walked into the formal dining room. There was a cherry wood table, already set with linen and crystal and china, and beyond it was a kitchen that would have been any cook's dream. There was a tile floor, modern appliances, a huge combination sink, and a counter big enough to use for dressing half a steer. Over the sink was a large window overlooking the pasture and forest behind the house.

"I'll bet you enjoy working in here," she remarked.

"I do. I like enough space to move in. Cramped kitchens are the very devil."

"Indeed they are, and I could write you a book on them," Violet confessed. "I bump into the refrigerator or the stove every time I turn around at home."

"What would you like to drink?" he asked, opening the refrigerator. "I've got soft drinks, iced tea, or coffee."

"I love coffee, if it isn't too much trouble."

He grinned at her. "I always have a pot warming," he said.

He got down two china cups and saucers and poured coffee into them. "Cream and sugar on the table."

He carried them to the places, which were already set, amid platters of fish, vegetables, fresh rolls and even a cake.

"This looks wonderful!" she exclaimed.

"I counted on your being punctual," he said with a glance. "You always are."

He seated her, and then himself.

"I like to make a good impression," she told him.

He chuckled. "Help yourself."

She looked around curiously as she helped herself to trout and rolls and a potato casserole that smelled delicious. "Where are the cats?"

"They're shy around people they don't know," he said nonchalantly. "They'll show up when I cut the cake. They beg for cake."

"You're kidding!" she exclaimed.

He laughed. "I'm not. You'll see."

They spoke about the upcoming election and the local political gossip during the meal. Violet was impressed with his culinary skills. He was an accomplished cook.

"Have you always been able to knock out a meal?" she wondered aloud.

"I was in the Army—special forces," he replied simply. "I had to learn how to cook."

"You were in Cag Hart's division, weren't you?"

He nodded. "So was Matt Caldwell. A lot of local guys turned up there."

She didn't know how far to push her luck. Someone had told her that he didn't like to talk about his unit's participation in the earlier Iraq conflict. But he got up to slice cake and two Siamese voices grew louder.

"See?" he asked, when the cats appeared on either side of him, their faces lifted as they meowed, sounding for all the world like little children.

"They have unique voices, don't they?" she asked, fascinated.

"They do. And Siamese have one other peculiarity—they can reach completely behind their heads. They have claws and they aren't shy about using them," he added with a warning glance. "Go slowly, and everything will be all right."

"Do you give them cake?" she asked.

He laughed. "Tiny little bites," he said, confessing. "I don't want to make them fat…"

Violet flushed red.

He ground his teeth and looked at her soulfully. "I didn't mean that the way you're taking it, Violet," he said gently. "I don't think you're fat. You look exactly as a woman should look, in every way."

"You said…" she began.

"I took a bad day out on you," he replied, "and I'm sorrier than you know. It was a vicious thing to do. I made you quit, and I never meant to."

For an apology, it was wholesale and flattering. She looked at him without blinking. "Really?"

He relaxed when he saw the combined pleasure and fascination in her face. She made him tingle just by looking at him. He wanted to drag her out of her chair and kiss the breath from her body. The thought shocked him. He stood with the knife poised over the cake, just staring at her.

The flush grew. She felt her heart racing like mad in her chest. Her lips parted as she tried to breathe normally.

"A lot of it was the way you dressed," he said tautly when he managed to drag his eyes back to the cake. "I like the new wardrobe. It fits properly. Baggy dresses and blouses aren't flattering for a full-figured woman."

She didn't take offense. He was looking at her as if he wanted, very badly, to kiss her. As he slid a piece of cake onto a saucer and put it in front of her, she looked up into his pale eyes with pure lust.

It had been a long time between women, but Kemp hadn't forgotten the way a woman looked when she wanted to be kissed. Absently, his lean hand went to the back of Violet's chair and he bent toward her confidently.

Her intake of breath made him hesitate, but only for a second. His other hand came up to her softly rounded chin and he tilted it up, just a fraction. "Don't make such heavy weather of it," he whispered as his mouth hovered over hers. "I want to kiss you as you much as you want me to."

"Re...really?" she choked.

He smiled gently. "Really."

His lips teased over her full mouth, nibbling her upper lip while he tasted it with a lazy stroke of his tongue. Violet jumped and shivered. The contact was completely out of her experience. She'd dated a few boys, but she didn't seem to appeal to any of them physically. This was different. She wished she knew what to do, so that he wouldn't stop.

He lifted his head and looked into her rapt, expectant eyes. She was breathing like a distance runner. Her breasts were shaking under the whip of her pulse. He'd thought she was at least a little experienced, but it seemed he was wrong.

His thumb moved to her lower lip and tugged it down gently as his head bent again.

"We have to start somewhere," he breathed as his mouth opened against her full, soft lips.

Violet shivered. Her hands went to his arms, her fingers digging in. He was muscular. He didn't look muscular in his suits, but she could feel the strength at this range. She moaned, a whisper of sound that drew his head up.

His eyes met hers, and there was no teasing in them now. They were intent, darker, hungry.

Her fingers lifted to his cheek, hesitantly. "Don't… stop," she pleaded in a soft, shaky whisper.

A muscle in his jaw tensed. He bent again, his own heart racing. "Violet," he whispered.

This time the kiss wasn't teasing, tender, or brief. He ground his mouth into her soft lips. She moaned again, and this time her hands met behind his neck and dug in. His mouth grew demanding.

There was another moan, but this one wasn't passionate.

His head jerked back. Violet reached down and grabbed her ankle just as Yow drew back, hissing.

"Yow!" Kemp exclaimed, moving around the chair to shoo the cat away while he knelt and examined Violet's ankle. It was bleeding. "I'm sorry! I wouldn't have had this happen for the world!"

"I must have stepped on her tail, poor thing," Violet faltered. It was exciting to kiss Blake Kemp. It was equally exciting to have him at her feet, concerned for her.

"You were kissing me," he corrected. "They're jealous of any attention I pay to other people."

"This has…happened before?" she asked miserably.

"Yes. Well, no, not like this," he said. "Mee sank her teeth into Cy Parks one day when he was having coffee with me in the kitchen."

"I see," she began.

He gave her a wicked grin. "I wasn't kissing him."

She burst out laughing.

He stood up, pulling back her chair. He tugged her to her feet and suddenly swung her up into his arms. She gasped and clutched at his shoulders.

He raised an eyebrow rakishly. "Now it's my ankles that will be in danger. I have to clean that and put antiseptic ointment on it," he mused as he turned and carried her down the hall toward the bedrooms.

"I'm too heavy!" she protested.

"You're not," he assured her. He looked down at her in his arms. He felt several inches taller. She was delightful close up. He enjoyed kissing her. He'd liked to have done it again, but this wasn't the time.

He put her down on the vanity in the huge, blue-patterned tile bathroom. There was a whirlpool bath and an enormous space that held commode, vanity, chair, and a linen closet, as well as a large medicine chest.

He fumbled in the chest for what he needed, tugged a washcloth out of a drawer and proceeded to clean and bandage the wound.

Yow peered into the bathroom, her blue eyes huge in her triangle-shaped face.

"No tuna for you tonight, young lady," Blake told her firmly.

She flattened her ears and hissed at Violet.

"And none tomorrow, either," he added curtly.

Yow turned her back and flounced out. Mee, in a conciliatory tone, meowed at the door and walked in, watching the byplay curiously but without much antagonism.

"Beautiful girl," Violet mused, lowering her fingers for the cat to sniff.

Mee sniffed them, rubbed her face against them, and then wrapped her lean body around Violet's legs.

"You can have tuna," Blake told the cat.

The purring grew louder.

Violet stroked the cat, but her eyes and her heart were on Blake's bent head as he put a sticky bandage over the scratch.

"It should be fine," he said.

"Of course it will be," she assured him, smiling down as he finished. "Thanks."

"I'm really sorry," he said again as he gathered up the first aid supplies and put them away. "Yow's spoiled."

"I love cats," Violet said, still stroking Mee. "I'd have loved to have some, if Mama wasn't allergic."

"I don't know what I'd do without mine. Although there are times when I'm tempted to try," he added, with a glowering look toward the door where Yow had reappeared and was hissing again.

"You live alone," she said. "It's natural that they'd resent strangers."

He bent down and drew her gently to her feet. "You're no stranger," he said huskily as his eyes searched hers. "I don't think you ever were."

She felt such elation that she could hardly get her

breath. Just weeks ago they'd been mortal enemies. Then, suddenly, they were almost intimate. It was a shock. It was...wonderful.

"Your eyes can't hide anything," he murmured, bending toward her.

She glanced worriedly at her ankles, and he laughed.

He picked her up again, shifting her in his arms. "Feel safer?" he murmured, staring at her mouth.

"Much," she agreed, and her arms tightened boldly around his neck.

With a long sigh, he bent his head and kissed her, very tenderly. His teeth nibbled at her lower lip until her mouth opened. He took immediate advantage of the opportunity, and she felt her whole body go hot as he dragged her closer, so that her full breasts rubbed against his muscular chest.

He groaned, and the kiss grew hotter, longer, more passionate. His arms contracted hungrily.

She gave him back the kiss with more enthusiasm than expertise, but he didn't seem to mind. She sighed under the hard crush of his mouth and sank into dreams. It was sweeter than she'd ever dared hope it might be.

She felt as if her whole body was shattering with pleasure.

Blake's head lifted. He turned it, listening. That hadn't been her imagination. Something really had shattered. "Yow!" he growled.

He put Violet down and rushed back down the hall ahead of her. He made it into the dining room just in time to see Yow feasting on Violet's piece of cake, on the floor, in the ruins of the saucer it had been placed in.

"Yow!" he bit off.

The cat jumped back and hissed at Violet. For good measure she hissed at Blake, too, and ran quickly out of the room.

Mee, seeing an opening, rubbed against Blake's legs while she eyed the cake on the floor.

Blake picked up the saucer pieces. While he was putting them into the trash, Mee grabbed up a piece of cake and trotted into the kitchen with it.

"That cat," he was muttering.

Violet was chuckling, happier than she'd been in years, despite the cat's antagonism. It was a rare look at Blake's private life, at the man he was when he wasn't working. She liked what she saw. His affection for the cats was obvious, even through his frustration with Yow.

"They're very different, aren't they?" she asked while he took the lion's share of the cake away from a frustrated Mee and put it in the trash, too.

"They're maddening from time to time," he admitted. "But I suppose they'd taste terrible, even if I do have infrequent visions of serving them up in a casserole."

"You wouldn't dare!" she exclaimed, laughing.

He shrugged. "Well, not sober," he confessed.

She grinned at him, her whole face radiant with the sudden, new relationship that was building between them.

She looked so pretty that Blake stopped what he was

doing and just stared at her. Why hadn't he realized how pretty she was? he wondered.

Violet saw the look and was mesmerized by it. She stood staring back at him, while time stood still around them.

# CHAPTER FIVE

VIOLET FOLDED HER hands in front of her, self-consciously. "I really like your house," she said, for something to break the silence.

He smiled. "I'm glad."

"I like the cats, too. In spite of everything," she added. "It's only a scratch."

He glowered toward the doorway, where Yow was looking in again. Mee was still twirling around Violet's ankles. "We'll have to work on Yow's social skills. Maybe she lacks proper company. I might buy her a dog."

"You wouldn't!" Violet exclaimed, laughing.

He gave her a wicked look. "A big, ugly dog with a bad attitude," he added.

"You'd turn up in court as a defendant."

"Not unless Yow can afford legal representation," he assured her.

She laughed. It was amazing how carefree she felt with him, a man who'd intimidated her from their very first meeting when she'd worked for him. He was another man entirely away from the office.

"Well, there's still cake," he pointed out. "We'd better get it while we can, before Yow tries again."

"What kind is it?" she asked as she seated herself at the table again.

"Pound cake. It's the only cake I can do myself."

"My favorite kind, too. I can make a layer cake, but I like these better."

He put a slice on a plate, and a fork, in front of her. "More coffee?"

"Please," she replied.

He poured more coffee and they settled down with their cake, but she noticed that Blake kept a careful eye on the doorway in case Yow made another appearance.

HE WOULDN'T LET her help with the dishes, insisting that he could do them later. Instead, he walked her out onto the porch and settled her beside him in the porch swing.

"I love this," she said. "We used to have a porch swing, before we lost everything," she mused. "I loved sitting in it, especially in the spring and summer. We had a big yard with pecan trees and a mesquite tree, and Mama had a flower garden, very much like yours."

He slid his arm behind her head and curled his long fingers comfortably into her hair. "It must be hard for both of you."

"We're getting by," she said softly. "I don't really mind. I'm just sorry about Daddy, and how he died." She looked up at him. "You haven't heard anything about the autopsy yet?"

"Maybe next week," he replied. "I'll tell you the minute I know for sure. Then we'll both break it to your mother."

"That's very kind of you," she said.

He bent and touched his lips to her forehead. "I'm

a kind man," he murmured, laughing softly. "I don't even kick cats when they deserve it."

She smiled back, leaning closer. She loved being near him, feeling his breath on her face, his fingers in her hair.

Blake was amazed at how receptive she was to his advances, how hungrily she met them. He hadn't analyzed his feelings for Violet. He wasn't going to. Not yet. But she kindled fires in his blood that he hadn't felt since Shannon Culbertson's death.

Shannon. His eyes grew dark and quiet as he stared over Violet's head and memories flooded in on him. He'd loved her. He'd given his heart completely, recklessly, without any thought for the future. Shannon had died, and his life had shattered overnight. He remembered that headlong passion with faint apprehension. It was dangerous to love. Very dangerous.

Violet didn't know what he was thinking, but she felt a sudden remoteness from him. She noticed that he was staring into space, thinking. Perhaps he was having second thoughts about the direction their relationship was taking. Was he sorry that he'd kissed her?

He felt her intent stare. He turned his head and looked down into her eyes, searching them slowly. The look was more intimate than a kiss. His body began to swell from the intensity of it.

"Is something wrong?" she asked after a minute.

His fingers touched her chin, drawing it up. "I have cold feet."

"I don't understand."

He drew in a long breath. "It's too quick, Violet,"

he murmured, looking at her. "I'm not sure I'm ready for this."

"For feeding me trout?" she asked, wide-eyed.

He shook his head. "No. For…this."

He bent and kissed her, very gently. He lifted his head. "I like kissing you."

She smiled slowly. "I like kissing you, too."

"To what end?"

She blinked. "Excuse me?"

"I don't want to get married," he said bluntly.

She felt all at sea, confused and uncertain.

He stared down into her wide eyes. She looked miserable and he felt confused. "Forget it," he murmured, dropping his stare to her soft eyes. "I'm just talking. I don't even know what I'm talking about."

"I know about her," she blurted out.

He scowled. "Her?"

"Shannon Culbertson," she said, averting her gaze to the budding rosebushes. "I'm sorry it happened like that. It must have been devastating for you."

He couldn't think of another single person he wouldn't have cursed for mentioning her name. But it didn't feel at all uncomfortable to discuss Shannon with Violet. She had a tender heart. He ached for comfort. He'd never had it.

"She was beautiful," he replied. "Young and full of fun and promise. I loved her until she was an obsession. I didn't think I could go on living when she died."

"But you did," she replied. "You're stronger than you realize."

"You have an odd effect on me," he murmured.

"What sort?" she asked, studying him.

One shoulder lifted and fell. His eyes went back to the landscape as he rocked the swing lazily into motion. "I don't talk about her. I haven't in years."

She sighed and rested her head on his shoulder, staring across his broad chest toward the distant highway. "You can't bury the past," she said absently. "It affects everything we do, everything we are."

He frowned. "Did you lose someone?"

She laughed. "Me? When I was in high school, I weighed even more than I do now. My parents sent me to a private school because they thought I might not get picked on as much. But I did. There are always the beautiful people who feel privileged to comment on the less fortunate. I hated school."

"I thought schools were cracking down on bullies."

"If they crack down very hard, they tend to get sued," she pointed out, with a speaking look in his direction.

He chuckled. "I don't take frivolous lawsuits," he reminded her.

"Plenty of other lawyers do. Then they get huge awards, which they keep the lion's share of. Then insurance, and everything else goes sky high."

He scowled. "Well, you have got a point."

"I make up in intelligence for what I lack in looks," she murmured.

He tilted her face up to his and searched her blue, blue eyes. "Violet," he said softly, "there's nothing wrong with the way you look. I had a bad morning and I took it out on you that day. I've been trying to find a way to apologize every since. You look like a woman should."

She studied him with big, curious eyes. He was very handsome. She was fascinated by the way he was looking at her, as if he really did find her enchanting. She smiled slowly.

"Ahh," he cautioned in a husky tone. "Looking at me like that will get you into trouble."

"It will?" she asked hopefully.

The humor went right by him. His eyes had dropped to her full, soft mouth and he was feeling a surge of hunger. Some tiny voice was urging caution. He ignored it and pulled Violet closer. His hard mouth curved down against her soft one, teasing lightly until she relaxed and leaned against his chest. His long fingers slid into her thick, soft hair, and tugged her head farther back on his broad shoulder.

His fingers were at her nape, teasing, tracing, while his mouth slowly penetrated the tight line of her lips.

She stiffened, but he persisted. When she still wouldn't give him what he wanted, his lean hand slid right over her full breast and contracted gently with the nipple trapped between his thumb and his hand. She gasped and shivered, giving him access to the dark inner softness of her mouth. She felt his tongue slide sensuously inside and a curious swelling sensation overtook her body.

His hand became insistent on her breast, searching for buttons. He made an opening and his fingers slid inside it, right onto the warm silkiness of her bare skin. She moaned huskily. Her arms reached up and enclosed his neck while she gave in to the unreality of being in his arms, being desired by him.

The kiss became passionate, demanding. She moaned

again. Vaguely, she felt him pulling her up. He bent and lifted her, his mouth still enclosing her yielded, hungry lips. He carried her into the house, kicking the door shut behind him.

He started toward the bedroom, but his body was in agony. Too many years of abstinence had left him powerless with Violet's mouth promising heaven. He made it to the living room and slid her onto the sofa, but there wasn't really room for both of them on it. She was as hungry as he was, and their restless movements landed them on the carpet between the sofa and the coffee table.

He started to lift his head, but she pulled his mouth back over hers. The sensations were like waves of pleasure that rocked her in his hard arms, and she didn't want them to stop. She didn't want him to stop. She'd never felt such physical delight in all her life, and she wasn't willing to give it up just yet.

Blake was feeling something similar. It had been a long time since he'd had such a willing, hungry partner. Even Shannon, although she loved him, had been receptive but not eager when he made love to her. Violet was different. She tasted of honey. He loved the feel of her mouth under his. He loved the feverish response of her body to his lightest touch. He loved the soft little noises she made, the tiny gasps that pulsed rhythmically out of her throat as his caresses became quickly more intimate.

She felt cool air on her breasts and opened her eyes just a breath. Her clothes were open all the way down the front, and her bra was unhooked. His eyes were a darkened, passionate blue as they caressed her bare

breasts, feeding on their ample curves and the taut
mauve rise of her nipples. He bent, his mouth opening as he eased down beside her again and took her
into his mouth.

She arched completely off the floor, sobbing. "Yes,"
she choked. "Yes!"

What little control he'd had left was gone at once.
She was as hungry as he was. He didn't think about afterward. He was too far gone to care about tomorrow.
There was only the painful need that stretched his powerful body like rope over her rippling, soft body. Years
of abstinence took control of his will.

His hands were deft and efficient. Within seconds,
the barriers were all gone, and his mouth was moving
hungrily over Violet's soft belly, down to the inside of
her thighs.

While he kissed her, he touched her, in ways and
places she'd only read about. She hadn't dreamed that
the sensations would be so overwhelming. When the
first ripples of ecstasy worked their way down her aching body, she was far beyond any sort of protest. She
loved him. He wanted her. She was becoming a woman,
truly a woman, for the first time. She wanted nothing
more than to go on being kissed and touched and caressed to madness in his arms.

Somehow, it never occurred to her that the first time
might be uncomfortable; or that he might not know it
was her first time. Most women were experienced by
the time they reached Violet's age. But Violet was a
late bloomer.

She felt the sudden penetration with a hungry delight that turned quite suddenly to discomfort, and then

pain. She stiffened and gasped, her nails digging into his back.

Shivering with desire, he managed to lift his head and look into her wide, shocked eyes.

He felt the barrier. Why hadn't he realized how difficult this might be? Because he was out of his mind with desire, that was why.

His knee pressed her legs wide apart, and his hand went quickly between them. He watched her face the whole time, watched fear and pain slowly give way to sharp pleasure.

Her nails bit into his back again, but not in pain this time. She was shuddering rhythmically with every sharp, deep downward movement of his hips. Her legs widened without any more coaxing. Her hips arched up to meet his. And still he held her eyes, watching her as he took her.

It was the most erotic experience of his entire life. Despite his experience, and he had some, it was new territory for him. He had inhibitions as surely as Violet had. Most of his encounters had been in dark rooms, at night. It was the first time he'd gone this far in broad daylight, and that was as erotic as the sight of Violet's pink nudity under him on the carpet. He began to shiver with each rough movement as he found his way ever deeper into her soft body.

"I've never done this…in broad daylight. And I've never watched, Violet," he bit off, his deep voice strained as he looked into her blue eyes.

She swallowed, hard. Her lips were parted on gasping breaths as the pleasure built and began to funnel up in her. She stared into his eyes, shivering, climbing some invisible ladder of pleasure toward what felt like an unbearable goal.

"I've…never," she choked.

His jaw clenched as the pleasure began to bite into him. "I know," he groaned harshly. His eyes closed on a wave of ecstasy that arched him above her, his hips pinning hers as he drove for fulfillment.

Violet's knees drew up on either side of him, enhancing the madness of delight. She arched again and again, her eyes wide, her mouth wide, as she looked into his eyes. They were almost black with desire.

"I feel you," she whispered brokenly. "I feel you… in me!"

The anguish tripled at the erotic little whisper. His body ground hers into the carpet with violent, urgent motions that were more desperate than experienced. Her back was going to be raw, he thought in one last burst of sanity. Then he felt her convulse under him and cry out, and contract around him. He exploded, his eyes closed, his body helplessly impaling her in one last furious downward movement that lifted him to a level of climax he'd never known.

Violet felt him, tasted him, bonded with him in that space of seconds. The pleasure slowly fell to bearable levels and she wanted to weep, because it was so exquisite, and so very brief. She looked at him while he gave in to his own need, her eyes hungry on the length of his body, rippling muscle and thick hair on his chest, down to the flat stomach that was pressed so close to hers, to the long, powerful legs lying between her white thighs.

It should have been embarrassing, to see them like

that. But she was only fascinated by the newness of intimacy.

She looked back up to see his face clenched, damp with sweat, as he slowly came back to himself. His eyes opened, dark, somber, sated.

She reached up and touched his mouth. She felt his body shivering in the aftermath, as hers was. He looked…shattered.

He collapsed on her, his forearms catching most of his formidable weight. His face pulsed at her throat, damp and sucking at breath. He shuddered. Her arms slid around him, cradling him. She felt him against every inch of her. She felt him, still inside her, still pulsing softly.

"Gosh," she whispered, awed. Her legs curved around the back of his and her body lifted in soft entreaty.

"Optimist," he murmured.

She laughed softly. She knew what he meant. Men spent themselves, and then it took a long time before they were capable again. She'd never indulged, but she'd heard other women talk.

"When I felt you stiffen, I could have shot myself," he said at her ear. "I lost it. I knew you were a virgin."

Her hands smoothed his dark, wavy hair. She looked up at the ceiling, vaguely aware of the cats moving around the room, of a breeze fluttering the curtains, of a distant car passing on the highway on the horizon. She'd never been so close to another human being. She knew, finally, what it was to be a woman. She'd never dreamed that it would be Blake who taught her how to make love.

He drew in a long breath and rolled over onto his back, bringing her over him so that he could look up into her wide blue eyes.

His hand went between them and came up with a faint trace of blood.

She blushed.

He searched her eyes for a long time. "I didn't have the presence of mind to think about protection, either."

She didn't know what to say. She was still halfway in and halfway out of a new reality.

His hands slid down her body to her wide, soft hips. "Lift up," he murmured sensuously.

She did, curious, until she saw his eyes go hungrily to her breasts. His hands slid up to them, cupping them softly. He eased her onto her back and his mouth made a meal of them, kissing and tasting until she rippled all over with renewed desire.

He groaned as his body responded with renewed arousal and sudden urgency. "Are you sore?" he asked roughly.

"I...well, I don't...ouch!" she gasped when he touched her where the tissues were torn from their first intimacy.

He ground his teeth together. "Sorry," he whispered.

She could feel how hungry he was. "You can," she whispered back. "It's okay."

He felt those words to the soles of his feet. She would have let him, despite the pain. It humbled him to know that.

He bent to her mouth and kissed her softly, with exquisite tenderness. She tugged at his hips, but he didn't respond.

"No," he said softly, and he smiled at her. "Not unless you can take as much pleasure from my body as I take from yours."

She was fascinated by the reply.

He kissed her again, very softly, and then rolled away from her. He tugged his clothes back on and stood up to finish the fastenings. He looked down at her as she pulled her discarded dress against her breasts and stared at him confusedly.

"I'll make some coffee," he said quietly, aware of her sudden embarrassment. "Then we'll talk."

He walked away. She struggled quickly back into her things, noting the curious stares of the twin Siamese cats, who probably had never seen such confusing behavior from their resident human pet. It made her self-conscious.

By the time he came back with a tray, she was sitting on the couch feeling waves of embarrassment and shame.

He sat down beside her, fixed a cup of coffee the way he knew she liked it, and handed it to her. He saw the tears she was trying not to shed.

He reached over for a tissue from the box he kept by the lamp and wiped her eyes with a tenderness that said more than words.

"I haven't had a woman for over two years," he said bluntly. "I'm sorry. I lost control the minute I started kissing you."

"It's all right," she choked, sipping coffee. "I didn't exactly fight for my honor." Tears started rolling again, staining her cheeks while she tried not to let him see how upset she was.

He took the coffee away from her, tugged her into his arms, and dragged her over into his lap. He held her while she cried, rocking her in the silence of the room. He felt satiated. His body was more relaxed than it had been in years. He felt young, vital, full of fire. He smiled at the difference a few torrid minutes had made in their tumultuous relationship.

"I'm sorry," she choked. "I'm acting like a child."

He kissed her wet eyelids. "First times are traumatic," he murmured, drying her eyes again with the tissue.

"Was yours?" she asked, curious.

He laughed. "The first time I tried to have sex, I was seventeen. I was dating an older girl and we were in the back seat of my parents' car at a country drive-in, one of the last few in Texas," he recalled. "We were going at it hot and heavy when my zipper stuck."

She stared at him, fascinated.

He laughed again. "I couldn't get it to budge. I couldn't get my jeans off with it zipped. And if I broke the zipper, I'd never have gotten past my mother to my room." He shook his head. "She was experienced, and furious. She called me a clumsy fool and said she couldn't imagine why girls went out with me. I took her home and never phoned her again. She didn't know it was my first time, which was all that saved my pride."

"I can't imagine you being clumsy," she said, fascinated by him.

He kissed the tip of her nose. "We all start somewhere," he mused lazily. He traced around her soft mouth. "But you were my first virgin," he whispered, holding her eyes.

Her lips parted. "I was?"

He nodded. He pushed back her disheveled hair. "I wasn't sure I knew enough to spare you the pain."

"You did, though," she whispered, and averted her eyes, flushing.

He'd noticed. He felt ten feet tall. He knew that she'd climaxed, and not just the one time. He'd given her fulfillment, despite the rough beginning. It made him proud.

He cradled her close, wrapping her up in his arms with her face in his warm throat. He rocked her hungrily, his body still tingling with remembered pleasure. "I'd forgotten how it felt," he whispered. "I suppose I've been half-alive, without knowing it."

"So have I," she replied drowsily. She curled closer into his powerful body.

He kissed her hair. "I'm sorry I made you sore," he whispered. "It was unavoidable."

"I know."

He sat holding her for a long time, so contented that he didn't realize how late it was getting until the automatic lights outside began to come on.

"Goodness," she exclaimed when she noticed, sitting up on his lap. "I have to get home. Mama will be worried." She stopped, aghast when she remembered her mother and her responsibilities. She remembered what she'd done with Kemp and she felt self-conscious and uncomfortable.

He knew that. He could see it in her expression. He didn't know what to say to make things right.

"If anything happens, we'll handle it," he said softly. "Don't beat yourself to death worrying. Okay?"

*We'll handle it.* Did he mean he'd pay for a termination? She felt sick at her stomach. What in the world had she been thinking? She'd just had sex with her former boss and he wasn't a marrying man. He wasn't going to start hearing violins if she turned up pregnant. He was going to suggest a practical solution. But she wasn't going to be able to agree with that. It just wasn't possible.

"I can see the thoughts in your mind, Violet," he said abruptly. "Let's not face problems before they appear."

She swallowed. "You're right, of course." She got to her feet unsteadily, and looked around as if she didn't quite know where she was.

Kemp got up, too. "Do you want me to follow you home, just in case?" he asked.

She looked up. "In case of what?"

"You don't drive at night much," he said. He scowled. "There are drunks on the roads at night around here."

"I won't have any trouble," she assured him.

"Except when it comes to living with what just happened," he remarked.

She picked up her purse and sweater and turned to look at him. "What?"

He shoved his hands into his pockets. "You're a Puritan, Violet," he said somberly. "You weren't a virgin by accident."

She colored. "I don't date much…"

He waved away the rest of the reply. "You're in love with me. I've always known it. There isn't any other reason that would make you give yourself to a man without marriage."

She glared at him. She hated being so transparent.

He moved closer, taking her gently by the shoulders. "You'll work for me until we find out, one way or another, if there are going to be any consequences."

"I should never have…!"

He kissed her mouth closed. "We're both human." He searched her eyes. "I love the way you were with me," he added huskily. "It was the most exciting encounter of my life, Violet. I think I could live on it, if I had to. You were…extraordinary."

"I didn't know anything," she blurted out.

"Instinct must go a long way, then." He bent and kissed her again. "Try not to be ashamed of something so beautiful," he added quietly. "We have a lot in common. I think we'll find even more, as we go along."

He was saying something incredible. She stared up at him, fascinated.

"I was happy being alone until you came along and shook up my life," he murmured absently, watching her closely. "I can't go back."

"You can't?"

He brought her soft palm to his mouth and kissed it hungrily. "In a few days, I think we might go and look at rings," he said hesitantly, and his high cheekbones took on a ruddy color.

"Rings?"

His thumb rubbed over her ring finger. "Rings."

She couldn't manage a single word.

His blue eyes were somber. "Today was a beginning. Not the end."

Her lips parted as she studied him, with love radiating from her face. He saw it, and felt humbled by it.

He'd never been with a woman who was so violently in love with him. He felt cosseted, valued, possessed.

He drew her against him, aware that he became aroused the instant he felt her soft breasts against his chest. That hadn't happened even with Shannon, when he was much younger. Violet lit fires in his body.

"Feel that?" he whispered as he bent to her mouth. "You arouse me so much that it hurts."

She opened her mouth when she felt his lips on it. He built the kiss, lifting her free of the floor in his embrace. "I would still let you," she whispered.

"I know," he whispered back. "You're part of me now. I'm part of you. Kiss me…"

The kiss was long, hard, passionate. When he finally put her down, she was trembling.

"Go home," he said firmly, leading her to the door with her purse in his hand.

"Throwing me out?" she teased.

He chuckled. "Saving you," he murmured wickedly. "I need a cold shower."

She touched his chest with her hand, dizzy and aching with new sensations, new joy. "I know you already know it," she said softly. "But I love you."

He traced her mouth with his fingertip. The words bit into him, made him feel guilty. He wanted her, but he didn't feel that emotion for her. Not yet. He just smiled. "Drive carefully. Call me when you get home."

He didn't say it, but he had to feel something powerful for her, she was certain of it. She beamed. "Okay. Good night."

"Good night, angel," he said softly.

He watched her walk away with feelings of utter

self-contempt. He'd taken advantage of what she felt for him, lost control and put her at risk. Now he had to stand by and wait to find out if she became pregnant, knowing that if she did, he'd be forced to marry her to save her reputation. It wasn't the best night of his life, despite the lingering pleasure that reminded him of the afternoon.

# CHAPTER SIX

VIOLET MANAGED TO slip into her house without being seen by her mother. She was disheveled and her hair was a mess. Her mother wasn't blind or stupid, she'd know that something torrid had been going on. To prevent any uncomfortable questions, Violet had called to her and then went straight to her room without letting herself be seen.

From there, she went to the kitchen, trying not to let her mind wander to the afternoon. Then she remembered that she'd promised to bring her mother some trout. She groaned inwardly. She heated her mother a bowl of soup and crackers for supper.

"I'm sorry about the trout," she began. But she was beaming and she couldn't help it.

Mrs. Hardy grinned. "Never mind that. Soup is fine. You've got feathers on your lips, my darling cat," she chided. "So what's going on with you and that dishy man?"

So much for deterring her mother's suspicions. Violet blushed, grinning back. "The boss man is talking about rings."

Her mother gasped. "Darling!"

Violet laughed. "Can you believe it? And we were fighting and giving each other fits just last week!"

"He didn't really know you before, though," the older woman pointed out as she sipped soup from a spoon. "You were too shy to be yourself with him."

"I was," Violet agreed, vaguely ashamed of what had happened, just the same.

"Did he mention a date?"

Violet shook her head. "We're going to take it one day at a time," she replied.

Mrs. Hardy only smiled. She knew that when couples got to the ring stage, weddings very often came quickly. "I've only ever wanted to live long enough to see you married and secure," she said absently.

"You'd better be around longer than that," Violet chided. "I can't do without you!"

"Bosh," the other woman murmured. "You've got your own life to live. I'm just about done with mine."

"Don't you talk like that," her daughter chided. "You're not nearly done. You have so much to look forward to!"

"Such as?" Mrs. Hardy asked, her eyes lackluster.

"Grandchildren!" she replied, and blushed again, because she could already be pregnant.

The older woman sat very still. "Grandchildren. Why… I hadn't thought…" She glanced at Violet. "Does he want children, then?"

"Of course," Violet said, smiling.

"He must have changed his mind," Mrs. Hardy mused to herself.

Violet felt a sinking sensation. "What do you mean?"

"Oh, it's just something he mentioned that day he came over to talk to me, dear," she said, sipping more soup. "He said that he'd never have a child."

Violet felt sick. "Did he?"

Her mother hadn't noticed Violet's sudden lack of color and enthusiasm. She was thinking. "Men often think like that, until they have a child. But he was rather emphatic about it, just the same."

"I wonder why," Violet murmured aloud, uncomfortable.

Her mother glanced at her worriedly. "You mustn't let on that I told you," she said.

"Told me what, Mother?"

Mrs. Hardy grimaced. "Mr. Kemp is a very upright man these days, but he was young and irresponsible once. I'd heard something about the Culbertson girl, from a nurse I know. I asked him about it. He was shocked enough to tell me the truth about her. She was pregnant when she died. It was his child. He hadn't known about it, although he would have married her sooner if he had. The coroner covered up her pregnancy, to spare her parents the embarrassment. But it affected him terribly. He lost not only his fiancée, but his child as well. He said that just the thought of a child gave him nightmares now, brought it all back to haunt him."

Violet sat down, hard. It was worse than she'd imagined. Blake didn't want children. She'd pushed him off balance and they'd had unprotected sex. He was making the best of things, but he'd never said that he loved her and he'd intimated that if she turned up pregnant, they'd have to make arrangements. Could that mean that he didn't want a child, ever, after what had happened with his fiancée?

She felt sick to her soul. What was she going to do?

"Dear, what's wrong?" Mrs. Hardy asked with a frown.

Violet forced a smile. "Nothing. I shouldn't be jealous of a dead woman, should I?" she added, leading her mother right into the false conclusion that she was thinking about Shannon.

Mrs. Hardy relaxed. "Yes, dear. You shouldn't."

Violet changed the subject. But she didn't sleep very much that night. She was sick with worry. How could she have been so blind and stupid? She was going to pay a high price for her one hour of passion. She'd thought it was worth anything at the time. Now, she wasn't so sure.

SHE WENT TO work Monday morning with uncertain feelings. She dreaded and anticipated seeing Blake again, both at once. Duke Wright smiled at her as he put her to work on new herd records, and he looked as if he might have known something about her day at Blake Kemp's house. But he didn't say anything.

Curt did. He grinned at her as he paused beside her desk. "I hear you were out at Kemp's place over the weekend," he murmured.

She gasped. "How…?"

"Jacobsville is a small town," he said pleasantly. "Kemp's driveway faces a major highway. Your car would stick out in a parking lot."

She grimaced. "I didn't think about that."

"Stop looking so tragic," he said gently. "You're both free and single. Nobody's going to make snide remarks to either of you about spending an afternoon together. Is it true about the cats?" he added quickly.

"What…about the cats?"

"That they're so jealous of Kemp that visitors can't get near him," he replied.

"They weren't so bad," she confided. "Well, I did sort of get scratched by one of them. But it was just a little scratch."

"The rumor is that the more Kemp likes someone, the worse the cats are," he told her. "In which case, you'd better wear body armor if you go over there very much."

"Siamese do tend to be temperamental, I guess," she said, wondering how many people had seen her car at Kemp's house.

"We had a dog once that hated Libby's boyfriend, when she was about fourteen," he recalled. "The dog sat and growled at him the whole time he was in the house. Then one day the boy brought him a beef bone. The next time he came over, the dog met him at the door and licked him half to death."

She pursed her lips and smiled mischievously. "I wonder if Siamese like beef bones?"

He chuckled and went on out to work.

VIOLET HAD HALFWAY hoped that she might hear from Blake during the day. After all, they'd been lovers. But he didn't call. It was a disappointment, and her self-confidence took a nosedive. All her hopes began to drown in doubt. She went through her normal routine, answering the phone and taking messages, and typing letters for Duke Wright after he dictated them. It was a normal day. Nothing out of the ordinary. She could have cried. Once, she almost picked up the phone and called his office. But that would never do. She couldn't look as if she were chasing him. Perhaps he just needed breathing space, in order to get used to the changed relationship between them. Surely, it was just that.

By the end of the day, she was feeling dismal. She wondered if perhaps Blake had phoned while she was briefly out of the office, because she had to run to town for Duke Wright and pick up a special delivery letter he was expecting, at the post office.

She had the opportunity to ask him as she gathered her purse and sweater to go home. He walked in with a sealed letter that needed a stamp.

"Could you drop that by the post office for me on your way home, Violet?" he asked.

"Certainly." She put on the stamp and gave him a shy glance. "Uh, there weren't any, uh, messages for me while I was gone earlier…?" she faltered.

He cocked an eyebrow and grinned. "From your ex-boss, you mean?"

She flushed. "Well…"

"There's a hard case, if ever there was one," he said. "You're taking a chance, Violet. A big one."

"Sir?"

"We all know you were out at his house," he replied easily. "News travels like wildfire around here. We've heard that those cats don't like company at all."

"They're sort of antagonistic," she confessed, without mentioning her scratches.

"Kemp took another lawyer home for supper one day and the man had to go to the emergency room. He was allergic to cat scratches."

She cleared her throat. "They are sort of possessive,"

she replied. "But I'm no threat. We're just friends," Violet said firmly. "He wanted to introduce me to his cats."

"That explains everything," Duke mused, grinning. "It's the cats who are interested in you, then?"

Curt Collins poked his head in the door, shamelessly eavesdropping. "And of course, Kemp loves his cats, so he brings home strangers that he thinks they'll like," he added.

"You two!" Violet exclaimed, laughing at the absurdity of it all. "I'm leaving. See you tomorrow."

They said their goodbyes and watched her go out the door.

She knew what they meant about the cats.

Mr. Kemp was a notorious loner. He never took women to his house. If he was entertaining Violet on the weekend, something was going on. She knew it was all over town if even Duke Wright knew about her visit. She wondered if the gossip had gotten back to Blake and that's why he hadn't phoned her. Of course, he could be feeling regret at his loss of control as well. She was feeling something similar. Her only excuse was that she loved him. Sadly, she knew it wasn't the same with him. Desire wasn't love.

VIOLET SPENT A sleepless night worrying about her lapse of judgment at Kemp's house, and his avoidance of her. She couldn't forget what her mother had said, about his attitude toward children. She hoped with all her heart that there wouldn't be consequences. Surely, she couldn't get pregnant from one brief interlude!

She went to work the next morning and found Duke

Wright making coffee. He glanced up when she came in the door, and smiled at her.

"I've got to be out of town today. Think you can hold the office together until I get back?"

"I'll do my best, sir," she promised.

"If Kemp shows up, you can have a long lunch hour," he added with a grin. "But don't let him know I said that."

"He's not a bad man."

"You don't have my perspective on him," Duke replied quietly.

She was aware of that. Duke's divorce had been a messy one, and he blamed Kemp for his wife's unreasonable demands. She didn't say a word.

He shrugged. "Sorry. I have bad memories. I'll see you tomorrow, Violet."

"Yes, sir," she said. "Have a safe trip."

"I hope to."

She watched him walk out with a sense of foreboding. She couldn't shake the feeling that something was going on.

AND IT WAS. Kemp walked into his office and motioned Libby Collins back down the hall with him.

He told her the results of the state crime lab's autopsy on her father, which was negative.

She was relieved, and showed it.

"But the opposite was true of Violet's father," he said quietly. "Don't tell her, and don't tell Curt until I've had time to get out to Wright's ranch. I'm going to tell Violet in person and then take her home and help her break the news to her mother. It's going to be an ordeal for them.

If we can catch Janet Collins, we'll charge her with first degree murder. Violet and her mother will both have to testify, and it will resurrect some terrible memories for old Mrs. Hardy. I'm not sure her heart will take it."

"What can be done?"

He shrugged. "The only thing I know is to try and reach a plea agreement, if I can talk the D.A. into it. If Janet can expect something less than life in prison, she might confess. I'll have to see. Right now, my priority is to make sure Violet doesn't hear it on the six o'clock news. There were reporters sniffing around this afternoon."

"Poor Violet," Libby said sadly. "Please, tell her if she needs me, I'll be there."

"I will. But I'm sure she knows it already. Hold down the fort for me."

"You bet."

ALL THE WAY to Duke Wright's place, Kemp worried about Violet's reaction. He was still aching from their brief interlude, and he was uneasy about facing Violet again. She was a shy, introverted woman who'd had no real experience with men. He'd taken advantage of that. She might hate him for it. Just the same, he had to do what he could for her and her mother. It wasn't going to be easy for either of them to face the fact that Mr. Hardy had been murdered.

VIOLET WAS JUST finishing the last of the new cattle herd files when she heard footsteps coming into her office.

She looked up, and her heart jumped wildly as she saw Blake Kemp for the first time since their passionate afternoon. She colored furiously as he came into the room and paused just in front of her desk. He looked very elegant in a pale gray vested suit, not a hair out of place. His blue eyes were quiet and sympathetic as they met hers.

"Is something wrong?" she asked at once, uneasy because of the way he looked.

"Yes, Violet," he replied. "We have to speak to your mother. Will Wright let you leave early?"

"He's not here today," she faltered. She stood up. "What's happened?"

"We just got the results back on your father's autopsy. He was poisoned, Violet. It wasn't a natural death. It was murder."

Murder. *Murder.* She felt the blood draining out of her face. Janet Collins had killed her father.

"That woman," she bit off. "That damned, greedy woman killed my father!"

He moved around the desk quickly and pulled her into his arms, wrapping her up tight. "It's all right," he murmured softly at her ear, contracting his arms when she began to shiver. "We'll make her pay for it. I swear we will."

She'd felt shock and then anger. Now she felt grief well up in her like water behind a dam. She'd loved her father, despite his faults. How in the world was her mother going to react to the news?

"It will kill Mama," she choked, sliding her arms around Blake's waist.

"No, it won't," he assured her. "She's stronger than she looks. But I think you and I should both break the news to her."

"Yes. Thank you," she added belatedly.

He drew in a long breath. Odd, how right she felt in his arms. He'd ached for her for the past few days. This was like coming home.

She loved the comfort of his embrace. Except for her mother, she'd had little real affection in her life. It was wonderful to melt into his muscular body and let him absorb all her worries, all her fears. He made her feel secure, protected.

His hand smoothed over her hair, enjoying its softness.

Footsteps interrupted them. Curt came into the room, stopped dead, and started to go back out again, faintly embarrassed.

Blake saw him and released Violet. "She's had some bad news," he told the other man. "It will be all over town soon enough, so you might as well know now. Her father was poisoned."

"By my stepmother?" Curt asked miserably.

Blake nodded. "Very probably."

Curt grimaced. "Violet, I'm so sorry."

She wiped her eyes with the back of her hand. They felt swollen and hot. "It's not your fault, Curt," she said sadly. "You and Libby have suffered because of her, too. We're all victims."

"And we can't find her," Curt muttered angrily.

"We will," Blake said firmly. "I swear we will."

"Is there anything I can do?" Curt asked.

Violet shook her head. "But thanks anyway. We're going to tell Mama. I hope it isn't going to be too much for her."

Blake smiled faintly as Violet went to gather up her

things. "I think you'll find that your mother is going to want vengeance more than sympathy when she knows the truth."

Violet smiled. "I hope so," she replied. "I really hope that's how she's going to feel."

Blake turned to Curt. "I'm going to follow Violet home. If Wright calls, can you tell him what's going on?"

"He left his foreman in charge," Curt replied. "I'll make sure he knows. There's nothing that can't wait until tomorrow. Violet, if you need anything, all you have to do is tell us. I know Libby would tell you the same thing."

"Thanks, Curt," she replied, managing a smile as she joined Blake. "I'm ready when you are," she told him.

"Let's go." Blake stood aside to let her go out the door first.

MRS. HARDY LOOKED up expectantly, and with faint surprise, when she saw Blake come in the door with her daughter. Both of them wore somber expressions.

She was propped up on the sofa with pillows. She gave them a wise look. "You have the results of the autopsy," she guessed. "That floozie poisoned my husband, didn't she?" she added, eyes flashing. "I want her drawn and quartered!"

Blake smiled at Violet. "Didn't I tell you?" he mused.

Violet nodded. "Yes, you did." She put down her things and went to sit beside her mother on the sofa and pull her close. "We're going to find her and send her away for years and years," she promised her mother. "It's just a matter of time and evidence."

"Evidence being the key word," Blake agreed. "Fortunately, the criminalists who processed the scene did a thorough job. They couldn't rule out homicide, so they did a good job of collecting trace evidence. There's more than enough for a DNA profile. If Janet was in that room, we'll be able to prove it. There's also an eyewitness who saw her come out of the room shortly before your husband was discovered," he added.

"Yes, but we don't know where she is," Violet murmured.

"Oh, that's just a minor detail," Blake said carelessly. "I have a private detective tracking her. It's just a matter of time."

"You didn't say anything about that," Violet remarked.

"Finding Janet is essential to Libby and Curt. They're fighting to keep their ranch, and it's not going well," he said grimly. "Janet has done everything in her power to take it away from them. She's absconded with all the money and tied up their finances so that they can hardly pay bills. They need her found, and quickly. So do both of you," he added. "The longer this drags on, the worse it's going to get."

"How can a human being be so cold?" Mrs. Hardy wondered out loud, her delicate features drawn as she spoke. "Money isn't that important."

"To some people it is," Blake replied. "I've seen men go to prison for life because they stole less than twenty dollars. A thief doesn't know how much money his victim is carrying, as a rule. Sometimes the victim resists, and dies, and the thief ends up with pocket change and a life sentence. Greed is its own punishment."

"I hope Janet Collins gets hers," Violet said quietly, hugging her mother. She glanced at Blake. "I suppose it will be in all the papers?"

"Undoubtedly," he agreed. He moved into the living room and dropped down into a comfortable armchair. "Personal tragedies have become popular entertainment. We've reached an all-time low in journalistic ethics."

"Where do you think Janet Collins went?" Mrs. Hardy asked abruptly.

Blake crossed his long legs and leaned back in the chair. "At a guess, somewhere close by. She won't want to let go of the ranch. Libby and Curt have had some threats already, probably at her instigation."

"I'm sorry they're having such trouble," Violet said. "Libby's the best friend I have."

"I won't give up until Janet is found," Blake assured her. "I've got one of the best private investigators in Texas on the job."

Mrs. Hardy was dabbing at her eyes. Anger had given way to grief. "I wondered about the coroner's report, saying that he had a heart attack," she murmured aloud. "He'd had all sorts of tests, and there was no trace of heart trouble."

"From what the medical examiner told me, the poison paralyzes the heart. Essentially, it stops it dead. Since no one suspected foul play, they didn't bother with an autopsy. But I credit those investigators in San Antonio with doing a great job of evidence gathering. When we finally catch Janet, we'll have enough to hang her."

Violet hugged her mother. "It will be all right," she said, although she didn't really feel it.

"The newspapers will have a field day, won't they?" Mrs. Hardy asked suddenly, her face contorted.

"We'll get through it," Violet assured her. "We're tough, aren't we?"

Mrs. Hardy hesitated, then she smiled. "Yes, dear. We're tough."

"We'll find a way around the publicity," Blake told them. "First things first. We have to find Janet."

"Thank you for coming with Violet to give me the news, Blake," Mrs. Hardy told him gently. "It made it easier."

"I thought it might," he said gently. "I'm sorry it turned out this way," he added.

"So are we," Violet replied. "But we don't get to choose our obstacles, do we?"

"How true," Mrs. Hardy murmured. She looked toward Blake. "Would you like to come to dinner?"

Violet flushed. She knew her mother was trying to play matchmaker, but she wished she hadn't. She was uneasy around Blake. She didn't know what he expected of her. She didn't know how she should behave.

Blake saw her indecision and averted his gaze to Mrs. Hardy. "Thanks," he said, "but I've got a lot of work to get through tonight for a client." The client was Libby Collins, but he wasn't going to discuss that with the women.

"Another time," Mrs. Hardy suggested.

"Another time," he agreed pleasantly. "I'd better get on the road. If you need me, call," he told Violet firmly.

"Of course, we will," she said without looking directly at him, and with a forced smile.

"My interim secretary is getting married," he remarked. "You might consider coming back to work. Libby and Mabel miss you."

Violet was surprised, because he hadn't been in touch with her since their dinner. She didn't even know that he'd hired an interim secretary. He sounded as if he wanted Violet to come back. But he didn't look desperate.

On the other hand, she missed seeing him every day. It was a wrench to work for Duke Wright. It guaranteed that she wouldn't see Blake on a regular basis at all. Today had been a rare event.

"Think about it, at least," Blake added quietly.

"Yes," she replied. "I certainly will."

He studied her for a few seconds too long, his eyes narrow and intent. She might mistake his invitation for something romantic, but that wasn't the case at all. He felt guilty for what he'd let happen at his house. Violet could be pregnant. He didn't dare keep his distance until he knew for sure. The woman hadn't a clue about relationships, and she'd be in a hell of a fix if she really had become pregnant.

He had to keep her close so that he'd know, whatever her condition turned out to be. If there was going to be a child…

He stopped the thought dead. He wouldn't think about that consequence. He had to look on the bright side. He wasn't ready for marriage and a family. He might never be. Certainly, Violet was hardly the sort of woman he envisioned marrying. She was sweet and kind, but she wasn't assertive. There were divisions between them that she didn't understand. He couldn't hurt her by pointing them out.

He had to bide his time until he knew for sure if there was going to be a child. That wasn't her fault, either. He'd seduced her, out of loneliness and aching hunger. He still felt the need for her. It was why he'd avoided her for the past couple of days. He'd hoped to get it under control.

But it wasn't. He looked at her and he wanted her. His body was already as taut as drawn rope, just from looking at her. He knew instinctively that if he touched her, he wasn't going to be able to pull away. The pleasure she'd given him was exquisite. He wanted it again. And he didn't dare have it.

"Violet, why don't you walk Blake out?" Mrs. Hardy suggested when there was a brief silence.

"I can find my way out," Blake said without making a big thing of Violet's hesitation. He even smiled. "Think about the job," he suggested. "We make a good team…you and me and Libby and Mabel," he added just when she thought he was talking about the two of them.

She nodded. "I will think about it," she promised.

"I'll be in touch," he replied. He didn't say goodbye. He simply left.

"See, dear, he misses you!" Mrs. Hardy exclaimed when they heard his car start up outside. "He wants you back! You'll do it, won't you?"

"I have to change clothes and get supper started," she interrupted to halt her mother's speculation. "What would you like? How about pancakes?"

"Pancakes? For supper?" the older woman exclaimed.

"Why not? We love pancakes!"

Mrs. Hardy smiled. "Then pancakes it is. And coffee."

Coffee reminded Violet of Blake and made her sad. She'd lost her job over coffee. But she didn't let it show. "Decaf for you," she teased, and went to change her clothes.

# CHAPTER SEVEN

BLAKE SPENT THE weekend working, trying to keep his mind off Violet. Monday morning, his private investigator called with some good news for Libby and Curt Collins. Their father's priceless coin collection had been located at a dealer's shop in San Antonio. There were bankbooks. There was also a copy of a new will, about which Blake had some suspicions. Blake phoned the dealer and arranged to drive up the following morning early and collect the coins and the documents. He told the dealer that he'd have Libby phone him as soon as she came to work—she could vouch for the fact that Blake was her attorney and authorized to handle her inheritance.

He didn't know if Janet Collins was aware of the coin collection's whereabouts and he considered that he might need backup.

He phoned the chief of police's office and talked to Cash Grier, who agreed to drive up with him. Grier would intimidate most people with evil intentions, Blake thought humorously, even without a firearm.

He told Libby about the trip and also asked her to go by Violet's house that afternoon with a pizza and cheer the women up. He also suggested that it wouldn't hurt for Libby to mention how badly they missed her in the office, and how short-handed they were since the interim secretary, Jessie, had given notice and quit. Libby laughingly agreed.

LIBBY WAS SURPRISED at Violet's new look and her nervousness when she stopped by Violet's house after work. She'd known Violet for a long time. She'd never known her to be anything except calm and collected.

"Mr. Kemp asked me to tell you how much we're missing you," Libby said, tongue-in-cheek.

Violet laughed softly. "Are you really, or are you just short-handed because Jessie quit without finishing out her notice?"

Libby's eyes widened. "How in the world did you know that?"

Violet chuckled. "Mrs. Landers who works at the newspaper office," she replied. "She's the best gossip we have, and she thought I'd like to know that poor Mr. Blake was short a secretary. She saw the baby shower announcement that Jessie brought in and Jessie mentioned that she was leaving the job early because Mr. Kemp was hopeful that his old secretary might come back if she knew how hard-pressed he was for help."

"Well!" Libby exclaimed on a laugh, showing her the box of hot pizza. "It's all true, of course. I brought you and Mrs. Hardy a pizza."

"You can have some, too, Libby, since you were nice enough to bring it," Violet said, hugging the other woman. "It was sweet of you. Mama and I have had a bad day."

"Mr. Kemp told me about it," Libby replied. "I'm so sorry."

Violet shrugged. "We all have hard times. We'll get through ours. It's just that it's brought back so many terrible memories."

"All my stepmother's fault," Libby said coldly. "Curt and I would love to get our hands on her!"

"Take a number and get in line," Violet mused with morbid humor.

"I see your point."

"Come on into the kitchen, and I'll find some plates. Mama, Libby's here, and she brought a pizza," she called to her mother in the living room.

"Hello, Libby," Mrs. Hardy called back. "That was sweet of you!"

"That's just what I said, Mama," Violet teased.

She led Libby into the kitchen.

"One way or another, my stepmother has made some terrible problems for all of us," Libby said somberly. "But she messed up."

"How?"

"My dad must have suspected something, because he made a new will and left it with a rare coin dealer in San Antonio," Libby replied. "The coin collection he had is there, too. Mr. Kemp says Curt and I will be able to pay off our mortgage and get our livestock back."

"Libby, that's wonderful!" Violet exclaimed.

"Yes. Wonderful. But Julie Merrill has been making my life hell lately. She's got her claws into Jordan and she won't let go. He thinks I'm just jealous and trying to break them up. But it's more than that," she said grimly. "She's dangerous. She's been spreading all sorts of rumors about Calhoun Ballenger. He got Mr. Kemp to file suit against her for slander."

"Good for Calhoun!"

Libby helped put pizza on plates. "I thought Jordan cared about me," she said miserably. "But the minute Julie turned on the charm, he dropped me flat. He even let her insult me without saying a single word in my defense."

"I'm really sorry," Violet told her. "I thought Jordan was smart enough to see through her."

"She's pretty and smart and rich," Libby murmured.

"And what are you, hideous?" Violet chided. "Your people were founding families of Jacobsville, and you're a paralegal. You're pretty, too. You're worth two of Julie Merrill."

Libby looked less stressed. She smiled. "Thanks, Violet. I really have missed you," she added. "I don't have anybody else that I can talk to, except my brother, and I couldn't tell him how I really feel about Jordan."

"Julie will fall into that deep hole she's digging one day," Violet told the other woman. "With any luck, Janet will fall into one just as deep!" She hesitated, remembering what Libby had said. "Mr. Kemp isn't going to go up there alone to get those things, is he? I mean, Janet might have an accomplice…"

"Cash Grier is going with him," Libby interrupted.

Violet laughed. "I'll stop worrying right now. Nobody is going to mess with our chief of police."

"That's gospel," Libby agreed. "Although you might remember that Mr. Kemp was an officer in the reserves until just recently. He's no shrinking daisy."

"I know," Violet replied, smiling. "Remember those two men he threw out of our office?"

"I'm trying to forget!"

They both laughed.

THE PIZZA WAS DELICIOUS. Violet walked out with Libby when she was ready to leave.

"Are you going to come back?" Libby asked the other woman seriously.

"Yes," Violet said. "I dread having to tell Mr. Wright, though," she added. "He was kind to me."

"Duke's nice. He won't mind. He may not like Mr. Kemp, but he likes you," she added with a smile. "I'll bet he won't even ask you to work a two week notice."

"That would be nice." She wrapped her arms around herself. The night was cool. "Has Mr. Kemp really missed me?"

Libby smiled. "He really has. He's set new records for hostility and impatience. I think Jessie quit because she reached the end of her rope. She couldn't please the boss no matter what she did. It seemed to Mabel and me that Mr. Kemp was trying to make her leave."

Violet smiled delightedly. "I've missed him, too," she confessed.

Libby hugged her. "We all know how you feel about him. I think you've got a good chance with him, Violet," she said gently. "I wouldn't encourage you to come back if I didn't. I know too much about unrequited love."

"You and Jordan are going to work out one day, too," Violet assured her friend. "I'm sure of it."

"Chance would be a fine thing," Libby sighed. "Well, I'd better get home. Curt's having a night out with the boys so I don't have to worry about his supper, thank goodness."

"Your brother's a nice man."

"He is, isn't he?" Libby grinned. "I wouldn't have minded you for a sister-in-law, you know. But you can't get past love. I know. I've tried."

"It will work out, Libby," Violet told her.

"Somehow," Libby agreed.

"Thanks for the pizza and the company."

"You're very welcome."

"I'll call Mr. Wright tonight," Violet added, full of excitement.

"We'll look forward to having you back whenever you can come," Libby called on her way to the car.

VIOLET DID PHONE Duke Wright, and he did waive her two weeks' notice. He was sorry to lose her, he added, but a blind man could see how she felt about Kemp. Not that Kemp deserved her, he added wryly. Violet thanked him and hung up. She was going to be sitting at her desk when Mr. Kemp came in the next morning. She could hardly wait to see the look on his face!

KEMP AND CASH GRIER were on their way back from San Antonio after a stop at the coin dealer's shop, a local attorney's office, and a quick lunch. Kemp had salvaged more than enough of the late Riddle Collins's assets to save Libby and Curt Collins from bankruptcy. They'd be able to pay off their outstanding loan and have plenty left over to put in the bank. The coin collection their father had left them was worth a fortune by itself. But in addition to it, Kemp had found two savings accounts and a new will that their late father had placed with the coin dealer in San Antonio. Apparently, he hadn't trusted his wife, Janet, one bit, and had planned for her legal shenanigans after his death. He'd assured that his children wouldn't be left penniless.

"Isn't greed amazing?" Kemp murmured aloud, having told Grier the bare bones of the shameful way Janet had treated her stepchildren.

"It is," Grier said. "I've never understood it. I like having enough to provide a roof over my head and the occasional night at the theater, but there are plenty of things I wouldn't consider doing even to make myself rich."

"Same here." Kemp glanced at the older man curiously.

"Something bothering you?" Grier asked.

"I'm surprised at the way you've fit in here," he replied with a faint smile. "You do know the whole town's talking about your defense of your two patrol officers—the ones the mayor is trying to fire."

"I like controversy if it's in a good cause," Grier said. He grinned. "I'm not letting them fire good officers for doing their jobs."

"You've got some drug traffickers on the run as well," Kemp mused. "You're shaking up our little community. I like the changes. So do a lot of other people."

"I'm glad, but I didn't take the job to win a popularity contest."

"Why did you?" Kemp asked evenly.

Grier sighed. "I'm tired of living on the run," he confessed, gazing out the window while Kemp drove. "I'm feeling my age. I think I might put down roots here."

"With Tippy?" Kemp fished.

Grier didn't fly at him, as he'd expected. The older

man frowned slightly. "She's not what she seems," he replied quietly. "I've misjudged her badly. I don't know that she'd be willing to take me on, once she's back on her feet and able to work again. In any case, I can't let her far out of my sight right now. Not until that third kidnapper is in custody," he added coldly. "If he turns up in Jacobsville and makes a try for her, he'd better carry life insurance."

"It would take a stupid criminal to do that."

"I've locked up a lot of guys who aren't rocket scientists," Grier said drolly, with a speaking glance at Kemp.

Kemp chuckled. "I've defended a fair number who weren't, too," he had to agree. "Which reminds me, if you want me to defend your patrol officers at the hearing, I'll do it pro bono."

"Thanks," Grier told him. "But I've got a big surprise for the city council when they meet for that hearing."

"I forgot. You're related to the Hart boys, aren't you?"

Grier grinned. "They're my cousins."

"And Simon Hart is our state attorney general," he added, laughing. "Then I don't need to offer my services. I won't try to guess who you're bringing with you."

"You won't need to guess," Grier said. He stretched lazily. "I need a few days off. Once the election is over and the disciplinary hearing is decided, I'm going to take some time off. Tippy's little brother is coming down here soon. He likes to fish. Maybe he and I can stake out a riverbank for a few hours and take some fresh fish home to Tippy for dinner."

"Can she cook?" Kemp asked, surprised.

"Indeed she can," he replied. "You'd be amazed at how domestic she is." His eyes were soft. "She looks right at home in a kitchen. I could get used to seeing her across a table for the rest of my life."

Kemp felt uneasy. Grier, an older and lonelier man than himself, was apparently thinking solemnly about a stable and shared future with a woman. Kemp thought of marriage and it made him uncomfortable.

"I'm not in the market for a wife," Kemp said aloud. "I like my own space, my own company."

Grier gave him a grin. "I used to be that way, too. There's always the one woman who can change your mind."

Kemp shrugged. "Not for me. I've been that route once. I never want to go over the same ground again."

"Nothing wrong with being a loner," Grier said. "Until recent days, I felt that way, too."

"Tippy's a beauty."

"She's got a good brain, and she's a quick hand in an emergency," Grier told him. "It's not about looks."

"Sorry," Kemp said belatedly. "I was thinking out loud."

"I hear your new secretary quit," Grier mused.

"She couldn't spell," Kemp muttered. "It's no loss."

"What are you going to do, have Libby and Mabel double up on work again?"

"Violet might come back."

Grier pursed his lips. "I thought she was keen on having you for a barbecue as the entrée."

Kemp shrugged. "We're speaking again." He tried not to let it show that they were doing a lot more than that.

"If you say so."

"I can get another secretary whenever I need one," Kemp added doggedly.

"Does the employment agency know this?"

Kemp gave him a glare. "Just because they hung up on me doesn't mean they don't want my business."

"I'm sure."

"Anyway, if Violet comes back, all my problems will be solved," he said. "And now that I've got Riddle Collins's secret stash in that suitcase, Libby and Curt Collins will be out of debt and back in their own home again."

"That won't suit Julie Merrill," Grier murmured coolly. "She's hot after Jordan Powell's money. Poor Libby."

"Poor Julie, if you can get her where we all want her," Kemp said.

"I'm working on that," Grier assured him. "One way or another, I'm going to put the last of the drug cartel out of business in Jacobsville."

"With my blessing," Kemp replied, smiling.

KEMP CAME INTO his office early the next morning with Riddle's stash and showed it to Libby, who'd come in early for the occasion. She was ecstatic as they went over the proof of her father's love for her and Curt.

A few minutes later, Kemp started out for the courthouse to file the revised will Riddle had left. When he walked into the outer office, the first thing he saw was Violet, sitting at her desk.

His expression was enough to feed Violet's hungry heart. She smiled, flushed and beamed up at him.

"You said I could come back," she reminded him brightly.

"Yes, I did," he replied, smiling. "Are you staying?" She nodded.

"How about making a fresh pot of coffee?" he asked. "Regular?"

"Half and half," he replied, averting his eyes. "Too much caffeine isn't good for me."

He went out the door, leaving Violet with her jaw dropping.

"I told you he missed you!" Libby whispered mischievously as she followed the boss onto the sidewalk.

As THE DAY went on, Kemp found himself looking for excuses to go to the front of his office. He went through two pots of coffee, because that was the best excuse he had. Violet was wearing a sassy blue dress that emphasized her nice, rounded figure. It was fairly low cut in front, and with her frosted dark hair and her improved use of makeup, she was enough to turn any man's head.

Libby and Mabel noticed his sudden interest in the coffeepot with subdued humor. They didn't want to embarrass Violet, who flushed every time the boss came close.

It was almost inevitable that Violet stayed just a few minutes longer than Mabel and Libby at the end of the day.

She tidied up her desk and slowly gathered her purse

and sweater. Blake came out to the front office and stood, openly staring at her, with his hands in his pockets and an odd, intent look in the blue eyes behind his trendy spectacles.

"Are you in a rush to get home? Can you phone your mother and tell her you'll be a few minutes late?" he added.

"Of…of course," she stammered. The way he was looking at her made her tingle from head to toe. She fumbled the phone to her ear and dialed, her eyes eating her handsome boss all the while.

She told her mother she'd be a few minutes late, trying not to react obviously to her parent's amusement.

Blake held out his hand. Violet dropped her purse and sweater on her chair and went to him, letting him lead her back to his office.

He closed the door and pulled her hungrily into his arms. She sighed with pure delight as his hard mouth found her lips and he lifted her into an even more intimate embrace.

"I've missed you," he ground out against her responsive lips.

"I've missed you…too," she whispered back.

"Come home with me," he suggested huskily.

She knew what he was really suggesting, and it wasn't supper. She wanted to go with him. She wanted to be with him. But she was hesitant.

He felt her hesitation. He let her slide down his hard body and he stared into her eyes hungrily. "Well?"

She swallowed. Her gaze was on his broad chest, because she couldn't look him in the eye and refuse him.

"What are you offering me, Blake?" she asked quietly.

He scowled. "Are we bargaining for sex?"

She stared up at him, dumbfounded. "Is that all you want from me?"

He was confused. Usually logical and cool in his thinking, now he was like a young man on the brink of his first affair.

"I don't want to get married, Violet," he said gently. "You know that."

She swallowed hard. "Yes. You've already said that. But I don't want to be your mistress."

His jaw tensed. "I don't recall asking you to be."

"What would you call it, then?" Violet asked sadly. "You want to sleep with me, with no ties, isn't that the truth?"

He stuck his hands in his slacks pockets and let out a long sigh.

"My mother is old-fashioned," she continued. "She raised me to think of sex as something that goes hand in hand with love and marriage. It would break her heart to have me settle for a purely physical liaison with any man, especially you." She looked up at him miserably. "Jacobsville is a small town, Blake. Everybody would know."

"I'm not a slave to public opinion," he said harshly, feeling himself lose ground.

"Yes, but I am," she replied. She stepped back, feeling a sudden coldness in his manner. It wasn't what she'd expected when she came in here with him. She'd hoped that he might come to love her. They'd been so close at his house. Now they were like strangers.

He was furious. He was confused. This woman had caused him more inner turmoil than he'd known since the death of his fiancée, years before. He loved his freedom. But he hated the thought of losing Violet.

"Violet," he began slowly, "I was engaged once. I loved her more than life. After I lost her, I didn't want to go on living." He frowned. "I...can't go through that again."

She looked up into his turbulent eyes. "Why would you have to? You don't love me," she said miserably. "You only want me."

She turned and went to the door.

Before she could open it, his hand covered hers on the doorknob. "Wait."

"I should never have returned here to work," she said. "I'll go back to Mr. Wright. You can get another temporary secretary to fill in until you replace me."

"No!"

Tears blurred her blue eyes. She'd never been so miserable in her life. "Just let me go, please!"

He moved his hand. Seconds later, she was out the front door and gone. He stood alone in his office, feeling empty and cold. She wanted something he couldn't give her. Why couldn't women be like men, he wondered angrily, and just enjoy the present without asking for solemn vows of forever?

He went home in a snit and made supper for himself and the cats. They gave him odd looks, as if they sensed his inner turmoil.

He glared at them. "Don't you start," he muttered. Mee rubbed against his legs. Yow sat watching him with blue accusing eyes. "Great," he muttered. "Now I'm talking to cats!"

He finished his meager supper and tried to get interested in a television program, but his body ached with thoughts of Violet in his arms. He wasn't giving in, though. If she thought she'd get him in front of a minister by holding out physically, she was dead wrong.

He couldn't forget their one time of intimacy, the beauty and joy of possessing her. It had been a perfect physical interlude.

Then he remembered something else he'd tried to forget. They'd had unprotected sex. What if Violet got pregnant?

He sat up straight, his eyes wide and stunned at just the thought. What would they do? He knew for a fact that Violet would never be able to go to a clinic. She'd insist on having the child. He had a horror of children. He'd never gotten over the fact that Shannon had been carrying his child when she died. It had warped his attitude toward pregnancy. He thought of children and he remembered how he felt when he knew his child had died with the woman he loved. It brought back nightmares of pain. Violet wouldn't understand that. She wanted happily ever after. All he wanted was relief from the nagging physical hunger that was taking him over.

But if she was pregnant, he couldn't desert her. Not only would it be unworthy of him as a man, it would reflect badly on his character in a town the size of Jacobsville. The gossip would ruin Violet's reputation and the shame might well kill her mother, considering Mrs. Hardy's fragile health.

He cursed under his breath. If he'd never invited Violet home with him, none of this would ever have happened. Why couldn't he have just let her go and left it at that? He'd landed them in hell with his uncontrollable passion. He couldn't blame that on Violet. All the same, he didn't know what he was going to do.

But he couldn't let her quit. Not until he knew about her condition. He picked up the phone and punched in her number.

VIOLET HAD MANAGED to hide her misery from her mother. She knew that Blake wouldn't mind if she quit again. It would probably be a relief to him. He wanted her and he couldn't have her on his terms. Perhaps it would make things easier if she went back to work for Duke. She should pick up the phone and call him, right now…

The phone rang, making her jump. She picked it up without thinking.

"Hello?" she said.

"Don't quit," Blake said quietly.

Her heart jumped up into her throat. "Excuse me?" she stammered.

"Let's take it one day at a time, Violet. All right?" he asked, and he actually sounded as if he was rethinking the future.

She felt reborn. Her spirit soared. She could hardly contain the happiness she felt. "All right," she said on a soft laugh. "One day at a time!"

# *CHAPTER EIGHT*

For days, Violet and Blake were hesitant around each other. He was the soul of courtesy. He didn't curse or yell. He didn't throw anyone out of the office. He seemed to be a changed man.

Violet loved the tenderness he showed her. He never raised his voice or made sarcastic comments about her work. But he wasn't forward in any way, either, and he didn't touch her. He seemed to be waiting for something, watching. Violet wondered why.

Julie Merrill was arrested for the attempted arson of Libby and Curt Collins's house the following Saturday, and Cash Grier had a big surprise for the city council at the Monday disciplinary hearing. The patrol officers were exonerated and the mayor was embarrassed for trying to force them to retract drunk driving charges against his uncle, State Senator Merrill.

The next day was the primary elections. Calhoun Ballenger won the Democratic nomination away from Senator Merrill in a huge upset, and the mayor lost his job in a special election won by former mayor Eddie Cane. It was a great day for Jacobsville.

But on Wednesday morning, Violet lost her breakfast at the office. Blake, walking past the bathroom, heard her retching. He felt sick himself. Violet was healthy as a horse. If she was throwing up, there could only be one explanation. She had to be pregnant.

It was the end of the world. Blake went around for the rest of the day in a daze. So did Violet. He overheard Mabel and Libby murmuring about Violet's bout of sickness and her upcoming doctor's appointment. They clammed up immediately when Blake walked into the room. It didn't take much to figure out that if Violet was pregnant, her boss was responsible. After all, who else had Violet been crazy about for a year? More importantly, who had she been alone with lately? It didn't take a lot of guesswork.

VIOLET WAS PANIC-STRICKEN after she lost her breakfast. She phoned Dr. Lou Coltrain's office and made an appointment, all too aware that Mabel and Libby could hear her doing it. She told them she thought she had a virus and she was afraid of giving it to her mother. But they were suspicious and it showed.

She drove to Lou's office after work, leaving Libby and Mabel to close up. She swore Dr. Coltrain to secrecy before she even mentioned her symptoms. Lou gave her a worried look as she had her nurse draw blood for a simple pregnancy test.

"One time," Violet choked when Lou gave her the results of the test a few minutes later.

"One time is all it takes," Lou said ruefully. "Oh, Violet."

"What am I going to do?" the younger woman groaned, with her face in her hands. "I can't even step on ants, Lou!"

The other woman patted her shoulder sympathetically. "I'm sure once Blake knows…"

Violet gave her a horrified look.

"Who else could it be?" Lou asked reasonably. "He's the only man you care about, and you spent half a day at his house," she added, smiling ruefully when Violet flushed. "Well, on the positive side, it won't be difficult to find your due date."

"He doesn't want children," Violet said. "He doesn't even want anything permanent. He said so…!"

Lou eased her back down into the chair she'd bolted from. "Don't panic."

"My mother has already had a stroke! She raised me to be good…!"

"People are human," Lou interrupted. "Your mother isn't going to disown you or throw you out into the street."

"Everyone will know," Violet groaned. She drew in a shaky breath. "I could move up to San Antonio," she began.

"That would make it even worse," Lou assured her. "And leave Blake to face the music all alone." She pursed her lips and her dark eyes flashed. "Maybe that's not such a bad thing. I thought better of him. He's intelligent enough to know about using protection. He couldn't have thought you were experienced!"

The flush got worse. "Am I wearing a sign?"

"It's a small town," Lou pointed out. "You aren't promiscuous."

Violet drew in another breath. "I don't know what to do."

"Go home and eat healthy. I'll prescribe vitamins.

You need to be in the care of a good OB/GYN specialist as well. I know one in Victoria I can send you to," she added when Violet looked even more terrified. "She's discreet."

Violet ground her teeth together. "This isn't how I planned my life."

"Life is what happens when you make other plans," Lou quoted. She frowned. "I don't remember who said that, but it's absolutely true." She gave Violet a long, smiling look. "You'll make a wonderful mother."

A mother! In the terror of the moment, Violet had lost track of things. But now she realized that there would be a miniature version of herself or Blake. She felt…odd. Her hands went to her flat stomach in wonder. There was a baby inside her!

"Now you're getting the picture." Lou laughed. "There's nothing quite like the feeling a woman gets when she realizes there's a tiny life inside her body. When I knew I was pregnant, I could hardly believe it," she added. "I was excited, and then afraid, and then I walked around in a daze of daydreams." Her eyes misted. "It was the happiest nine months of my life. I can hardly wait to do it all over again, but we wanted to wait until our little boy was older. It's hard to handle a baby and a toddler and a profession, all at the same time."

Violet smiled, feeling torn by emotions. "I've always wanted children. I just hoped…well, I'd have liked being married."

"Tell Blake and you will be," Lou suggested.

Violet shook her head. "I can't tell him. Not now. Maybe not ever."

"He has an obligation to help support his child, Violet," Lou said firmly. "You didn't get pregnant all by yourself. As for keeping it from him, that isn't going to be possible. Not in a town this small. For one thing," she said, "when you get this prescription filled, everybody in the pharmacy is going to know what's going on," she added, writing it out. "It's for prenatal vitamins."

Violet had that base covered, at least. "I'll drive up to Victoria and get it filled," she said doggedly.

"All right, ostrich, hide your head in the sand while you can," Lou said amusedly.

"I can do this," she said firmly.

"Sure you can," Lou humored her. She handed Violet the prescription. "No heavy lifting for the first trimester. And get plenty of sleep."

"Plenty of sleep. Right," Violet muttered, foreseeing sleeplessness that might never end, from worrying about her condition and her mother's health.

Lou patted her shoulder. "You won't believe me, but in five or six months, you're going to look back on this day and smile."

"If I were a gambler, I'd take you up on that," Violet said heavily. "But thanks, Dr. Lou."

Lou watched her go with worried eyes that Violet didn't see. She wondered how in the world Violet was going to manage.

BLAKE KNEW THAT Violet had been to see Lou Coltrain because he'd seen her coming out of Lou's office on his way home from work. The visit, combined with the hunted look on Violet's face when she came in to work the next day, told the whole story. He cursed himself for what he'd done to them both. If he'd kept his head, if he'd used protection, if, if, if…! Now he was going to be a father and he had to marry the mother of his child or disgrace himself and Mrs. Hardy as well as Violet. He hated the whole idea of giving up his freedom. He hated the idea of a child in his life. He wasn't family man material.

But he was a responsible man and he had a conscience. He was going to have to act. He didn't want Violet doing something desperate.

If he told her that he knew about her condition, she'd know that he was asking her to marry him out of duty and she'd refuse. So he had to hide his real feelings and pretend to have a change of heart while there was still time. He had a poker face. He could pull it off. After all, what choice did he have?

When it was quitting time, he went out to the main office. "Violet, how about a cup of coffee and a steak and salad at Barbara's Café?" he asked carelessly. "You can take a salad home to your mother."

Libby and Mabel hid delighted smiles, said their good-nights, and left at once to give the couple some privacy.

Violet stared at her boss curiously. "Supper? With you?" she stammered.

He forced a smile. "Supper with me. Are you game?"

"People will talk."

He shrugged. "So?"

She felt a little better. At least he liked her enough that he wasn't backing away from gossip. Maybe there was a little hope for the future after all. She smiled. "I'd love to!"

"Good. Call your mother and we'll walk over to Barbara's after we lock up."

"I'll do it right now!"

BARBARA SERVED THREE meals a day, and her café was always crowded after quitting time. Today was no exception. When Violet walked in with Blake Kemp, conversation muted at once and all eyes turned toward the couple in the buffet line.

They chose steaks and salads, and Violet placed an order to go for her mother. But she insisted on paying for her own order, to Blake's dismay.

"Talk about independent women," Blake murmured dryly as they sat down to eat.

"Mama raised me that way," Violet said simply, smiling. "She said we need to depend on ourselves and not impose on other people."

"I never thought of steak as an imposition," he mused.

She laughed. "Thanks for the offer, anyway," she replied.

He finished his salad in short order and started on his steak. He didn't use condiments. He noticed that Violet didn't, either.

"What sort of music do you like?" he asked abruptly.

She hesitated with a piece of steak halfway to her mouth. "I like country-western and classical. And some hard rock," she added impishly.

He laughed. "Actually, so do I."

"Do you like to read?"

He nodded. "I like ancient history and biographies."

She smiled sheepishly. "I like women's fiction and books about gardening and gourmet cooking."

He searched her eyes. "Your mother said you like astronomy."

"I do," she agreed. "But I can't afford a telescope."

He leaned forward. "I have a twelve-inch Schmidt-Cassegrain."

That was an expensive composite telescope, part refractor and part reflector. She'd dreamed of owning something so large and efficient. She gasped. "You do?"

He laughed. "I spend a lot of time outside at night. Since I live so far out of town, I don't have problems with light pollution."

"I'll bet you can see the craters on the moon," she sighed.

"I can see inside them," he corrected.

She whistled softly. "I'd love to look through it."

"We can arrange that. Think you could get used to two warlike Siamese cats?"

"I like Mee and Yow," she replied, curious.

He stared down at his plate. "I've been giving a lot of thought to our situation," he said finally. "Since you left and went to work for Wright, my priorities have changed. I'm not as happy being alone as I used to be."

She put down her fork and sat just staring at him. Her heart was beating her to death. Could he mean…?

He lifted his eyes to hers. "I said that I wasn't a marrying man. And at the time, I believed it. But I like having you around." His gaze fell to her mouth and his eyes darkened. "In fact, I'd like having you around more than just at work."

"I don't understand," she faltered.

He reached for her hand and curled her fingers into his. He looked into her blue eyes and felt as if he were drowning. "I think we might get engaged," he said, trying to find the right words and failing miserably.

"You and me?" she exclaimed.

"You and me," he agreed. He slid his fingers over hers. "Violet, we have a lot in common. I think we'll find a lot more as we go along." His voice lowered. "And physically, there's no question of compatibility."

She flushed softly. "But, you said you didn't ever want to get married, and that you'd never want children…"

"A man says a lot of stupid things when he's trying to hold on to a comfortable routine, Violet," he replied. "I'm a loner. It's been hard for me to even think about changing my life, in any way."

"You don't love me, though," she blurted out.

He couldn't pretend to. It would look like a lie. Violet was perceptive. His fingers curled around hers. "Friendship and affection can lead to it," he said gently. "I can't give you any guarantees about happily ever after. But I can promise you affection and companionship and respect. The rest will fall into place. I know it will. Give it a chance. Say yes."

She hesitated. It didn't sound genuine. He wasn't pretending undying love, but he wasn't promising much. She could get companionship and affection from a dog or a cat. What she wanted from Blake was much more. What sort of marriage would it be if he didn't love her, as she loved him? He obviously enjoyed her physically, but everybody said that passion wore itself out eventually. After it was gone, what would Blake have left if he didn't love her as well as want her?

"You're thinking it to death," he accused. "Listen to me. I'm tired of living alone. I'm willing to take a chance if you are. If things don't work out, it's no problem. We'll go our separate ways." He was already thinking ahead; if she turned out not to be pregnant, there was no reason to think he'd have to stay married to her. But he wasn't about to admit that.

"You mean, we'd get a divorce," she said.

He shrugged. "Sometimes things don't work out. I'm not saying I think we wouldn't make it, Violet. I'm offering you a way out, just in case."

"Isn't that sort of like having a fire engine stand by in case there's ever a fire?" she fished.

He chuckled. "No. It's not." He studied her warmly. "Come on. Give in. You can have any sort of engagement ring you like, and I'll even let you sign an iron-clad agreement that you'll never leave me to work for anyone else ever again."

"Why would I sign such an agreement?" she exclaimed.

"For my peace of mind, of course," he told her dryly. "You'd want me to be happy, wouldn't you?"

She lost her apprehension and laughed with him. "That's awful."

"Give me time. I'll get even worse with age," he promised.

"What a horrible thought!"

"I'll promise not to throw dictionaries at you," he added.

"You've never thrown one at me," she recalled. She hesitated. "You didn't throw one at Jessie?"

"It was a thin one," he assured her. "Paperback, and abridged."

She burst out laughing. "No wonder she quit!"

"Oh, that wasn't about the dictionary," he said easily. "That was after I poured coffee over a brief she typed."

She gaped at him, waiting for an explanation.

"It had two spelling errors per line. I wanted to make sure she knew to redo it."

"You couldn't have just asked?"

"Too demeaning," he said. "My way worked much better."

"Your way made her quit!"

"So you could come back," he pointed out. "She wouldn't have quit if I'd just asked her to retype the brief, would she?"

She really liked him. It was surprising how comfortable she felt with him, now, even though he excited her almost beyond bearing. It would be taking a chance, she supposed, to marry him. But she didn't have enough willpower to refuse. Perhaps she could teach him to love her, if she worked at it. At the moment, she felt as if she could do anything. Her heart was soaring with delight.

Her free hand covered his. "I must save other women from you," she said facetiously. "So I suppose I'll have to marry you, after all."

He felt funny in the pit of his stomach. He was willing to marry her out of a sense of duty, although she wouldn't know it. But when she agreed to it, he felt suddenly lighter than air. He felt like the luckiest man alive. That was absurd. He didn't love her. He wanted her. He remembered suddenly the feel of her eager, untried body under his on the living room carpet and his cheeks reflected a ruddy color.

"What is it?" she asked, curious.

"I was remembering my carpet."

It took a minute, but she remembered, too. Her own face flushed.

He laughed softly, wickedly. "At least, in that department we're very compatible, aren't we, Violet," he taunted.

"Devil!" she accused, glancing around to make sure nobody heard him.

"It's okay. We're alone on the planet," he assured her in a mock whisper. "We're invisible to the rest of humanity. That being the case, how do you feel about linoleum?" he asked with a speculative glance toward the floor.

"Blake Kemp!" she exclaimed, smacking him on the arm.

He grinned at her. It was a genuine smile. He'd never felt such pleasure in a woman's company. Well, not since Shannon. The thought of Shannon wiped the smile from his face and left him haunted.

She saw that, and her face fell. "Something's wrong, isn't it?"

He couldn't tell her the truth. "I was thinking about your mother," he lied.

"Oh. Oh, dear!" She bit her lip. "Blake, I can't leave her alone. I wouldn't dare."

"How would you feel about having someone stay with her, around the clock, if we visited her often?" he asked, looking for compromises.

"I don't know…"

"We won't get married in the next two days," he said with a comforting smile. "We've got plenty of time to work something out."

"Yes," she murmured, but she was wondering what he meant about plenty of time. He didn't sound as if he was expecting to marry her soon.

He let go of her hand and reached for his coffee cup. "Don't borrow worries, Violet," he chided gently. "Everything falls into place, given time."

"I suppose so."

"Want dessert?" he asked.

She grimaced. "Not really," she confessed. "It's too hard to work it off once I gain it." Then she remembered that she was going to be gaining a lot of weight, soon, and her spirits drooped. Her hormones were already reflecting her pregnancy. She was going to go through a lot more changes in the near future.

"I like the way you look," he said, his voice deep and soft.

She lifted worried eyes to his. "Do you, honestly?"

He nodded.

She finished her own coffee, just as Jan, the young woman who worked for Barbara, brought Mrs. Hardy's supper in a bag for Violet.

"Should we tell Mama yet?" she asked Blake.

He hesitated. He was still getting used to the idea of having to get married. He didn't want to tell anybody.

"We could wait, a few days, at least," she suggested.

"Do you want to?" he replied, surprised.

"Yes," she said firmly. "I need time to get used to the idea myself," she confessed with a shy smile. She didn't add that she didn't think he was serious about getting married, and she didn't want her mother to be disappointed in case he found a reason to back out of it. Maybe it had been an impulse, asking her to marry him, and he was already regretting it.

"If that's what you want," he agreed easily.

HE WALKED HER to her car. The parking lot was crowded and he wasn't keen to give local citizens any more reason for gossip. He caught her hand and touched it to his lips. "I'll see you in the morning," he said.

"Right. I enjoyed supper," she added with a shy smile.

"So did I. We'll have to spend more time together. I don't know much about you, do I?" he asked gently.

"I don't know a lot about you, either."

"All the more reason." He checked his watch. "I've got to go. I'm expecting a phone call about a case, at home. It's almost time. See you tomorrow."

"Yes." She would have said more, but he was already walking away. He didn't break stride until he reached his car, and he didn't look back.

Violet watched him drive away with an odd sense of foreboding. He didn't act like a newly engaged man. He didn't act like a man eager to marry, either. She got into her car and drove home. She was more determined than ever not to mention their so-called engagement to her mother.

THE REST OF the week dragged on, with Violet successfully hiding her morning sickness both from her mother and her co-workers, and Blake.

It worried her that Blake didn't announce their engagement, or treat her any differently. She grew depressed, and it showed.

Blake noticed. Friday afternoon, he held Violet back after Mabel and Libby left. He locked the front door, drew her into his office and closed that door, too.

Sometimes, a sacrifice was called for. That was what he told himself when he drew Violet into his arms and bent to kiss her with forced enthusiasm.

But the minute he felt her soft mouth open under his, it stopped being a sacrifice. He lifted her body against his and deepened the kiss. She moaned under his lips. He caught his breath, his arms contracting hungrily. It had been a long, dry spell, and he was reacting badly to it. He felt himself go taut as the kiss moved into deeper, more urgent dimensions.

He bent to lift her, his mind no longer on pretense or fabrication. He had only one thought in his mind, to relieve the need that was drawing his powerful body as tight as a cable.

"Blake, we…shouldn't…" she tried to protest when he laid her out on the sofa and melted down onto her.

His mouth stopped the halfhearted little protest. His hand was busy on fastenings. In seconds, she felt her bare breasts under his equally bare chest. It was so sweet that she couldn't even manage a defense.

One lean leg inserted itself between both of hers under her skirt and he groaned harshly as he dragged her briefs down and found the fastenings of his slacks.

"I'm sorry," he ground out into her mouth as his hips moved down and she felt him in growing intimacy. "I'm sorry, Violet," he groaned, shivering. "I can't hold it…!"

He was genuinely out of control. His body impaled hers with quick, deft movements that should have been uncomfortable. But she was hungry for him, too. She opened her legs with a shaken little sigh and arched her hips to encourage him.

Her hands found their way into his thick, wavy hair and caressed it while he moved on her in intense passion.

In some ways, it was far more exciting than a slow seduction. He was at fever pitch, and she was quickly following him into the fire. It made her feel oddly protective that he was that desperate for her. It was honest. No man could have pretended the passion she felt in him.

"Here," he whispered urgently, shifting her leg with one lean, strong hand. "Lift it over…mine. Hurry. Yes. Yes!"

He pushed down against her, lifting his head so that he could see her face, her eyes. They were open, dark, almost shocked. But her body was encouraging him. He felt her lift to meet each deep, hard thrust. He felt her softness envelop him, cradle him, in that secret warmth. He was flying. He was burning alive. His whole body was one long, throbbing ache.

The tension built to insane proportions. He gasped with every hard thrust, his eyes blazing with desire, his body rigid, shuddering, with it.

His fingers contracted on her soft thigh, pulling her up to him. His teeth clenched as he looked into her wide, shocked eyes.

"I've never watched…with anyone else," he managed in a deep, shaken whisper.

She couldn't answer him. She was spiraling up with
him into some dark, hot pleasure that built and built
with no relief from the tension that strained her muscles and left her shivering with every movement of his
lean hips.

"This is insane," he managed harshly.

Her breasts pushed up against his chest, rubbing
hard against it while her hands went between them and
stroked down to his flat belly.

He groaned harshly and shuddered. "Yes," he
choked. "Yes, do that…do it!"

He arched up, feeling the throbbing pleasure like
a knife in him. He couldn't think. He could barely
breathe. He hoped she was going with him, because
he didn't want to stop!

He cried out, his voice hoarse and strained as his
body convulsed over hers. She watched him, fascinated, feeling the deep throb inside her as he shivered
and stiffened and then, suddenly, collapsed and gasped
for breath.

She was still tingling, but he hadn't given her enough
time. She felt sad; cheated. She didn't want to say anything. At least he needed her, if nothing more.

He managed to steady his breathing, although he was
still fiercely aroused. He lifted his head and looked at
her taut, drawn face. She hadn't gone with him. She
was still hungry.

He felt a tenderness toward her at that minute that
he'd never felt in his life. She wasn't even complaining. She loved him.

Loved him. The thought made him humble. He

reached between them and touched her blatantly, his body controlling her when she jerked in protest.

"Oh, no," he whispered softly, his hand moving gently until he found the place, and the pressure, that made her gasp and lift up. "No, I'm not stopping until you go as high as I did, no matter what it takes." He bent and brushed his mouth slowly over her lips. She shivered as his touch became more insistent. "I'd do anything for you," he whispered into her mouth.

"Blake," she moaned, her fingers gripping his shoulders painfully as the pleasure grew.

"Yes, you're ready now," he whispered, lifting his head to look at her. "I'm going to watch you this time. I like the way your eyes go black when I take you over the edge. I like the way your breasts swell under my mouth. I like feeling you shiver, inside, and ripple around me when you feel that exquisite fulfillment."

The words were as exciting as the way he was touching her. But she was far beyond answering him. Her body was lifting rhythmically, pulsing, her eyes fixed on his face as the pleasure grew so tight that she felt as if she might blow apart from the tension.

Her legs drew apart and she sobbed, her nails biting hard into him as the silvery delight suddenly became dark and throbbing and urgent. "Blake, now," she pleaded, gritting her teeth. Her eyes closed on a wave of pleasure. "Now! Please, please, please...!"

He moved, thrusting deep inside her. The single, hard motion was enough to take her right into the sky. She arched up, shuddering again and again as the ecstasy rippled over her in savage waves. She couldn't see him. She felt him in her body as she exploded like a meteorite.

"Yes," he whispered, unbearably excited by her explosive climax. He ground his teeth together and moved harshly on her, driving for his own fulfillment. They strained together in a hot, fierce silence as the pleasure melted their bodies together for one long, aching instant of perfect communion.

She cried when it was over. The other time it hadn't been so intense, so overwhelming. She cried and couldn't stop.

Blake lifted his damp head and looked at her, his body still trembling faintly from the violence of their coming together.

She opened her eyes and looked into his, and saw something she never expected. She saw utter shock.

# *CHAPTER NINE*

VIOLET STRUGGLED TO BREATHE. She was suddenly aware of the closeness of their bodies joined together so intimately that she could even feel the faint pulsation of him inside her.

He propped himself on his forearms, still fighting to get his breath, and looked into Violet's blue eyes. He'd never felt such a primitive urge to possess a woman, not even Shannon. His feelings for her had been tender, protective, almost passive. He'd never wanted to ravish her. But it was different with Violet. He felt an aching, violent hunger for her. It seemed to grow by the day in strength and power.

But even so, there was tenderness. Her body was soft and pliable, and he breathed in her faint perfume with delight. He traced her eyebrows with a long forefinger, his eyes searching over her face, her throat, her swollen breasts. He touched them tenderly. He thought about his child in her womb and shivered. Would she nurse the baby? he wondered, and he felt suddenly the magic and fear of creation. She was carrying his child. His child…

His breath caught. He bent and touched his mouth to her eyes, closing them tenderly. His fingers speared into her thick hair and tilted her face so that he could close his lips over her mouth.

Violet didn't understand. It wasn't like last time. He was different, suddenly.

He lifted his head and smiled at her. "So much for abstaining until the ceremony," he murmured ruefully.

She flushed.

He laughed softly. "Embarrassed?" he teased. "You shouldn't be. This is one of the most important parts of any marriage. I've seen couples who were compatible in every other way end up in divorce court because one couldn't satisfy the other in bed."

"We don't seem to have that problem," she agreed shyly.

He traced her cheek. "You should have told me that you weren't satisfied," he said softly. "I could see it, fortunately for you. But I don't like thinking you'd let me leave when you were still aching for satisfaction."

She studied him curiously. "I thought men were only concerned with their own pleasure."

"Not this man," he replied, his voice deep and soft. He smiled quizzically. "You enjoy me, don't you?" he asked conversationally. "I'm glad. I thought you might have hang-ups because you'd abstained all your life."

"So did I," she confessed with a soft laugh. "I can't think when we're like this."

"I noticed," he replied. "You dive in headfirst and give it everything you've got." He kissed her softly. "I love the way you are with me, Violet," he said seriously. He drew away slowly, aware of her faint embarrassment. He smiled, because he liked that little sign of insecurity. He liked knowing he was her first man.

She fumbled her clothes back into place. When she finished, he was already opening the door.

"Your mother is going to be worried," he said, glancing at the clock. "You should call her before we leave."

She went to the phone and made the call, inventing a few letters that had to be done after hours. Her mother wasn't worried, and sounded amused. Violet gave Blake a wry glance when she hung up.

"She didn't buy it, did she?" he asked, amused.

"She was young, once."

"So she was." He drew her into his arms and held her for a long moment, his expression worried. He'd only just thought about the baby and how rough he'd been. It was a protective impulse that had just started. She was carrying his child...

"I didn't mean to be that rough," he said suddenly. "I just...lost it when I started kissing you," he confessed quietly. "I didn't hurt you, did I?"

"Of course not," she said, and thought immediately of the baby. Would sex hurt her child? Surely not. Lou had said not to lift. She hadn't said anything about sex. It would be all right. Of course it would.

She followed Blake silently to the front of the office and waited while he turned out the lights and locked up.

"Go straight home," he said softly. "I'll follow you to the turnoff."

"You don't have to do that," she said, surprised by his concern.

"I know. Come on."

He helped her into her car and then got into his. She saw him in her rearview mirror until she turned off on the short road that led to the house she shared with

her mother. She felt warm and secure until she pulled
into her driveway and remembered that he hadn't said
one word about seeing her again during the weekend.

HE DIDN'T CALL, EITHER. She drove up to Victoria Saturday to get her prenatal vitamins and spent the weekend
making an afghan while she kept her mother company.
She'd been sure that Blake would at least phone her.
But he didn't.

She felt oddly used by Sunday evening. He'd needed
her Friday night. It had been sweet, but completely
physical on his side. She could feel that he had no
strong emotional bond with her. It was physical, and
that wasn't going to last. She wondered why he'd asked
her to be engaged to him. He couldn't know she was
pregnant.

At least, that's what she thought until Monday morning. Mabel and Libby were hard at work on documents
for court. Violet had gone back to Blake's office to carry
him a message from a caller, because he was on the
other line and she didn't want to interrupt him in what
might have been a private conversation.

She hesitated outside the door, which had been left
cracked. What she heard caused the written message
to fall to the floor. It broke her heart.

"What else could I do?" he was asking someone in
a heavy, hunted tone. "Her mother is in seriously bad
health and she's already upset about the manner of her
husband's death. If she knew that Violet was pregnant
out of wedlock, it might kill her. Besides all that, it's a
small community and everybody knows us. There's no

way Violet would agree to a termination, so marriage is the only possible resolution."

He paused for several seconds before he spoke again, obviously listening to the person on the other end of the line. "I know," he said, and sounded worn. "I know. But she won't find out. I'll never tell her. I can give her enough to make her happy. She and her mother will never want for anything. After the child is born, we'll make whatever decisions have to be made. I'll make sure she's taken care of, whether or not the marriage continues. Yes. Yes, I know."

Violet bent to pick up the fallen piece of paper. His voice droned on. Whoever he was talking to seemed long-winded.

She turned and went back down the hall to the waiting room. She wasn't thinking clearly at all. It was impossible to make any rational decision until she could sort out her priorities.

She sat down at the computer and put the phone call memo on top of a stack of papers beside the printer tray. She felt numb for the moment. That was good, because she was going to have hysterics when she could reason again.

The front door opened and Libby came in. She glanced at Violet and hesitated.

"Are you okay?" she asked at once. "You're white as a sheet!"

Violet swallowed hard and then swallowed again. "I feel a bit woozy," she confessed, feeling her forehead. "There's some sort of bug going around. I'll bet I've caught it."

"Can I get you anything?" Libby asked, concerned.

"What's wrong?" Blake asked, coming into the room, frowning.

"Violet's feeling ill," Libby said. "Maybe you should go home," she told her co-worker.

"Not a bad idea," Blake agreed. "Do you want me to drive you?" he added.

"I can drive," Violet managed in a husky, soft tone. She didn't meet his eyes. "I'm just a little sick. It's nothing. Really."

Blake helped her up and walked outside with her. "Call me when you get home," he said firmly. He hesitated. "On second thought, I think I should go with you."

"No, there's no need for that," she said at once. "I'm fine," she repeated. "I just need to lie down."

He looked uncertain, and he frowned. "You look pale."

She had a good reason to look pale, but she couldn't tell him what it was. "I'll be fine tomorrow," she replied.

"Violet…" he began softly.

"See you tomorrow, boss man," she interrupted with a faint smile, and walked away.

Blake watched her go with odd twinges of guilt. If he'd been a proper fiancé, he'd have picked her up and carried her to his own car and driven her home. He'd have stayed with her, too. He didn't understand his own nebulous feelings. He'd spent a miserable weekend trying to resolve them. The futility of his situation had made him moody. He resented the knowledge that Violet was pregnant. He resented the trapped feeling he'd had all weekend, which had kept him from phoning her, despite their passionate interlude in the office. The baby was as much his fault as hers, of course, but he wasn't facing facts well. He was being selfish. It was just that his whole life had turned upside down. He was uneasy about being a husband, much less a father. He'd been alone for so long. But that was no reason to let Violet suffer for something that was his own fault. She was sick, and it was his responsibility to take care of her now.

Resolutely, he turned and started toward her car, but it was only in time to see her drive out of the parking lot. She was gone in a heartbeat and he felt like the world's biggest louse. She was sick and he was letting her go home alone.

While he was debating his next step, and reaching into his pocket for his car keys, Libby stepped to the door to tell him he was wanted urgently on the phone. One of his clients had been arrested.

He went back inside, fate having decided the next move for him.

VIOLET CRIED ALL the way home. She'd hoped that Blake really cared about her, that he wanted her for keeps, that he'd be thrilled when he learned about the baby. But he already knew, God knew how, and he wasn't thrilled. He was only marrying her for appearances. He felt trapped. He didn't want Violet in any way at all, except perhaps physically. It was a harsh blow.

She stayed in her car until the tears stopped and she was able to act with some sort of normalcy. She checked her eyes in the mirror to make sure they weren't red. She didn't want to alarm her mother. About one thing

Blake was right: her mother would be horrified if she knew about the baby.

With a forced smile, she called to her mother as she walked in. Mrs. Hardy looked up from her soap opera and waved and smiled absently, going right back to the action on the screen.

It was a reprieve. Violet went into her bedroom and changed into loose jeans and a sweatshirt. She did lay down for a few minutes, certain that her mother wouldn't be moved by a hurricane until her program went off.

She had to make a decision, and quickly. She couldn't hop on a bus and leave town. It would be impossible to move her mother right now, and not only because of the impending legal problems if Janet Collins was ever found and prosecuted for the death of Violet's father. She couldn't leave because her mother wouldn't survive being uprooted. She loved Jacobsville.

That being the case, temporarily Violet had only one possible course of action. She had to get out of Blake's office. She was uneasy about calling Duke Wright back and going to work for him again, but she didn't have a list of potential employers. She wouldn't be able to hide her pregnancy for a long time, but for several weeks at least she wouldn't show. That gave her a little time to make decisions.

She picked up the phone and called her former boss.

MINUTES LATER, SHE walked into the living room. The credits were rolling on Mrs. Hardy's soap opera, and the elderly lady was drying her eyes.

"It was so sad," she told Violet. "Harry had loved

Eunice for years and years, and just when he asked her to marry him, he died of a heart attack."

"Yes, that's sad, all right." She bent and kissed her mother gently. "How are you feeling?"

"I should be asking you that, dear," she replied with a pointed stare. "You look very pale. Are you all right?"

"I think I've picked up a bug," Violet told her. "I came home early. It was okay with the boss man," she added with a forced smile. "I'm going to fix something nice for supper."

"If you like," Mrs. Hardy said, but she looked worried.

Violet wasn't about to tell her the rest, that she'd just agreed to go back to work for Duke Wright. Her former employer hadn't been able to replace her, and he was overjoyed that she was willing to come back.

The only bad thing was that she'd agreed to be in his office Monday. Now she had to tell Blake Kemp that she was leaving again, and why. It made her sick at her stomach even to contemplate it.

BLAKE PHONED HER as soon as he'd pacified his worried client, but Mrs. Hardy answered the phone and said she was sorry, but Violet had gone to bed with a headache. He hung up and went home. But he didn't sleep.

All night long, his selfishness haunted him. Violet was sweet and kind, and she loved him. He could look for the rest of his life and never find a woman half as honest as she was. Ever since she'd come to work for him, she'd nurtured him, cared for him, to the extent that his heart lifted just at the sight of her in his office. Since they'd become intimate, his body ached for her night and day. He knew that he was her first man, that she wanted no one else. And now she was carrying his child under her heart. After all that, he'd proposed to her only because he felt an obligation, not because he wanted her or his child.

Now, with his mind finally functioning again, he realized what a lucky man he was. Why had it taken him so long to know it?

He got up before dawn and made himself a big breakfast. He was going to the most exclusive jewelry store in Jacobs-ville and he was going to buy Violet a diamond so big that it would blind her. Perhaps he'd felt trapped into proposing before, but he was only beginning to see what a wise thing he'd done. He was going to make Violet believe that she was the luckiest woman on earth. He'd bring her flowers, take her to the theater, buy her presents. He laughed at his own lightheartedness. He'd never felt so happy.

VIOLET SAT DOWN at her desk, somber and quiet on the following Monday morning. Her demeanor made her co-workers nervous. Especially when she started cleaning out her desk.

Blake walked in the door, smiling.

Violet looked up at him with an expression he couldn't comprehend.

"What are you doing?" he asked suddenly, when he realized she was putting her things into a cardboard box.

"I'm going back to work for Duke Wright," she said quietly.

He stood completely still, his mind not working at

all as he stared at her, uncomprehending. "You're quitting, again?" he exclaimed.

She glared at him. "Yes, I'm quitting!"

Mabel and Libby exchanged glances and rose at the same time from their desks. "We're going over to the bakery for bear claws!" they announced, and ran for it.

"You just came back to work here!" Blake burst out, barely noticing the front door close behind the two women.

"And I'm just leaving!" she said, slamming down a stapler on the desk.

"Why?"

"Why?" she exclaimed. "How can you ask me that? You're only marrying me because you know about the baby!"

His indrawn breath was all the confirmation she needed.

"Yes," she said coldly, her anguish in her blue eyes as she looked up at him. "I know, Blake. I heard you talking on the phone."

Talking on the phone. Talking… His mouth opened as he met her sad eyes. Dusky color tinted his high cheekbones and his teeth clenched. Damn fate for letting her overhear that indelicate conversation with Dr. Lou Coltrain. Why, why, hadn't he closed the door?

Violet felt her last hope fly away as she saw his guilty expression. He had meant what he said, she thought. He was only marrying her to give their child a name and keep her mother from having a fatal stroke from the shame.

"A lot of marriages start with less than we have," he said after a minute, choosing his words carefully.

"But we'd have been starting without what matters most, Blake," she told him. "Love."

He almost blurted out that she loved him and he knew it. But that would put the last nail in his coffin. He didn't dare say it.

He drew in a long breath. "I won't try to stop you," he said quietly. "If this is what you really want. But I wish you'd reconsider."

She shook her head. "I don't want to stay here with you feeling sorry for me and everybody speculating on why."

"If you leave, you'll hear plenty of speculating," he replied with visible impatience.

She turned back to her desk, feeling empty inside. "I can't stay."

"Well, don't expect me to try to stop you," he replied furiously. "If you'd rather go out there and tell the whole planet that you're pregnant and you won't marry the father of your child, be my guest!"

"And that lovely sentiment is exactly why I'm leaving!" she raged. "You aren't concerned about me, you're concerned about what people think! Your reputation might be ruined, isn't that it? You might lose clients!"

His eyes blazed at her. "What about your mother, Violet?" he shot back, seeing the point hit home as she winced. "How is she going to feel when she finds out?"

She bit her lip. "Mama will understand."

"Think so?" he replied sarcastically. "How about Duke Wright?"

"Excuse me?"

"When you start showing, what is he going to think? And his employees, not to mention his ex-wife!" He glowered at her numb expression. "They'll think it's his!"

She gasped. "They...won't!"

"Bull!"

She glared at him. It was just too much, all at once. She didn't want to believe what he was saying, but it was the truth. Her face grew redder by the minute.

He glared right back. His eyes narrowed on her thickening waist. His expression changed. He'd never thought of children. At least, not since Shannon's death. Now, he began to wonder what a child of his might look like. Would it have dark hair like his and Violet's? Would it have blue eyes? Would it be a boy, or a little girl?

"You look...odd," she commented.

"I was thinking about the baby," he said absently, his eyes still on her waist. "I never really thought about being a father. I've been alone most of my adult life."

"So have I," Violet confessed.

"What do you want?" he asked, meeting her eyes levelly.

She blinked. "I...haven't thought about that. Not much anyway."

He moved a step closer. "What would you like to have?"

She was lost in his eyes. "Little girls are nice," she ventured. "I like to knit and crochet and quilt. I could... teach her."

His breath caught. A little girl. He thought about Rey Hart's little girl. The family had come to see him about a minor legal matter and Celina came with them. She was barely six months old, dark-haired and fascinating to Blake. He'd watched her like a hawk, noting that Rey was a pushover for his daughter, to his wife, Meredith's, amusement. The same could be true of Judd Dunn and Christabel's twins. Everyone in town was indulgently amused at how easily a tough guy like Judd Dunn was reduced to putty when he held those babies.

"Little girls are nice," he agreed softly.

"But I wouldn't mind a boy, either. I like baseball and soccer," she continued. "I can still bat and catch and kick."

He smiled. "So can I."

Her face fell as reality came rushing back. "You don't really want a child, Blake," she said sadly. "You're doing the right thing, offering to marry me. But it wouldn't work."

"You don't know that," he said. "A lot of couples start out with less than we have. I said some stupid things on the phone, and you heard them. But I'm still in the early stages of this. You've had time to think about the baby. I haven't." He stuck his hands in his trouser pockets. "I don't react well to change," he said flatly. "I have to have time to work through what it's going to mean."

Violet sighed worriedly. "Yes, but you'd feel trapped."

He shrugged. "Honestly, maybe I do, a little," he confessed. "But that's temporary. I just need a little time, Violet."

"I know that. So do I." She turned and went back to her desk, to the box she was packing up. "Duke's willing to let me come back. I'm going. In a few weeks, when you know what you want, we can talk."

"In a few weeks, you'll be showing, Violet," he replied shortly.

She turned. "I'm plump," she said without heat. "I won't show for a while."

"Plump." He smiled gently. "Womanly is a better adjective. You look lovely."

Her eyebrows arched.

"I'm not trying to win you over," he said when he saw her expression. "I actually mean it. There are a lot of things about you that I like. Besides, the cats like you."

"Does that win me points?" she ventured.

He chuckled. "They don't like many people. And they attacked a pizza delivery guy one night, one cat climbing up each leg. I have to pay extra now to get him to come back. And I have to promise to lock up Mee and Yow before he pulls into the driveway."

"Ouch."

"It could have been the anchovies, I guess," he said in hindsight. He eyed her quietly. "All right, if you're determined to leave again, I won't stand in the way. But you have to do some thinking yourself. The person we both need to consider is the baby. He, or she, has no choice at all about this."

She grimaced. "I didn't think about…precautions."

He smiled slowly. "We were both a little preoccupied. Both times."

She flushed.

He laughed. "It was very good. I imagine I could search for the rest of my life and never find a woman who suited me so well, physically."

She shrugged. "I thought men could find pleasure with anybody."

"So they say. But I've stopped looking."

The way he was looking at her made her toes curl in her shoes. He seemed to be genuine about his feelings. But he didn't love her. And she did love him. It would be a poor match.

"I plan to call you, often," he said. "I'm giving advance notice. Don't think because I'm agreeing to let you leave, that it means I'm giving up on you. I'm not."

Her eyes widened. "Oh."

"And I'd prefer it if you didn't tell your mother we're having problems," he added. "She doesn't need any more upsets."

"Yes, I know. I won't tell her," she agreed, her head bent over the box.

"There's a rumor that Duke's wife may be coming down with their son, for a quick visit," he added. "It may be for legal reasons, but I think she's heard about the new lady vet who's working for Wright."

Her eyes twinkled. "Jealousy?"

"Who knows? But it would be nice if they could patch up their differences. A child needs two parents," he added firmly, and he wasn't talking just about the Wrights, Violet guessed.

"Yes. A child does need two," she agreed.

He moved forward and picked up the box for her. His eyes were solemn. "I should have gone with you, the afternoon you left sick," he said unexpectedly. "I was going after you when the phone rang and I had to placate a frightened client."

"You were?" she exclaimed, surprised.

"I was. Open the door."

She did, and he followed her through to the outside.

SHE EASED HER mother past the fact that she was going back to work for Duke Wright with a simple explanation—she and Blake weren't getting much work done staring at each other, so she was solving their problem until they got married and settled down.

Her mother gave her an odd look, but she smiled and let it go.

True to his word, Blake called Violet every day. She was shy at first, but he related the day's happenings and the office gossip, and after a couple of days, it was very nice to have someone to talk to who knew everything that was going on around town.

BUT THEN JANET COLLINS was arrested in San Antonio and charged with the murder of Violet's father.

As he had when the autopsy results on Mr. Hardy came in, Blake didn't phone Violet. He went to Duke Wright's house and delivered the news in person.

Violet's expression wasn't easily read. "What now?" she asked slowly, her hands poised over the keyboard of the computer.

"Now she gets formally charged with first degree murder. She'll be arraigned next Monday in San Antonio."

"Should Mother and I go, do you think?" she wondered, hoping not. It would be an ordeal to have to see the woman who'd killed her father.

"That's not necessary," he replied. "Although your

mother will probably have to testify at the trial in order for us to get a conviction."

"What good will that do?" Violet asked miserably. "It will only upset her. She never saw Janet with my father, anyway."

Blake held up a hand. "I'm afraid she did," he replied, watching her expression turn from worry to shock. "She never told you, but she walked in on them in the motel, just before your father collapsed and was taken to the hospital."

"That's where police got the trace evidence that linked her to poison," Violet recalled, still battling shock about her mother's secrecy all these years.

"Yes, and it was fortunate for us that your mother did walk in on them, because she's not only an eyewitness, but her very presence shocked Janet into running for her life. In the process, she left behind the glass the poison was in. Her fingerprints are on it," he added, "although nobody knows that except the crime lab, the police, and me. And now you," he amended. "There's more than enough evidence to convict her of murder. Your mother will provide the motive and eyewitness identification that links Janet to the motel room, your father, his bank account and her penniless state. They'll try to introduce evidence from the previous poisoning of a patient in a nursing home who left her his estate. The old man's son is more than willing to testify."

"You've been busy," she exclaimed, when she realized that he'd been investigating the status of the case against Libby.

"I have, indeed." He slid his lean hands into his

slacks pockets, smiling slowly at Violet in a way that made her toes curl up in her shoes.

Harley Fowler walked in with Duke Wright, talking about a bull Harley's boss, Cy Parks, had bought and sent Harley to transport, when they spotted Blake.

Duke's big fists curled at his sides. "What are you doing in my house?" he demanded of Blake.

Blake glanced at him with a rueful smile. "Just talking to the mother of my child," he said, dropping the bombshell. Just as well, he was thinking, to get two birds with one stone, especially since both men were temporarily single. No way was one of them going to mess around with his Violet.

# CHAPTER TEN

BUT IF BLAKE was feeling smug, Violet was trying to rein in a totally different emotion. She glanced from Harley's amused expression to Duke's shocked one, back to Blake's arrogance.

"How dare you!" she raged at Blake, pushing to her feet.

It was a mistake. She was already weak from the effects of pregnancy and lack of sleep. She started to fall.

Blake moved like greased lightning to catch her as she slumped. He hefted her in his arms and cradled her close, smiling. "It's still the first trimester," he told her gently. "You have to watch making sudden moves like that. You could fall."

She glared at him, furious and with no way to retaliate.

Duke's threatening stance had relaxed. He looked at Blake with conflicting emotions. "It's your baby?" he asked slowly.

Blake gave him a look that could have started a brushfire. "How dare you!" he repeated Violet's own earlier statement, and managed to look indignant as well as angry. "What sort of woman do you think she is?"

Duke cleared his throat. "Sorry."

Violet was trying not to smile. It really wasn't funny. But Blake's defense of her made her feel warm all over.

Blake relaxed a little, but he wasn't putting Violet down. "You have to make sure she gets frequent breaks," he told Duke. "So that she doesn't get too tired. I'll come by at lunchtime every day and take her out to a nice restaurant where she can get plenty of protein." He looked thoughtful. "Nothing with hormones or antibiotics, of course, we have to think of the baby."

"Blake!" Violet gasped, hitting his shoulder.

"And she positively can't work late," Blake added belligerently.

Duke was smiling now, and trying to hide it. "Okay," he said agreeably.

Harley was shell-shocked. He'd really liked Violet. But the way Blake Kemp was looking at her made his feelings almost tangible. And she was pregnant. Harley sighed wistfully. He didn't have a lot of luck getting women, despite his history for helping crack a major drug ring in the area.

Blake looked back down at Violet. "Feel okay now?" he asked softly, and smiled at her.

She wanted to curl into his strong body and kiss him until she stopped aching. That would never do, of course. "I'm much better," she said primly, and shifted to let him know that she wanted to be put down.

He eased her onto her feet. "We have to tell your mother."

"About the baby?" Duke wondered aloud.

"About Janet Collins being arrested in San Antonio," Blake corrected. "She's being charged with first degree murder in the death of Violet's father."

Duke and Harley both let out a whistle. "I'm sorry, Violet," Duke said gently. "If you need to leave early, you can. I'll get a temp out here to fill in for you."

"No, it's better if I don't upset Mama by altering my routine," Violet said. "I'll do it when I get off work."

"I'll go with you," Blake said easily.

She met his eyes and it was like lightning striking. She cleared her throat. "Thanks."

He nodded, lost in that soft, hungry gaze.

Duke whacked Harley with a big fist. "Speaking of routines, we've got cattle to move." He glanced at Blake. "I didn't realize why you were here. Sorry about the reception."

Blake shrugged. "No harm done."

Duke hesitated. "I'll make sure she gets enough breaks," he added. "I remember how my wife was, before our son was born." His face closed up.

"We heard she's coming down for a visit," Blake said, fishing.

Duke's poker face was hard to read. "We're discussing a revision of the custody rights. She's spending a lot of time in the air, and the boy stays in a day care center or with a sitter most of the week." His eyes flashed angrily. "I want to bring him here to live."

"Will she do it, do you think?" Violet asked gently.

"It was a messy divorce," he replied. "But I'm just beginning to realize how much of it was my own fault. I ran her off." He shrugged. "Maybe we can work things out better now." He stared at Blake. "You tried to tell me that, and I punched you."

Blake chuckled. "No harm done. I punched back."

Duke managed a smile. "He was a captain in the

special forces, did you know?" he asked Violet. "He and Cag Hart served together."

"I don't talk about that," Blake said curtly.

"Well, excuse me," Duke said easily. "It wasn't as if you hid in a foxhole and looked for ways out of combat, you know."

Violet was looking at Blake curiously.

Duke grinned. "He'll tell you one day, I suppose," he said. "Or show you the medals, if he's in a good mood."

Blake's eyes were blazing.

"I'm going!" Duke said, palms out. "Come on, Harley, we'll go load up that bull your boss wants."

"Yes, sir," Harley replied, with a wink at Violet. Blake glared at him. He held his palms out, too, chuckling, and followed Duke out the door.

Violet stared after them, then at Blake. He didn't look guilty. He looked smug, standing there with a grin on his face and his hands in his pockets. He wasn't a man who smiled often. He seemed to do it a lot with Violet, she noticed. It eased her embarrassment.

"Now you'll marry me, won't you?" he mused with pursed lips.

Her eyes narrowed as she sat back down. "That wasn't fair."

His eyes twinkled. "Neither is walking around town with my baby under your heart, smiling at other men. Especially Harley Fowler," he added, just to make it clear.

She blinked. "I'm not interested in Harley, that way."

"Well, he's interested in you. Or he was."

"You're not serious."

"I am." The smile faded as he looked at her, and felt

a new and tender protectiveness for her. "You don't have much of a self-image. I've been a bad influence on you, and I haven't given you the support you need. That's going to change."

"Do you feel all right?" she asked warily.

"Maybe Duke isn't the only one who'd done some soul-searching lately," he replied. "I spent weeks putting you down, when you came to work for me. You'd never given me anything except concern and kindness. I resented it. I suppose I knew even that long ago that you were under my skin. I fought it, of course."

"It might just be the baby," she began.

"It might not."

She smiled at him, her eyes softening. "Well, well."

He smiled back. "I'll come by when you get off work and follow you home. We'll both break the news to Mrs. Hardy."

"Mama's tough," she told him. "She seems very frail, but she's got grit."

"So have you. I'm afraid you'll need it, too, when this case goes to trial. It will bring back some painful memories for both of you."

"We faced all that when Daddy died," she said sadly. "Including the loss of his money and our home. At least we'll get some satisfaction at seeing her brought to account for killing him. I hope she'll go to jail."

"So do I, but you can't second-guess a jury. We'll have to supply the prosecutor with as much ammunition as we can get," he added. "I don't want her to slip out of this."

"Neither do I," Violet agreed. She smiled at him. "Thanks."

"I'll see you at five." He winked before he went out the door. Violet sat staring after him, sighing, until she realized that she had work to get done.

MRS. HARDY KNEW something was wrong when she heard two cars pull up in the driveway, and especially when she saw Blake and Violet come in together looking somber.

She sat up straight in her chair and folded her hands on her lap. "Okay. What's going on?"

They both started.

"Two cars? Both of you here just after work? It's something big."

"Well…" Violet began.

Blake moved closer. "They caught Janet Collins. She's in jail in San Antonio."

"Hallelujah!" Mrs. Hardy burst out, grinning.

Blake and Violet exchanged puzzled stares.

"Am I supposed to faint or something?" Mrs. Hardy asked. "Sorry. I'm very happy they got her, and I'll be more than happy to testify to everything I know."

"It will be stressful," Violet began, sitting down on the sofa across from her mother.

"Letting her get away with it would be more stressful." She looked at Blake solemnly. "And speaking of stress, when are you two getting married?"

Blake's lips fell open.

"It had better be soon," she added firmly. "I do not want my daughter waddling down the aisle in maternity clothes."

"Mama!" Violet exclaimed, horrified.

"She thinks I'm deaf," Mrs. Hardy told Blake. "I'd

have to be, not to hear her throwing up every morning." She studied him belligerently. "Well?"

Blake actually laughed. "I just told her new boss about the baby."

"It will be a scandal," Mrs. Hardy wailed.

"It will be a baby," Blake corrected, smiling tenderly at Violet. "With two parents who'll love and want him very much."

"Indeed they will," Violet agreed, smiling back at him.

"So?" Mrs. Hardy persisted. "When?"

"I suppose if we hurry, we can manage next week," Blake said. "Under the circumstances, the sooner the better. But it won't be a big wedding. I've got cases I can't postpone, so there won't be time for a honeymoon just yet."

"Never mind the honeymoon, you have to legalize my grandchild," Mrs. Hardy continued.

"I'll get right to the arrangements," Blake said. "She can go shopping for a dress and I'll arrange the flowers and the reception."

"What about the minister?" Mrs. Hardy asked.

"We could have a civil service," Violet began, worried.

"We will not," Blake interrupted. "We're having a church wedding. Violet," he continued softly when he saw her face, "it's not as if we're being forced into it." He glanced at Mrs. Hardy and cleared his throat. "Well, we're sort of being forced into it, and we did jump the gun. But we're going to have a good marriage, and it needs a good foundation."

"I'd be self-conscious in church," she murmured.

"Even the Puritans crossed the line when they were engaged," Blake said. "God doesn't expect people to be perfect. Luckily for us all."

"I suppose so," Violet replied.

"People will talk," Mrs. Hardy murmured unhappily.

"They're already talking, and smiling, and laughing," Blake told her with a grin. "It's an open secret all over town. The only thing they're curious about is where we're being married."

"I suppose that's the beauty of small towns," Violet agreed, smiling back. "There are no real secrets. We're all family."

"Exactly," Blake replied. "Now to the next important issue." He watched their faces grow attentive. "Who wants Chinese take-out?" he asked, chuckling.

HE WENT TO get the order and brought it back to Mrs. Hardy's. She and Violet already had the places set at the table and they were all hungry. They talked over the potential case against Janet Collins, and the forthcoming wedding. By the time Blake was ready to leave, Mrs. Hardy was smiling and seemed to have no more misgivings.

Violet walked him out to his car, noticing how bright and clear the night sky was. The stars were brilliant. All around there was the fragrance of the old-fashioned roses Mrs. Hardy grew in her small garden.

Mrs. Hardy had already announced her opinion of living with the newlyweds—and especially Blake's delinquent Siamese. She said she'd prefer torture. So they'd compromised on having a nurse-companion stay with her. Blake would call an agency and have them send over people for Mrs. Hardy's approval.

"She'll be much happier here, I know," Violet told him on the porch. "She loves puttering in her roses. We can visit her a lot."

"We'll come over often and bring supper, too," he said. "She'll have someone qualified to look after her, so you don't have to worry about that." He looked at her curiously. "See how easily things work out, when they're meant to happen?"

She nodded. She moved a step closer to him. It was chilly, despite the usually warm spring nights. She looked up at him quietly. "You won't end up resenting the baby because it forced us into marriage?"

He caught her by the waist and pulled her close. "If I didn't care about you, I'd make provisions for you and the baby and we wouldn't get married," he said surprisingly. "I don't like the idea of divorce. It's messy and it leaves a trail of sorrow behind it. You and I have a lot in common. We're basically the same sort of people. We have the same attitudes. We both love children and animals. There's enough there to start with, and a physical compatibility that I never expected in a million years. I want to marry you. The baby is going to be a bonus."

Tears stung her eyes. "You've thought about this a lot."

"I have. That's why I'm sorry you overheard me talking to Dr. Lou Coltrain," he added, identifying his confidant for the first time. "I wasn't choosing my words, and I was confused. I'm not anymore."

"You're sure about that?" she asked gently.

He nodded. He traced a line down her soft cheek.

"I've been alone for a long time. I'm tired of it. I'll adjust, and so will you."

She nodded, but she still looked worried.

"What now?" he asked.

"I'm scared."

"Of getting married?" he asked with a quizzical smile.

"Of the baby," she replied. "They don't come with instruction manuals. They're so tiny, and so fragile..."

He drew her close, laughing softly. "Everybody's afraid of being parents," he said easily. "But babies are tougher than they seem, and there's always Dr. Lou. She's had lots of experience with pregnant people, and she knows a very good obstetrician."

"So I heard."

"Stop worrying," he told her. "We're in this together."

"I suppose we are, at that," she conceded. "We'll have company, too—well, about marriage. Libby and Jordan Powell are getting married."

He grinned. "That's no surprise. He's been in and out of the office several times trying to get her to forgive him."

"Serves him right that she took her time about it," she pointed out. "He and Julie Merrill were a venomous pair. Will Julie go to prison for that arson charge, do you think?"

"She'll probably try to let her employee swing in her place. Don't worry. Chief Grier has another pending charge, one that she won't escape so easily."

"Are you going to tell me what it is?" she fished.

He chuckled. "Not now." He bent and kissed her gently, tugging her close into his arms. They were warm and safe against the chill of the evening. She sighed and kissed him back. His mouth felt as warm as his arms. He was perfect to her.

"Go back in," he said after a minute, running his lean hands over her arms. "You're freezing out here."

"It's supposed to be spring already," she pointed out, shivering.

"If you don't like the weather, wait five minutes," he repeated the standing local joke.

"I believe that." She smiled. "Are we really getting married next week, or was that just to placate Mama?"

"It was to placate me, too," he replied somberly. "I don't want people making snide remarks about you, the way they're talking about Tippy Moore moving in with Chief Grier."

"She was badly hurt," she stated. "Nobody sane is going to think anything of it. Besides, Mrs. Jewell is staying there around the clock. So is Tippy's little brother. There are too many chaperones for much to go on."

"Still, there's talk," he countered. "And they'll have more ammunition with you than they did with Tippy, even considering her miscarriage. It won't take long for someone to notice that you had prenatal vitamins filled up in Victoria."

She gasped. "How did you know that?"

"Lou told me," he said simply, and he smiled. "Well, I am a concerned party," he reminded her. "It's my baby, too." He hesitated, frowning as he looked down at Violet and then at her flat stomach. He felt…odd. He'd never thought about children, except once, long ago, with Shannon. Since then, since the fatal poisoning that had claimed her and her unborn child, he'd been belligerent about not wanting children. But now...

"You're upset," Violet said softly, moving a step closer. "What is it?"

He looked worried. "You know that I've been adamant about never wanting children. I'm not sure you know why."

She'd forgotten that, and it made her heart sink. She knew he was making the most of a bad situation, but she hadn't wanted to remember how he felt about children. "Some men just don't like them," she began.

He put his forefinger over her mouth. "Shannon was pregnant when she died," he said bluntly. "It was my child."

She didn't look shocked, as he'd expected. He frowned.

"Small towns," she explained softly. "Everybody knows everything."

"You knew that?"

She nodded. "I'm sorry it happened that way."

He drew in a long breath. "Yes. So am I. It was a blow that I never quite got over. Every time I saw Julie Merrill, it brought it all back. She killed another human being for no more reason than she wanted to be class president. She didn't even seem to be bothered by it."

"There are people who feel nothing at all," she replied. "I don't understand it, either. But someday, she'll pay for the evil she's done."

"The sooner, the better," he replied.

She reached up and touched his cheek. "Did you know, about the baby?"

His face went taut. "No. I'm not sure she was comfortable telling me about it. I was more adamant in those days about families than I am now, and that's saying something. That made the guilt worse. I wondered if she'd been tormented, thinking I wouldn't want the child. As it is," he added heavily, "it's a moot point. The baby died with her."

"Did Julie know?" she wondered.

"I never asked. It would make no difference now. But I'd still love to see her lining up for payback, for the things she's done. She shouldn't be allowed to get away with it."

"People don't get away with things, Blake," she said, sounding much more mature than she was as she looked up at him. "It may take years, even a lifetime. But eventually people who hurt other people get it back, doubled."

He traced her mouth softly. She made him feel comforted, safe, secure. He was a tough ex-special forces captain and he really did have the medals to prove it. But she melted him. He wondered if she had any idea what he felt for her. It was like what he'd felt for Shannon, years ago. Shannon. He saw her face, in the casket, white and still, her happy blue eyes closed forever. He felt sick.

It wasn't Violet's fault, and when he saw her uncertain stare, he felt worse. He bent and kissed her tenderly. He was anguished, but he didn't want her to think she was responsible for it. He was remembering Shannon, as he'd last seen her, when the light had gone out of the world. He had to get out of here, to have time to himself to come to terms with the past. "Get some rest. I'll phone you tomorrow," he told her.

He'd promised lunch, but she could tell that the discussion about Shannon was wounding him. She only smiled. "I'll look forward to it," she said. "Drive carefully."

He nodded absently, turned, and went to his car. He didn't look back as he drove away.

Violet hesitated before she went back into the house. She wasn't really worried. He wasn't lying about their physical compatibility, and he did seem to want their child. But he hadn't completely settled the past. He needed time, and she was going to give it to him. She wanted him desperately. But he had to want her just as much. He had to let go of the memory of Shannon.

Somehow, she knew, he would manage that.

SHE AND HER mother had an early night. She dreamed about the baby, and awoke feeling flushed and excited about the prospect of bringing a new little life into the world. She didn't care which sex it was. She only wanted a healthy child.

She wondered how she was going to manage to work and raise a family, or if Blake really wanted her to. She liked her job, but she loved the idea of being with her children while they were small, taking them places, reading to them, being with them. Her mother had given up work to be a stay-at-home mother, and she'd never regretted it. Violet knew that she would feel the same. If Blake had been a common laborer, and she had to work to help make their living, she knew she'd cope. But they were in different circumstances. She wanted to try it.

As she walked into Duke Wright's office the next morning, she noticed that her boss was looking uneasy. He glanced up at her approach, and he didn't smile.

"Did I do something wrong?" she asked uneasily.

He shook his head. "Beka's on her way."

"Excuse me?"

"Beka. My...almost ex-wife. And our son."

"Oh." She put down her purse. "Do you need me to do anything?"

"There isn't much to be done," he replied. He moved away from the desk with his hands in his jeans pockets. "I hope she meant what she said on the phone, that she's willing to consider leaving Trent with me."

"Maybe she did," Violet said, trying to be reassuring.

He shrugged. "It's just that she may change her mind if she finds out I've got Delene working here in the lab," he blurted out.

"Does she know Delene?" Violet wanted to know.

He grimaced. "They only met once, at my college reunion. Delene didn't like her, and it showed. See, Beka had barely graduated high school at the time. It was before she went back to college to get her law degree. Delene was in my graduating class—a science major, at that. She always was brainy."

Violet's eyebrows arched. "Well!"

"If she thinks I'm involved with Delene, she may take Trent right back to New York," he said uncomfortably. "What can I do? I can't very well fire the best biologist I've got!"

"You could have Delene go off on a fact-finding trip to Colorado," she suggested.

He looked at her blankly. "Colorado?"

"Isn't the National Cattleman's Association sponsoring some sort of workshop for artificial insemination experts this week?" she wondered.

He pursed his lips. "Why, so they are! There was a brochure about it in the mail last week, remember?"

"Yes, I do." She checked her watch. "You could get her on a plane by noon, if you hurry."

He chuckled. "Violet, you're a wonder!"

"Just a suggestion, boss."

He sighed. "Now, if she'll just go...!"

"Ask her. But you'd better hurry," she pointed out. "You don't have much time."

"I'll do it right now. Uh, those letters on the desk need answering, but I haven't got a minute to dictate them right now. Just catch up herd records, okay?"

"Okay."

He was gone before she had a chance to even answer him. She sat down, amused, and turned on her computer. It was going to be an interesting day.

TWO HOURS LATER, she was deep in a spreadsheet program, listing daily weight gain quotas and measurements from the new bull yearling crop, when the door opened and a tall, blond woman walked in with a small boy in a suit in tow.

She stopped short when she saw Violet at the desk. She frowned, and peered at the woman. "Do I know you?" she asked slowly.

"Are you Mrs. Wright?" Violet replied politely, and then grimaced, because she was about to be the ex-Mrs. And that might not be a politically correct way of addressing her. Violet flushed.

"I'm Beka Wright," the other woman replied tersely. She moved forward, with the little boy. "Are you new?"

"Yes, ma'am," Violet agreed. "I've been working for Mr. Wright on and off for just a few weeks."

"On and off?" Beka queried, while the child at her side fidgeted and leaned against her leg in its elegant black slacks above high heels.

"Mr. Kemp fires me periodically," she replied. "Or I quit. But I'll be going back pretty soon, I guess, because we're sort of engaged," she added quickly, before the other woman could get the wrong idea about her presence here. She smiled shyly.

"Blake Kemp is getting married?" Mrs. Wright asked. She felt her forehead. "I must feel worse than I thought. Or maybe I'm hearing things."

"No, it's true," Violet assured her. "We're sort of having a baby."

"A baby. Now I know I need to sit down." Mrs. Wright plopped into the chair in front of the desk and hoisted the little boy onto her lap. "Where's my husb… my ex-husband?" she corrected curtly.

"I think he drove Miss Crane to the airport," she replied, and then could have bitten her tongue out for mentioning it.

"Delena Crane?" Her face tightened. "What's she doing here?" Beka demanded.

"Uh, she's going to a conference in Colorado. She's a biologist." She didn't dare add that she worked for Mr. Wright, too.

Beka relaxed, but just a little. "Does she spend much time here?" she asked suspiciously.

"Not much, no." Violet hoped she wouldn't get in trouble for lying.

"Good. I mean, I wouldn't want my son around her," Beka qualified. "She has an attitude problem. When will Duke be back?" she continued.

Violet looked past her and grimaced. "Any second," she murmured uncomfortably.

Beka turned around. Duke Wright was standing in the doorway, his hat cocked low over one eye, his face as rigid as steel. And he wasn't smiling.

## CHAPTER ELEVEN

DUKE MOVED FORWARD into the room, his expression changing when he saw the blond-headed little boy in his wife's lap.

"Hey, Trent!" he called, grinning.

"Daddy!" Trent struggled away from his mother and made a beeline to the tall man who waited, stooping, with his arms open. The child launched himself into them and hugged the man for all he was worth. "Daddy, I missed you so much!" he wept. "Why didn't you come to see us in New York?"

Duke looked tormented. He wouldn't meet his wife's eyes. He kissed the little boy. "I'm glad you came to see me," he replied, smiling at the child. He looked up, meeting Beka's dark eyes evenly. "Hello, Beka."

"Hello, Duke," she replied, not quite meeting his accusing gaze.

"I'm sure you have a motel room by now, but I'd love it if you'd let Trent stay here," he said quietly. "I have a live-in housekeeper, Mrs. Holmes, who loves children. She's a wonderful cook."

Beka seemed uncomfortable. "I…there aren't…well, there isn't a motel room vacant in Jacobsville…" She looked up at him.

"You're welcome to stay here, too," he replied. "I just didn't think you'd want to," he added bitterly.

"I can stand it if you can," she told him. "Our suitcases are in the car. I'll just go get them," she said, rising.

"I'll have one of the boys bring them in for you," he returned curtly. "If that's all right," he added unexpectedly, and without antagonism.

Her thin eyebrows arched and she looked shocked. "Yes. That would be fine. Thank you."

"You're welcome." He put Trent down and smiled at him. "Want to come with me? I'm going out to the corral to get one of my cowboys. He's working a new filly on a leading rein."

"What's a filly, Daddy?" he asked.

"A filly is a young female horse," he replied. "She's an Appaloosa. She has striped hooves and spots on her back," he added with a grin.

"I thought you sold all the Appaloosas!" Beka exclaimed.

"Not all of them," he replied. His eyes went over her red silk blouse and down the black slacks to her small feet in high heels. "You're welcome to join us. It's pretty dusty out there," he added.

She moved toward him, a little hesitantly. "Clothes can be cleaned," she said. She took Trent's hand. "I'd like to see her."

Duke's eyes softened and he smiled. "She's a beauty."

Beka smiled back, following the man and the boy out the door.

Violet watched them go with hopeful feelings. She knew it had been a messy divorce, because she'd been working with Blake at the time. Her personal opinion had been that Duke Wright was an overbearing, unreasonable tyrant. She had no sympathy for him at all. A woman who married a man like Duke could expect to be owned like a horse. He never asked anyone else's opinion; he gave his. He threw out orders like a military commander, and the first day Violet met him, she'd have liked to see him upside down in a barrel of dirty water.

But he'd mellowed just recently. It was obvious that he was trying to be polite to his ex-wife, even if it was only to help his case with his son. Delene certainly seemed to like him. She grimaced. When Mrs. Wright found out who the new biologist was, she wasn't going to be smiling. It was going to be an explosion of some magnitude…

BLAKE HAD GONE home in a black mood. Mee and Yow curled up beside him in bed that night and purred while he brooded. He couldn't get that last vision of Shannon out of his mind, lying so still and beautiful in her white coffin. All the long years, he'd wondered if he could have saved her if he'd just agreed to go to the party with her. She'd asked him to, and he'd wanted to go, because even back then he didn't trust Julie Merrill.

But he'd had a court case the following Monday and he'd wanted time to work on his defense. While he was writing up gambits for his opening argument, Shannon was drinking a drug that worked like poison. He hadn't known a thing about it until early the next morning, when her mother had phoned from the hospital to tell him the news.

He'd gone around in a daze for weeks afterward. He hadn't been able to think, much less work. His reserve unit, like Cag Hart's, had been called up in 1991 when Operation Desert Storm sent soldiers to Kuwait to liberate it from invasion. He'd volunteered without a second thought, not at all concerned that he might die.

He'd waded right in with his company, in the thick of the fighting, a captain in a forward unit. During a memorable firefight, he'd propelled a tank into the thick of an enemy position and used it like a battering ram to shut down a machine gun nest that was killing his men. He'd been awarded a Purple Heart, because he'd been wounded in the ensuing firefight, and a Silver Star for gallantry in action. Few people around here knew about it. He didn't talk about his military service. Well, except to Cag Hart, who understood. Cash Grier was rumored to have been in Iraq during the same period, but it was a subject Cash didn't encourage. He was even more reticent than Blake, and that was saying something.

He tossed and turned all night, finally giving in around daylight. He got up and made coffee and toast and brooded at the table. Shannon, the war, all that was in the past. He couldn't go back. For all the wonder he'd felt with her, there had never been the spontaneous rush of passion that he felt when he was with Violet. He and Shannon had loved one another, but with a quieter, less tempestuous love. What he felt with Violet was something else again, a whirlpool of delights that left him breathless even in memory.

He thought about the baby. He wondered if it would look like him or like Violet, if it would be a boy or a girl. He could picture himself with a little girl on his lap, reading her bedtime stories, or with a little boy, showing him the telescope and distant planets, and teaching him about rocks. He loved rocks even more than astronomy. He had samples of crystals and meteorites and fossils and all sorts of minerals. He had a metal detector, and in his spare time he loved wandering around the property with it, looking for metallic meteorites. He'd found several over the years. He'd never told Violet about this odd hobby. He wondered if she liked rocks, too.

He finished his coffee and stretched. The cats sat watching him, puzzled at his change of routine.

"I couldn't sleep. Don't you have bad nights?" he asked them.

They blinked. For all the world, they seemed to be listening. Of course, they seemed to watch television, too. Obviously, his lack of sleep was playing tricks on his mind.

"I'm going to marry Violet," he told them. "And there's going to be a little tiny human being here in a few months. You'll both have to adapt."

They blinked again. But this time they looked at each other and then back at him.

He shook his head. He was doing it again, talking to the cats. Violet and the baby would be good for his mental health. Any day now, he was going to think the cats actually understood him.

He got up and went to the sink. Just as he put his coffee cup and plate under the running water, separate sets of teeth dug into separate ankles.

*"Eyoowch!"* he burst out, and started cursing.

The two cats moved quickly away, in different directions, with their ears back and their tails as rigid as flags. He rubbed the marks, glaring after them.

"I said, you'll have to adapt and I meant it!" he yelled after them.

They walked faster.

He wasn't going to tell Violet about this, he decided as he doctored the small incisions. She'd have him locked up before the wedding!

WHEN BLAKE WENT to pick Violet up at Duke's house for lunch, neither Duke nor his wife and son were around.

"Has she left?" he asked Violet covertly.

She shook her head. "They were stiff and polite at first. Now, they're walking around each other like wrestlers looking for a good hold."

He sighed as he tucked her hand into his and they headed toward his car. "I was afraid it might go like that. People don't really change, you know," he added thoughtfully. "They hide traits that bother potential mates, but bad habits always show up eventually."

She stopped walking and looked up at him with twinkling eyes. "Do tell? And what hideous traits are you hiding from me?"

His own eyes twinkled. He bent down. "I'm a rock fanatic."

Her eyebrows levered up. "You like rock music?"

He shook his head. "I like rocks. Meteorites. Fossils. Crystals. Right now, I'm keen on iron meteorites. I go out looking for them with a metal detector on weekends."

She began to smile. "I've got a box of projectile points in my closet," she said. "I picked them up on my grandfather's farm when I was a little girl. Some are big and some are little. I don't even know much about them, but I treasure them just the same. And I've got quartz crystals of all sorts, from amethyst to rose quartz…!"

He hugged her close, laughing. "Of all the coincidences," he burst out.

She hugged him back. "I can see us now, hiking up a mountain with the baby in a backpack and a metal detector," she chuckled.

He drew away so that he could see her face. "We'll take turns carrying him," he mused. "Or her."

"He feels like a boy," she said. "I don't know why."

He bent and kissed her nose tenderly. "We'll love whatever we get. Maybe he'll like rocks, too. And astronomy."

He took her hand again and led her toward the car. He favored his left leg a little and winced as he moved.

"What's wrong?" she asked immediately. "Did you hurt yourself?"

He paused by the passenger door of his car and studied her.

"Don't you want to tell me?" she persisted when he hesitated.

"You might want me locked up when I tell you," he mused.

"Be daring."

He laughed. "I told the cats we were getting married and expecting an addition to the family. They looked at each other, and at me. One got on either side of me and they bit both ankles at once and flounced off in a huff."

She didn't say anything. She gave him an odd look.

He shrugged. "I told you you'd want me locked up."

"Do they like tuna?"

He shook his head. "Salmon. They're crazy for it."

"I know where we can get some fresh salmon," she murmured dryly.

He pursed his lips thoughtfully. "It might just work."

"Let's see!"

"First thing after lunch," he promised, putting her in the car.

CHIEF GRIER WAS in Barbara's Café when they got there, sitting with a somber Leo Hart. They both looked up when Kemp walked in. Grier motioned to him. He left Violet in line to keep his place and paused by their booth.

"Something's going on, I gather?" he asked.

"Something big," Grier agreed. "Leo's brother Simon got some news about Julie Merrill. Remember the drug lord who tried to set up shop here before I came to work on the force?"

"I do," Blake replied. "He was bad news."

"Well, a female drug lord has replaced him, and we think Julie Merrill is her lieutenant. I've been watching a house out of town on the Victoria road where drug smugglers had a hideout that the DEA busted. There's some new activity. I think Julie's involved, along with some prominent local politicians."

Kemp whistled. "Got her in custody?"

"Chance would be a fine thing," Grier replied. "She made bail and got out, but a couple of days later, she made bush bond." In other words, Blake translated, she skipped town.

"If you need help tracking her down, I know a good P.I."

Grier grinned. "Thanks. But I think my contacts are even better than yours. What I'd like to know from you is something that may be painful," he added, and the smile faded.

"You want to know about Shannon Culbertson," Blake said perceptibly. "Julie put something in her drink and she died. But I could never prove it. I tried, believe me!"

"If you have any notes on the case, I'd appreciate a look at them, if it isn't a confidentiality matter," he added.

"Not at this late date," Blake replied solemnly. "Drop by my office in the morning and I'll have them for you. I'd love nothing better than to see Julie Merrill in stripes."

"That makes two of us," Grier agreed. He glanced at Violet, who was looking at Blake with wide, soft, loving eyes. He grinned. "You've got good taste in women, I might say," he told the other man.

"I do, don't I?" Blake said complacently, smiling at Violet, who blushed.

"I hear she's taking prenatal vitamins," Grier murmured wickedly.

Blake didn't fire from the hip. He actually laughed. "Abundantly," he agreed, "or she goes to sleep in her plate." He glanced from Grier to Leo Hart, who was also grinning. "You can both come to the wedding, if you'd like. We decided on the Methodist church. We're announcing it in the paper. No time for invitations.

Mrs. Hardy has loaded her shotgun and made significant threats."

"As if that would matter to you," Leo chuckled.

Blake smiled. "I never thought I'd get married, much less be a parent. But it all seems to be falling into place naturally." He eyed Grier. "I hear you're already taking Tippy's brother fishing with you."

"He's quite a boy, Rory is," Grier agreed. "I like having him around. I like having her around, too."

"So?" Blake prompted.

Grier just shrugged. "We're waiting for a major complication to resolve itself."

"I heard the kidnapper was still on the loose," Blake told him. "You don't think he'd be crazy enough to show up here in town?"

Grier met his eyes evenly. "Without Tippy, there's no case. Kidnapping is a federal offense. It means hard time. The guy is a professional contract killer. I don't have any illusions about Tippy being safe just because she's in my house. I sleep light these days."

Blake nodded. "I hope it works out."

"It will, one way or another," Grier said grimly.

"What about your cats?" Leo asked curiously.

Blake blinked. "What?"

"We've heard some strange stories from people who visited you at home," Leo replied with a chuckle. "They say most all of them came out running."

"And bleeding," Grier added wickedly.

"A few scratches here and there, that's all."

"Yes, but Violet will be living with them."

"She has some ideas that involve fresh salmon," Blake replied, grinning. "They do take bribes."

"Good luck," Grier said.

"Amen," Leo added.

Blake just smiled and went back to Violet.

HE TOLD HER on the way out of town about Julie Merrill jumping bail, and about the evidence Grier wanted to see.

She looked at him with soft compassion. "It's hard for you to look back, isn't it?" she asked gently. "Shannon meant a lot to you."

He nodded solemnly. "She did." His head turned toward her. "But the past is gone, Violet. I've made mistakes, trying to live in it. She was a kind woman. She wouldn't have wanted me to be bitter."

She smiled. "You were just hurt," she said. "It takes a lot of time to get over losing people. I know. I still miss Daddy."

"I miss both of my parents," he said unexpectedly. "My father died when I was little. I took care of my mother all the way through school. She died of a stroke the week after I graduated from law school. Shannon was there, with food and comfort, kindness. I was almost out of my mind with grief already. Then, just a few months later, I lost Shannon, too." He glanced at Violet. "I've been hiding, I suppose."

"It isn't hard to see why." She leaned back against the seat. "Leo looks different."

"He's married," he said, laughing. "He's definitely mellowed. All the Hart boys have. It's just amazing. I'd have bet real money that they'd end up crusty old bachelors."

"They said the same thing about the Tremayne brothers," she pointed out. "And look at them!"

He smiled. "Marc Brannon, Judd Dunn, there are two other bachelors I'd have bet on staying single." He shook his head. "Now Cash Grier's about to fall."

"You think Tippy could settle down in a small town?" she asked, aghast.

"You've seen them together. What do you think?"

She sighed. "I think they're crazy about each other, but neither of them is willing to admit it. She's been through a lot, including the miscarriage. That must have been tough. What if the tabloids find out she's here and start on her again?"

His eyes twinkled. "Oh, I think Cash can handle the press."

"Matt Caldwell certainly did, they say, when a reporter targeted his Leslie some years ago, before they were married."

"This is not a good place for outsiders if they ruffle feelings," Blake reminded her.

"I'm glad. I like living here." She sighed worriedly. "Blake, they won't try to make some big news story out of Janet Collins when her trial comes up, will they? She poisoned Daddy and was suspected in still another murder in a nursing home. There aren't that many women serial killers. What if the press comes in here and starts making snacks out of me and Mama?"

"Not a chance," he promised.

His tone was curious. She glanced up at him. "Do you know something I don't?" she asked slowly.

"Let's just say, I'm working on something," he replied. He stopped at the town's only fish market and parked the car. "Fresh salmon," he said as he turned off the engine with a grin. "Let's hope they take bribes!"

THE CATS WERE both sitting in the front window when the car drove up.

"That's odd," Blake remarked. "They never wait for me like that unless it's grocery day."

"Maybe they smell the salmon!" she teased.

He made a face. "Fat chance."

Violet picked up the fish and they both went in the front door together.

"Hi, guys," Violet said, wafting the brown-wrapped fish above their heads. "Hungry?"

They both started yowling, sounding for all the world like crying babies as they stood on their hind legs trying to swat the package out of her hands.

"That has to be a good sign," Violet told him.

"We'll see. Come on, girls," he called to them, leading Violet through the living room and into the spacious kitchen. "I'll get their bowls."

He pulled them out of the dishwasher and settled them on the counter. Violet opened the brown package and split the salmon down the middle. The cats were all but climbing the cabinet.

"Here you go, babies," she said softly, and put the fish down.

They both glanced at her with big blue eyes, but only for a minute. They started eating and growling at the same time, determined that each was going to get her own fair share without having her bowl raided.

Blake and Violet moved away while they ate, watching them. It didn't take long. The cats licked their bowls clean and then started bathing themselves. They ignored the humans completely.

"Ungrateful wretches." Blake laughed. He picked up the bowls and put them in the sink, shaking his head.

But Violet had more confidence than before, and she squatted down next to them on the floor. "Beautiful babies," she said softly, smiling. "I'll make sure you have salmon any time you want it."

They stopped bathing and looked at her with those piercing blue eyes.

"Honest," she added.

Mee called to her, got up, and rubbed against her knees. Yow blinked, hesitated, then moved closer, too, but stopped at one brief head-butt against her thigh.

She looked up at Blake. "It's a start," she said optimistically.

He grinned from ear to ear.

THEY WENT TOGETHER to Libby Collins's wedding. She married Jordan Powell in a beautiful church service, with most of the leading citizens of Jacobsville for witnesses. As her brother Curt led her down the aisle, she glanced at Violet, sitting so close beside Blake Kemp, and grinned. They grinned back.

It was a nice ceremony, brief but poignant, and a reception was held afterwards in Barbara's Café. Tippy and Cash waved to them from across the room. So did the Ballengers. Calhoun was euphoric after having soundly beaten old Senator Merrill for the Democratic nomination for state senate in his district. His wife, Abby, was there, too, clinging to her husband's arm. After three children, all boys, they were still very close. Justin Ballenger attended as well, with his Shelby. Like Calhoun and Abby, they had three sons of their own. Shelby was a direct descendant of Big John Jacobs, who'd founded Jacobsville and Jacobs County.

Violet had felt uncomfortable around all the bigwigs at first, but she learned very quickly that they were just ordinary people, and they didn't put on airs. She liked them. It wasn't going to be hard to fit in here.

But she worried about the case against Janet Collins. There was DNA evidence, of course, but there were ways a good defense attorney could twist the truth. She didn't want the woman to get away with what she'd done to Violet's father.

Blake noticed her distracted expression. "Cheer up," he whispered. "People will think it's a wake instead of a wedding!"

She moved, and smiled up at him, clutching her small cup of punch. "Sorry. I was thinking about Mrs. Collins."

He moved closer, tilting her chin up to his blue gray eyes. "Let me worry about it," he said softly. "I promise you, she's not going to get away with it."

She sighed. "Okay, boss man," she said. She stood on tiptoe and touched her lips to his hard mouth. "Whatever you say."

He smiled, pulling her close to kiss her back, very emphatically. When he drew away he was aware of a faint silence around them.

He looked around and discovered that everyone was watching them instead of the newlyweds.

"Better get a ring on her finger by sundown," Cash

Grier whispered as he walked by. "Or you may be the next tabloid centerpiece."

Blake grinned at him. "The wedding's next week," he told the police chief. "You're invited."

"I'll bring my whole department," Cash promised.

Blake's eyebrows arched. "All of it?"

Cash nodded thoughtfully. "And I'll have something very nice planned for your wedding day," he added.

Marc Brannon overheard him and drew his very pregnant wife, Josie, closer. "Run for the border," he advised Blake and Violet. "He was waiting for us at my ranch after our wedding, with half the county law enforcement personnel, and I had to threaten him with a shotgun to get rid of him!"

Grier glared at him. "I did not have half of them." He shifted. "Some people I called refused to come. They didn't want to impose on newlyweds. Can you believe that?"

"We're leaving town right after our wedding," Blake promised Violet at once.

Grier really glared then, at Blake and the Brannons. "Hmmmph!" he muttered. "Some people have no sense of humor."

"Some people have no sense of privacy," Marc shot right back.

Grier glanced at Josie and grinned. "Didn't I warn you about him?" He pointed at Marc. "And you didn't listen!"

Josie leaned closer to her husband's tall frame. "Oh, he's not so bad," she said complacently. "In fact, neither are you," she added to Cash, "despite your far-reaching reputation."

"What reputation?" Tippy Moore asked with a soft laugh as she walked to Cash and was gathered against him gently. "He's as pure as the driven snow," she drawled with a mischievous flash of green eyes.

Cash bent and kissed the tip of her nose. "Pest."

She smiled back at him and it was like fireworks. "And I planned to make you beef Stroganoff tonight," she said. "But here you are calling me names…"

"Nice pest," Cash qualified.

She shrugged. "Okay. I guess I can live with that. Good to see you," she added to the others as she let Cash lead her away to the punch. She still had plenty of cuts on her pretty face, and some bruises, and she was a little shaky. But what she'd lived through in New York had gained her a lot of sympathy around Jacobsville. It was pretty much an open secret how Cash felt about her, and vice versa.

"There goes a prospective bride and groom, or I miss my guess," Marc Brannon mused.

"Same here," Blake replied. He curled Violet's fingers into his. "I suppose it's contagious," he added, looking warmly into her eyes.

"What about your cat harem?" Marc asked.

"They take bribes," Violet said before Blake could speak. "Fresh salmon."

"Way to go, Violet," Josie chuckled. "Leave it to a woman to find a way around a difficult situation."

"She'd know," Marc replied, smiling at his wife. "She's just joined the local D.A.'s office as a prosecutor. After the baby comes, that is."

"What do you want?" Blake asked curiously.

"Well, we already have a little boy. I'd love a daughter next. But we'll settle for whatever we get," Josie said warmly, smiling up at her husband, who readily agreed. "I can hardly wait."

Blake looked down at Violet with a softness in his eyes that made her heart float. "Neither can I," he said gently.

Violet blushed scarlet and nuzzled her cheek against his chest.

"We're expecting, too," Blake told the Brannons with a quiet smile. "It's going to be a wonderful year."

"You can say that again," Marc replied. "Congratulations."

"You, too."

Violet closed her eyes as the conversation drifted away. She wondered if she could die of happiness.

## CHAPTER TWELVE

VIOLET WAS NERVOUSLY waiting in the hall for the organ to sound. Her mother was in the front pew. Half of Jacobsville was seated in the rest of the pews. She noticed that big Cag Hart was acting as best man for her husband-to-be. She had nobody to give her away. But it was something of an archaic custom, she tried to remind herself. She wasn't being given or sold to any man, regardless of how much she loved him.

She plucked nervously at the waistline of her beautiful white satin gown, hoping the slight swell didn't show too much. It wouldn't matter a lot. Most people already knew she was pregnant. She smiled. She and Blake would love their child. She had no more doubts about him, or herself. It would work out.

The organ sounded and she jerked her mind back to the occasion, tightening her grip on her bouquet of baby's breath, white roses, and lily of the valley. She took a deep breath and stepped out on her right foot, just as a big, gentle hand caught her left hand and tucked it into his elbow.

She looked up, startled, into twinkling green eyes.

"I'm not quite old enough to be your father," Cy Parks said in a loud whisper, "but Blake said you wouldn't mind."

She grinned up at him. "I won't mind at all, Mr. Parks. Thank you!"

"That's okay. You can do the same for me one day," he said, tongue-in-cheek.

She started giggling and only stopped when "The Wedding March" was belted out on the piano.

"Straight faces, now," Cy murmured.

"You bet!" she agreed.

They walked down the aisle, to where Blake was waiting with his heart in his eyes when he saw Violet in that vision of white lace and satin, the veil delicately covering her pretty face. He thought his heart might burst.

The ceremony was brief, poignant, and unforgettable. Blake lifted the veil to kiss his bride, and Violet's blue eyes brimmed over with tears as she returned the kiss with pure joy.

They walked out of the church into a soft rain of congratulations, confetti and rice.

"The rice is for fertility," Libby Collins whispered loudly.

"It worked!" Blake exclaimed in a stage whisper, with wicked eyes.

Violet whacked him with her bouquet and winked at Libby.

They climbed into the waiting limousine and sped away to Blake's house, to change clothes before the reception.

"WHAT A GOOD thing the reception isn't for another hour," Blake groaned as he kissed Violet hungrily in the big king-size bed.

"And you think we'll still make it in time? Optimist!" Violet panted, lifting up to the hard, measured thrust of his body.

He laughed, but the sensations caught him unaware and he arched, groaning with pleasure so deep it felt like pain.

Violet went with him, flying up into the sky like a rocket, exploding in sudden, fierce delight.

He increased the rhythm, and the pressure, and seconds later, he was right there with her, burning up in a fiery satisfaction that was vaguely shocking in its length. It seemed to go on forever.

When he was finally able to breathe again, he was wet with sweat and shaking all over. So was Violet.

"Wow," she whispered reverently as she met his eyes.

He nodded, bending to kiss her delicately. "See what a week of abstinence does to a normal man?" he murmured against her swollen lips.

"Want me to lock the bedroom door for a week to make it better…?" She jumped and cried out as he pinched her bottom.

He wrinkled his nose at her. "You lock it, I'll break it down," he challenged. "I hate abstinence!"

She wreathed her arms around his neck and smiled contentedly, although her heartbeat was still shaking her. She was wet with sweat, too, and working just to breathe.

"It's better every time," she said, dazed.

"I improve with practice," he informed her.

She grinned and slid her legs around his. "Do you, really? Let's see…!"

THEY KNEW THE party was already underway before they got out of the shower. They dressed quickly in the clothing they'd laid out for the reception, a lacy pink dress for Violet and slacks with a white shirt, tie, and sports coat for Blake.

They were barely dressed, still smiling at each other in a daze of pleasure, when there was a loud rap on the front door.

They stared at each other. "Are we expecting anybody?" Blake asked curiously.

"I don't think so."

They went together to the front door and opened it.

Outside was most of the Jacobsville Police Department, with Chief Cash Grier, in uniform, leading the rest. He had a paper in his hand and he was grinning mischievously.

"Lady and gentleman," he began, "your friends in the Jacobsville Police Department would like to congratulate you on your recent nuptials and remind you that if you are ever in need of assistance, we are only as far away as your telephone. We have…"

"I'll call the governor!" Blake began, interrupting the speech.

Grier glared at him. "I have six pages to go."

"I have ten pages," Assistant Chief Judd Dunn announced, displaying them.

"I have a loaded shotgun," Blake told him.

Judd and Cash looked at each other speculatively. "How many years could he get if he pointed it at us?" Judd wondered aloud.

"That wouldn't be nice, on his wedding day," Cash agreed, but he gave Blake a rakish grin.

Blake's eyes narrowed. "Trespassing on private property," he began, "creating a public nuisance, terroristic threats and acts…"

"I am not a terrorist!" Cash informed him.

"But you are a public nuisance," Judd told Cash.

"Me?" Cash exclaimed.

Officer Dana Hall cleared her throat and elbowed both superior officers out of her way. She was holding a cake.

"This is the wedding cake from the reception," she told them, giving it to Violet. "I'm really sorry, but it was all we were able to save."

Violet was staring at her blankly.

Officer Hall cleared her throat. "Somebody spiked the punch. Harden and Evan Tremayne drank it before they realized. One of the local cattlemen also drank some and made a very loud, unpleasant remark about lunatics who raised organic cattle just as Cy Parks walked in with J. D. Langley."

Cash cleared his throat. "Judd and I had to, sort of, shut down your wedding reception and lock up a few of your guests. But we saved your cake. There was some punch, too, but Officer Palmer there—" he noted a tall, handsome blond officer with odd-colored highlights in his hair "—is wearing it."

Blake burst out laughing. Only in Jacobsville, he was thinking.

"Anyway, you're leaving right away on your honeymoon, right?" Judd asked them. "So you can get all the sandwiches and punch you want where you're going."

"Your jail is full, I guess?" Violet teased.

"Uh, yes it is, and he—" Cash indicated Blake "—

represents Cy Parks and the Tremaynes. They want him to come down and get them out."

"That explains the cake," Blake told Violet.

She grinned at him. "We can detour through town on the way to the airport, can't we? After all, Mr. Parks did give me away."

"Good point." He sighed. "Okay, tell them I'm on the way. And thanks for the cake."

"And the punch," Violet said with a glance at Palmer, who grinned back.

The police force got into its cars and left. Violet put the cake in the freezer. The house was quiet without Mee and Yow, who were being boarded for the honeymoon. Mrs. Hardy was staying at her house with a nurse.

"Would you like your wedding present now?" Blake asked as they were turning off the lights.

She turned and looked at him. "What is it?" she asked, surprised.

He pulled her close and kissed her. "Janet Collins cut a deal with the San Antonio D.A. She pled guilty for a reduced sentence, so there won't be a trial. You and your mother won't have the stress of a court trial."

"Oh, Blake!" She kissed him hungrily. "You had something to do with that, didn't you?"

He nodded, smiling. "I've been working on it for two weeks. It came through yesterday. I saved the news for today."

"Thank you," she said, and meant it fervently. She'd dreaded the idea of dredging the painful episode in public.

"I have to take care of my best girl," he whispered.

"And the mother of my child." His big hand rested softly on her slightly swollen belly. "You were the most beautiful bride who ever walked down an aisle."

"And you were the handsomest groom." She kissed him back. "Well, shall we go and rescue some prominent local citizens on our way out of town?"

"Works for me," he chuckled.

They walked to the car hand in hand.

"Today is the first day of the rest of our lives," Blake mused.

"The rest of those days will be wonderful," she said softly.

They were.

* * * * *

# SPECIAL EXCERPT FROM

## HQN™

*Garrett Sterling has a second chance at love
with the woman he could never forget.
Can he keep both of them alive long enough
to see if their relationship has a future?*

*Read on for a sneak preview of*
Luck of the Draw, *the second book in the
Sterling's Montana series by New York Times
and USA TODAY bestselling author B.J. Daniels.*

Garrett Sterling brought his horse up short as something across the deep ravine caught his eye. A fierce wind swayed the towering pines against the mountainside as he dug out his binoculars. He could smell the rain in the air. Dark clouds had gathered over the top of Whitefish Mountain. If he didn't turn back soon, he would get caught in the summer thunderstorm. Not that he minded it all that much, except the construction crew working at the guest ranch would be anxious for the weekend and their paychecks. Most in these parts didn't buy into auto deposit.

Even as the wind threatened to send his Stetson flying and he felt the first few drops of rain dampen his long-sleeved Western shirt, he couldn't help being curious about what he'd glimpsed. He'd seen something moving through the trees on the other side of the ravine.

He raised the binoculars to his eyes, waiting for them to focus. "What the hell?" When he'd caught movement, he'd been expecting elk or maybe a deer. If he was lucky, a bear. He hadn't seen a grizzly in this area in a long time, but it was always a good idea to know if one was around.

But what had caught his eye was human. He was too startled to breathe for a moment. A large man moved through the pines. He wasn't alone. He had hold of a woman's wrist in what appeared to be a death grip and was dragging her behind him. She seemed to be struggling to stay on her feet. It was what he saw in the man's other hand that had stolen his breath. A gun.

Garrett couldn't believe what he was seeing. Surely, he was wrong. Through the binoculars, he tried to keep track of the two. But he kept losing them as they moved through the thick pines. His pulse pounded as he considered what to do.

His options were limited. He was too far away to intervene and he had a steep ravine between him and the man with the gun. Nor could he call for help—as if help could arrive in time. There was no cell phone coverage this far back in the mountains outside of Whitefish, Montana.

Through the binoculars, he saw the woman burst out of the trees and realized that she'd managed to break away from the man. For a moment, Garrett thought she was going to get away. But the man was larger and faster and was on her quickly, catching her and jerking her around to face him. He hit her with the gun, then put the barrel to her head as he jerked her to him.

"No!" Garrett cried, the sound lost in the wind and crackle of thunder in the distance. After dropping the binoculars onto his saddle, he drew his sidearm from the holster at his hip and fired a shot into the air. It echoed across the wide ravine, startling his horse.

As he struggled to holster the pistol again and grab the binoculars, a shot from across the ravine filled the air, echoing back at him.

*Don't miss*
Luck of the Draw *by B.J. Daniels, available June 2019*
*wherever Harlequin® books and ebooks are sold.*

www.Harlequin.com

**HQN**™

Save **$1.00**
off the purchase of
*Luck of the Draw*
by B.J. Daniels.

Available wherever books are sold,
including most bookstores, supermarkets,
drugstores and discount stores.

---

# Save **$1.00**

off the purchase of *Luck of the Draw* by B.J. Daniels.

Coupon valid until October 31, 2019.
Redeemable at participating outlets in U.S. and Canada only.
Limit one coupon per customer.

**Canadian Retailers:** Harlequin Enterprises Limited will pay the face value of this coupon plus 10.25¢ if submitted by customer for this product only. Any other use constitutes fraud. Coupon is nonassignable. Void if taxed, prohibited or restricted by law. Consumer must pay any government taxes. Void if copied. Inmar Promotional Services ("IPS") customers submit coupons and proof of sales to Harlequin Enterprises Limited, P.O. Box 31000, Scarborough, ON M1R 0E7, Canada. Non-IPS retailer—for reimbursement submit coupons and proof of sales directly to Harlequin Enterprises Limited, Retail Marketing Department, Bay Adelaide Centre, East Tower, 22 Adelaide Street West, 40th Floor, Toronto, Ontario M5H 4E3, Canada.

**52616378**

**U.S. Retailers:** Harlequin Enterprises Limited will pay the face value of this coupon plus 8¢ if submitted by customer for this product only. Any other use constitutes fraud. Coupon is nonassignable. Void if taxed, prohibited or restricted by law. Consumer must pay any government taxes. Void if copied. For reimbursement submit coupons and proof of sales directly to Harlequin Enterprises, Ltd 482, NCH Marketing Services, P.O. Box 880001, El Paso, TX 88588-0001, U.S.A. Cash value 1/100 cents.

5 65373 00076 2 (8100)0 12421

DPCOUP0419

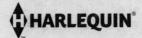

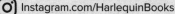

*Love Harlequin romance?*

## DISCOVER.

Be the first to find out about promotions, news and exclusive content!

Facebook.com/HarlequinBooks

Twitter.com/HarlequinBooks

Instagram.com/HarlequinBooks

Pinterest.com/HarlequinBooks

ReaderService.com

## EXPLORE.

Sign up for the Harlequin e-newsletter and download a free book from any series at **TryHarlequin.com.**

## CONNECT.

Join our Harlequin community to share your thoughts and connect with other romance readers!
**Facebook.com/groups/HarlequinConnection**

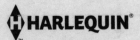

**ROMANCE WHEN
YOU NEED IT**

HSOCIAL2018